VANISHED

AMELIA BLAKE

BRUDNICKI-PENN PUBLISHING

Cover Art by *DDDesigns*

Editor *Tracy Stephen*

This book is a work of fiction. Names, characters, places, brands, media, and incidents are either the product of the author's imagination or are used fictitiously. The author acknowledges the trademarked status and trademark owners of various products referenced in this work of fiction, which have been used without permission. The publication/use of these trademarks are not authorized, associated with, or sponsored by the trademark owners. Any resemblance to actual events, locals, or persons, living or dead, is coincidental.

First Edition, 2018

To Bru and Tyler who believed in me when I didn't always believe in myself. Thank you for the encouragement. I love you guys.

CONTENTS

PROLOGUE

A lonesome foghorn sounds on the riverfront announcing a vessel's presence. I envy it - envy the ability to be heard and to be seen. In dim seclusion, I lay in a formless heap, blood oozing from my wounds. I ache. The assault has ended for now; I pray forever. But I know within reason that this will never be revenge enough for him. He blames me, blames the article . . . blames everyone but himself.

The sickly sweet aroma of flowers still hangs in the air and reminds me of death. I lowered my guard for only a moment when the courier approached. Only he was no delivery boy, a fact that cruelly revealed itself.

I'm a fighter and proved that when I dug my nails into his face, hollowing out a chunk of skin. It only intensified his rage. I fought him with everything I had, but now I'm weak, so weak, and don't have the strength to battle him a second more.

I hear the water lapping at the bank as I watch his shadow disappear into the foggy mist. Either no one saw him drag me here, or they just didn't care. I'm scared. I feel the scream welling up inside me, but only a soft whimper passes my lips. "Help me, please," I whisper, but no one hears me. How could they? Discarded like a rag doll, a tear spirals down my cheek.

A veil of darkness falls over my shivering body as my eyes fall closed. I feel the metal bench below me. It's cold and unforgiving, much like the blade that repeatedly sliced me.

My heartbeat slows now and sounds fade away. Maybe this is shock. Maybe it's death. Either way, I embrace it.

A soothing voice calls to me, pulling me from my slumber.

"Stay with me," he urges, "I've called for help." His hand gently closes against my shoulder, jostling me lightly and repeating his gentle reassurance.

I hear the wailing sirens come to a halt and know my prayers have been answered. The relief that washes over me comes in the form of tears and broken sobs.

I'm safe for now. I pray, forever. But will I ever truly be safe? Or is this only the beginning . . .

CHAPTER 1

A desperate scream shattered the silence, its haunting melody echoing off the walls. Jolted awake, Emma scrambled back against the headboard, drawing her knees tightly against her chest.

She felt wildly for the lamp on the desk beside her. Her hand falling on the cool surface, she clicked it on, illuminating the darkness. Emma surveyed the dreary room, sweeping her eyes from side to side. Labored breaths blew out through her trembling lips. "It's just a dream, only a dream," she coached herself, like she'd done so many times before. With a shaky hand, she reached up to push a sweat soaked strand of hair from her face.

Her heart raced inside her chest and her stomach churned like a brewing hurricane, the weights of despair that always accompanied a dream of him.

He dominated her fears during waking hours and tormented her subconscious at night. Would she ever be free of him, of the stalker whose goal in life was to make her pay?

Silent prayers spilled from her lips as she willed it all to stop. "Please, God. No more. I can't take anymore," she mouthed as she rocked back and forth. Snippets of her dream flashed through her mind - the cruel laughter and imageless face of her attacker taunting her. A raspy sob escaped her throat.

Her vision began to tunnel. Emma attempted to redirect her thoughts in an effort to stave off the inevitable panic attack that would soon encompass her body.

Clasping her eyes tightly shut, she breathed in and out - in and out, over and over. *Her mind carried her to a meadow. She could hear the babbling brook as she watched the water wind its way over protruding rocks and between the narrow confines of its banks. Turning, she walked through waist-high grass and wild-flowers, stopping to pick a bouquet on her way to the two-story white farm house. The soles of her sneakers squeaked noisily across the wide plank porch as she approached the door. She turned the knob, pushing it open. The smell of freshly baked cookies wafted past her nose, and she was greeted by the sight of her grandparents in a curious game of cards. She watched as her granddad tugged his glasses down his nose then leaned across the table to inspect the current discard. His eyebrows shot up, and he captured his partner's gaze. A joyful giggle filled the air, the one her granny always made into the back of her hand when she'd been caught cheating.*

A content sigh pulled Emma from her daydream, bringing her back to the present and to the reality that she had successfully averted a panic attack for the first time. "Thank you," she whispered, grateful for the reprieve.

Even though she missed her grandparents terribly, thoughts of them and the farmhouse she loved would remain vibrant memories that would live on in her mind forever.

Emma opened her eyes and smiled. She noticed her chest rising and falling at a rhythmic pace. Shallow breaths feathered across her lips of their own accord. *I'm gonna beat this one day at a time . . .*

With visions of her daydream fleeing from her mind, she took in the lackluster room before her. So much had changed in the last year, for the worse. She had a hard time fathoming all that she'd lost - family members, peace of mind, her dream job, and the home she loved.

In her quest for independence after moving back to her Kentucky hometown, Emma had rented the only place she could afford on a broke journalist's salary - a room in a dilapidated boarding house deceptively named Dillingham Manor.

It sounded stately and at one time, it had been. Dillingham Manor was once the home of wealthy Thorough-bred breeder, Samuel Dillingham and his wife, Elizabeth. In the early nineteen hundreds, it had been brimming with Brookfield royalty – aristocrats of the ages who attended lavish balls in the exquisite home. What once had been the talk of the town now was the shell of a home that time had forgotten.

The grandeur of its rumored hidden passages was long eclipsed by its current choppy layout into boarders' quarters. Most of the house was off limits to tenants, a fact Emma became familiar with on the same day she formed a mutual dislike with her less than lovely landlady, Nancy.

Once again, her appraisal fell on the room. The dingy white walls and faded wood floors were representative of the rest of the house, lackluster in every sense of the word. Modifications of any sort were prohibited. That included painting, hanging art, or adding anything that would breathe life into an otherwise desolate home. The only positive was that it smelled nice - now. When Emma first moved in, the room had smelled of must and mold, the telltale signs of a closed off space. She'd scrubbed her fingers to the bone assuring that every inch from floor to ceiling was clean. That much she could do. If only she could wash away its bleak reality. She reminded herself that it wouldn't be like this for long. She lived here in order to save money. She would have her own place again. In the meantime, drab, depressing Dillingham Manor was where she laid her head at night but would never be the place that she called home.

Reaching for the clock on her desk, she groaned when she saw the time. It was hours still before dawn. Too early to shower for work and with sleep evading her, Emma pulled the photo album from her desk drawer. She settled down under the covers and opened the leather bound book. Memories poured off the pages, eliciting emotions of every form. She laughed at silly pictures, cringed at others, and yearned for simpler times.

As she continued through the album, the lump in her throat continued to grow. She took a deep breath when the final page was turned, knowing the heartache that would be revealed. The crinkling plastic filled the silence as she ran her fingers over the clipped article and photos of her grandparents. Tears stung her eyes as she gazed upon the words: *Elderly couple perishes in house fire.*

The pain too much to bear, she closed the album and pulled it close to her chest, resting her face across the top of it. *I thought running from the pain of their deaths was the answer. Had I only known the horror that awaited me in Louisville.* She blew out a shaky breath and attempted to purge the thought from her mind.

~

It was a cool, crisp morning in the rural town of Brookfield, Kentucky. The orange and red leaves of fall streamed down like a rainbow covering the streets and walks, the sunlight reflecting off of every glorious hue.

Autumn was Emma Saint-Claire's favorite season, and she took every opportunity to enjoy the harvest of colors that was all around her on her walk to work. The cool breeze nipping at her skin and sounds of leaves crunching under her feet brought a smile to her face as she basked in the changing season.

The morning breeze swept her chestnut hair all around her shoulders. Pulling a tie from her bag, she secured it in a messy ponytail.

Emma watched as people rushed past her in a huff trying to reach their destination quickly, but she rather enjoyed her leisurely stroll. Being in the fresh air was better than being at dank Dillingham Manor and was certainly better than being at The Brookfield Journal where she worked as a journalist. It wasn't that she disliked her job, but the office was too small and dark for her liking.

She supposed she should just be thankful for employment since so many people had had to leave the area in an effort to support their families. Small towns equaled little opportunity on the job front.

She had tried the big city for a while; however, not only was she *not* cut out for the busy pace, she wasn't cut out for stalkers, either.

Emma had moved back to town six months ago and was lucky that her former employer welcomed her back in. With the exception of her living arrangement, small town living suited her fine.

As she passed an oak tree with a marker to its side, it occurred to Emma that even though she'd grown up in Brookfield, she knew very little about the town's history.

She only knew about the boarding house's past from a waitress at the diner. The topic of the home had never piqued her interest. With its features masked by neglect and time, Dillingham Manor was just another building that sat deteriorating.

Emma had lived there for three months but often wondered what the rest of the house looked like. Her land-lady, Nancy, had an all seeing eye that had thwarted Emma's attempts to explore the house on several occasions. The reporter in her was itching to see the rest of the house. She was certain that stark Dillingham had more to offer than the bleak existence that sat off Penn Way.

As town square came into view, she knew her stroll to work was nearly over. Emma crossed the street and climbed the steps to the main street shops. As always, she glanced at her reflection in the plate glass window of the jewelry store. She wore black from head to toe, which made her five foot ten inch frame look even taller. Her gaze immediately settled on her full hips. She placed her hands on them and frowned at herself, contemplating a diet for half a second. Then she shrugged her shoulders. *I'll take pleasantly plump over hungry any day!* Smiling at the thought, she continued on her path.

Emma entered the dusty, dim entryway of the newspaper office. Making her way past several unoccupied desks and a fax machine that noisily spat out papers, she walked into her office.

Sunlight shone brightly through the windows when she

pulled the cord to open the blinds. She traced dust particles as they lazily drifted about through the stream of light.

As she peered out the window, she saw her cousin, Cat, unlocking the door to her shop across the street. Her dark auburn hair cascaded in fiery waves down her back, reflecting the sun's rays. It was a perfect contrast to her ivory skin. At five foot nine inches tall, Emma always thought her cousin might choose to be a model someday, but Cat had decided to go the route of permanent art, opening a tattoo shop.

Cat's hand blocked the sun, shielding its blinding rays from her eyes as she gazed across the street. Emma shuttered her blinds a few times - their customary morning hello. Cat waved enthusiastically then disappeared through the door.

Turning her focus back to her office, Emma pressed the power button on her dinosaur computer. While it groaned to life, she picked up the stack of messages that the office manager, Lisa, had left on her desk.

The first message was about covering a chili cook-off at the festival. The second was from Tank. Emma held the paper in front of her face and laughed as she read the message. "Tank stopped by on Saturday. He wants you to marry him and asks that you not say no – *again!*"

Well, at least he's consistent, Emma thought to herself as she placed the note in a stack behind the previous message. The third message was from a Colton Graves. He was requesting a meeting to discuss a masquerade ball. She paused for just a moment before moving on to her final message - a citizen requesting that she start an advice column in the paper.

Being that Emma had had a very bad experience with an advice column while she lived in Louisville, she decided she would *not* be returning *that* call. At this point, the chili cook-off was the only do-able task. She looked at Tank's message again and chuckled. Tank had asked Emma to marry him nearly every month for a year. Even when she moved away, he'd sent word by Cat that his offer still stood. She laughed at the image in her head of them standing side by side at the wedding altar.

He stood about five feet tall with unkempt, mousy brown hair and bleak eyes. He wore black rimmed glasses that always sat a little crooked on his face. He seemed like he would have made a good assistant to a mad scientist. Again, her mind drifted back to them at the altar, and she imagined the wedding ceremony ending with a kiss that she would have had to bend down nearly a foot to get. She shuddered at the thought.

Message two was quickly filed in the circular bin. Message three was nearly as laughable as the proposal. Shaking her head, Emma decided that Colton Graves must not know the first thing about Brookfield, Kentucky. *No one in their right mind would plan to have a grand ball here in Mayberry.* She'd call him just to see what he had planned, but the chili cook-off was looking like the only thing that Emma had to look forward to reporting on.

Pulling out the folder labeled "Festival," she glanced over her notes of things she'd covered in the past.

She found town festivals to be delightful and was looking forward to the Brookfield Harvest Festival. It was held the third Saturday in October every year. She always enjoyed seeing the booths that each vendor had created. They ranged from quilt exhibits, pottery, local blacksmith demonstrations, glass blowing, woodworkers, and, of course, the food peddlers. She thought that the foodies got better every year. In addition to the booths and food, Emma always looked forward to the carnival that came to town a few days before the festival.

Even though Brookfield was a sleepy town, it was a great place to live. The crime rate was low, the people were true, and she had always felt a sense of pride living there.

She thought she could be happy living in Louisville, but that happiness was short lived. It took three months of trying only to discover that the city was too big and too fast-paced for Emma. It also turned out to be quite scary. The gentle caress of her thumb across her wrist brought her focus back to her messages.

With the festival being three weeks away and knowing she didn't have anything pressing to talk to Mr. Sizemore about regarding the chili cook-off, Emma thought she'd take the time to call up Mr. Colton Graves and inquire about this fancy shmancy ball.

His name didn't seem familiar. Another glance at the digits revealed that it wasn't a local number. And even though she'd never seen one before, she knew it was not a United States number either because there were too many numbers. *Well, only one way to find out who he is.* Emma dialed the number listed on the message and waited for him to answer.

After a long delay, the tone was interrupted by a greeting, "Regal Engineering, Eleanor speaking."

"Hi, this is Emma Saint-Claire returning a call for Mr. Graves. May I speak with him please?"

The receptionist clarified that the call was for Colton Graves then placed her on hold. As she waited, Emma pictured a formal gala in her mind. She thought it would be fun to dress up, maybe even dress a little risqué. She'd be wearing a mask after all, so no one would know that she was plain Jane Emma who didn't even have a middle name. *That's my claim to fame - I don't even have a middle name.*

"Sorry for your wait," the pleasant female voice sounded over the line, "Mr. Graves will be with you momentarily."

Again, her mind drifted with the silence. *A fancy ball. What would I wear? Emma imagined a long skirt with its train flowing down the steps as she descended an elegant staircase-*

" . . . Miss Saint-Claire? Are you there?"

Embarrassed by her daydreaming, Emma crinkled a piece of paper in the phone. "Yes, sorry. I think we have a bad connection."

"I'm pleased you returned my call so quickly."

An accent. A British one? Oh, Lord. Emma cleared her throat. "What can I do for you, Mr. Graves?"

"The reason that I contacted you is because I would like to employ your services for a masquerade ball. I assume your town still has the annual festival?"

"Well, yes, we do." Emma hesitated for a moment, her confusion settling in. "But Mr. Graves, I'm a journalist, not an events planner. I don't know the first thing about a ball." She thought for a second. "And how did you come about my name for this, anyway?"

"I'm afraid that you misunderstand my intent. Allow me to clarify, but first let me say that I came about your name in a very scientific manner. I didn't know where to start, so I Googled it." Colton laughed when he admitted this and Emma did, too. "When I entered 'Brookfield, Kentucky' into the search engine, the Brookfield Journal popped up with your contact information. I also received contacts for the Historical Society and a court records office, but they have yet to return my calls. So, I thank you for taking me seriously. As for your part in this, I'm not asking you to coordinate the event. I need you to look into the venue for me.

There is a stately home in the town of Brookfield named Dillingham Manor. My great, great grandparents once owned the property, and I'm curious to know who owns it today. Our knowledge is limited – consisting of a couple boxes of memorabilia that were discovered in my parents' attic. The home has a rich history – one that the current owner may be unaware of. I'd like to shed some light on that fact."

Emma closed her eyes and pinched the bridge of her nose, trying to take in the arsenal of information he had hurled her way. "You realize you can't just waltz into someone's home and insist they have a party. Right?"

Colton laughed. "Yes, I imagine that's universally unacceptable – regardless of which side of the pond you're on. While I understand I have no right, I'd like to speak with them just the same. I'm looking at a photograph as we speak. Being that I'm an engineer, I appreciate the complexity, the grandeur-"

"Excuse me, Mr. Graves."

"Please, call me Colton."

"Ok. Colton, I don't mean to be rude and cut you off, but I think you're sadly mistaken. Dillingham Manor is not a place for a ball. It's barely inhabitable as it is. The only 'grand happening' at The Dillingham is when the hot water lasts through a shower! I'm sorry to have to be so blunt, but I would hate for you to waste your time planning a mega blowout for the town when this property is two steps above being condemned." Emma heard long silence on the line.

"Miss Saint-Claire, would there be a way for you to take photos of Dillingham Manor in its current condition and message them to me? I have trouble imagining this glorious property in the throes of ruin. Understand that I do not doubt what you're saying to me, it's just that I can't believe it

13

to be the same property that my ancestors cherished, the one I've read about."

Emma asked if he would, in turn, send her some photos of the home in its pristine condition. She was certain that they were, indeed, speaking of two separate pieces of real estate. *How could he not know what happened to the house? If this land was in his family and supposedly "cherished," how could they not know what had happened to it?*

It was a slow Monday morning. Since she had little to report on for the first part of the day, Emma decided to do some research on the owners of the land. Her friend, Kimberly, was a property valuation officer, so she started by contacting her. It took a couple of hours to hear back, but Kimberly determined that the property had never actually been sold and that it belonged to the heirs of Samuel and Elizabeth Dillingham.

Emma thought that Colton would be pleased to hear this since he'd clearly been upset over the news of the current state of the home.

Ending the call with her friend, she checked her messages and stared wide eyed at the stately manor in the photos. Colton had sent them right away, and she could see why he was so astonished to hear of its apparent demise.

There were pictures of the grounds, one of which was a pond and flower garden surrounded by children playing. In the background, three ladies wearing long, flowing gowns caught her attention. They were the epitome of elegance. Another picture showed a foggy morning with horses next to a split rail fence.

Emma's gaze fell on the next set of images that allowed her to see inside the walls of Dillingham Manor. It was a stark contrast to the current condition. She saw the dining room filled with family on a holiday; it was like peering into a vintage catalogue. The room itself had tons of character with its vaulted ceiling and magnificent columns. Not only was the room impressive, but the individuals gathered around the table were too. Their wardrobes and postures exuded class.

Taking the virtual tour deeper into the home, she saw the bedroom of a privileged young girl. Emma's focus fell on a cameo brooch on the girl's antique dressing table.

She saw many photos of a masquerade ball. Even though they were in black and white, she could clearly see the details in their features and the life beaming from the home. She was taken aback. The home was gorgeous, the people were gorgeous, and the grounds were gorgeous. Even though she fashioned herself a journalist, all Emma could say was that it was all incredibly gorgeous. She was spell bound.

Her mind darted between the photos on the screen of a magnificent place in time to the thought of the mundane boarding house that now stood in its wake. The comparison between the two was immeasurable.

As much as she hated to be the bearer of bad news, Emma walked the short distance to Dillingham Manor to take the pictures Mr. Graves asked for.

Emma ran her fingers across the columns. Of all the times she had walked through the entryway of the boarding house, she never once had taken the time to revel in the intricate carvings on the pillars. They were so caked in decades of dust and dead vines that she never noticed their markings. The once exquisite home sure didn't exist today.

She wondered where the ballroom was located. *Whoever*

would have thought that the Dillingham would have a ballroom? There was so much that Emma wanted to know about. Maybe it wouldn't be today, but Nancy wouldn't stand in her way of exploring now that she had gotten a peek into the Dillingham's forbidden corridors.

Emma looked at the leaves collecting in every corner of the porch, spider webs, too. It almost hurt her to see this home in its current condition having seen evidence of what it once was. With much hesitation, she pulled her camera from her bag and began to click the images. From the conversation they'd had, she knew that Colton Graves would be devastated to view the photos of the neglected home – a home that he had spoken of so fondly.

As she walked around the perimeter, Emma captured as many photos as she could manage. She tried to find anything about the home that he might view in a positive light. She tried, but there was nothing. *It hasn't been leveled by a tornado. Maybe he'd think that's a positive revelation . . .*

Taking one last look at the battered home, Emma walked back to the Journal where she emailed the images right away. She could almost imagine him comparing picture after picture as his heart fell like a lead ball into the pit of his stomach.

Thinking of his stomach made Emma think of her standing lunch date with Cat. They always met for lunch on Monday at the diner. All the walking that she had done today really had her ready to devour a burger and fries. *I've been good – maybe a milkshake, too!*

Glancing at her watch, she grabbed her bag and walked toward the door. Before she reached it, the phone on her desk rang. She turned to look at it. The growling in her stomach told her to ignore the call, but the incessant ringing on her dedicated line had her curiosity piqued. Emma crossed the room and picked up the receiver.

"Brookfield Journal, this is Emma."

"Hello, again, Miss Saint-Claire. Colton Graves here."

This time there was no excitement in his voice. She could almost feel the despair in his tone.

"Hello, Mr. Graves. I take it that you received the photos that I emailed to you?"

"Yes. And as you can expect, I'm quite shocked. I suppose I'll be looking for another venue for the ball."

"Mr. Graves, I-"

"Colton. It's Colton," he said smoothly. "And I'm sure you're curious of my intent."

"Actually, I am. It's not every day that we have someone ask about a having a fancy ball, and especially not a man. But hey, I don't judge."

Colton barked out a laugh at her misconception. "First of all, there is a purpose to my request. Through my grandmother's letters and the photos, I almost feel like I've been there. The engineer in me can see what it was, and even though I clearly see what it is now, I can also envision what it can be. It has potential. If you could only read the letters, you'd have a better understanding."

Emma could hear the sincerity in his voice. "I would love to read those letters someday. Have you ever thought about sharing them with the Historical Society of Brookfield?"

"I think that I just may do that someday. That brings me to the other reason I would like to resurrect the masquerade ball at Dillingham Manor. In my online research, I've found that the historical society doesn't list the manor as a historic property. It clearly is and should rightfully be documented as such. If I can convince them to acknowledge my family's former home as being part of the National Register of Historical Places, then Brookfield can receive grant monies to preserve it. By the way Miss Saint-Claire, did you have any luck securing information on the rightful owner?"

"It appears that you are!" Emma blurted out excitedly. "Well, sort of."

"Care to clarify?"

"The property was never sold and remains listed as belonging to the heirs of Samuel and Elizabeth Dillingham." After all the bad news that she had been pelting him with, Emma was relieved to finally have something encouraging to say.

"Hmm, that's an interesting turn of events, and one I certainly didn't foresee. It looks like a trip to the States is in order sooner than I had planned. If it is owned by the Dillingham heirs, I'm curious as to who has maintained the property all these years?"

"Part of that is something that I can help you with. I think I also forgot to mention that I rent a room at Dillingham Manor. That's where I live along with two other tenants. We're required to pay our rent in cash to the landlady on the first of every month. She lives there as well. "

"That's interesting, indeed."

"Is there anything else you can tell me about Dillingham Manor, Colton? I know I shouldn't have to ask you since I live there, but town history has never seemed interesting to me, until now." *And with you telling the story, that accent could cause me to willingly listen to the stock reports.*

"... and did you know that in the early nineteen hundreds, the masquerade ball was part of the festival?"

"The Brookfield Harvest Festival?"

"Yes. According to my grandmother's journals, the who's who of the town would come together for a masquerade ball on Halloween night to signify the end of the harvest. I take it that it was the talk of the town. This was before prohibition, so alcohol flowed freely – although, according to her journals, alcohol still flowed freely during prohibition, too." He chuckled at his grandparents' rebellious streak.

"Colton, I really would love to read those letters, maybe even do a piece on town history and include some of the Dillingham's letters and journal entries, if you would approve."

They chatted a few minutes longer. After shuffling appointments, it was determined that Colton would arrive in Kentucky in three days. He requested her freelance investigation skills - of which she possessed none. It was Brookfield. What could he really ask for that she couldn't figure out?

Her duties at the Journal were always minimal, at best, so she knew that she could fit in some freelance work with no problem. Emma couldn't imagine that Colton would take up too much of her time once he actually saw Dillingham Manor, so she would show him around Brookfield and try to do some research on things that he may find interesting . . . because she surely found him to be. *Which I shouldn't. He's probably old enough to by my father. A girl can dream, though.*

CHAPTER 2

*T*he rumble in Emma's stomach made her painfully aware that she was nearly famished. All the hustle and bustle of the morning's running around had her running on empty, and she couldn't get to the diner fast enough. Emma usually had absolutely nothing to report to Cat when they met for lunch. Boy would Cat be surprised today! Cat loved nothing better than an excuse to dress up. Neither of them had ever been to a masquerade ball. As adults, opportunities to dress up for Halloween hadn't presented themselves very often.

Emma entered the diner and saw Cat sitting in their usual booth. She was talking on her phone and drumming her fingers. She wore a long purple dress with a fitted black jacket over top. She looked gorgeous, as always. Spotting Emma, she ended her call.

"Well, if it isn't Saint Emma finally deciding to grace me with her presence. What's your sorry excuse for being late today?"

Emma slid into the booth. "Oh Alley Cat, you'd never guess in a hundred years!" Emma was clearly beaming with excitement.

Cat narrowed her eyes as possibilities danced through her mind. "Did you go and get yourself laid? I didn't think this day would ever come!" She laughed at her own joke, but Emma was not as amused. "Are you gonna take a headline out in the paper? Maybe sign it, Emma SINclaire?" Again, she laughed and Emma did, too. That was Emma's preplanned evil penname if she ever decided to take a walk on the wild side.

The presence of their server halted her response.

"Girls, you'll never believe what I heard." This was how Bonny always greeted them and anyone else who passed through the doors of the diner. She gave a sideways glance to a neighboring table before leaning closer. "Now, don't tell anyone 'cause just me and few other people know. But I have it on good authority that they're selling knock off purses at the warehouse on East Street." She straightened, flashing a smile. "They hardly look fake at all. Now, what can I get you?" This was also typical behavior. She could deliver town gossip then switch back to waitress mode in the blink of an eye.

After ordering their food, Emma proceeded to tell Cat all about her morning. For the first time in a long time, she was excited about work. She hardly knew where to focus her energy. Suddenly, she had a lot to do - usual Journal stuff, freelance stuff for Colton, helping plan a ball, and last, but not least, she would finally get a peek deeper inside Dillingham Manor. Her mental note taking was interrupted by Bonny.

"Here you go, ladies. Two cheeseburgers, bacon cheddar

fries, and chocolate milk shakes." She looked at the food and then back to them. "You girls eat like truckers, you know. If you don't slow down, you're gonna end up looking like Sal in there!" She thumbed over her shoulder toward the kitchen where he was grumbling about something.

Emma looked down at her belly and giggled.

"What are you laughing at, sugar?" Bonny asked.

"Well, I'm just trying to imagine myself balding on top and with a pot belly, like Sal."

Bonny snorted out a laugh, but waved away the declaration before tucking a lock of curly, blond hair behind her ear. She always wore her hair piled on top of her head and twisted around with a pencil holding it in place.

Having fulfilled her duty, Bonny trotted off to the next table leaving the cousins to their discussion.

"So let me get this straight," Cat said as she ticked the points off on her fingers. "This Colton owns the place, wants to have a fancy ball, and wants you to be a freelance assistant in addition to all that you're covering for the Journal with the festival coming up?"

This *was* more excitement and responsibility than Emma had seen in a long time, so she could understand Cat's hesitation.

"Emma, I don't mean to be a downer, but what do you know about this guy, really? I can't stand the thought of what happened to you in-"

"Stop. Right there!" Emma ordered. "We agreed not to discuss that again, ever. You and I are the only ones here who know what happened. Besides, the emotional scars are healing and-"

Cat reached her hand across the table and gently rubbed her thumb over Emma's left wrist. "Not all scars heal, babe." They both stared at the marred flesh.

Emma pulled away from Cat's grasp. She dropped her

wrist to her lap and held it against her body as if to shield it.

"Seriously Cat, we're not discussing it."

With that, Bonny popped back out and asked if they had heard about plans for the old Williams' bridge, over Drowning Creek, to be dismantled. Soon they were all reminiscing with stories about the swinging bridge.

Emma suddenly found one more thing on her to-do list, an article about Williams' bridge. She was sure to come up with a haunted story or two just in time for the Brookfield Harvest Festival edition of the Journal. Townspeople had always told stories of Williams' bridge being haunted, but never seemed to say much about the metal trussed bridge that sat just a few feet away – likely because the swinging bridge scared people into imagining all sorts of wild realities.

The next couple days passed in a blur. Emma kept herself busy interviewing Brookfield neighbors and collecting their stories about the Williams' bridge. She decided she would title the article *Haunted Brookfield*. Everyone knew someone who'd seen the ghost of Little Victoria, although, Emma couldn't find *anyone* who'd actually seen her themselves. She was always described in a similar manner – strawberry-blond hair that she wore in long spiral curls, a flowing white dress, and a giggle that echoed through the night fog. Legend had it that little Victoria was crossing the bridge one stormy, foggy night when a plank loosed and she fell through the crack to the water below. With the raging storm and pounding rain, the current was fierce and Victoria drowned – hence the name, Drowning Creek. To be granted safe passage, according to legend, Victoria's name had to be chanted three times before crossing the bridge or travelers would never make it across. According to others, safe passage was only granted if a toll was paid in the form of tossing gifts and toys to little Victoria. A small price to pay for remaining alive. It was rumored that when the bridge swayed violently during storms that little Victoria was waiting on the other side for playmates.

Once *Haunted Brookfield* was complete, Emma gathered information for *Historic Brookfield*. She visited the older generations and recorded whatever they were willing to share about their past. She learned a lot. Many spoke of their youth - games they played, who taught them to drive if they drove, and who their favorite teachers were. Others told her stories of what school was like for them, what they packed for lunch or if they went home to eat. They talked about their clothing and transportation.

She asked about their occupations. Many had grown up to become teachers. Others worked in the medical field but most were coal miners, mill workers, or farmers.

Emma also asked what they knew about the Dillinghams and Dillingham Manor. Many recalled the history of the home and its grandeur, but unfortunately, none reported having attended a ball.

The most colorful interview of all came from Loretta Townsand. Emma decided she *must* have been hitting the bottle, heavily, before she shared her stories. They were so scandalous that they would never make it off the pages of her notepad. They certainly were entertaining, though.

Mr. Graves had inadvertently opened a corridor in her mind and suddenly, town history was something she couldn't gather fast enough.

~

Thursday arrived at last and Emma wondered why she had butterflies multiplying in her stomach in mass quantities. The walk to work hadn't calmed her nerves in the least. Not only was she late, but she was as giddy as a school girl. Sure, she was excited to meet Mr. Graves, but these feelings? How strange for her.

She thought she'd stop by Cat's shop for outfit approval. Emma's sense of style bordered on dreadful at times, and Cat always could pair up something to make her look better. As Emma entered, Cat gave an approving nod at her attire. Her black slacks and shoes complemented the formfitting crimson top that was a tad lower cut than Emma would normally wear. A leopard print scarf tied loosely around her neck completed the ensemble. Her long, chestnut brown hair shimmered in the sunlight as it shone through the floor to ceiling window.

Cat let out a whistle. "Looking good, Saint Emma."

"Are you sure?"

Cat nodded as she motioned for her cousin to spin so she could see the complete outfit. "Someone's been shopping!"

"New shoes and all." Emma lifted up her pant leg to show Cat.

"Girl, you need to dress like this every day. I'm telling you, the people of Brookfield are going to pass out when they realize you actually have some boobs. I don't know why you hide those things! Seriously Emma, you look beautiful!"

"Thanks," Emma said as she drew in a shaky breath. "I can't tell you how nervous I am. I'm meeting him at noon today."

"Do you even know what he looks like?"

"No, but he's coming to the Journal – shouldn't be too hard to recognize a British newbie over there." They both glanced across the street. "I think he may be older, though. The words he uses and his phrases are something I wouldn't expect a young guy to have. He's probably some hunched over, stocky, old, bald guy." She giggled at that image.

"Why are you so nervous then?"

"Well, for starters, his voice is to die for! I could just listen to him forever. You know I've always had a thing for guys with an accent." Cat nodded. "But even though I know he's not going to be some gorgeous young guy, for the first time in a long time, I'm excited because I feel like I have a purpose." Emma glanced at her cousin, almost embarrassed to continue. "I really can't wait to find out about Dillingham Manor. I want to read his letters and the journal entries that his grandmother kept about her time at the estate. I want to plan a ball that I'm going to get us into somehow. And I'm excited to do a historical write-up on Brookfield. I've actually already started that. I don't even recognize me and this fire that has been ignited!" Scrunching her nose, she looked at Cat and winced. "Ok, you can call me a dork now!"

A smile played across her lips. "Babe, it's good to see you like this. By the way, I just saw the door close at the Journal." They both pressed their noses to the glass of the tattoo shop. As hard as they looked, they couldn't make out the shadowy figure that had just passed through the door.

Emma rubbed the palms of her rapidly sweating hands on her slacks. "Well, here goes nothing. Let's just hope that I don't trip walking across the street. These hoochie-mama shoes make me six foot tall!"

"You're almost six foot tall anyway. You'll be fine, now scooch. I'm expecting Hayden."

"Hayden," Emma sighed. Hayden McAllister was the eldest of the McAllister brothers and quite handsome. Sometimes Emma was jealous that she wrote on flimsy note pads while Cat wrote on strong, gorgeous specimens like Hayden.

Walking to the door, she cast a nervous look over her shoulder. "Wish me luck."

Emma took a deep breath and threw her shoulders back. Holding her head high, she crossed the street to the Journal. Her heart thrummed in her chest so hard that she heard the roaring in her ears. Her legs felt like jelly. She contemplated her first meeting with Colton happening in the emergency room because she was sure that this was what a stroke must feel like.

When she reached for the door to the Journal, it swung open instantly. *Oh God! I'm gonna pass out!*

"Hi Emma, beautiful day we're having."

And exhale . . . she could finally catch her breath. Standing before her was Tank. The closing door hadn't been Colton Graves after all. It had been Tank, no doubt to see if she got his message. "Hey! Yeah, it is a beautiful day." He held the door for her to enter. When she turned to thank him, he quickly walked away.

Emma gazed down at her new clothing and couldn't help but shake her head. *When Tank doesn't even notice me, it's a sad, sad day. I swear! Sometimes I think I spray on 'Guy be gone' before stepping out in public.* Tank was the only guy in town who actually pursued Emma romantically. *Actually, that's the sad part!*

She walked into the Journal where there were several staff members mulling about. No one called her out for being late, and she was thankful for that.

Emma called over her shoulder as she walked by the office manager's desk. "Lisa, Colton Graves is supposed to meet me at noon. Will you give me ample ogling time before sending him in?" Emma laughed. "I'm eager to see what I'm up against." Lisa didn't say a word, but Laura, her sister, fell into hysterics.

She continued into her office without acknowledging Laura. She was a strange one anyway.

Emma glanced out the window when the church bells rang out, signaling that it was twelve o'clock. The echoing vibrations served as an audible reminder that she'd barely made it in time for her meeting. It was then that the 'ding' sounded from her computer. She turned to view the instant message that had popped up on her screen.

It was from Lisa. "Red alert - *hottie* in the house!"

Emma's mind raced. Surely Lisa wouldn't be so cruel to pretend that it was Colton that was here already and actually nice looking. "Wait, what? You mean Colton Graves? Are you joking?" she typed back.

"Girl, I'm not even going to ruin the surprise for you. INCOMING!"

Emma felt her pulse speed up as her throat went completely dry. *Did Lisa mean that the hottie was Colton? Don't be stupid, Emma!* She reprimanded herself. Not only was this reaction ridiculous, she knew within reason that he was an older man, right?

The light rap captured her attention, her eyes falling on the stranger in her doorway. Her lips parted, and her chest rose as her gaze traveled up and down his frame. Heat began to rise into her cheeks. The words that she willed to come out of her mouth failed her. Again, she took in the features of the short, stumpy, bald, and old British gentleman that she had imagined.

Only what she was expecting came in a totally different package than what was delivered. Nearly eclipsing the seven foot doorway of her office was a man with broad, muscular shoulders. He was every bit of six and a half feet tall with tousled, dark hair that stopped just inches above his shoulders. Sun-kissed skin graced his face as did the remnants of sexy stubble.

"Miss Saint-Claire, I realize that your request to, and subsequent alert to, 'ogle Mr. Graves' may not have come with ample warning." He tipped his coffee cup to his lips, staring at her over the rim. As he pulled it away, Emma could see the smile he tried to suppress. Tilting his head, he said, "I'd be happy to have a seat until you're finished if you do, indeed, need more 'ogling time.'" A smile crept across his face as amusement lit up his emerald eyes. "Colton Graves, very nice to make your acquaintance."

Emma stood and crossed the room as she smoothed invisible wrinkles out of her slacks, her face still flushed. She opened her mouth to speak, "Mr. Graves, I'm Emma Saint-Claire and am very pleased . . . and somewhat embarrassed, now, to meet you. Listen, I had no idea you were already here when I said that to Lisa. Again, I'm very sorry. It was unprofessional of me."

He walked further into the office, extending his hand. "Colton, luv. It's Colton," he said with a crooked grin.

Being that he was clearly amused with the situation, Emma decided to make the best of it, too. She gave her best smile and shook his hand. Now they just had to figure out where to begin.

"Well, I know you're curious to see Dillingham Manor, so why don't I take you there now?"

Colton nodded his head. "I'm eager to see what I'm up against."

Emma glanced up at him and smiled, recognizing the words he echoed.

Colton made a sweeping motion toward the door. "After you, Miss Saint-Claire."

"Look Colton, it's apparent that I lack professionalism. I think we've moved past the formalities. Call me Emma, please." *Unless you want to call me "luv" again, because I'm surely fine with that!*

"Emma it is."

CHAPTER 3

*A*greeing to go the distance on foot, they set out on their journey. Emma's focus fell on the handsome stranger to her side. Her eyes quickly poured over his simple style of dark jeans and a long sleeved waffle knit shirt the color of night. Motorcycle boots completed the ensemble, lending an edge to his look.

She inwardly groaned. *Of all the times to forget my camera bag!* Her initial face to face encounter with Colton had knocked her off kilter a tad. Time to regroup. Thinking about the task at hand, she eased into conversation. "Would you like a tour as we go, or do you want to go straight there?"

Colton nodded his head, his eyes darting from one shop to the next. "I rather enjoy history, so I'd like a tour. I imagine this quaint town has quite the story to tell."

Indeed. And she'd enjoy telling it. Emma followed his gaze as it locked on hers. "You'll find that every person and every place has a story to tell, Mr. Graves, if you just take the time to hear it."

"Then I look forward to the discovery, Miss Saint-Claire.

Afterwards, perhaps you'd like to have a bit of a nosh and discuss the masquerade."

Emma nodded, "Sure, we can go to the diner when we get back. It's just a few blocks from here, and they have excellent *nosh*." She smiled at Colton's fancy word. "And even if it's not, Sal's burgers are."

Colton glanced to his side, clearly amused with her playfulness. "Perhaps Mr. Saint-Claire will be joining us for lunch?"

She laughed. "Sorry to disappoint, but you're stuck with me. Mr. Saint-Claire's in Texas . . . and is my father."

Colton glanced at her left hand as if to validate what she said, making a slight nod of his head when he saw that she wore no rings, as if to say, *noted*.

Yep, that's me. Brookfield's last remaining old maid!

Redirecting his focus off her solo status, Emma pointed to the ironwork above each shop door. She explained that the figures depicted the nature of the business. As he looked from shop to shop, she could tell by his expression that he appreciated the little town's rich heritage.

Hoping to ease any apprehension that he may feel, Emma shared funny stories about Brookfield to help take his mind off the rubble that he'd see all too soon. Motioning to the Cathedral on the corner of Main and Vine, she explained that the toll of the bell tower could be heard throughout the town and had once been thought to be possessed by the Devil.

"A devil possessed bell tower? That's different," he mused.

"Oh, yes. Bobby Couch, who was Mayor Couch's little brat of a son - and mean as the devil himself - had stolen the keys to the tower and piped in satanic sounds that he'd recorded. They echoed all across town. So the running joke for a while was that in Brookfield even the Devil went to church. Since everyone brushed it off, so did the Mayor. Bobby continued to be a brat. Until he became a preacher. He likes to tell everyone that he scared religion into them."

"Interesting town you have here," Colton laughed.

Continuing on their scenic walk, Emma motioned to the business up ahead. "And there's the glass-smith's. Would you like to watch them for a minute?"

"Actually, I would. It reminds me of a shop that my mum and I would pass on our way to the market near our home when I was a young boy. I have always found it to be a fascinating art."

I pass by these windows every day that I walk to work; surely I can come up with something to say about these guys. Emma peered through the window and saw what looked to be a wine glass in the making. *Thank God! I can wing this!* "Looks like Michael and Tim are making a wine goblet. Sometimes they donate items to local restaurants. It exposes more people to their products and they get more business that way."

The more they watched, the bigger the glass became. Emma wanted to hurry along because it was becoming painfully obvious that what they were making wasn't going to end up being a wine glass, but Colton seemed very interested in staying. They watched as the crafters pulled, stretched, and smoothed the hot material. When the "wine glass" became a large bowl on a pedestal, Emma was horrified. She shot Colton an embarrassed grin and shrugged her shoulders.

"Emma, do they serve beer and wine in those 'goblets' at the diner and other local eateries?" He pointed to an array of bowls in the window display case. "If so, I think I may like this town just fine." The lines on the outer corners of his eyes appeared when he smiled. Colton was clearly enjoying the moment. Emma bit her lip, trying, but failing to suppress a smile.

As they proceeded on the path to the Dillingham, she continued on about this fact and that one when she finally stopped walking and turned to him.

"Colton, I'm sorry. I'm a jumble of emotions today. I'm excited to show you the town you've only heard of through letters, nervous about you seeing the house for the first time, and anxious about helping plan a ball. When I get like this, I talk. A lot. I know it probably sounds like gibberish. So I'm gonna be quiet now and let you ask me anything that you can think of. So just whatever's on your mind, you know – anything you see that interests you or just has you curious." *Well, Miss Saint-Claire, I was wondering if you are on medication. If not, perhaps you should be because you tend to ramble on and on.*

"I was actually thinking that I'm rather enjoying your company and your stories. And while I don't follow everything completely, I like listening to your accent."

Hmm. I did not see that one coming! "And here I thought *you* were the one with the accent." She titled her head slightly and smiled. *I could see myself being so comfortable with him.* Emma quickly shook the thought out of her head.

They rounded the corner off Penn Way and entered the property to the boarding house. The wrought-iron gates stood open, calling them to enter. As long as she could remember, the black iron gates had been secured in the open position. Emma tried to think of something interesting to say about them.

These . . . are gates. Yep, that about sums it up. There's nothing interesting about a dilapidated fence and two chipping gates. Still, he probably appreciates that they're old. No, that's not the right word. Antique? Rustic? Vintage? Weathered? Yes, weathered.

Calling his attention to the top of each gate, Emma pointed out the words 'Dillingham' that sat atop the left gate and 'Manor' that sprawled across the right one.

"They're pretty weathered. A lot of etching can be seen on the ironwork."

Colton nodded his head as he ran his hands lightly over the rough, flaking material, "Yes, they're quite old."

Old? Grrr! That was my first thought! Stop over thinking stuff, Emma!

The winding driveway ahead was heavily lined with maple and oak trees, the path strewn in autumn colors. Emma couldn't resist the urge to kick her feet through the fallen leaves, nor did she miss the smile that tugged at Colton's lips when he witnessed her carefree stride.

He commented on how beautiful the foliage was with its red, yellow, and orange hues.

"Autumn's my favorite season," Emma said. "I love everything about it – the ever changing color palette, cooler weather, and an excuse to wear boots. It's perfect."

Colton agreed that he could see why she would think so.

As they continued on, a squirrel darted past her feet. Startled, Emma lost her balance and began to stumble. Colton's arms shot out in an effort to catch her, but it was all in vain. With her hand wound tightly around his arm, he ended up tumbling to the ground right beside her. A thick blanket of leaves cushioned their landing.

Rather than being embarrassed, Emma found herself laughing hysterically as she glanced over at Colton. He was laughing, too. She was sure she was quite the sight being all sprawled out on the ground. Emma turned to her side and propped herself up on her arm.

"Mr. Graves, this was all part of my research, you know."

"Well, yes, of course. The evil squirrels of Kentucky," Colton said, feigning concern.

Emma was dragged from her blissful moment by a sound that she hated. Nancy was coming down the drive and sounding that annoying horn that grated on her last nerve. The bun of Nancy's salt and pepper hair was the only thing that could be seen over the steering wheel.

Colton stood and extended his hands to Emma to help her up. They stepped aside as the landlady drove past. She stopped abruptly and lowered her window.

Staring at the taillights of the car, Emma attempted being polite. "Hi, Miss Nancy. How are you today?" She called out and waited for the retort. *I can only imagine where this will go. That old bat hates me!*

Nancy poked her head out the window, looking back at them. "Emma, if you must frolic about on the ground, can you do so somewhere other than the drive?" Nodding to Colton, she continued, "And take your boyfriend elsewhere. The Dillingham has a reputation to uphold."

Emma pursed her lips and narrowed her eyes, but said nothing.

Quirking a brow, Colton looked at Emma, "Friend of yours?" he whispered, clearly amused.

"Foe! That would be Miss Nancy, the crazy old bat with the all seeing eye." At his puzzled expression, she continued, "And, the worst landlady and neighbor in history!"

"Ah, yes, the landlady." His eyes narrowed, but only briefly. Colton had a job to do and tipping his hand to the fact that she was there illegally was not part of the plan. He had to find out why.

Nancy motioned for him to come to the car. "And who are you," she asked, looking up at his tall frame.

"My name is Colton Graves. Pleased to meet you." With this, her eyes lit up. It was clear that she, too, appreciated a man with an accent.

She nodded at Emma, "You should stay away from that one. She's nosy. Always snooping around where she's not wanted and asking questions.

"That's because I'm a *reporter!*" Emma murmured under her breath. She was sure her nostrils flared at the same time her fists clenched.

When the landlady had delivered her warning, she drove further down the drive and stopped, rather than exiting.

Colton looked from the car to Emma. "What's she doing?"

"She's watching us in the rearview mirror. Some nosy neighbors try to be discreet. Not her. She doesn't care if you see her spying."

"Will she leave?"

"She will. There's one thing she hates worse than me and that's people *enjoying* themselves! I'm just going to move a little closer to you, she'll draw her own conclusions about my intentions, and she'll tear out of here in no time."

Instead, Colton closed the distance between them. He snaked his arm around her waist and pulled her flush with his body. Even though she knew this was pretend, Emma couldn't help the breath that hitched in her throat.

Colton placed the opposite hand on the back of her neck

and lowered his head. His gaze traveled over her lips which were full and parted.

With their bodies so close, she could feel the rise and fall of his chest against hers. Emma's eyes fell heavy as she inhaled his scent. He smelled good – a clean, fresh scent that could only be described as one hundred percent masculinity.

Barely registering the hum of a motor over the roar of her heartbeat in her ears, Emma was vaguely aware of Nancy's presence.

Colton pulled her closer leaving less than an inch between their lips.

Oh. My. God. She thought as she felt his warm breath feather across her lips. That image was all the landlady needed. She shot down the drive like a bullet. *Damn that woman! Why does she have to be so predictable?*

Suddenly, thoughts of Nancy faded away when Emma found herself still folded in Colton's arms, his appraisal lingering on her lips. His gaze traveled back up to her eyes before he slowly released her.

They walked toward the house.

Well, hell. She willed her heart to stop racing. She hoped he hadn't picked up on her obvious appreciation of his closeness.

Trying to shake her mind of the awkward encounter – awkward only because she wanted the kiss - Emma said, "You know, with you and your family being the rightful owners of this house, you could send her packing!"

"Emma, I have no proof in hand that any of that is true. I can't just storm the castle and slay the dragon."

Emma glanced at him. "No? Well, it would really help the princess if you could! Miss Nancy's a nasty old bitty."

He smiled.

When Dillingham Manor was almost in sight, Emma tried to prepare him for what he was about to see.

"Colton, I just want you to be prepared when you see the house, and again, I am so sorry that it's in this condition. I know it's going to be so much worse than you expect."

When they walked around the final bend, there was no postponing the inevitable. There before them stood bleak Dillingham Manor with its faded white wood and fractured exterior. As he walked, he took in the condition of the house. He took photos with his phone and made notations about this and that. She could tell that the property had changed a lot from the photos that he had seen. Emma watched as Colton walked up the stairs. He ran his fingers over the columns and tested them for strength. He noted the carvings on each post and then checked the railings that ran along the edge of the porch.

Even though Emma thought that he would be devastated, he didn't seem to comment much. Colton walked into the yard and glanced up at the windows. She watched as he circled the house and touched every surface that he could. He checked the siding, the window sills, the down spouts . . . Everything that he could touch, he did. He took more photos and notations as he checked the boundaries of the property.

Once he finished assessing the exterior, Colton requested they move inside. Emma told him about Nancy's ability to halt her attempts.

"How many times have you tried to explore?"

"Three. And she caught me every time! Either she's

synched her schedule to mine or she really never goes anywhere."

Colton looked around with a wicked grin, "Well, she's not here now . . ." He extended his hand in her direction, and that was all the encouragement Emma needed.

The weathered entryway door looked to be original to the home with its faded walnut finish and prominent oval window in the center. Sheer fabric, the color of cream, distorted the view within. With a look back at Emma, Colton pushed inside.

From his grandparents' photo albums, he'd painted a mental picture of what the house would look like. Only that wasn't at all what he saw. Colton's brows drew firmly together - equal parts shock and anger. The open foyer he expected with a semi-winding staircase in the distance simply didn't exist. Instead, the panel of doors that greeted him more closely resembled an apartment building than a stately home.

Emma saw his expression. As much as she wanted to ponder the design with him, there simply was no time to discuss the "whys." Nancy would be back soon, and she wasn't about to miss another opportunity to explore. Fanning her hand to the side, she began familiarizing him with the layout. "To the right you'll find our renters' rooms. Here's our 'commoners' bathroom, as Nancy likes to call it." She pointed cattycornered to the left of where they stood. Beyond that was a sitting room the landlady strictly forbade anyone else from using.

From his appraisal of the exterior, Colton knew that the home was deeper than the boarders' quarters allowed for. Knowing within reason that the door leading into the rest of the house wouldn't be where renters had access, they went to the side that Nancy deemed her own.

The small sitting room, which was located beside the landlady's bedroom, had an entirely different feel altogether. It was warm and inviting with framed portraits gracing the cream colored walls and an oriental rug covering the wood floor. Soft light poured out beneath the shade of a floor lamp giving the alcove a homey appearance. A bookcase with well-worn titles flanked one side of a wingback chair. On the other side sat a wicker basket containing skeins of yarn, crochet needles, and a rose colored afghan two shades darker than the chair. Colton's eyes were drawn to the tapestry that hung above the chair. More specifically, to the three inches of hardwood that peeked out below. Common sense guided his steps.

With his hand grasping the armrest, he pulled the furniture aside. Just as Colton suspected, the chair and tapestry concealed an entryway. It had been a clever move, but his keen eye for architecture quickly detected the ruse. He reached for the handle. His smile mirrored Emma's when it provided no resistance.

Inching around the chair, they stepped inside, closing the door behind them. Even though there was nothing they could do about the skewed furniture, with the tapestry mounted to the frame of the door, at least having it closed would make their presence less obvious.

Colton and Emma were greeted by darkness and a thick, musty odor. Emma hugged herself tight, running her hands up and down her arms to ward off the chill that hung in the air. Colton illuminated the space using the light from his cell phone. Three locked doors - one on each side and the other at the end of the hall - denied further access.

"I have a mean drop kick," Emma joked. "Just let me know if you need me to kick down any doors."

The deep baritone of his laughter echoed off the walls. "Perhaps we could employ a less barbaric method to begin with." Handing her the phone so she could aim the light, Colton tugged his wallet from his back pocket then produced a shiny credit card.

Turning his attention to the matter at hand, he grasped the handle on the left. Wiggling the card back and forth between the frame and the lock assembly, he worked it until it gave way. With the door creaking open, a splinter of light filtered toward them. Emma drew in a shaky breath. The thrill of discovery always excited her. And *this* was exciting. She'd seen the pictures and now was about to witness Dillingham Manor's forbidden corridors firsthand. Colton hesitated for only a moment, glancing back at her.

As he pushed inside, the corner of the warped door dragged across the floor making a loud scraping sound. And just like that, the magic was lost. Emma had thought it wasn't possible for the Dillingham to get any worse. She was wrong. Moving deeper into the room, she saw a haunting reminder of the beauty it once held.

Beams of light shone through twin columns of windows, highlighting dust particles in the air. The curtain rods had long since concaved, gathering the long drapes into V formations. Maybe they were brown. Maybe they were blue. One thing was certain; whatever hue they were originally was now caked with a powdery gray film. The entire room was in disarray.

Colton was silent as he took in the surroundings. Even amidst the ruins, he saw the beauty. Short strips of ceiling debris hung like streamers overhead. They were plentiful, a multitude having fallen down to litter the floor in a sea of crumbled plaster. The crystal chandeliers were strewn with spider webs, dust, and debris.

Movement caught his attention. In the far corner of the

room, Emma stood in front of a broken down piano. Green mold inched up one side, the wood pulling away in small sections of curled strips. She fingered a key. It depressed, but no sound emitted.

"I wish I had my camera," she said softly.

It was then that she heard the click of his. She looked over her shoulder in time for Colton to capture another image. When she smiled, he took one last photo. He could see it, too. Could hear and feel the untold story in the room.

"From the accounts in the letters of the piano and the staircase, I've every reason to believe *this* is the ballroom."

Emma lit up with excitement. She stripped away what she saw and imagined the room in another place in time. Her appraisal turned to the semi-winding staircase that flanked the right side of the room. Its handrail topped balusters to the left of the stairs and turned into a swirl at the end. She knew it had been a beautiful sight at one time. Emma imagined the room in another era brimming with Brookfield royalty at the annual Harvest Ball. She could almost hear the gasps as she imagined a parade of beautiful woman and handsomely clad suitors. She envisioned the breathtaking ladies as they descended the staircase in their long, flowing gowns. She thought maybe they wore masks with feathers and bright colors. Maybe some of them had the masks with holding sticks that gloved hands would grasp. Urgent words tore her from her daydream.

"Emma! Did you hear me?"

"What? No."

"I said she's coming." They looked around the room. With no place to hide, they decided their only course of action was to ascend the staircase. When they heard the clicking of Miss Nancy's heels in the corridor nearby, they bound up the stairs as quickly and quietly as they could.

Once at the top, they entered through the first door they

found unlocked. Vintage architecture greeted them with low, slanted dormers extending from the ceiling as older homes of that era often had. The focal point of the empty room was an enormous window draped in flowing layers of fabric. The dust engrained cobalt curtains spanned the distance from the floor to the ceiling.

A creaking step alerted them to the fact that someone was close by. Colton motioned across the room then pulled his finger to his mouth as a reminder to proceed quietly. Rushing for the cover of the drapes, Emma hit the corner of her forehead on a dormer. A blue indention was visible immediately. Colton took her by the hand and easily folded them in the layers, disappearing into the curtains fully.

Nancy's accusatory voice echoed off the walls of the hall outside the door, "I know you're up here, you nosy little woman!"

Emma's head hurt so badly, but all she could do was lay it on Colton's chest and chuckle, quietly. She was certain that he found her to be the clumsiest woman alive. While waiting for the landlady to leave, they spoke in whispered tones.

"You hit your head pretty hard. Are you ok?"

"Bruised my ego more than anything," she whispered. *God he smells good!* Once again, Emma found herself pressed against his body. And once again, she liked it.

"Let me take a look," Colton said softly. He tilted her chin up, brushing her hair aside. The gentle glide of his thumb over the knot sent chills racing through her body. He leaned closer, the gap between them closing.

Her heart leapt from her chest. *Oh my God.* Emma's gaze dropped to his lips.

"Let me get that for you, luv." Colton reached over and removed a leaf from her hair.

Damn. She closed her eyes and bit back a smile. *Has it really been so long since I've been in a man's embrace that I'd*

mistake any form of attention for affection? First aid, grooming . . .
She had little time to ponder her feelings further.

They both went completely still when they heard the
door creak open. Emma gazed up at Colton who winked in
response. The smile on his lips made it apparent that he was
enjoying the game of cat and mouse.

Emma jumped when the slamming door caused the
windows to rattle. His arms tightened in silent reassurance
around her.

It was apparent that a quick sweep of the room was all
Nancy was interested in. When the clicking of her heels
against the hardwood floor grew fainter, they realized it was
clear to exit their hiding spot.

"That was fun," Colton said with a laugh. "A refreshing
change to my usual work duties."

"My usual work duties don't normally involve breaking
and entering either, but it'll sure look impressive on my
resume. Or rap sheet."

"You're quite funny," Colton said with a chuckle.

His hand that now rested on the small of her back made
her smile. It was an innocent gesture, but one she liked.

As they moved toward the door, they looked back in the
direction of the windows where a gap in the curtains
revealed Nancy walking in the yard, looking for them, no
doubt. They made their way back into the ballroom and then
into the common part of the house. When they exited the
front door, Nancy was waiting for them.

"Emma, you'd do well to stick to your room, your
commoner's bathroom, and not anywhere else, understood?"
She shot them a hateful look, then walked past into
the house.

When the door closed behind them, Emma looked at
Colton and placed her hands in a praying motion, "Please
slay the dragon!" They both laughed at her plea.

Colton closed his hands over hers for a brief moment before uttering a single word, "Soon."

With their investigation of Dillingham Manor thwarted by the unwelcomed return of Nancy, they headed back to town to have lunch.

CHAPTER 4

On their walk back to town, they discussed the house and the condition that it was in.

"It's apparent that we won't be holding a masquerade ball at Dillingham Manor," Colton said.

"Yeah, the ballroom was in pretty bad shape. It's *all* in pretty bad shape."

"As bad as I know it looked to you, Emma, I think it could be fixed relatively easily."

"You mean you could still have the party there?"

"Sadly, no. Not at this time, anyway." Colton turned to look at her. "But if my freelance assistant, or whatever we're calling you, could point me in the right direction, we could still have one on Halloween."

"I'll put you in touch with a realtor who's a friend of my dad. Her name is Peggy. I have no doubts that she'll come up with the perfect spot for you." Emma pointed up ahead. "We'll get the number off the office window as we pass by."

"Is the rest of your day busy?" Colton asked.

Emma nodded. "A little. I have to meet with my boss, Phil, when we get done with lunch. He's on the festival committee and has asked for my help. We're finalizing activities they'll be doing this year. With this being the one hundredth annual Brookfield Harvest Festival, they're bringing back activities they've had over the years. This should be interesting."

"I should imagine so," Colton agreed. "What sort of activities will they have?"

"I'm not sure. But as long as we're not greasing pigs, I'm good with it!" She bumped his arm with her shoulder as laughter poured from them both.

Colton stopped and entered Peggy's number into his phone as they passed the window of Brookfield Realty. "In addition to a venue for the ball, I would also like her to look into a place for me to rent for the next few weeks."

I like the thoughts of him being around for a few weeks. A lot!

Colton thought for a moment. "I really dislike hotels. I've done extensive travel with my job and am often away from home for weeks or months at a time. I hate the impersonal feel of hotel rooms."

"I think the Pennington place is available at the river. It would be pricey since it's fully furnished, but that would be a lovely place to spend time. Speaking of time, how are you getting weeks off of work? Won't your boss be upset?"

He grinned. "*Being* the boss has its advantages."

Wow. "Yeah, I imagine it does. Tell me about your business."

"When I started Regal Engineering seven years ago-"

"Seven years ago?" Emma interrupted, her gaze pouring over him. "But you can't be more than-"

"Thirty-five," Colton provided with a nod. "I've always been driven, Emma. I know what I want, and I go after it. As I was saying, I started Regal Engineering seven years ago. I began as an electrical engineer, but furthered my education when I realized I preferred the design aspect of it. So to answer your previous question, no, the boss won't be upset in the least if my stay is extended."

"Oh, well what about your wife or girlfriend?" *Please say you're single!*

Colton smiled, pausing only for a moment. "Miss Saint-Claire, are you inquiring about my status?"

She was embarrassed, but chose to be coy. "Well, an investigative reporter covers every angle. When the news breaks that you're responsible for reestablishing the town ball, the ladies will be curious." She looked him up and down, "And I'm guessing some of the guys!" She wiggled her eyebrows.

He continued the conversation, leaving her hanging, "If Peggy finds a venue for me, would you be able to meet tomorrow to discuss details? You've made it perfectly clear that you're not an events coordinator, but I would value the help. You're the only one I know in this town, and I enjoy your company."

Emma wasn't used to accepting compliments. She usually fired back with a witty comment when someone gave her one. She wasn't sure why she was like that. She just was. *Wait, that makes twice that he said he enjoyed my company.*

When Emma and Colton arrived at the diner, Cat was just entering as well. She tugged her sunglasses down her nose giving Colton a once over. An appreciative nod was given to him and a wicked smile to Emma. Gesturing to Cat, Emma said, "Colton, this is my cousin, Cathryn Morgan. Everyone calls her Cat."

"Hello, Miss Morgan. Nice to meet you," he said as he extended his hand. "I'm Colton Graves."

"Colton, honey, just call me Cat." When she turned to address her cousin, she noticed the blue knot popped out on the side of Emma's forehead. "Uh, Em, what up with your head?"

"Occupational hazard," Emma answered as she shared a laugh with Colton. Cat knew there was a story, but let it go.

"I'm starving. Let's eat already!"

"Sorry, Alley Cat. We're working," Emma frowned. But when Colton insisted that it would be ok for her to join them, they happily piled into their usual booth - Emma and Colton on one side and Cat on the other.

"Let's talk about this fancy ball that you're planning," Cat said excitedly. When they explained the Dillingham would not be hosting the ball this year, she was disappointed.

"Don't worry, babe. He's gonna find another place to have it. All is not lost. Hey, can you think of any place that would accommodate a good deal of people? Since Dillingham Manor is out of the question, we need a place that is both beautiful and ready right now for a Halloween ball."

"Well, the McAllister's have that sprawling mansion at Cross Creek. Maybe I could ask Hayden. He's meeting me here for lunch."

"Cathryn Leanne Morgan! Do tell!"

"What?" Cat asked. "The guy just needs some grub."

"Mmm hmm. Yeah, I'm not buying that one! You sure seem to be spending a lot of time with Hayden lately."

Cat's gaze fell away from her cousin, but her guilty smirk spoke volumes. Emma agreed to let it drop. But only for now.

The three of them chatted about funnel cakes at the festival, music, and a story about a three legged chair from their youth that the girls had tormented a teacher with. She would throw it out and they would haul it back in. Since they were always good girls, the teacher never suspected that they were the culprits. They joked about making prank calls when they were teens and fondly remembered Emma stealing baby Jesus from the manger during a Christmas program when they were just three years old. Colton chimed in, "So the mayor's son put the devil in church and you took Jesus out? Perhaps it was you who was mean as the devil!" Their laughter was cut short by the dinging of the bell.

Suddenly, Cat sat up and a different kind of smile crept across her face as she looked toward the door. Emma turned to see who had elicited such a reaction from her cousin when she spotted the sandy haired police officer. His broad muscular frame filled the doorway. When an equally broad smile touched his lips, Emma heard movement across from her.

Cat rose and greeted Hayden as he entered the diner. Emma was shocked when she met him with a kiss and then they chose another booth. She gave Colton a shoulder shrug, "And that would be Hayden McAllister. I'm as much in the dark as you are about this one."

"They haven't been dating long?"

Emma glanced back at the duo, "As far as I knew, they didn't date at all! I guess we see how much I know."

Focusing her attention back on Colton, Emma remembered that British people liked hot tea. At least they did in the movies, so she excused herself and found Bonny.

"Bonny, my friend over there is from England-"

"Sugar, I noticed your friend the second you came through the door, as did every other lady in here. He seemed to be enjoying the story you were telling, so I've kept my distance. Can I get you something?"

"Would you mind bringing him a cup of hot tea?" Emma was so proud of herself. She knew he would notice how thoughtful she had been. Bonny came right away with the drink and Colton looked surprised, but thanked her. He was very kind. He sipped the hot tea and engaged Emma in conversation about Nancy. They ordered their food, but Emma was running late for her meeting with Phil, so she didn't get to finish it.

Saying goodbye to Colton, she hesitantly rose to leave. Emma walked over to Cat's table, hugged her cousin good-bye, and whispered in her ear. "You've been holding out on me, Cathryn. I'll collect those details, soon!" She was certain that Cat had withheld details about her relationship with Hayden to shield Emma. *Great! Now even my best friend is treating me weird! But I'm so happy for her.* With one last look in Colton's direction, Emma gave him a wave and went back to work.

CHAPTER 5

*E*ven though she wanted to stay at the diner and learn more about the handsome stranger she'd just met, Emma now found herself perched on the corner of Phil's desk awaiting a teleconference with the festival committee. He hurriedly tried to complete a game of solitaire before the call. It was more of a "for your information" meeting rather than a brainstorming session. Emma had been living in Louisville when planning first began and had only recently been asked to join them. She was curious about the activities. *No greased pigs, no greased pigs . . .*

Emma tried to imagine booths that would've graced the streets of Brookfield over the last hundred years. The cup of water on Phil's desk brought a dunking tank to mind. She glanced over at her boss and imagined him plummeting into the frigid water. She couldn't help but smile as she pictured his short, plump frame flailing his arms and legs as he tried to find his footing on the slippery bottom. His curly red hair would-

The beeping of the fax machine pulled her from her thoughts. Emma rose and refilled the empty paper cartridge.

Within seconds, out popped the list of activities that the committee members planned for the festival. She walked back to Phil's desk, and they read it together.

One Hundredth Annual Brookfield Harvest Festival:

Hey guys, here's the list of activities that we came up with. I hope they're ok with you all. We asked a few townspeople to give us ideas of events they would like to see. We made a list of eight activities that have been at the festival over the years. Brookfield Journal will man two booths. You guys have number three and four on the roster. We think that these activities along with the vendor booths, the haunted house, and the carnival will make for a great festival.

Each group has taken two activities. Here's the list -pony rides, wagon rides, kissing booth, sack race, bobbing for apples, costume contest, face painting, and dunking tank.

Emma looked up and gave a sheepish grin to her boss. "The sack race isn't bad. But the kissing booth?" She capped her hand over her mouth. Through a muffled voice, she continued, "I know one thing; it ain't gonna be me in that booth!"

"I'd volunteer . . . but we'd have to pay them money," Phil said with a snort. "These are activities that were around a long time ago. I suppose it could've been worse."

"I don't know, Phil. Nothing says cooties like kissing booths and bobbing for apples!" Emma studied the list again. Her mind drifted to the masquerade ball. That was something that was around a long time ago and if Colton had his say, it would be back again this year. She wondered if the old tradition would be adopted again. *How fun it would be to plan such an event every year.*

"Emma, you're being quiet. Are you upset about the activities? I know apple bobbing is kind of gross, but I remember when I was a kid, and we did it. Everyone really enjoyed it. They enjoyed kissing booths, too." A distant memory caused a smile.

"No, I'm not upset. It's just a germaphobe's worst nightmare!" She shrugged her shoulders, "It's not like you or I will be in that kissing booth, so what do we care?" They both laughed at someone's misfortune.

With the two of them refusing to run the booth, they had to choose who would. Laura was pregnant. *And weird.* Ryan would be out of town, so the obvious choice was Lisa. With her glossy black hair, olive skin, hazel eyes, and slim figure, they would have no trouble getting people to line up. Not only was she beautiful, but charismatic, too. They knew they'd hit pay dirt with that idea.

"We could charge for her kisses and give the money to charity. I suppose we could donate the proceeds to the fire department or the police department to purchase toys for children at Christmas. And since it appears my cousin is dating the police Sergeant, I should have no problem finding out if they're doing that again this year."

Phil was still thinking about the likelihood of Lisa manning the booth. "Do you think Lisa'd agree to be in a kissing booth? Maybe you should try to get Cat instead." Everyone in town knew that Cat loved the men, and they loved her.

"Cat might be a little preoccupied. Besides, I think Lisa will do it. As for the sack race, I think we'll have a contest to determine the finalists. We can't have seventy kids trying to race. Someone will get hurt. We have to narrow it down. I want it to be a contest that they win – not their parents - so no coloring or poetry writing or crafts. Oh, maybe we could have them eat as much as they can and . . . no wait. That would turn into a puking contest." Emma quickly attempted to shake *that* visual out of her mind. She rose to her feet. Sometimes pacing helped her thought process. Or at the very least, it got her moving which might get her brain moving in a new direction, too. Spotting a framed article on Phil's wall gave her an idea. "On second thought, let's have them do a junior journalist segment at school with no prior notice. That way, they won't be coached and any idea that they come up with will be theirs and theirs alone."

"Sounds great, Emma! What would they report on?"

"Hmm, well how about-"

Emma was interrupted by the phone ringing. This was the conference call they were waiting on. They discussed the activities with the committee, only making minor changes here and there. Emma and Phil told the committee that they already knew who would be in charge of the kissing booth and that they would discuss the sack race further then call them when the details had been ironed out.

Once the call was finished, they discussed the logistics of the contest. Emma suggested that their junior journalists would tell the most creative story, truth or fiction, about Brookfield or a town event. They would publish the five winning stories and those five children would have the chance to be in the sack race.

With Phil's focus returning to a game of solitaire, Emma walked back to her office. She sat down at her own computer and clicked on the email icon. She couldn't suppress the smile that lit up her face when she saw a message from Colton.

Dear Emma,

I wanted to thank you for taking the time to meet with me today. I enjoyed the tour of Brookfield and the manor. While the estate was in poor condition, I rather enjoyed our escapades avoiding Miss Nancy. Also, thank you for putting me in contact with Peggy. She plans to show me several properties. If all goes well, I will contact you tomorrow, and we'll start planning the ball.

Sincerely,

Colton

Clicking on the message, Emma dragged it to the folder labeled "Personal." She had every intention of reading it over and over.

As she was preparing to go home for the day, Emma stopped by Lisa's desk and informed her about the festival activities and that she had been chosen to "man" the kissing booth.

"Why me?" Lisa asked.

"Because you're the obvious choice. Ryan will be out of town at the athletic conference. Laura will be on maternity leave soon and the other option is me, and I'm not doing it. Then there's Phil . . . but we won't go there!" That in itself was self-explanatory. Lisa didn't put up too much of a fight about it, which Emma was happy for.

"Oh Lisa, one more thing, will you send a fax to the elementary schools in the morning asking them to have their students do a writing segment for us?"

Handing her a sheet of paper, Emma outlined what they

would like the students to write about. She stated that the winners would be chosen by Brookfield Journal staff members. The entries were to be delivered or picked up after school tomorrow, and the winners would be announced to the schools on Monday. Emma knew that any children who were absent from school on Friday would automatically be out of the running, literally, but that was the best they could come up with. She also knew that this meant that she would be working the weekend. Entries from the five elementary schools would be divided by four of the five staff members: Phil, Emma, Lisa, and Laura. Since Ryan would be out of town, the staff member who got two schools would be chosen from a draw. *Please let it be Laura . . .*

Each staff member would choose a winner from their respective schools. Emma always loved seeing how little minds worked and enjoyed hearing their stories, so it wouldn't be a bad weekend.

Emma shouldered her satchel, stepping out into the fresh autumn air. The evening sun, although beautiful, assaulted her eyes after being in the dark office. She lowered herself to a park bench while she dug blindly through her bag for her sunglasses. The aching in her feet reminded her that she'd sleep well tonight. Emma had had a full day of running all over town, meetings, and, of course, her latest job as a free-lance- Well, she really didn't know what her title was, but as long as she was working with Colton, she didn't care. She concluded that meeting Colton Graves certainly was the highlight of her day. No, make that year. She recollected every detail about him – his tall frame, muscular body, handsome face, tousled hair, and devine scent. *Has anyone ever smelled better? I think not!*

Emma recalled the smile that lit up his gorgeous eyes, the

way her heart had thumped wildly in her chest as they were pressed together while tricking Nancy into thinking they were going to kiss. *Miss Nancy . . . Geez! That woman is the bane of my existence.* Emma knew that if she and Colton had actually kissed, that it would have been a sweet escape that she would never have wanted to return from. She closed her eyes and sighed heavily.

~

The rumble in her stomach having guided her steps, Emma exited the doors of the Chinese restaurant. She glanced into the paper bag at the white box that contained her beef and broccoli and fished out her fortune cookie. She ripped it open with her teeth, placing the plastic inside the paper sack. As she walked, she chomped on the treat and read her fortune. *"Life is what you make of it - make yours count. Wait not for the perfect moment, for that moment is now."*

"Well, that's certainly fitting," Emma said to herself. *I think I'll heed that advice and not let a moment pass me by again. Like Daddy always said, "You better get it the first time around, 'cause you don't know if it's coming back."*

Emma wondered what Colton was doing for supper tonight. He had left her hanging when she questioned him about a significant other. It occurred to her that she knew very little about him. He spoke of his business, his mother, and that was it. She would have to do more adequate questioning when she did see him again. She couldn't help but hope that would be tomorrow. The thought of tomorrow made her think, once again, of a grand ball that she hoped to help plan. She thought of the costume that she'd wear. She knew it would be red. She wanted it to be risqué – low cut and form fitting. With her mask, she could be anyone she wanted to be. She pictured Colton in a black tux. Actually, she'd prefer if he wore nothing more than a Speedo . . . and maybe a bowtie. Her eyebrow hitched up at the thought.

～

As Colton settled in to his hotel room, he reflected on his day. Meeting Emma Saint-Claire had been a pleasant experience. He found her to be quite attractive, easy to talk to, and fun to be with. He liked how she handled the situation when they fell on each other in the drive at Dillingham Manor, how she laughed heartily at it rather than fretting about it like most ladies would have. He recalled how the sun had reflected off the highlights in her hair and the golden specs in her hazel eyes. He liked how she called the landlady "the dragon" when he referred to Dillingham Manor as a castle.

He was hoping against hope that the estate would be in better shape, but he knew it wasn't near condemnation as Emma had reported. He applauded himself for not moving too fast by kissing her while they were pressed together first in the driveway, then in the drapes, although it took all the self-control he could muster. He suspected that Emma had no idea how beautiful she was, and he didn't want to spook her.

He was also pleased that Peggy had not only come up with some properties for him to view in the morning, but had also secured a location to host the ball. He had given her his specifications, and she narrowed them down to a bed and breakfast, three houses to rent, and the only location in town that would work for a last minute masquerade ball. She assured him that it was sure to be a crowd pleaser as many of the townspeople had always yearned to gain access to that particular venue.

Colton hoped that Emma would be willing to help him in planning the event. He was eager to put his plan in motion. If all went well, the exposure would force the hand of the historical society, and his ancestors' home would become part of the national registry.

~

With her belly full, Emma climbed into bed. One of her nightly rituals was to work Sudoku puzzles. She'd only solved one block before her eyes fell heavy and she quickly drifted off to sleep . . .

Saving the document she'd been working on for the last few hours, Emma rubbed her strained eyes, relieved the project was finally done. She was done, too, and was looking forward to a long, uneventful weekend. Pulling her hair into a ponytail, she shut off her computer, gathered her things, and moved toward the door. She had the honor of locking up since she was the low man on the totem pole and therefore, the last one there on a Friday night. With her hand on the light switch, she looked back at the office, noting how cold it felt. The blaring fluorescent lights and bare white walls held no warmth. The white cubicles were crammed so tightly together, they better resembled mazes for lab rats than a conducive work-space- Emma shook her head, halting the thought. She hated this place. Who wouldn't? With the flip of the switch, she cast the room into darkness, blocking out the glaring reminder that this was what she chose.

Emma dropped the keys in her bag after locking the door and turned to descend the concrete steps leading to the water's edge. Heavy fog rolled across the river, anchoring her to her spot. It reminded her of home, and she took a moment to appreciate the canvas before her. Outlines of docked vessels stood out against the thick fog while the pale lights of the riverside restaurants blinked faintly in the distance. It was a beautiful sight.

Sliding her bag off her arm to get her camera, she wondered if there was enough background light to capture the image.

A whipping sound snapped the silence as a fluttering movement caught her eye. Panic welled deep inside her, and she shrieked, dropping the bag. She bolted, glancing back over her shoulder in fear. But the boogeyman she expected simply wasn't there. She clapped her hands over eyes, shaking her head and laughing in relief. It was the flag. She gripped the handrail and laughed again. The good ole American flag had nearly given her a heart attack.

"Delivery," an ominous voice called out, shattering her relief.

Emma turned toward the stairs to see a courier holding a package. The long, rectangle box was shimmering silver with a red translucent bow tied around it. "For you, Amanda." She quickly forgot the beauty of the package as the words fell from his lips.

The icy stare in the stranger's pale eyes was pure evil. He was no delivery boy. It was him - the stalker who'd promised to make her pay. And she was cornered, like helpless prey. Emma tried to move past him, but he caught her arm.

"You fucking look at me when I'm talking to you," he screamed, digging his fingers into her arm painfully.

With an elbow to his ribs, she jabbed back with all her might in an attempt to get away. But it had little effect.

His hand shot forward, grabbing her ponytail. The stranger dragged her down the steps then tossed her face first onto the park bench at the base of the stairway. The box fell to her side.

As she turned, his fist crashed into her face, sending jarring pain shooting through her. In an effort to move him off her, Emma began kicking and hitting him. She could feel the weight of his body pressing her down, silencing her fight. In a last ditch effort, she clenched her hand against his cheek. Digging her fingernails into his flesh, she ripped out a jagged chunk.

The stranger stumbled backwards, grasping his face.

Reaching down, Emma searched for something, anything, to defend herself with. Her fingers closed around the box. Springing to her feet, she swung with all her might. Red rose petals rained down on the man, an Ebony Rose falling untouched to his feet. Death.

The significance of the flower dawned on her as searing pain tore through her wrist, over and over.

Masked by darkness, the stranger dragged her by her hair to a bench at the water's edge. With his hand closing around her neck, he began to squeeze. "You took everything from me, bitch . . . now I'll return the favor."

Sights, sounds, fears - they all began to fade . . .

Emma bolted awake, her heart thundering in her chest. With every passing breath, with every rise and fall of her chest, the images of her nightmare drifted into the night like a feather riding the currents of the wind. Little did she know that the *dream* she was so quick to dismiss was no dream at all but the actual occurrence of her last night in Louisville – the night she came face to face with her stalker.

CHAPTER 6

$\mathcal{C}$olton met the realtor at her office. She was excited to show him the properties, and he was eager to see them. She thought they would start with the easiest task first – approval of the banquet hall.

Peggy explained that Victorian Gardens was a privately owned estate situated on the lakefront just outside of Brookfield. Invitation was extended to any prominent figure that could or would cast Meg and Thomas Lewis in the limelight. Peggy described them as being eccentric and shallow. Colton's only concern was that they had a space to rent, not with their personality flaws.

The realtor suspected that she'd have a satisfied customer the moment the Lewis' heard her client speak. With his British accent, she was certain he could charm them into anything he wanted.

Colton and Peggy drove to Lake Brookfield Estates. The homes that dotted the landscape in the exclusive lakeside subdivision were impressive in grandeur as were their immaculate grounds.

Victorian Gardens sat just off the lakefront to the left and was every bit as exquisite as Peggy had promised. In Colton's line of work, money was no object for his clients, and as he gazed upon the home they had just pulled in front of, it was clear that it was no problem for the Lewis' either.

After a tour of the banquet hall, Colton and Peggy were shown to a sitting area around the back of the home by a staff member. The warm morning sun spilled onto the veranda, autumn hues the perfect backdrop to the peaceful morning. Colton inwardly groaned as he shifted in the uncomfortable white chair. The wrought iron material might be pleasing to the eye, but the bum was a different story.

The Lewis' joined them for coffee and pastries. With small talk and pleasantries exchanged, negotiations began. Colton lowered his cup to a dainty saucer. "As Peggy informed you, I would take great honor in reserving your banquet hall for a Halloween night masquerade ball."

"Oh, just like they did in the old days," Mrs. Lewis inhaled excitedly, clasped her hands together and held them to her chest. "I think that's a splendid idea!"

It was apparent to both Colton and Peggy that Mrs. Lewis wanted to renew more than town history with this endeavor.

"There's just a few bits of business we have to take care of, our conditions and such," Meg offered. "Our fee is three thousand dollars to secure the room for the evening."

Peggy looked to Colton to see if that was a deal breaker, knowing the fee was much too high. Colton knew it as well.

"Mrs. Lewis, I'm willing to offer fifteen hundred for the evening and not a penny more." Without giving her a chance to interrupt, he continued on. "I have journalism connections who will announce the event publicly. Only those receiving an invitation would have the honor of attending. Those are *my* conditions."

Colton had no trouble getting Meg to lower her price. He played on her weakness, which was the need for notoriety. Both she and Mr. Lewis agreed to his offer.

Having made plans to return tomorrow to finalize contractual obligations, Colton and his realtor made their way back to her car and drove back to town.

Even though he was disappointed that Dillingham Manor couldn't host the ball this year, the publicity would draw attention to him, allowing him the opportunity to tell the history of Samuel and Elizabeth's home. Nothing would get the historical society involved faster than a town abuzz.

Now that the masquerade ball had a temporary home, it had to be planned. He would call Emma to tell her the good news, but he realized that he didn't have her number with him.

"Peggy, would you happen to have the number to the Brookfield Journal? If not, I can look it up. I'd like to call Emma and tell her the good news about securing Victorian Gardens."

"How do you know Emma anyway?" She asked.

"She's assisting in planning the event and is being very helpful."

"I just love Emma. Everyone does. We were all so happy when she came back."

"When she came back? Where did she go?"

"To Louisville; it's not that far away, but worlds different than here! She moved back here several months ago. She wasn't gone very long. Rumor has it that she had a bad experience there and that someone treated her real bad. She had a run in with some crazy man. No one knows, really, what happened – just that it was bad. I can't imagine anyone harming Emma."

"Nor can I." Colton honestly couldn't fathom it.

"She's always been so helpful to everyone in town. Before she left, she rented a cute little house nearby on Oakland Hills Road. She always loved the water and the wide open space. It's a shame she had to move into the Dillingham when she came back. I know she hates it there with it being so closed-in and dark, but there's just no other place in town that she can afford right now. In order to leave her new job in Louisville, she had to pay back her sign on advance. They didn't care that she was in danger. It made more business for the paper she wrote for. She came back here without a penny to her name. If Cat, that's her cousin, if she hadn't taken her in, well, I don't know what she would've done. Those two have always been thick as thieves."

Colton felt like his head had become a permanent attachment to the headrest. Not only had Peggy taken every curve at a high rate of speed, she'd passed a car without any regard to the "no passing zone." Even though he had a penchant for fast cars, he realized that only held true when he was the driver. He needed a steering wheel in front of him . . . not a gripper bar. Settling his nerves, he took a moment to reflect on the multitude of information Peggy had flooded him with. He'd always heard that small towns were like this, everyone knowing everyone else's business, he guessed that was a fair assumption.

The realtor continued. "If you've aligned yourself with Emma Saint-Claire, you've found yourself a gem!"

He couldn't disagree. There was something about Emma that Colton really liked. He wondered what really had happened to her in Louisville.

"If she dislikes Dillingham Manor so, why wouldn't she reside with her cousin?"

"I think as much as she loves Cat, she wants independence and privacy – to give it and to get it." Peggy thought for a moment. "It's no secret that Cat has many . . . *sleepovers* with her gentlemen friends." She chuckled at her crafty wording, but Colton had no trouble grasping the meaning.

Trying to determine if she was repeating facts or rumors, Colton asked for clarification. "With all due respect, Peggy, how are you aware of her misfortune? I assume she hasn't discussed it with you since you're unsure of some details."

"Mr. Graves, this is a small town. Everyone knows everyone else's business - it's a blessing in times of hurt the way we all rally around each other and then again, it's also a curse when you need time to heal. Emma needs time to heal. Her father, Daniel, and I go way back. When he and Claire moved to Texas, I was asked to keep an eye on Emma. I haven't told him about her experience in Louisville – partly because I don't know all the facts and partly because I know Emma wouldn't want her daddy hovering around her, smothering her."

"That's very thoughtful of you."

"Like I said, we all love her."

"Peggy, about that number?"

Emma made it to her eleven o'clock appointment at the Town Square Gallery. She'd been invited to an art exhibit. After all her years in journalism, she still felt slighted when she was *invited* to the most talked about events in town. She knew that it was expected that she would come as a journalist and not as a guest of honor. *For once, I'd like to come to*

something without my camera and note pad. I'd like to just be a guest.

Emma mingled about the room chatting with this person then the next, taking pictures, and making notations. The Maggards were a talented bunch of artists, and it really was neat to see how their minds worked. John helped out in different treatment centers, bringing his Art Therapy into existence.

Light music drifted through the air from unseen speakers, soothing the crowd as they focused on John. With graceful fluidity, he quickly transformed a blank canvas into a stunning sunset. His perfectly choreographed moves and velvet voice captivated the attention of his audience.

Turning, he scanned the crowd then locked eyes on her. With a twitch of his lips, he began to speak. "Emma, I'm looking for a volunteer. You'd love to help, wouldn't you?"

She pointed to herself and shook her head exaggeratedly, "Not exactly."

John smiled. "I think our little journalist needs some encouragement."

Artist and audience alike were relentless. Caving to peer pressure, Emma rose to her feet and reluctantly joined him on the platform.

She had a problem – a big problem. Even stickmen looked bad when she attempted to draw. Emma was a craftsman of words. But of images? Not so much. John told her to draw anything she wanted and as she drew, he would tell the story of what she painted. She thought her intended image would be a lollipop, but knew that the guesses from the crowd would be more along the lines of *hot air balloon plummeting to the ground, perhaps a tornado, maybe it's the apocalypse . . .*

She could just imagine their guesses and knew that whatever she tried to draw, it would not be successful.

John fanned his hand out toward her, "The reluctant Emma Saint-Claire, everyone." The crowd applauded and Emma took her place in front of the easel. Funny they should call it an easel because she felt nothing close to *ease*!

John explained that this was a new therapy technique they were using at his treatment facility. He said that much was revealed about a person's reaction when their drawing was altered. He prompted her to begin drawing any image she chose.

Emma began. She drew a straight line down the page. John explained that that line represented the journey of life. She made a loop at the top of the line. He said that the loop represented a life coming full circle, the end of an era. Even though she had planned to make a sucker, John interjected a few swirls and shadows and her stick man lollipop had transformed into a rose. She frowned at the image.

He asked how she felt about that.

"I don't like flowers." In a small voice, she added, "Especially not roses." As Emma stared at the shadows cast by the charcoal crayon, tears stung her eyes. She was reminded of the black rose that haunted her dreams and the attacker whose intentions were equally as dark. Her memories of that fateful night were sketchy. Maybe that was a blessing.

John's voice broke her concentration when he asked if she wanted to add color to the rose. She reminded him that it was not a rose. When she grabbed the paint and swirled circle after circle in bright, alternating colors of yellow, pink and blue – completely covering the "rose" and making it disappear - John smiled. He said it was clear that she was in charge of her destiny. She thought that was an artsy fartsy response, but his audience seemed to buy into it with their loud applause.

"We all need to be more like Emma. Don't ever let someone alter your course. Staying true to who you are and keeping with your own thoughts, that's what sets you apart from the rest. Very good, Emma." Everyone applauded, again.

Looking back at her lollipop, Emma was proud that she hadn't freaked out over the rose. As she stepped down from the platform, she noticed pink paint had dripped on the bottom of her gray shirt. She excused herself and went to the restroom to wash it out.

As she stood at the hand dryer drying her shirt, her mind traveled back to the nightmare she'd had the night before. These senseless dreams that taunted her every night, would they ever end? Would his course ever be altered and would she survive it? Emma squeezed her eyes tightly closed and gently shook the memory of the nightmare from her head.

She opened her eyes and glanced in the mirror again. "I am in charge of my own destiny, and I will rise above this!"

Being that Brookfield was a small town, it hadn't taken long for Peggy to show Colton the handful of properties available for short-term rental.

He was eager to talk to Emma and tell her about his successful day. He called the Journal and got her voicemail.

"Good afternoon, Emma. This is Colton. I just wanted to share with you that I have been successful today in securing a banquet hall and a rental. I'm eager to get started planning the masquerade ball. I hope that you can still find time to lend a hand." After leaving his number, he hung up and went back to his hotel room.

A call to his secretary at Regal Engineering revealed that Kane, his second-in-command, was running things smoothly in his absence. There had never been any doubt that his brother was capable of handling the responsibility. *He's always made a better business partner than brother, anyway!*

Colton took out a note pad and wrote Dillingham Manor across the top. He first had to prove that he owned it. He had the document that Emma faxed him when she told him that the home belonged to the heirs of Samuel and Elizabeth Dillingham. But he knew he would need a deed to uproot Nancy and the other tenants when the time came. He also knew Emma would be happy to hear that news.

Another ticker on his to-do list was to investigate how Nancy had come to collect the rent money. Tracing cash would be hard, but something wasn't adding up about that. Colton was pulled out of his thought by the telephone ringing. *Eleanor must have forgotten something.* Without looking, Colton answered, but was pleasantly surprised to find Emma on the other end. She explained that she was famished and asked if he would he like to have a working lunch. They agreed to meet at the diner.

CHAPTER 7

*H*aving arrived first, Emma had a steaming cup of tea waiting for Colton when he joined her at the diner.

After placing their order, Colton slowly sipped his tea while listening to Emma explain that her day had started on a bad note. She had overslept after a nightmare induced ninja session had sent her arms flailing and her alarm clock careening to the floor, inadvertently shutting it off.

"I'm sorry you had a nightmare. Do you want to talk about it?"

"Colton, if you lived in the Bates house, you'd have bad dreams, too." Emma chuckled and then stopped, abruptly. It was out before she could stop herself. She knew that his feelings for Dillingham Manor and the reality that she lived would never align, but she really regretted being herself sometimes. "I'm sorry, Colton. I'm just no good and pure rotten sometimes," Emma frowned.

"Miss Saint-Claire, I assure you that there is nothing rotten about you. Why are you calling the estate 'the Bates house?' What does that mean?"

"Oh, just a creepy old movie," Emma dismissed the thought with a wave of her hand. "Anyway, that's not the least of it. I had another horrific experience today. I had to paint."

"At Dillingham Manor?"

"Oh, heavens no! I don't mean paint a room. Miss Nancy would never allow that! I had to paint a picture at an art gallery . . . in front of people."

"Oh, I didn't realize you were an artist."

Emma snorted. Everyone looked their way, but she ignored them. "Artist and Emma should not even be uttered in the same sentence. I swear, Colton, I can't draw anything. At all. I was so embarrassed." She shrugged her shoulders, "I drew a lollipop."

"A lollipop sounds simple enough. I'm sure you were brilliant."

"I was not."

Colton bit back a smile. "Why don't you draw me something now and I'll be the judge of your artistic abilities? I'm sure you're not as dreadful as you pretend to be."

Emma knew he would never be the same after viewing her abstract art. She pulled a pen and spiral-top notepad from her bag. Holding the paper so that the front cover was straight in the air, shielding her "canvas," she began to draw. Emma pretended to put great passion into the rendition, just like John had done at the gallery. When she was finished, she picked up her masterpiece, held it in front of her face at arm's length - as if checking for final approval - then nodded appreciatively. When she handed it to Colton, a huge smile spread across his face at the stickman she drew.

"You're right, Emma," he said nodding his head. "This *is* dreadful."

"Hey!" Emma protested with a scowl.

They both laughed.

Colton studied it for a moment longer, "But it certainly is a stick*man*." Emma snatched the tablet from his hands, feigning disgust at his mockery. That's when she saw that the line for his body extended a little too far between his legs.

She was embarrassed, but laughed it off. Pointing to the 'man part' of the stickman, Emma added, "Merely my attention to detail, Mr. Graves."

Colton appreciated their ease of conversation and that she would be herself around him. He was aware that his looks often made women behave in a way that he found unappealing. He concluded that Emma was either completely uninterested in him personally, or she was without a clue at how truly interesting he found her and how much more he wanted to know about her.

Emma noticed that Colton's drink sat basically untouched. "You haven't finished your tea."

"I was enjoying your story and let it get cold."

"Well, then let's order you a fresh one."

Colton had gotten far in business by being quick on his feet. He hoped that ability spilled over to redirecting the beautiful brunette across from him because he simply could not choke down another swallow of that dreadful tea. "I think I would prefer a cold drink with my lunch. Perhaps a bowl of beer?" Colton's lips quickly tugged into a devilish grin.

Emma blushed then cleared her throat as if preparing for a speech. "Again, another part of my research, Mr. Graves. I was merely checking to see how receptive you were. You know, how easily you could be swayed to agree with me."

Colton leaned in closer, hitching a brow, "Miss Saint-Claire, I think you'll find that I am easily swayed if the right idea presents itself."

Emma felt heat rise into her cheeks. She had no idea what Colton was referring to, but she knew the direction her mind had just headed - south.

"Are you feeling ok, Emma? Your cheeks are flushed."

Hot and bothered, luv . . . hot and bothered. "Yes, I'm feeling fine. It's just really hot in here!" She fanned herself and was more than relieved when Bonny popped to their side, balancing a tray of food.

Colton watched as the normal color returned to Emma's cheeks. His comment had caught her off guard, proving she wasn't *completely* unaffected by him. He smiled, unable to hide his satisfaction. Immersing himself back in the moment, Colton listened to a *scandalous* report of a Mrs. Brown. He suspected it was gossip by the way the waitress lowered her voice and tapped her ring finger when she spoke of the woman no longer wearing her wedding band.

Once the food was served, Bonny scooted off to the next table.

"Mr. Brown, the poor chap," Colton said with feigned concern.

"Mrs. Brown no longer wears her wedding band because she's gained a bit of weight. She probably can't get it on. I'm sure it has nothing to do with marital trouble." She shook her head. "You gotta love Bonny, anyway."

Emma wanted to talk about something that would interest them both. "So, let's hear about the banquet hall you rented."

"Peggy suggested Victorian Gardens, and I was fortunate to find it available."

In all her years in Brookfield, Emma had never been invited to Lake Brookfield Estates for any reason. She felt like the Lewis' looked down their noses on her professionally. She didn't even know what that part of town looked like. The gated community ensured that lowly townspeople would never have a peek inside. "I've always wondered what it looked like out there. Tell me about it."

"You mean you've never seen the Lewis' estate? I assumed you covered many events for them."

"We'll just say that they aren't the kindest people . . . or not my kind of people, anyway. What's it like out there?"

"It's exquisite. It's one of the most extraordinary places I've ever seen, and I see and design a lot. For people who want to keep others away from them, as Peggy alluded to, the Lewis' certainly have spared no expense in designing this property. Where do I begin describing it?" Colton gathered his thoughts for a moment. "Of course, it's situated on the lakefront. The driveway is a piece of art in itself and provides a prelude to all that lies behind the gates. Close your eyes, Emma. Allow me to paint a picture for you."

She did as he asked.

"I want you to imagine every detail as I describe it." When Emma nodded her head, he continued. "The long driveway is beautifully stained in hues of marbleized taupe and chocolate brown. It carries you into a picturesque garden of weeping trees, small labyrinths, and bright, stunning flowers. The circular driveway in front of the mansion runs alongside a raised patio. Its railings feature thick cement balusters as well as stone pillars. The masonry work is incredible. To the left, winding paver stones trail a path to the lakeside gazebo and also to the banquet hall entrance. A wide brick staircase leads you up to a set of double doors. Once inside, you step down into the three thousand square foot banquet hall. I couldn't help but marvel at all the details the room had to offer. Magnificent turned pillars with intricate carvings spanned the space from floor to ceiling where they rested against tin ceiling tiles. Panel moldings were all about the wall as were tall niches that housed expensive statues and floral arrangements. In the center of the room, the marbled staircase spills out onto mahogany floors offering a beautiful contrast to the beige walls. The handrails of the staircase reach into the ballroom and wind around in a swirl. On the west side of the room, there are crimson and cream flowing sheer drapes that I can't imagine would ever be closed because they encompass window lined walls that showcase the lake. I imagine it makes for a mesmerizing view as the sun sets into the water.

It's just perfect, Emma . . . and everything I had hoped Dillingham Manor would prove to be."

Emma opened her eyes. Extending her hand, she gently closed her fingers over his. She knew he was devastated over the manor, and she wanted to offer support in the only way she could - understanding. She listened attentively as he continued.

"It gives me incentive to work diligently so we can have the masquerade in its rightful place next year."

"I look forward to it and to helping you in any way I can." Emma changed the focus of the conversation. "Thank you for describing Victorian Gardens to me. I wish I could've been there with you to see it."

"I return tomorrow morning to finalize the contract. Would you care to accompany me? You could photograph the Lewis' and myself, and perhaps write an article for the paper about the masquerade ball. I want to plant the seed in the historical society's collective mind about Dillingham Manor."

Emma couldn't help the butterflies that soared into her stomach. "Yes, I'd love to go with you. This is starting to get exciting!" She squeezed his hand then released it just as quickly. Emma had forgotten her hand rested on his. "Dang it! I forgot I have to work tomorrow."

"Is Saturday a normal work day for you?"

"No, it isn't. But we have a writing contest that we extended to elementary students. So I'll be reading their entries and selecting a winner. Each staff member has to choose a winner from the school they are in charge of. It will be a long weekend for me."

Not wanting to lose the chance to spend more time with her, Colton made an offer he hoped she wouldn't refuse. "Perhaps I could assist you in choosing the winner? Not that you need help, but-"

"I would love the help," Emma interrupted. "You may find it interesting because the children were instructed to write about a town event – real or fictional - or a local person. It should be fun to see what they come up with. The reason they're writing this is because the Journal was given an event to host in the festival. Actually, we were given two. The first is a kissing booth."

"That's interesting," Colton grinned.

Emma chuckled, "Yeah. I'm not in charge of it, so I'm perfectly fine with it as an event! The second activity is a sack race. The reason the students are doing the writing segment is to win a chance to be in the race. They have no idea about the physical competition. They just think the winning five articles will be printed in the paper."

"That's a brilliant plan. However, the activities themselves are rather-"

"Ancient," she provided. "There's also apple bobbing." He raised an eyebrow in question. "Remember, it's the one

79

hundredth town festival. So they're bringing back activities that we have had throughout the years."

"Ah, that's right," he nodded in acknowledgement.

"Sounds like an exciting weekend ahead."

"Indeed. I'll assist you in sorting entries, and you'll accompany me to the Lewis estate."

"Absolutely. There's no place I'd rather be. Do you want to go together or meet there?"

"Unless you object, I'll meet you at Dillingham Manor first thing tomorrow morning. I suspect the Lewis' might frown upon my Harley. Perhaps you can drive us there."

"You have a Harley?" *Damn, you continue to get better and better.*

"I've leased one for my stay in the states. I thought it would be fun to ride the open highway and feel the freedom that only a motorbike can provide. Or at least that's what the salesman told me." Colton smiled a crooked grin.

"Easily swayed there, Mr. Graves. Easily swayed."

"Would you like to ride with me sometime?"

Oh, God yes! "You know, I think I'd like that very much," Emma smiled sincerely. There's nothing she could think of that she'd like more than the opportunity to spend more time with him.

With lunch finished, Emma returned to the Journal to wrap up some articles that she was working on and to wait for her entries from the school to arrive.

"When are you going to tell me about Mr. Tall, Dark, and Studly?" Lisa asked as she entered Emma's office. "I've given you plenty of time. Now spill the beans, chicka!"

"Well, aside from his obvious ... qualities, he's ... he's ..."

"Do I need to remind you that you're a writer? Come on, woman!"

Emma had become as giddy as a school girl. She felt her pulse race, and she was wringing her hands as she thought about him. "He's just perfect, Lisa. I can't find anything wrong with him, and you know I look for people's flaws."

"How hard have you been looking? To hear Miss Nancy tell it, you two were sinning up the Dillingham yesterday!"

"We were *not!*" Emma's eyes narrowed. "Oh, how I hate that woman! She's forevermore looking for ways to irritate me *and* to see the worst in me!"

"I know she's a busybody. And I also know that you would have told your favorite co-worker if you two had done the nasty."

"Sorry to disappoint, Lisa. Nothing to report on that front!" *Damn.*

Once the entries were delivered and her day was finished, Emma drove to Cat's place. She used her key to let herself in and rummaged through the closet. She'd be meeting the Lewis' tomorrow as Colton's - well, she didn't know the title - but she wanted some fresh new duds to wear.

Cat had more clothes than she could possibly wear and didn't mind her cousin's impromptu stealing sprees.

CHAPTER 8

*E*mma heard the Harley pull up in front of Dillingham Manor. With one last check in the mirror, she gave an appreciative nod at the outfit she'd pilfered from Cat's closet. Deciding that a nearly all black ensemble was the route she would go, she carefully chose a black sweater with a high neck, a gray skirt that hugged her frame, black leggings and knee boots. Yes, Cat's closet was much more fun than her own.

Passing through the entryway and down the porch steps, Emma pulled in a breath of fresh morning air. Her gaze traveled to where she'd parked the night before . . . and now to the man admiring her vintage black car.

When he saw her, he motioned to it, "Nice fastback. Is it yours?"

Emma nodded as she walked toward him. "Thanks. It was my Granddads."

Lost in his appraisal, Colton spoke without making eye contact. "A sixty-seven, right?" He peered through the window.

"Yep, it's a nineteen sixty-seven with standard transmission. Not a typical 'girl' car, but that's one of the things I like about her."

Colton smiled. He found it amusing that Emma called the car "her." It seemed that he found something new that he liked about her every time they met. "Does she have a name?"

"Of course she does. Other than needing a tune up and a paint job, Shelby's a good car."

"Shelby," he repeated, "Of course that would be her name."

Colton turned his attention back to Emma, "And I'd say she's as special as her owner."

Emma slowly raised her gaze to meet his and lightly bit her lip. He had just doled out a blatant compliment, and she was trying her best not to smile. She swallowed hard when Colton's gaze didn't sway from hers.

Her heart beat a little faster as he crossed in front of the car to the driver's side where she stood. Emma backed up against the door, unsure of his intentions. Colton moved closer and lowered his head. Her lips parted of their own accord. He extended his hand beside her hip, his lips tugging up into a crooked grin. "Let me get that for you, luv," he said with a wink as he reached for the door handle.

Damn. Emma almost had to laugh at her own stupid, hormone induced delusion. Of course he was going for the door handle. Of course he was. He's a gentleman. *Double damn!*

Placing his helmet in the backseat of her car, they set out for Lake Brookfield Estates. On the way, they talked about everything from their jobs to their hobbies. She liked photography; he liked restoring things.

Emma knew at once when they had arrived because

Colton's description made her feel as if she had already been here, like a vibrant memory in her mind.

Having arrived a few minutes early, they followed the pavers down to the water's edge. Colton stood to her right as she gazed out at the lake. Emma was mesmerized by the sunlight that reflected off every ripple of the water's tiny waves – like shimmering diamonds. "Can you imagine what this looks like when the evening sun hits it, Colton?"

Mr. Lewis cleared his throat behind them. They turned to meet a condescending glare. Emma wanted to tell herself it was due to the unforgiving reflection off the water, but suspected it had more to do with her presence.

Without a greeting of any sort, he crept into cold conversation. "Mrs. Lewis has been called away unexpectedly and won't be available for an interview until late afternoon." Lowering the clipboard he held clutched to his chest, he addressed Colton, extending it in his direction. "You'll find the contract to be a standard agreement."

Colton combed through the legal terms with ease. Having read the agreement and signing in the appropriate place, he handed it back along with the check he pulled from his back pocket.

Emma listened as they finalized the return visit. For a man who had just received fifteen hundred dollars, he sure was glum.

With their business squared away, for now, they walked back to Emma's car.

"We have a good bit of time to kill before we come back," Colton said. "Would you like to get started on the entries from the school?"

"Sure. Do you have a preference of where you'd like to go?"

"Where do you normally do things like these?"

She laughed, "Well, I normally sit on a pillow on my bedroom floor with my back to my bed and papers that I'm working on spread out all around me. Of course, I'm usually in my pajamas and sometimes my hair is up in rollers. It's quite the sight, Mr. Graves."

"I'm sure it is. Perhaps you would like to go to my rental after we stop and get the papers?"

She thumbed behind her. "We don't have to stop anywhere. They're in the trunk. I didn't take them in when I got home last night because my arms were full."

It was a beautiful day. Had she had a convertible, they would have ridden with the top down to soak up the morning sun. Instead, they had to settle for the warm breeze whipping through the open windows. Emma drove as Colton directed. Soon they wound up at the river. She stopped in front of the Pennington place. "Is this where you will be living for the next few weeks?" Emma had always loved the Pennington house and had visited many times when she was younger.

Colton shook his head. "No, just keep driving." As they drove, it was clear to her where they were heading. Most of the river homes sat clustered together, but the further you traveled, the more spread out they became. Emma determined that Colton must have rented a room in the Jacobson's Bed and Breakfast, which was nearly impossible to do at the last minute. The historic home was the epitome of southern grace and beauty, often times booked a year in advance.

Even though she had been there many times, its beauty never failed to captivate her. As they parked, Emma stared in awe of the home that sat atop the beautiful hillside. She could hear the gurgling sounds of the water as the river gently flowed. The massive home was surrounded by mighty elm trees with an impressive yard that allowed for ample bench seating throughout the lawn as well as flower and rock gardens. Various stone lined paths disappeared into the nature trails behind the house, adding to its charm.

The long porch was outfitted with wicker furniture and generous pillows. The railings were low and wide and doubled as additional seating. It was a beautiful sight to behold.

Emma looked at Colton over the top of the car when they exited. "The Jacobson place? Nice! How on earth did you get an extended reservation? They are always booked solid."

Emma opened the trunk and grabbed the canvas bag containing the children's written entries. When she slammed the lid shut, Colton reached out and unburdened her of the load. *I sure could get used to having someone like him around.* "Thanks," she said with a smile as they climbed the stairs and pushed through the heavy wooden doors.

The smell of bacon from the morning's breakfast buffet wafted past their noses. That coupled with the slight chill of the old home made Emma think of her grandparents' house. The view within was where the similarities stopped.

Expensive antiques and vintage furniture were carefully strewn about the large parlor. The pieces ranged from single wingback chairs with button leather designs to Victorian sofas and loveseats covered in era appropriate tapestries. A large fireplace flanked the center of one wall with various framed art on all the others. The paintings depicted men who looked important. Emma hoped Colton wouldn't ask because she sure didn't know who they were.

A wonderfully ornate piano sat near a double set of

French doors. The doors led onto the wrap-around porch overlooking the river.

Colton's velvet voice pulled her from her appraisal of the picture perfect room. "They actually had a cancelation," he continued as if there'd been no lull in conversation whatso-ever. "Peggy stressed how fortunate I was to find this partic-ular accommodation available. I explored last night and found that there are several great places for me to work here. I spoke with the owner and she assured me that her clientele avoided the common areas, which she felt was distasteful. Francine wants her guests to explore the entire property as well as the house itself. She said that guests typically spend the day sight-seeing and kayaking and at the end of the day, they generally retired to their rooms. So I think it safe to assume that we can get to work in here and not be distracted."

Emma nodded her head and motioned to a large, round coffee table that sat low to the floor. She suggested that the easiest way to do these things was to categorize them, placing like titles into a pile. She explained that most students chose to focus on topics that they knew. "Facts are always easier to report on than fiction. Fiction requires more concentration at keeping your story straight."

"So we are to make like subjected columns and then break them down into fact or fiction?"

"No, they can be either fact or fiction. We'll just place each school into similar categories."

"We have two schools?"

"Yes, luck of the draw! Ryan, our sports editor, should have had a stack too, but he's out of town. Yay me!"

As they began working, Colton pulled the couches and the table closer together. Emma sat on one side of the round table and he sat on the other. As she squirmed, he asked if everything was ok. *You mean other than the fact that I'm wearing a skirt and trying my hardest not to flash you?* "Yes, everything's fine. I'm just a tad uncomfortable in this skirt. You can't be very ladylike sitting like this and get your work done, too." She motioned to the close quarters.

"Then why don't you change into your jeans?"

"What jeans?" Emma asked curiously.

"The jeans on your backseat floorboard."

It was her lucky day. She couldn't wait to get out of that skirt! Emma went to the car and grabbed the jeans. She went back inside and found a restroom. As she slid the jeans up her legs and past her hips, it quickly occurred to her why they were in the floor of her car. They didn't fit anymore. She looked down and stared at three inches of legging covered ankle hanging out the bottom of her pant legs. She had herself a pair of Capri's that were never intended to be. When she was at the Laundromat last, some good Samaritan had "paid it forward" and tossed her laundry into the dryer, paying for the session while she was away. In theory, it was a terrific idea. But what he didn't know was that Emma's jeans hadn't seen the inside of a dryer since she was in junior high. Tall women don't have the luxury of pulling a pair of warm, soft jeans from the dryer. Emma always had to hang her pants to dry to keep them from getting too short. She decided that all was not lost. She would tuck her pants legs into her borrowed knee boots and Colton would be none the wiser. *Now I just hope this sweater is long enough to cover my granny panties...*

With her fashion emergency averted, she sashayed back to the parlor. She *had* to sashay since her pants were a bit too tight for proper walking. Colton seemed unaware that anything was wrong with her ensemble. As a matter of fact, she thought he rather enjoyed her change of clothes. When she sat down and leaned forward, she was pleased that the ratio of 'back of the shirt hike to the top of the pants pull' worked out and her panties didn't show.

After all that, she was ready to get to work. She saw that Colton had already gotten started, and he had plenty of questions over what was fact and what was fiction. "Please hold all questions until the tour is over, Mr. Graves," Emma jokingly directed.

He smiled. "Of course, Miss Saint-Claire. Please forgive me. I'll try to save only the most important questions until the end."

They decided that the best way to proceed was to choose a winning entry from each category and then select a winner from the finalists. Emma knew that most of Colton's questions would be answered by the narrowing down process. She couldn't help but be drawn to the total fiction entries, and she hoped that he would enjoy them, too.

When the stories were sorted, they decided to take a break and stretch their legs. Emma couldn't wait because her rear-end was numb from sitting so long. She was pleased to discover that her jeans had loosened up a bit, too.

"Emma, would you like to sit on the veranda for a while and get out in the fresh air?"

"I would very much like to feel the fresh breeze, but sitting is the last thing I want to do. You're welcome to, though."

Instead, they walked out into the yard and took in the view. It was a beautiful fall day without a cloud in the sky. Emma watched as Colton walked ahead and leaned against the pergola. His tall frame looked even taller with his black slacks, black long sleeved shirt, and his raven hair falling near his shoulders. As he turned, she noticed his chiseled facial features. She thought that he looked the part of a movie star, and she could take in this movie forever. But rather than standing there gawking at him, she decided to join him and take in the view that he was appreciating.

Colton's gaze traveled the undeveloped mountainside on the other side of the river. An autumn canvas in shades of orange and red graced the hillside, as did the melody of a far away bird. "It's very peaceful here with all the wildlife and trails." He looked to his side. "Do you hike, Emma?"

"Not on purpose!" she quickly answered, chuckling at a thought. I don't have a great sense of direction. I start my survival eating three steps into the hills just to be safe! I'm a modern day Hansel and Gretel . . . only, I eat the crumbs rather than drop them!" They both laughed at her description.

"You're an interesting little thing, Miss Saint-Claire."

"How about you tell me something about yourself?" She urged. "You know more about me than I know about you, and that's not fair."

Colton turned to face her. "Right. Well, as you know, I started my business seven years ago. I live alone, but have always dreamed of having a large, close-knit family someday. I was born in Shanburg, England, where I still reside. My mother, Mildred, is a retired nurse. My childhood dog was named Betty. And my father, Henry, was a history professor. He passed away several years ago. I have a brother named Kane that a lot of people mistake for my twin. That's bloody annoying! He's the same height as me with dark hair, but has brown eyes."

Good Lord in heaven. There are two of them? Mercy! Ok, he

lives alone but still hasn't said if he's single or not. Wait. "Wait, your puppy was named Betty?" Emma couldn't suppress her laughter.

"Actually, no. My mother was dreadfully allergic to pets. I was just seeing if you were still listening, luv." He winked and playfully tugged on her chin.

After a few moments more, they decided that it was time to get back to work.

After sorting through all the entries, they looked at the stories in the running for the winning spot. The winning ghost story was about Little Victoria and the Williams' bridge. Emma was very familiar with the local folklore, but chose it because it had an original ending. In this rendition, Little Victoria fell through the bridge into the water and died as before, but was revived when sheets of music were thrown into the creek. Victoria was rumored to love music. So when the sheets were offered as toll, it spoke to her heart and she awoke.

The winning townspeople entry was about Tank. In this story, he was a mighty prince who slayed the dragon at button bridge and then took off on his horse named Star. He and the princess rode into the sunset where they lived happily ever after in the haunted house down by the river.

The final nominee was the story about the town of Brookfield and the fictitious way in which it received its name. In this story, a young boy was falsely imprisoned for cheating on a test. From his underground cell, he would look up at the feet that passed by on the street and wish someone would stop and talk to him. A mighty eagle came forth, spoke to him, and determined that he was not guilty of cheating.

The eagle told him to hold out his hand and close his eyes. When he suddenly felt something there, he opened his eyes and saw that the understanding eagle had offered his talon to pick the lock and set himself free. He then nudged a piece of paper – a map - toward the boy before flying off. When the prison keeper came to do a head count, he found that the boy had disappeared. All that was left in his place was the forgotten map which contained only a brook and a field. And therefore, the town was named Brookfield.

With the finalists chosen, Emma looked at Colton and asked if he would like to select the winner. He said that honor should go to her.

"Very well, Mr. Graves-" At this, he gave her a tsk and she corrected, "Very well, Colton. I'll choose." He smiled, and she thought she'd do anything it took to see that award winning smile every chance she could. "Ok, Colton, before I select the winner, would you like to ask your questions?"

"Indeed. I have burning inquiries," he said with a crooked grin. He thought for a moment then continued. "The Victoria story, was it based on an actual person?"

"It's hard to say. I might chalk her up to town legend since that has never been proven. She's been described so many times, I can almost see her strawberry-blond hair and flowing white dress. I think you can talk yourself into believing anything if you hear it enough. I think that's why so many townspeople think she was real."

"And speaking of townspeople. This Tank, is he real?"

"Tank is very real, my intended, as a matter of fact."

"You're engaged?" Colton immediately glanced at her left hand.

"Only if Tank had his way about it," Emma laughed. "Tank has asked me to marry him for a year straight." Colton looked as if the wind had been let out of his sails, which she was pleased about. *Could he be interested in me?* Emma glanced across the table at him and pondered. *Yes, he seems a bit deflated at the thought of me and Tank.* She smiled at that revelation.

"What's so amusing?"

"Oh, I was just thinking of Tank and me. And trust me when I say, it is laughable! He's very much not my type."

"I see," Colton said, and he seemed relieved about that.

"Tank is a guy who has been around Brookfield for as long as I have."

"I'm to assume that Tank is not his given name?"

"And you would be correct. Everyone calls him Tank, but his real name is Curtis. Curtis Meadows. They also think that he's the town drunk, and they're all afraid of him. All my years of questioning everyone about everything has led me to believe that he is neither a drunk nor anyone to fear. As far as I know, he doesn't drink at all. This goes back to hearing a story so much that you believe it."

"One final question, Miss Saint-Claire."

"As charming as it was, Mr. Graves, the naming of *Brookfield* had nothing to do with a lost map and a jailbreak."

With a hearty laugh, Colton assured her that that was not his question.

"Who's the winner, luv? That was my question."

"Oh," Emma laughed. "Colton, I know you want me to decide, and I will. But I'd like to hear which story you think's best."

"I like them all, but if I had to decide, I think I'd choose the naming of Brookfield. I could see a children's book written about that."

"I agree, and that was my favorite, too. I remember stories that I wrote as a kid, and I could see myself having written that one. I used to get in trouble all the time for daydreaming."

"Nothing wrong with curiosity," Colton countered with a wink.

Emma gathered all the pages, placing them in a neat stack. "Ok, that's settled. Little Tyler has our winning story from Brookfield Elementary with the naming of Brookfield. And Madelyn is the victor from Riverside Elementary with her Little Victoria and the music notes story."

With the winning stories selected, Emma and Colton could now focus on the delightful chicken salad sandwiches Miss Francine had prepared for them. As soon as she overheard the mention of lunch, she had been fast at work. She was so happy that they were utilizing the facilities and the grounds at the bed and breakfast, "as they were intended to be used," that she eagerly volunteered to make a picnic lunch for the two of them. When Colton thanked her for her generosity, she said it was nice to feel needed. Emma suspected that Colton would dream up many ways to make her feel useful and was certain that Miss Francine would spoil him in his time in Brookfield.

After a quick wardrobe change, Emma and Colton traveled back to Lake Brookfield Estates to meet with the Lewis'.

CHAPTER 9

When Emma and Colton arrived back at Victorian Gardens, they pulled into the circular drive where the Lewis' were waiting for them on the brick staircase. Mrs. Lewis was dressed to the nines in a shimmery gold hued outfit that screamed, "Look at me - I think I'm important." The bead encrusted top caught every ray of sunlight, and her flowing pants looked elegant. Her reddish-brown hair was cut short, the layers teased to disguise the sparse areas of her scalp. She'd obviously been out that morning getting her hair styled since it looked just so. Her jewelry was large, the topaz stones in her earrings accenting her clothing beautifully. Mr. Lewis wore a black suit and a scowl upon his face. Emma suspected that if she lived with Mrs. Lewis, she'd wear the same glum expression.

Meg looked at Emma like she was yesterday's trash. Emma could never remember doing anything to her, but for some reason, Meg Lewis couldn't stand the sight of her.

"Hello, Mrs. Lewis. We are so pleased that you could join us for this afternoon's meeting," Colton offered pleasantly. "I've brought my publicist, Miss Saint-Claire. She'll conduct the interview and take some photos of us for the Brookfield Journal to announce the event."

"She'll do no such thing. When you said you had journal connections, I assumed you were referring to a *real* journalist, Mr. Graves – not a two bit local wannabe."

Colton drew his eyebrows tightly together. "Mrs. Lewis, I suggest you watch how you speak of Miss Saint-Claire."

Emma was taken aback by the insult as well, but tried to muster any remaining professionalism that she had.

"Mrs. Lewis, I assure you that I am a professional and have been trained in photography." *Yep, Amy Pennington showed me how to point and shoot in junior high. So technically, I was trained.* "I've written for the journal for nearly four years."

"Yes, Emma, I'm aware of your biased work and how you shun anyone who has an opinion other than yours."

What the hell? Emma's eyes narrowed and her fists clenched. "What are you talking about?"

With a look of condescension, Mrs. Lewis delivered her accusation. "Let me refresh your memory, *dear.*"

Somehow I don't think she meant that as a loving sentiment . . .

Meg continued, "Think back to the story you did on the growing homeless problem that we have in Brookfield."

"Not exactly as I recall the story, but please continue," Emma said through seething teeth. Yes, the pieces were falling into place. For years, she wondered why the Lewis' treated her as they did, but now it made perfect sense. Emma had conducted so many interviews that she had forgotten the 'Beacon of Hope' story about a home for homeless veterans.

"You wouldn't print my interview when I gave my honest and humble opinion."

"That's because you called them vagrants and said they were a blemish on Brookfield and society in general! They are veterans of the United States who have fallen on hard times. If anyone should have the right to access the shelters, it's them – the very people who sacrificed so much for your snooty ass freedoms and for mine. So yes, Mrs. Lewis, I refused to print that story and given the chance, I'd do it again!"

Colton didn't know this side of sweet, humorous Emma. All he had seen was agreeable and polite. Now he was getting a first-hand glimpse at the professional side of his new assistant, and he thought he liked it.

"And that's precisely why I have brought in my own."

"Your own what?" Emma spat.

"My very own journalist – a true professional. When Thomas told me that you were here with Mr. Graves this morning, I knew that I had to intervene on the poor man's behalf. He has no idea the way you let stories be dissected or dropped altogether."

Meg motioned to someone inside.

Emma immediately recognized the man who came out the door. *Of course she'd choose him.*

Charles Jackson, a journalist with Kentucky's premiere paper, came to stand beside Mrs. Lewis. The well-known journalist was of average size with sandy hair and blue eyes. He was dressed impeccably in a heather gray suit. As his eyes shifted to each person in the group, his smile quickly faded. Their body language spoke volumes, as did the look of unease now on his face. Tension was high. It was about to get worse.

"Mr. Jackson, I would like you to meet Colton Graves, the coordinator of the Brookfield masquerade ball. You will interview him, Mr. Lewis, and myself for this article and take pictures of the three of us."

Emma cleared her throat.

"And feel free to ignore this woman." Meg made a disgusted face and gestured in Emma's direction.

"If you have any hopes of conducting this interview, Mr. Jackson, you'll do no such thing," Colton interjected. Charles glanced from couple to couple, clearly uncomfortable with the situation. "Miss Saint-Claire is my assistant and co-planner and has worked diligently on coordinating this event. We are a package deal and if you want to interview me, you interview her as well. No exceptions." Colton knew this was a brazen move and one that may cost him Victorian Gardens. He didn't like the way Mrs. Lewis spoke to Emma, and he refused to put up with it. However, he was fairly certain that fifteen hundred dollars would smooth things over, anyway.

"Let's begin anew," Charles suggested clasping his hands together. In an obvious attempt to diffuse the situation, he suggested separating Emma and Meg. "I would like to speak with each couple as I conduct my interview." He turned to the Lewis'. "I think I'll start with the two of you."

"Splendid idea, Charles. I think the gazebo would make a gorgeous backdrop for the photo," Mrs. Lewis offered.

"Perhaps we'll go inside and speak? I'd like to photograph the ballroom."

Emma hated that Meg was trying to direct the path of the interview. Had it been her, she wouldn't have asked. She would've told Mrs. Lewis that they were going into the ball-room – the obvious place to conduct the interview in the first place.

Emma and Colton watched as the trio disappeared through the doors.

"It's apparent that she's been stewing over this for years, and I had no idea. It makes perfect sense to me, now, why I've been shunned and never once asked to cover an event out here - out here in the chosen land," she motioned all around her.

"I noticed Mr. Lewis didn't say a word. Is that common for him?"

"I actually think he's a decent person, but paired with the ice princess in there," she pointed toward the estate, "he comes off as cold as she does. I'm really thankful that I didn't blow this for you. I turn into a different person when I'm working. I'm not meek Emma. I also want to thank you for standing up for me. I truly appreciate you doing that, even though it could have cost you everything."

Colton smiled. "Indeed."

"What?" She asked, not following his comment.

"Emma, you don't have to thank me for anything. It was my pleasure." Colton shrugged his shoulders. "She was rude to you. If that's all there is to the story, I think you were justified in saying what you did. I was simply agreeing that you turn into someone else altogether when you're cornered. Such a brave girl."

He knew they had to get straight to work covering the details. "With you not conducting the interview, we have to come up with some details of the ball that you can discuss." They decided it would occur on Halloween night at eight in the evening. The guest list would remain anonymous simply because they hadn't gotten that far in the planning yet.

"Why eight o'clock? Was that traditional in your grand-parents' events?"

"Because these parties usually last four hours and even though guests may dance with whomever they choose, it's customary for couples to share the last dance of the evening and a kiss at the stroke of midnight."

"Now I have two problems," Emma said, defeated. But before she had the chance to explain, Charles appeared. It was their turn to be interviewed.

He decided he wanted their conversation to occur further away from the house. As they walked, Emma wondered how such beautiful grounds could belong to such hateful people. Once they reached the flower garden, Emma had a seat on the curved stone bench. Charles told them that he loved the idea of the Brookfield masquerade ball. Colton corrected that it would be called the Brookfield Harvest Ball in honor of the town's history and the conclusion of the Brookfield Harvest Festival.

Charles laughed. Apparently Mrs. Lewis had claimed the idea as her own. Colton explained that the ball was last held in his family's former home at Dillingham Manor nearly a century ago. Emma was about to correct him to clarify that he was the owner. Colton held up a hand, where Charles couldn't see it, in a motion for her to stop. He would explain later that he wanted to investigate further, with the element of surprise, where the money was going for rent.

"How long have you been planning this event?" Charles asked.

Not wanting it to seem like a last minute deal, Emma provided some evasive answers. "We work on it daily. But to be honest, I'm not sure how much time we have into it. I know we worked for about five hours today alone." She directed an innocent smile toward Colton.

True, they had worked for that amount of time today, but not on masquerade ball business. Colton shot Emma an amused look before interceding.

"Mr. Jackson, this event is instrumental in getting Dillingham Manor back in the limelight and getting the Historical Society of Brookfield to recognize my family's former home as a notable structure. It pains me that it is not being maintained by the current owner, for whatever reason, and I have great hopes that monies will be granted to resurrect and maintain Dillingham Manor to its former beauty and stature."

When Charles asked if he could go to Dillingham Manor to take photos, Colton said that he thought it best that a blemish not be associated with this event since the home was not in pristine condition. Charles agreed and said he wanted to check on the Lewis' to see if they were ready for their photo and to see if they had any knowledge of the Brookfield Harvest Festival's annual ball from their parents and grandparents. He explained that people with knowledge of town history made for a better story. "This is certain to grab the attention of the historical society. I would expect great changes and soon."

Once he left them, Emma noticed how the sunset reflected off the lake. "Let's take a walk," she said to Colton. Rising from her seat, she moved toward the gazebo to get a closer view.

Emma laid her hand on the column, her head gently resting against it. Gazing out onto the lake, she watched as ripples licked at the setting hues like dancing flames of fire. The sunset that the lake had captured was mesmerizing. Without pulling her eyes away, she spoke softly, "Have you ever seen anything more gorgeous?"

Colton's breath feathered against her ear, anticipation running down her spine when she realized how close he was.

"Never have I seen a sight more lovely than this."

Emma glanced at him over her shoulder. She realized that he was looking at her, and felt like he had been the whole time. She didn't know where this was going, but she was willing to see it through. Desire directing her steps, she turned to face him.

As if he were on the same wavelength, Colton moved closer, placing his hands on either side of her hips on the railing. With her back to the lake, her hair reflected the last golden rays of nature's easel. He watched as her eyes grew heavy with desire, his closeness affecting her in ways that couldn't please him more. As if a magnetic force pulled them together, Colton pressed his body to hers. He cradled her face in his warm hands, caressing her cheek with his thumb. Emma wound her fingers through his hair, pulling him closer. She could feel the rise and fall of his chest. Only a hint of their lips touched before they were torn apart by the sounds of an explosion.

They jerked around in the direction of the blast. They saw someone in a boat out on the water. "Sorry 'bout that, kids," Dave called out with a wave. "Just practicing for the festival."

"Who is that, and what is he talking about?" Colton asked with an edge to his voice.

"That's Dave Scott. He's the local pyrotechnics guy who does the firework shows for all the events we have in town. He's also the one person I want to kill right about now," Emma laughed weakly.

Colton understood. Their perfect moment had been interrupted. "Besides having wretched timing, it's not even dark yet."

"Yeah, Dave's a drinker. His reasoning is different than ours sometimes. But still yet . . ." Emma groaned.

Colton chuckled. He found himself wanting to hold on to her, but remembered their earlier conversation. As if he was forcing himself to move in another direction physically and mentally, he pulled away. "Emma, when we were discussing the formalities of the ball, you mentioned having two problems."

Why are you putting the man brakes on? Guy-be-gone's at work tonight! "Refresh my memory, please."

"You said you had two problems when I mentioned dancing with your partner and kissing at the stroke of midnight."

Pretty sure I'd have a stroke at midnight if you kissed me! "Oh yes, it's coming back to me now."

"So what are your problems?"

"I can't fancy dance. At least, I don't think I can."

"Miss Saint-Claire, I can teach you to dance. It would be my pleasure." Colton reached for her hand, which she extended, and he led her to the center of the gazebo. "But you mentioned having *two* problems."

"My second and greatest problem is that I won't have a date to *need* to learn to dance for. I could probably force Cat to dance with me, but I assure you that she would not take kindly to me kissing her at midnight!" Emma laughed at the thought. Colton did, too.

"Why are you so certain that you won't have a date, Emma?" He moved them around in a lazy dance.

"History, my dear Colton, history. I haven't had a date in- Well, we won't go there. So there's nothing to make me think that I might stumble upon one by Halloween night."

"As fate would have it, Miss Saint-Claire, I find myself without a date on Halloween as well."

"So we should go alone, together?" Emma teased, but hoped that he was planning to ask her.

"If you would do me the pleasure of accepting my offer, Emma, we could go together." Taking her hand, he coiled her in to his body, her back resting against his chest. Swaying to silent music, he continued, "As proper dates."

She bit back a smile. "But there's the midnight kiss, remember?" she looked over her left shoulder at him.

"If I have my way, luv, that midnight kiss will happen long before Halloween night." At this, he spun her out of the embrace and kissed the hand that he still held. "I'd say your first dance lesson is going well, would you not agree?"

"I'm enjoying it very much, but I think I'd need a lot more work before the night of the ball."

"You didn't answer my question, Emma."

"No? What question was that?" *You're lucky I can speak at all! Don't expect me to think, too.*

"Miss Saint-Claire, would you do me the pleasure of accompanying me to the masquerade ball?"

Before Emma could answer, Charles summoned them to the ballroom. She was starting to dislike his timing. A lot.

Once inside, Emma was spellbound by the beauty. Even though Colton had explained every detail, vividly, seeing it first hand was breathtaking.

"It's gorgeous. Is it not, luv?" Colton asked as he sidled up beside her.

"It's amazing and is going to be so perfect for the ball."

Mrs. Lewis walked past Emma and scowled as Charles motioned for them to meet on the impressive staircase for a photo. Colton and the Lewis' posed for pictures as Emma looked on. Charles turned to face Emma. "Miss Saint-Claire, I think you should be in this photo as well since you are co-contributor of the masquerade ball."

In an effort to play nice, Emma was about to object when Mrs. Lewis spewed her nastiness.

"Absolutely not! She will not be a part of this photo. This

is about Thomas and me . . . and Mr. Graves, of course. Not this woman," she said as she gave Emma a repulsed glance.

Emma was livid. *How dare she treat me like this! How dare her.* Before Emma could fire back with her insults, Colton, being the suave diplomat that he was, suggested that all parties of the committee be present and represented. When everyone agreed, except Meg, Emma bound up the stairs to stand beside Colton. She really wanted no recognition for this, but she wanted Mrs. Lewis to be as uncomfortable as she possibly could be. Emma felt a devilish satisfaction and smiled proudly for the camera as she stood tall by Colton's side. She suspected that Charles didn't like Mrs. Lewis any more than she did, and she was going to test this theory.

"Mr. Jackson, I think it only fitting that Colton and I stand on the steps below Mr. and Mrs. Lewis so that there will be no confusion as to who planned this event." Yes, Emma was putting Meg on the back burner and she couldn't be more pleased. When Charles bit his lip to suppress a grin, Emma knew her theory had been correct.

Emma and Colton stood on the ballroom floor with the Lewis' behind them on the staircase. Emma thought they looked good as she glanced over at Colton dressed in all black and she in her gray and black.

With the interview finished and the Lewis' rushing them out the door, Charles tucked his camera in its leather case then shouldered the bag. Emma and Colton walked out with him. "If I get the story submitted in time, it'll go out in Sunday's paper."

"Sunday," Colton repeated with a nod. This meant that locals would be expecting their invitations in the next few days. They still had much planning to do.

Shaking hands, the trio parted ways.

On the drive back, Colton had been on the phone with Charles with last minute details for the article.

Emma drove the narrow driveway leading to Dillingham Manor. With every turn that pushed them closer, the butterflies in her stomach increased. She knew this wasn't a date, but she couldn't help but wonder if Colton would kiss her. They had been so close in the gazebo.

With his phone call finished and his helmet retrieved, they exited the car. "One more," he said.

"One more what?" Emma asked.

"Earlier today when we were working on the entries, I told you I'd save the most important questions for last. Now I have one more to ask, well, two actually."

"Ok, ask away."

"Emma, would you do me the great pleasure of accompanying me to the ball?"

An insuppressible smile tugged at her lips. *Breathe in, breathe out, breathe in . . . No, stop it!* "No."

"No?" he asked, puzzled.

"No - *yes!* I mean yes." she pulled in a breath. "Yes, Colton. I would love to accompany you to the ball." *I'm such a dork!* "And your second most important question?"

"Can I see you tomorrow, Emma?"

"No."

"Do you mean 'yes'?" he laughed.

"Sadly, no. I have to say no. But I don't want to. I promised Mrs. Loretta that I'd help paint her kitchen. I interviewed her for the paper. She told me some crazy stories – including one about Nancy. I'm hoping to find her sober this time and see if there was any truth to the story."

"Then perhaps you could help me paint my kitchen on Monday?"

"I'd love to help you paint your kitchen on Monday, Mr. Graves, but you don't have a kitchen. Actually, I'm terrible at painting, but I'm real good at eating," she laughed. "So would you like to meet for lunch on Monday?"

"I would. May I see your phone?"

Emma handed it over. Colton pushed some buttons, then handed it back.

"What did you do?"

"I entered our lunch date into your calendar, just in case you needed a reminder." He smiled a handsome grin and she felt a grin creep across her face, too.

"Good night, Colton."

"Monday." That's all he said as he reached for her hand, placing a delicate kiss to it.

She walked inside.

Just before he climbed on his bike, he received a text message. Colton pulled the phone from his pocket. It was a simple message, but one that made him smile.

"Monday.

Emma"

CHAPTER 10

*E*mma was awakened by the sound of rain drops pelting her window. She turned and pulled the covers over her head, but the assault continued. She grabbed her pillow and added that to muffle the sounds as thunder boomed loudly, jolting her upright. As she rose to look out the window, she could see the gray skies and wished she could go back to sleep.

Last night was a dream-free slumber that she would give anything to repeat. It wasn't often that she went without nightmares, let alone dreams of any kind. Emma thought that Colton may serve as the barrier that her mind needed.

For far too long, the imageless face of an angry man dominated her thoughts, night and day. She was thankful for the mind block. She knew she'd seen his face, but the mind sometimes does a powerful service in the face of trauma, as it had in her case. The man, whose name she did not know, had a face that she could not see in her memory. She couldn't imagine envisioning those eyes day after day. She knew they were piercing and cold, but was thankful to not have an image to go along with that account.

When she began straightening the covers, her phone slid off the bed onto the floor. Emma reached for it, glad she hadn't stepped on it, shattering it like the last one. She checked her messages and realized that the phone was still on silent from last night.

That's when she saw the message from Colton. *"Good morning, Emma. I wish you luck in your painting endeavors today. I've been working on creating invitations for the ball and plan to have them printed later today. We can work on the guest list over lunch. Until tomorrow, Colton."*

Now that's a way to start the day. When she saw what time it was, she decided she may as well get dressed. Since she was painting, she wore her "Capri's that weren't supposed to be," as she liked to call them now, a pink t-shirt that had *Chicago* sprawled across it, and a pair of canvas shoes that had an "air hole" for her pinky toe. She reached for the hair tie that she kept on the door knob and pulled her hair into a loose pony-tail that she fed through the hole of a ball cap.

As she turned to look in the full length mirror, she laughed at the sight. "Some might consider this a hot mess," Emma said to herself as she smoothed her hand down her torso and twisted from side to side, "but I like to say, 'I'm stylin!' Now, if Mrs. Loretta will let me in is another question. I kinda look like a hobo."

When Emma arrived, she was greeted by Shiloe, the fierce wiener dog with a wicked bark.

"Emma, is that you?" Loretta asked through the closed door.

"Yes, Mrs. Loretta. I'm just wearing my finest painting duds. I understand why you didn't recognize me." Emma laughed. Loretta unfastened two separate deadbolts, the door knob lock, and a chain lock. Since her husband, Cliff, passed away, she had been frightened of everything and took extra measures to protect herself. Or, at least, that's what the rumor was. When she opened the door, the aroma of freshly brewed coffee drifted out. Emma had always loved the smell of coffee but detested the taste. She knew that she'd be drinking coffee when she saw two mugs beside the coffee pot. It was simply rude not to take what was offered.

As Emma choked down her coffee, she stared across the little metal table at Loretta. She recalled that every time she had gone to her house for an interview, or whatever the reason may be, Loretta always looked exactly like she did this morning. Her jet black hair was a mess from the night before. Emma could tell by the large curls, albeit every which way on her head, that Loretta had styled her hair with rollers of some sort. She wore a thick beige terrycloth robe and matching slippers. Emma referred to her as her sleepy headed friend, but only to herself, of course.

"Emma, I'm so happy that you didn't back out on me this morning. Most people would have turned over and sunk into a deep slumber with the weather like it is. But this kitchen hasn't been painted in years and could use some attention."

As Emma looked around, she was pleased that the pictures, towel racks, and whatever else those shadowed areas were had been removed from the walls.

"I promised you help if you gave me an interview. I would hate to be known as someone whose word was no good. I'm happy to help you." *My word's good. I didn't say I was truthful! I would soooo rather still be sleeping. That's what would make me happy!*

When Loretta had changed into her painting clothes, she came back into the kitchen. "Would you like to get started, Emma? Or do you need another cup of coffee?"

Oh Lord, anything but that! "I'm ready to get started. Let's do this thang!"

Loretta shot her a strange glance.

"You'll have to over look me. I think the coffee just kicked in."

When Emma poured the paint into the tray, she was pleasantly surprised that Loretta had selected a sunny yellow hue. She knew it would brighten up the drab space instantly. Priming each roller, she handed one to Loretta. As they started painting, Emma tried to figure out a way to bring up the Nancy story again. "It's nice to sit around the table in the kitchen and chat sometimes. That's what Mom and Dad always did when I was little. All the adults would come over, and they'd all sit in the kitchen."

"And drink coffee and chat?" Loretta asked.

"More like drink coffee and gossip about the friends who weren't there," they both laughed. "Anyway, I miss that. We don't have a kitchen at Dillingham Manor. Miss Nancy refuses to update the place."

"She has no authority to update the place," Loretta said as she continued to paint, "but that's never stopped her from overstepping boundaries before."

Here we go . . . "She doesn't like me. I've been as nice to her as I can manage, even though I didn't want to. My only notable offense was when I tried to explore Dillingham Manor. She nearly blew an artery. She acts like she's holier than thou - way better than me, anyway."

"Trust me, my dear. That's all an act. In order to be holy, you must be without sin, and Nancy Reardon is anything but."

"Really?"

"Nancy had an affair years ago with her husband's friend. Her husband was a good man and Oliver, the man she cheated with, was a ruthless womanizer. I didn't like him much, but if anyone deserved Oliver, it was Nancy."

"Miss Nancy has a husband?"

"He passed away many, many years ago. But yes, she had a husband who was a good, hard working man and loyal to fault. He worked in the mills and sometimes had to travel, too. That's when she would visit Oliver."

"Did he ever find out about the affair?"

"He didn't, and for his sake, I'm glad for it. But a few people knew and one is still blackmailing her today. Or so I've heard. Emma, when people assume you're the town drunk, they say things in your presence that they should keep to themselves. I've learned a lot over the years. They assume that I'm mellow with spirits and won't remember anything. Here's some advice for you, dear. Never tip your hand. You can go far with the knowledge you collect if you don't."

"That's good advice. Do you know who's blackmailing her?"

"The details are sketchy. But I do know that it's someone from the historical society. A man. I overheard them talking some years ago but didn't see him. He put Nancy in the position of landlady when it was determined that the home was owned by a long list of heirs. I hear the rent is paid in cash." Loretta looked over her shoulder at

Emma for confirmation then continued, "The cash is collected by Nancy and given to him. What I'm not sure of is how many people are involved. I think they want to tear the house down. If it's placed on the historic registry, it'll be maintained, and that will never happen. I don't know how a family home goes unnoticed, but for some reason, no one is claiming to be the owner." She thought for a moment then shook her head. "And if memory serves me correctly, the statute of limitations is drawing near. Once the home is deemed abandoned, the city of Brookfield becomes the rightful owner. It's a real shame, too, given its history."

Emma had stood in silence as Loretta shared the details. But she was confused by a few of them. "I don't completely follow. If Miss Nancy's husband is dead, why is she still being blackmailed? Why would she *care* if this mystery man shared her secrets?"

Loretta offered an understanding smile. Someone of Emma's generation couldn't possibly understand. "Emma, when you lose everyone in life, your social connections are all you have left. If her judgmental ladies' group found out that she cheated on Gene Reardon, the kindest man this town has ever known, she would be shunned. She can't handle being an outcast."

"The Nancy I know sure doesn't crave acceptance. She's nasty to me."

"That's because she doesn't want you getting close and finding out her secrets, Emma. She also doesn't want you snooping around Dillingham Manor and risking exposure. They want the home forgotten."

"Well, that's not going to happen. As a matter of fact, as early as today, it may be thrust into the spotlight." Emma continued to paint as she explained about Colton, the Lewis estate, and the masquerade ball. Loretta listened intently.

"Your Mr. Graves is a clever man." Loretta dipped her paint roller into the pan before returning to the conversation. "The publicity that the gala receives will bring Nancy's house of cards tumbling down. And it won't be long before her co-conspirator is revealed. These are exciting times ahead for your friend. For the whole town, I suppose."

Even though she spoke of excitement, Emma detected sadness in her voice. "Mrs. Loretta, would you like an invitation to the ball?"

She looked at Emma, a tear streaming down her face. "Do you know how long it's been since I've been invited to anything, Emma? I would appreciate that so much more than you will ever know."

When the painting was finished and they were cleaning up, a knock at the door interrupted them. Loretta went to answer and greeted a neighbor. He had brought over some muffins that his wife made. As always, she started spouting gibberish. Emma knew at this point, that the drunken confessions of earlier in the week were all an act by a very clever woman.

When it was time to leave, Loretta walked her out. She watched Emma stroll away from the house then called out to her, "Emma." When Emma turned, she continued. "Remember, never tip your hand, my dear." They both smiled and Emma gestured a salute.

Well now, that was an interesting encounter. I can't believe they want to tear down Dillingham Manor. I also can't believe that all

*this time, I thought Mrs. Loretta was loony. Who knew she'd actu-
ally be an ally?*

As much as Emma wanted to hurt Nancy with the information that she'd attained - merely returning the nastiness that
she'd been handed - she knew good advice when she heard it.
She also knew that waiting until tomorrow to talk to Colton
would not happen. *Now what? Do I call? Do I text? Maybe I'll
just drop by.* With one glance at her attire, she decided a stop
at Cat's house was in order.

～

Emma stood knocking at Cat's door. When it became
apparent that she wasn't home, Emma used her key to let
herself in. *This is like having a key to the mall!*

After a leisurely shower, Emma wrapped herself in a plush
peach towel and plundered through a shopping bag on Cat's
dresser. Emma laughed when she pulled out a pair of tiny
underwear by a very wimpy string. *Well, I won't be wearing
these! Has the woman never thought of giving granny panties a
try?* The next pair was more to her liking – a lacy pair of boy
shorts. Sexy but sensible. *I can't wait to see what's waiting to
choose from in the bra department. Pasties? Maybe some of those
cone-shaped Madonna bras that would put someone's eyes out?
With Cat, you just never know.*

Emma looked the room over, but couldn't find a bra
anywhere. *Where the heck are your bras, child?* Then she had
the horrific thought that there were none. She pulled open

one last drawer which contained a single lacy black bra - one cup size too small - with a smiley face sticker on it. She knew that Cat had done this on purpose just to torment her.

Emma crossed the room to her favorite boutique – Cat's closet. When she pushed the closet door open, she read the note on the floor:

Saint Emma, I don't mind you borrowing my clothes, but would it kill you to return them now and again? I'd change the locks, but I'm afraid you'd be forced to run around this town naked. And with your aversion to stylish undergarments, I think you'd frown upon that. xoxo, Alley Cat

Emma laughed at her cousin's note and then rummaged through her closet. She chose a burgundy cowl-neck sweater that looked good with her stripper boobs. She now knew how bra models achieved that look – a bra that's too small. She also knew that Cat had made that purchase just for this occasion because there was no way that Cat could ever fit her "assets" into it! She pulled on a pair of dark jeans and was thankful for the slimming effect. Remembering that her shoes had a hole in them, she grabbed a pair of brown boots and a brown Newsboy cap to complete the ensemble. Emma's hair was styled in a loose ponytail that draped over one shoulder. She decided that she could pair clothes nicely if they were narrowed down for her. *Now to call Colton and see if I can meet him . . .*

CHAPTER 11

*E*mma scrolled through the contacts in her phone. When she came to Colton's name, she selected the number and was hopeful that he'd be available to meet on such short notice. The phone rang twice before his voice sounded on the line.

He was at the print shop with the invitations to the ball and asked her to meet him there.

Emma walked to her car, pleased that the storm had passed, leaving a gorgeous day in its wake.

When she arrived at the Printer's Press, she saw Colton's bike outside. Her heart did that little flutter that she'd come to know when she thought of him. She smiled as she exited the car. Approaching the door, she saw him inside. So tall and so very handsome. He wore a simple button down shirt and jeans. And even though he was dressed in simple cloth-

117

ing, she noticed how all the ladies watched him, including Shelly Arnold.

She had been a thorn in Emma's side since high school, Cat's too. Shelly was *that* girl - the one who was pretty, always had a boyfriend, and always had a date to the dance. She was the captain of the cheerleading squad and valedictorian. Just once Emma wanted her to know what it felt like to be the *other* girl. Just once. Maybe twice.

Maybe today was the day because as she peered inside, she could clearly see that Colton was ignoring Shelly. Emma couldn't suppress the smile that crept across her face. *Is this the day that I, Emma Saint-Claire - the girl who took herself to her senior prom - comes out the winner?*

The door "dinged" as she entered. When Colton turned and saw her, a broad smile spread across his face. Emma could tell he was happy to see her.

"I'm glad that plans changed and you could see me today," Colton said as he walked toward her then hugged her casually. Emma deepened the hug then raised up on her tiptoes to kiss his cheek. His curiosity piqued, he smiled, but said nothing. Emma watched Shelly out of the corner of her eye and was pleased that she had caught the embrace. "Care to tell me what that was about, luv?"

"Later."

Colton held her at arm's length to get a better look at her. He smiled, "I like the cap."

"Why, thank you, Mr. Graves. Now, can I see the mock-up for the invitations?"

"They're printing right now."

Emma looked confused. "Ok, but I thought I was going to see them first?"

"That was the original plan, but I wanted you to receive

the very first glance when you opened your invitation. You'll be the first in town."

And how could she argue with that?

"Mr. Graves, your order is now complete."

Hearing his name, Colton and Emma walked to the counter where they found eight rectangular boxes waiting for them. Colton looked at Emma and laughed. "I didn't forsee them being printed so quickly."

"Easily swayed there, Mr. Graves, easily swayed. Maybe I should've been a motorcycle salesman."

"Emma, I'm afraid I'd own twenty of them, then. I don't think I could tell you no."

"Good to know," she said with a grin. "You seem to be in need of my help, so I'd be happy to oblige."

They loaded the boxes in her car and each drove to the bed and breakfast. When they arrived, Miss Francine was mulling about the house and asked Emma if she could help her reach a bowl on the top shelf.

"Normally, I'd stand on this stool, but it broke last week, and I haven't replaced it yet." As Emma listened to the story of how the stool broke, she took in Francine's features. She was a robust African American woman of short stature. She had the kindest eyes that Emma had ever seen. When Emma retrieved the mixing bowl, she heard Colton call her name.

"Oh Emma, I have something for you."

Emma entered the parlor, "Your royal highness summoned?"

Colton smiled.

Sitting on the floor surrounded by boxes, invitations, and envelopes, he cleared a spot in front of him for her to sit. Emma accepted the card he handed her as she sat down facing him.

It was addressed to her: *Emma Saint-Claire, the loveliest maiden in all the land.* She smirked when she read it.

"Pardon? It's an invitation to the ball. Don't all little girls dream of receiving one and having a royal title?"

For once, I don't feel so much like Cinderella, before the ball. This is a good feeling. Emma opened the envelope and saw a beautiful cream colored invitation with apricot ink. But it was the printed caption at the bottom that caught her attention. *"The curator humbly requests that you not wear green."*

"Colton, it's beautiful. But can I ask a question? Have something against green, much?"

"You amuse me, Miss Saint-Claire. That message does not apply to you. It is customary for the curator's attendant to wear green. The fairest maiden in all the land shall wear the color that all will envy. And besides, with you as my partner, it'll look good with my eyes." He batted his lashes.

Emma shook her head. "You're such a goof. One with too perfect hair!" She shot her hand forward to roughly tousle his locks at the same time Colton leaned back, purposely throwing her off balance. They both fell to the floor laughing, Emma on top of him.

"It sure is nice to hear laughter in this old house again."

Emma slid off Colton's chest when the robust voice filled

the room. They sat up, turning toward Francine who stood in the doorway holding an hors d'oeuvres tray.

The smile on her face contradicted the pain in her voice. Walking toward them, she handed over a silver platter containing herb-tomato crostinis, cheese wedges, and grapes. "I know you're hard at work, but I thought you might like some refreshments."

They thanked her for her thoughtfulness as Emma lowered the tray to the table beside them.

"I won't keep you. It's just when I heard Mr. Graves laughing, it reminded me of my Jesse and the laugh he used to have. I just-" she stopped herself. "Sorry for the intrusion." She turned on her heels, intent to walk away.

"Wait," Emma urged softly. "Would you like to talk about him, about Jesse?" When Francine turned back to the conversation, tears had welled up in her eyes.

Taking a deep breath, her hands spanned out in front of her. "He could fill a room with his laughter, my Jesse, and command a crowd with his word," she smiled at the thought. "People, they were drawn to him and had predicted great things for my boy, yes they had. But he- well, a car accident took him from me, he wasn't even eighteen. Sometimes it seems like such a long time ago, and other times it feels like only yesterday."

"Miss Francine, we're very sorry to hear about your son."

"Thank you, Emma. Even though he's been gone a good long while now, some hurts never heal."

Emma rubbed her wrist at that statement. She knew all too well that some hurts left imprints long after the physical wounds had healed.

Francine continued, "Losing a child is an emptiness that can never be filled. Sometimes I still sense him. I feel like I see him round the corner or can smell him. I just miss him so much." She looked at Emma and Colton. "It's good to have you two here. Let me know if you need anything."

"Thank you for the refreshments. Emma and I will enjoy them while we work."

"You're welcome. It's nice to feel needed."

"I understand."

She smiled a tight smile. "I really don't think you do, Mr. Graves. When I lost my Jesse, I lost my purpose in life. All I ever wanted to be in this world was a mom. Jesse's dad left us when he was just a baby, so my job was to be the best momma that I could be to that boy. And I loved it. When Jesse's life ceased to exist, so did my sense of purpose." She motioned to the room around them, "So when this place came available, I bought it. I'm good at cooking and cleaning. And I enjoy meeting new people. It was a perfect fit. There's nothing I want more in this life than to be needed. So Mr. Graves, it is I that should be thanking you."

"I appreciate you telling us your story," Emma said.

"Miss Francine, do you have a laundry service that I could bother you with? It appears that I'll be in town for longer than I originally perceived."

With a smile that lit up her face, Francine replied. "I can do that for you. I'd be happy to."

"Also, I'd like to stay on here for a couple more weeks. If you have a room available, that is?"

"I do. You can keep your room. I always keep one room in reserve." She brought her finger to her mouth. "Shhh. Don't tell anyone, though. This will be our secret."

Emma noticed how Francine's eyes lit up with the mention of having Colton stay longer. Emma had originally thought that she would spoil him, but it appeared as if Colton was going to be the one to spoil Francine.

As she turned to leave, Colton called out to her. "Miss Francine, would you be interested in attending a masquerade ball?"

Emma turned around and playfully swatted him on the arm, "Hey, I thought I was your date for the evening!"

He smiled at her and winked then explained to Francine the details of the Halloween ball.

"Yes, I would love to go. You two have pleased me more than you will ever know. Now, I have chores to do." She turned again and walked away. "Enjoy your snacks," she called over her shoulder.

As they sat side by side nibbling on the finger food, Colton reminded Emma that she needed to tell him about the kiss on the cheek at the print shop.

Popping a grape in her mouth, she led into her story. "Ok, so Shelly Arnold was the "it girl" in high school. She always looked down on me, treated me like a second rate citizen, and things haven't gotten better as adults. She was in the store today and was clearly noticing you. I just wanted to see her get knocked down a peg. I don't know why it matters, but sometimes, it just does. When I noticed that you weren't paying attention to her," Emma shrugged her shoulders, "I thought maybe you weren't interested in her. So I pretended to know you better than I do, for the simple reason of goading her. There, I said it. I know it's shallow. But I wanted her to see you with me, and it felt good. Cat and I can't stand her, but we'll save that story for another time."

Reaching over to stroke her cheek, Colton smiled. "Emma, I'd very much like to know you better."

"How about we start right now?"

He looked intrigued. "What did you have in mind, luv?"

She cocked her head to the side. "Do you ever get fortune cookies from Chinese restaurants?"

"I do."

"Well, I had a fortune that said, *'Life is what you make of it - make yours count. Wait not for the perfect moment, for that moment is now.'* Also, it said my lucky numbers were 22, 7, 11 and 10." They both laughed.

"*Are* you making the most of the moments in your life, Emma?"

Without answering, she rose to her feet, extending her hands to help him up. Emma had every intention of making the moments count starting now.

Colton placed his hands in hers, pushing himself up to his feet.

"Let's go for a walk," she suggested as she turned and walked slowly toward the veranda doors. Emma reached behind her for his hand, but instead of fingers intertwining with her own, a strong hand wound around her waist, pulling her body against his.

Emma's eyes, heavy with desire, fell closed. She basked in the feel of his strong arms around her, his hard body behind her, and the warm breath that danced across her neck. He was close enough to kiss her, but didn't, which only caused her to want it more.

They swayed in silence, her hands resting on his. "I like you," she whispered. Peering over her shoulder, "And I like spending time with you."

She saw a hunger in his eyes that she was certain mirrored her own. "It seems we have that in common, luv."

Twisting free from his grip, Emma turned fully then

slowly walked backwards. With the French door to her back, she soon found herself toe to toe with a sexy Brit.

"Emma, is *this* what you had in mind about making the most of the moments in your life?" Colton gently removed her cap and laid it on the table beside them. With his attention back on her, he watched her heavy laden gaze drop to his lips. He could tell that this was exactly what she had in mind.

She pushed her hands into his hair, drawing him closer. With one hand wrapped around her holding her firm to his body, Colton placed the fingertips of the other under her chin, gently lifting. "You're beautiful," he whispered.

Emma's heated gaze rose to meet his own.

His hand slipped behind her head as a single word feathered across her lips, "Beautiful."

Desire enveloping her, Emma's eye's slid shut as Colton's lips brushed against her own. *Heaven.* As he deepened the kiss, she found herself thinking that this could be one of her last first kisses.

Breaking away, he said, "Wait not for the perfect moment, for the moment is now." He cupped her face in his warm hands and lowered his head, taking full possession of her lips again.

The butterflies that she had felt in her stomach quickly subsided giving way to sheer desire. The feather soft touch of his lips had grown more deliberate, more passionate with every pass. He dominated her, thoroughly capturing her lips.

Colton's hands slid down her back. He could feel the cool glass against his knuckles as his wandering hands rested on her backside.

She had never experienced anything like this. She wanted this kiss . . . wanted this man. Passion clouding her composure, she instinctively ground her pelvis against his as she wove her hands roughly through his hair, refusing to allow even an inch between them.

He wanted her - a fact that was becoming blatantly obvious from the uncomfortable constriction of his jeans. Breaking the kiss, Colton pressed his forehead to hers.

With his hands cradling her face, he captured her gaze, "What is it about you?" He ran his thumb over her bottom lip. "That was quite a kiss, and one that I've wanted for days."

His seductive voice did nothing to quell her desire.

"Never have I wanted anything more."

Emma groaned when her phone sounded from her pocket.

Colton gently brushed her lips with his one last time before putting space between them. "I'll give you some privacy." As he walked onto the veranda giving his libido a mental reprimand, he heard Emma's sweet voice greet the caller.

"Hi, Daddy."

When her call ended, she remembered the very reason she had called Colton to begin with.

"There's something big I forgot to tell you," Emma said as she walked out into the fresh air to stand by his side. "When I was helping Mrs. Loretta, who's not the quack I pegged her to be, she told me some disturbing information about Nancy. There's a long story behind this, but if what she heard is correct, someone wants to tear down Dillingham Manor. Oh, and I invited Mrs. Loretta to the ball."

Colton stood in silence for a moment. "That's fine that you invited her. We'll place her on the guest list along with

Miss Francine. Now, explain about the house being torn down."

Emma pulled her cap back on as she continued. "Mrs. Loretta didn't know who or why, but they are trying to let the house sit deteriorating so they can deem it abandoned. It'll then belong to the city of Brookfield, and they can tear it down and do with the property as they please. All I know is that it's someone at the historical society who's behind this, and they're also the ones who placed Miss Nancy there as the landlady. She's being blackmailed into doing his bidding, whoever 'he' is. I'm not sure who works there now. Apparently, Nancy had an affair with Mrs. Loretta's husband's friend a long time ago, and in order for her friends not to find out, she's going along with this plan. Mrs. Loretta thinks that the rent money goes to this guy at the historical society. So you know what this means?"

"No, Emma, I'm barely following any of it."

"It means that once that article comes out, we have to get you proven as the legal owner of the estate. I can call my friend, Kimberly, first thing tomorrow morning and get her to look into getting the proof you need. When I go back to town, I'll check the Lexington Herald paper box and see if the article is in it." *And exhale.* "But being that so many heirs own it, it'll be hard to prove ownership."

"It actually won't. I contacted my cousins and have written proof that they have no interest in a home that sits deteriorating in the United States. I emailed them some of the photos that you sent me. They all agreed that a heap of rubbish was more to my liking than theirs."

"What about Kane?"

Colton laughed, "As of now, he has no interest in the home but has reserved the right to change his mind after viewing it. In true Kane fashion, I'll do all the leg work and then he'll try to come and bark orders when we start renovating the house."

"So I'll meet him?"

"Yes, and my mother, too. They'll be here for the ball."

"I look forward to meeting them." Emma thumbed over her shoulder to the work they had abandoned, "I guess we should get started on the guest list."

Colton opened the door for her. "Which you'll have to do the majority of since I only know three people in this town."

When they had invited as many people as they could think of, they called Miss Francine in to see if she'd like to help them stuff envelopes. She was eager to help, and they were glad to have it.

With everything but the address labels adhered, Emma and Colton decided to move back outside and enjoy the day.

CHAPTER 12

*C*olton sat in the middle of the swing in the yard overlooking the river. Emma joined him, bumping his left hip with her right as she sat down. He scooted over about an inch, which drew a hearty laugh from her. "Thanks for making sooo much room," she joked.

"I made as much as was necessary." He punctuated his comeback with the crooked grin that she was starting to love.

As she basked in the warm rays of the sun, Emma stretched her legs out in front of her, one ankle crossed over the other. She couldn't help but smile. For the first time in a long time, she was happy. Completely and totally happy.

She was aware of the way Colton stole glances at her when he thought she wasn't looking. When he did it again, she turned to face him. This time, he didn't look away.

"What are you thinking?" Emma asked.

"I was thinking that I rather liked the way the sun reflected in your hair last evening. Beautiful red highlights shone through as the sun set behind you. Let's remove this cap and your hair tie so I can see them again."

Emma shrugged her shoulders, "It'll probably be wild as a buck in this breeze, but we'll give it a shot." When she lifted her arm to remove the hat, her left sleeve came down, revealing her scarred wrist.

Furrowing his brow, Colton took her wrist into his hand, gently dragging the pad of his thumb over the raised, intersecting lines. "Emma," he said softly as he stared in disbelief. "What happened to you?" He knew he shouldn't have asked the question, but it was out before he realized what he was saying.

She stared down at the wrist he still caressed. "It's something that happened not too long ago . . . something that I really don't discuss." She caught his gaze. "I will say that it's not what you think. Someone did this to me when I was trying to defend myself. Maybe we'll discuss it someday, but not this day."

Colton nodded his head in understanding. He knew instinctively that it had to do with the man in Louisville that Peggy had mentioned. He also knew that Emma was unaware he knew about that, and he would keep it that way.

He tried to change the subject to a more pleasant topic. Looking across the yard, Colton pointed out some squirrels busying themselves gathering nuts. They joked about the evil squirrels of Kentucky that stole people's composure and tossed them to the ground.

"Brutes, they are," Emma joked.

"How about that walk?" Colton asked, leading Emma across the yard. As they started down the meandering stone steps that led to river's edge, Colton broke the silence. "Emma, tell me about yourself."

"Ok, what do you wanna know?"

"Tell me something that I don't know."

"Well, look at you being all inquisitive," she said as she playfully tugged on his shirt.

"Yes, it's fun to switch roles sometimes."

"I assure you, Colton, that you wouldn't want me designing or building anything! So we'd better keep these roles right where they are."

"Humor me," he said as he stilled their downward progression toward the water. "Tell me three things that I don't know."

"Let's see. Ok, I hate my name."

"Why do you hate your name?"

"I don't think you want to start there. You'll use up all your questions. Just let me finish. Please hold all questions until the tour is over," she said playfully.

"Oh, yes, Ma'am. I forgot the rules."

"Ok, three things you don't know about me," Emma held her fingers up and started ticking them off as she made her points. "I hate my name. Autumn is my favorite season. And I've always wanted to go on a horse drawn carriage ride or sleigh ride, or both."

She continued her stride down the long path. Once they reached the bottom, they sat on the edge of the dock.

"Why do you hate your name?" Colton continued as if there'd been no break in the flow of conversation.

"My name is Emma Saint-Claire. No Emma Sue, Emma Lou, or even Emma Pooh - just plain old Emma. I don't even have a middle name. Have you ever met anyone in your life who didn't have a middle name? I haven't."

"Why didn't your parents give you a middle name if it's customary to do so in the United States?"

She laughed and explained. "When my Mom was pregnant with me and my parents were trying to decide on names, she hated every combination that my dad came up with. He wanted to name me 'Taylor' if I was a boy and 'Amanda' if I was a girl. Being that I came early, there was no time to agree upon a name, so they named me Amanda Taylor Saint-Claire."

"That's a beautiful name, Emma. Why don't you go by that name?"

"Again, another story. When my parents sent off for the birth certificate and it came back, Amanda Taylor had become Emma. Just plain Emma. As you will recall, my mother hated the given name that my father came up with from the very start. So when the birth certificate came back as 'Emma,' my mother took it as a sign from God and left it alone. Emma was her grandmother's name and would become mine. So there you have it. Just plain Emma, at your service."

He reached for her hand, pulling it to his mouth to place a gentle kiss on it. "You're anything *but* plain, Miss Saint-Claire. But you cheated."

"How so?" She snapped her head back as the question rolled out.

"I said tell me three things that I *don't* know. But on the very first day I met you, you told me that Fall was your favorite season. So you must confess something else."

She thought for a moment and then continued. "Ok. Since I *cheated*, I'll give you one more, but only 'cause you asked nicely."

"That seems fair," Colton agreed, amused.

"Number three - never in all my time as a journalist, have I ever referred to a person as 'extraordinary.'"

"That's a perfectly respectable sentiment. Why have you not?"

"When I was in elementary school, it was either fifth or sixth grade, we had a school newspaper-"

"And you were the editor, no doubt," Colton interrupted.

"Actually, no. I was the child who was invisible. I avoided drawing attention to myself at all cost. Anyway, this particular edition of the school paper had every child's name in one column and an adjective in another column beside their name. My description was 'extraordinary.' But to a child with low self-esteem, what I saw were the words *'extra ordinary.'* So I thought to myself that it wasn't bad enough for me to just be ordinary, but I was *extra* ordinary. The rest of the day, in my little world, I felt like everyone was laughing at me because I was so plain and then everyone knew it because of the paper. Of course I know that that's not how they meant it, but it is for that reason that I have been careful to never use that word when describing a person or anything they've created. If I had to say 'wonderful' eight hundred times, I would, just to avoid saying 'extraordinary.' So, there you have it. Are you ready for me to leave yet? I'm sure you're getting some weird vibes," Emma laughed weakly.

"Not weird vibes. Just happiness at meeting an extraordinarily beautiful, kind, and funny lady. And make no mistake, Emma. I'm an educated man. I have a firm understanding of the word, and I believe that it fits you perfectly."

"Thank you," she said softly. "You're very kind." In all her life, she had never felt so at ease with anyone. Even though she had only known Colton a short while, Emma was starting to catch herself imagining things moving forward. She liked the thought of that.

"You know, we have to get those invitations out tomorrow. We want people to have plenty of time to get dresses and tuxes or whatever they're to wear." *Good Lord! What am I going to wear? I have to raid Cat's closet for daily clothing!*

Colton caught the worried expression on her face. "Is something the matter?"

"Oh, I was just thinking about what I would wear and

where I would find something. I'm really not all that good at being a girl." Emma's slumping shoulders demonstrated her point and Colton laughed.

"I'm certain that you'll come up with something stunning."

You'd do better to be a realist, Mr. Graves. All that's coming to my mind is, "Toga Toga!"

~

They walked back toward the house, admiring the colorful scenery as they went. They explored the yard, and Colton stopped to admire the workmanship that went into the stone wall. Emma motioned toward a walking path and suggested that they take it sometime. "You never know what kinds of surprises you'll stumble upon just off the beaten path."

"Sounds like a wonderful idea. Speaking of 'off the beaten path,' do you have plans for dinner tonight?"

"Ravioli - straight from the can. That's a tough act to follow, Mr. Graves." Even though he laughed, Emma could tell he wanted to say something more.

"I saw a place today on my way to the printers, an Italian restaurant. It was quaint and tucked into a nook near town."

"Oh, you're talking about Portabella's. They have wonderful Italian food."

"Emma, would you like to go there with me tonight? We could ride my bike if you'd like."

Breathe, Emma, just breathe . . . "I think I'd like that very much." *The thought of having my arms wrapped around you makes Emma a very happy girl!*

Wrapping his arms around her, he groaned as he pressed a kiss to her head. "On second thought, maybe you could drive to your place and then I could pick you up there. I have to call my secretary, Eleanor. We have a meeting scheduled for tomorrow and need to tidy up loose ends before video chatting with the client."

Colton started to let her go, but pulled her back. "And Emma, wear the hat. I like it." Without asking permission, he ducked his head leaving her with a kiss she wouldn't soon forget.

CHAPTER 13

*O*nce she arrived back at the boardinghouse, Emma kicked off her boots and lay back on the bed. Thinking back over her day, over the last few days, she realized that she couldn't remember a time when she had been so happy. Everything was going well for her. She'd had the best kiss of her life today. Her job was keeping her busy. Her other job with Colton was starting to keep her away from Dillingham Manor and Nancy as much as possible, and that was certainly a plus.

She couldn't be more pleased with Colton – not just his looks, but he was courteous, respectful, and he truly seemed to enjoy spending time with her. Emma was also happy that things were going well for Cat with her budding romance with the very sexy Hayden McAllister.

And last but certainly not least, I have a date tonight. I haven't had a date in . . . longer than I care to admit!

The sound of a text message pulled her from her thoughts. Emma looked at her phone and smiled when the familiar name displayed on the screen. Emma had known that she'd hear back from Cat as soon as she'd listened to the voicemail. Emma had been bursting at the seams when she'd left the message on her way home.

"You kissed?"

"Oh, yes. And I acted like a wanton whore during the whole thing!"

"'Bout damn time! Where are you anyway, and where are you going tonight?"

"In my room. I'm stretched out on the bed, resting a little, then we're going to Portabella's."

"And we both know how that'll turn out! You'll wake in the morning having stood up the sexiest man you've ever known!"

"I have my door open. I'll hear him."

"I trust you look stunning?"

"Oh, yes. I think you'd just love what I'm wearing."

"No doubt I would, since I likely bought it. Maybe you'll let me wear it sometime. Have fun, babe."

Emma switched the light on beside her bed and examined her nails. She was thankful that they were presentable, but made a mental note to get a manicure soon.

Pulling the hair tie free from her hair, she placed it and her cap on the desk beside her. She didn't know what time he'd be there, but knew he wouldn't be long. She thought she'd just close her eyes for a minute and when she heard him pull up, she'd go out and greet him. Emma was excited to ride his motorcycle. *Who am I kidding? I'm just excited to wrap my arms around him!*

She thought she could get used to this tranquil feeling of everything lining up in her life just perfectly. Her thoughts drifted to Colton once again. She could only imagine what Kane looked like, too. Colton said people mistook them for twins, so she knew he must be over six feet tall as well, with dark hair and gorgeous features.

Her eyes sliding shut. Emma replayed the kiss in her mind over and over and . . .

∾

Colton's bike roared to a stop. He kicked down the stand and shut off the engine. As he hung his helmet on the handlebars and dismounted, he stared at the dark house. A single light spilled from the shadows, casting a lonesome beam onto the ground.

He still couldn't believe that this was his. He chuckled at that thought. *Most people would be disappointed if they found out that they had a heap of rubbish across the pond, but I'm looking forward to the challenge of restoring it.*

After tomorrow, he would be able to show ownership and halt the plans to tear down the place, should that come to light.

Walking up to the weed infested porch, Colton wondered how many times his grandparents had stood in that same spot. He often thought about things that most people would overlook. He thought that made him a better engineer - his attention to detail. As he went through the door, he laughed at his previous thought. *Someone who pays attention to detail might have asked Emma which room was hers.*

Colton walked down the dark hall to the right and spotted her room with no problem because he could see Emma inside lying on her small twin bed. Its bright bedding was a stark contrast to the rest of the house.

Walking closer to her room, Colton realized she was asleep. He thought she was the loveliest woman he had ever met. She was smart, funny, and someone he wanted to get to know better.

Emma lay sleeping on her left side, her knees slightly bent. One hand was wedged between her cheek and pillow while her other rested on her torso. Colton didn't know if he'd ever get the chance to watch her sleep again, so he took pains not to wake her.

He entered her room, easing the door shut. When she didn't wake, he took in her surroundings.

Her bed was nestled against the wall, catty-cornered from the door with a floor fan near the footboard. He noted that the placement of her bed assured she could see into the hall. He thought that the lime green and pink accessories of her bedding revealed her playful side. Her white wooden bed was old and worn. It had a matching desk that sat underneath the wide window beside the head of her bed. Colton wondered if the furniture was hers or if they were already here when she moved in. Turning his attention to the right of where he stood, he noticed a door, most likely a closet. A chest of drawers was to its right. Her stereo sat atop the cabinet with many CD cases beside it. *She likes music.* He quietly walked over and glanced through the titles. He could clearly see that she appreciated an eclectic blend of music ranging from Southern Rock to country to metal.

Her tidy room with only a couple pair of boots out of place seemed fitting. Moving across the room, Colton peered down at her full desk calendar, which sat open. He noticed that every Monday in October had "lunch with Cat" written on it. He knew they liked to eat at the diner, so he suspected that's where they would be. His mind wandered to a day when the calendar would read, "lunch with Colton." *I don't know what the hell's wrong with me! I barely know this woman. But the more I learn about her, the more I like and the more I want to know.*

Colton pulled out the chair to her desk, lining it up with the lime green shag rug that ran alongside her bed. He hoped that the chair wouldn't scrape the floor or creak when he sat down. He bore his weight on his legs as he squatted and eased into the seat. *I hope it's not as old as it looks. It may crash to the floor under my weight. That would be interesting to explain.*

To his relief, the chair held up. And to his amazement, Emma continued to sleep. He thought that painting must have exhausted her today, and she was just catching up on her rest, albeit unintended.

Colton looked to the far wall. He noticed a toaster, minimicrowave, and small refrigerator all stacked on top of each other on the opposite wall near the door. He quickly realized why she ate out so much; she didn't have a real kitchen. He also now had an understanding of why she disliked Dillingham Manor so much. He stared at her dingy white walls, without any pictures, and remembered her saying that Nancy didn't allow modifications of any type. The bedding hues suddenly made sense as well. He thought Emma was determined to brighten the room the only way she could, through accessories.

His attention came back to the sleeping beauty lying before him, her lips parted. His mind returned to the kiss they shared earlier. When she began giggling in her sleep, he couldn't help but smile. He liked watching her. *Here I sit, like a stalker, watching her sleep.* The thought of that made Colton ill at ease. He never wanted to be viewed as anyone that Emma would fear.

When he started to leave, he accidentally skidded the chair leg across the floor. Colton thought he had woken her, but Emma just turned over and continued sleeping. *Now what? I don't want to leave making her think I've forgotten our date. I suspect that's universally unacceptable no matter where you are. I can't text her because that will wake her up. If I look for something to write on and she wakes up to me rummaging through her desk, she'll think I'm a stalker and a thief. And suddenly, having stood her up is sounding like the best plan of all!*

Even with the understanding that he should go, Colton couldn't bring himself to leave. He didn't want her to think that he'd forgotten their date.

He decided that the only thing he could do was to wait it out. Stretching his legs out as quietly as he could, he crossed one ankle over the other one. With nothing to do, he turned his phone to silent, accessed the e-reader, and thought this was as good a time as any to read a new book. He didn't usually read for relaxation because it always put him to sleep. He found a book that would interest him and began reading . . .

$$\approx$$

Emma awoke, having taken the best nap of her life. When the bedside light filled her room, she knew it was dark outside. She also knew he hadn't shown. The sinking weight of disappointment pooled deep in her stomach. She didn't bother turning over. She just lay there staring at the drab wall that had been her only regular companion in this dank room for months. So much about the room was lackluster, including the grooved indentions that she now traced her fingers over on the wall – a years old repair that she had always wondered why it was there . . . wondered why *she* was there.

She was too embarrassed to have anyone over, so no friend other than Cat had seen her room. *Cat. She thinks I'm living it up somewhere tonight.* The reality of the situation cut her deep. Emma knew she'd been stood up. Being stood up was the worst feeling on earth. It was the moment in time when you realized the person you made time for neglected to make time for you. *I thought he was different. I mean, I think he is different. I'm sure he just got held up with work.* She couldn't help but feel the familiarity of making excuses for the dates of the past that didn't bother to show. *Somehow, I know he didn't mean to do this. I just know he's different.*

Emma turned over and was startled to see someone at her bedside. Her first reaction was to scream and strike out, but realization hit before panic set in. Sitting at her bedside was a sleeping beauty that the fairytale didn't portray – tall, dark, and handsome with his phone in his lap and his chin to his chest. *Well, what do I do now? Do I wake him up? Let him sleep? Scoot over and let him lie down beside me?* She thought for just a moment before deciding that sharing a bed with Colton was exactly what she wanted. *Yes, that sounds like a delightful idea, right after I make sure my mascara hasn't smeared.*

Emma's covert attempt to slip out of bed was cut short when she bumped his foot with hers. Colton sucked in a breath, his eyes fluttering open as his mind made sense out of the fact that he had fallen asleep.

"Did you have a good nap, sleepy head?" Emma asked, sinking back down on the bed.

"I didn't mean to fall asleep. I was just going to wait until *you* woke up."

"I didn't mean to fall asleep, either," she smiled at her sleepy giant.

"I tried to read, but that always puts me to sleep. I'm so sorry, Emma. I guess I just got here later than you expected, and you were asleep when I arrived."

"Are you still tired?"

"A bit," he yawned, "and my neck feels like it's been in a vice." Colton wrenched his head from side to side.

Emma shifted, drawing her knees up underneath her until she sat back on the heels of her feet. "Let me help you with that," she offered, motioning for him to sit in front of her.

Without pause, Colton rose, turned, and then sat on the

edge of the bed. Emma moved closer until the front of her thighs rested against his lower back. Bringing her hands to either side of his neck, the pads of her thumbs traced small circles against the tense muscles as she slowly worked invisible knots out of his shoulders.

~

Colton's fingers dug repeatedly, painfully, into his thighs as he tried to reign in his desire. Did she have any idea what she was doing to him? Was she purposely trying to drive him mad by pulling his body against hers with every ministration? She may have succeeded in relaxing the muscles in his neck, but she was doing a number on the one between his legs . . . and her hands had yet to touch him there.

Emma's breasts pressed against him. He shifted uncomfortably. Her hips tilted into him. A silent curse fell from his lips. Did she even know she was doing that? *Bloody hell, is she trying to kill me?*

~

God, he feels good. Emma's ministrations became stronger, deeper . . . slower. Did he have any idea what the feel of his strong muscles beneath her hands was doing to her? His scent wafted towards her. She inhaled and closed her eyes. She knew her body pressed against his, and she knew she couldn't stop it. Every time she squeezed the ridge between his neck and shoulder, she couldn't help but imagine what it would feel like to close her hand around his-

A low moan inched into her awareness. Eyes that she didn't realize had slid shut now opened. Did that sound spill from her throat . . . or from his?

Colton looked over his shoulder, his predatory eyes traveling her body. He looked away, clearing his throat. He knew exactly how he wanted the night to end, but did she want the same? He had to get out of here. "We should go before the restaurant closes."

A smile tugged at her lips. The innocent gesture of a simple massage had clearly stoked a fire within him, the same one that burned within her. Emma placed her hands back on his shoulders, kneading his muscles. Colton groaned.

"We *could* go," she stilled her hands. After a moment, he felt warm breath on his ear as she uttered the open ended invitation, "Or maybe we could find something *here* that would interest you."

The sound of her husky voice was his undoing. It took only a second for Colton's strong arm to snake around, readjusting her until she straddled his lap. "It seems you're in luck. I've already found something that interests me." His heavy lids rose ever so slowly to capture her gaze, "Interests me very much." Colton threaded his fingers into her hair pulling her just shy of a kiss. "Come here," he commanded seductively as he crushed her lips down on his.

The kiss traveled from her mouth to her neck. "I don't know what it is about you," Colton said between kisses. "On the first day I met you, I wanted to kiss you then, but I was afraid of moving too fast. You didn't know me. You still don't-"

Emma tugged his chin upward. "But I want to," she interrupted, dropping a soft kiss to his lips. With every pass of their lips, the kiss grew more passionate.

Did she mean to rock against the growing bulge in his pants? *Is this what she wants, too?*

Pulling away, Colton began to speak, his strained words a testament to the control he struggled to hold on to. "You're driving me mad, luv." He held her gaze to make his point clear. "I want more than a kiss, Emma, and I'm not going to stop unless you ask me to."

Her smile provided silent confirmation.

Emma knew that this night would be one that she would never forget. She also knew that this would be the night that she would finally lose her virginity.

Shamelessly, she ground against him when his lips claimed hers once more. Emma found herself enveloped in arms of steel. His kisses were soft and gentle at first, but as her body responded, they became more urgent.

Butterflies soared through her stomach when she felt his fingers breach the hem of her sweater. Warm hands fell against her back, first holding her close before slowly inching around. Emma couldn't suppress the moan that escaped her throat as his thumb dragged deftly across her nipple, repeatedly, awakening the tip to a tight point and sending jolts of need straight to her core. His left hand mirrored the motion giving both breasts equal treatment.

Slowly, she slid button after button from their restraints, freeing his shirt. *Beautiful,* she thought, her fingers gliding over the corded muscles hidden within. She ran her hands along his chest, up to his shoulders where she pushed the fabric until it slid down his arms. Colton shrugged it from his body, tossing it to the floor.

Watching her tug her bottom lip between her teeth in reaction to the sight of his body, Colton dragged her sweater over her head, letting the soft material fall from his hands. She sat before him in a lacy, black bra that perfectly displayed ample cleavage. He pulled her close for a kiss, his experienced hands releasing the hooks of her lingerie.

In a swift motion, he rose to his feet, taking her with him. Emma's arms wound around his neck as her legs wrapped around his waist. He marveled for a moment at the way they fit together, thinking that she felt perfect in his arms.

A shiver ran down her spine when he tugged her bra strap down with his teeth, repeating the motion on the other side. Pert nipples held the fabric in place, hiding her from his view. Pressing a kiss to the swell of each breast, he turned, lowering her to the bed.

Desire coursed through him as he pulled the lace away, tossing it to the floor. She was gorgeous. Curvy in all the right places, and absolutely gorgeous.

Heat rose into her cheeks as she felt the weight of his gaze. Automatically, she brought her hands up to cover herself.

"Don't hide yourself from me, Emma," Colton urged as he lowered his body to hers, effectively shielding her. "You're beautiful," he said pressing a kiss to her neck, "and your body is beautiful."

Like most women, Emma did have insecurities about her shape, but there was nothing she could do about it now. Besides, she felt like he was telling the truth. If the bulge in his jeans was any indication, he honestly did like the way she looked.

"Lean back," she whispered in his ear.

Colton sat back, his thighs resting between hers. He was unsure what her intentions were.

Emma watched his reaction as her hands slid from her breasts, down her belly, and settled on the waistband of her jeans. She popped the button free then slowly slid the zipper down. He felt her pelvis tilt upward against his and took the cue, stripping the jeans away and tossing them in the growing pile of clothing on the floor.

Colton turned back, settling his full appraisal on her body. Lying before him, wearing nothing but a pair of lacy boy short underwear, she was beautiful.

His eyes poured over her, igniting her own desire. Emma leaned forward and placed her hands on the back of his neck, tugging him down into a passionate kiss.

The click of the lamp let her know that he'd shut the light off. "I think you're still over dressed," Emma said playfully.

Colton chuckled, and she felt the weight of his body lift off hers. The sound of his zipper slowly tugging down had her sucking in a breath of anticipation. This was really happening.

"Emma," Colton said as he lowered himself down, clearly still clothed, "We don't have to do this, luv. It's ok if you want to wait."

"I've waited long enough."

"Me too. It's been a while," he said as he brushed his lips against hers.

"Really? Well, it's been about twenty-seven years for me. I think I win."

Silence. The room was thick with silence, and the forward progression of the best night of her life was now wrought with total stillness. Colton's body continued to press down on hers, but no words passed between them. She felt him shift slightly, heard the teeth of his zipper gently pull together, then watched as luminous light flooded the room.

"Colton, what's the matter? Did I . . . Did I do something wrong?"

With his head against her neck, he began showering her with gentle kisses. "Emma, are you saying that you're a virgin?"

"Well, not if that's a deal breaker. I . . . I've slept with lots of people."

"Really. How many?"

"How many? Fi . . . fifty-seven."

"You've slept with fifty-seven people?" He looked amused.

"Absolutely. Now turn that light off, and we'll pick up right where we left off." Emma tried to kiss him, but he held her away.

"Please tell me the truth, Emma. Are you a virgin?"

She could visualize the brakes to an Amtrak train being placed on emergency stop – jackknifing cars and all. Emma exhaled a frustrated breath, embarrassment rolling over her. "Yes, Colton, I am. I'm the last remaining virgin of Brookfield. Maybe you could check out my exhibit at the festival. I'll be beside the two headed chicken!" *Because clearly, I'm a freak!*

His body shook above her in silent laughter.

"I never would have told you if I'd thought you'd stop." She tugged his head back to capture his gaze, hoping to make her plea more effective, "Please, Colton."

Lowering his head, he placed a long lingering kiss to her lips. Colton propped himself up on his elbows, gazing down at her. "Emma, there is nothing on this earth that I would rather do than spend the night making love to you. But if you give me the chance, I can promise you that your first time will be special and will be something that you'll want to remember."

"It would've been special . . . Will be special. Being with you would've made it that way. Nothing has changed for me."

"Nothing has changed for me either, luv, as far as wanting you," he lightly ground his hips against hers so she could feel the truth in his statement. "But I know that women remember their first time, and I don't want your memory to be of being on a single bed in an apartment that you hate with a man you barely know."

"You had a dog named Betty. I know lots about you."

"I want this to be special for you, Emma."

"Please, Colton."

"I'm not saying that we won't. And believe me when I say I'd love nothing more than to be your first," he stroked her cheek. "I'll plan a night that you will never forget." He leaned down and kissed her softly.

Emma's nails dug into his back as her breasts pressed harder against his chest. He knew she'd been pushed to her limit, and he sure as hell had. Colton reluctantly pulled his lips from hers. They were soft and pliable, just like her body beneath him.

Her bated breaths feathered across his lips.

Colton answered the question her pleading expression demanded.

"I haven't always made the right choices in life, Emma. I want to change that. Can you trust that that's what I'm trying to do now?" He searched her eyes, waiting for her response.

"So the virgin meets the gentleman . . . Just my luck!" Emma looked away, defeated.

Colton pulled her chin back, holding it in his grasp. A wicked grin tugged at his lips. "I won't always be a gentleman, luv."

The gentleness in his touch contradicted the promise in

his words. *Do I want a gentleman?* No, she thought. She wanted this man – whatever form he presented himself in. The throbbing between her thighs intensified when he shifted between them.

"Now, get some sleep. All that rest will be needed one day very soon." Colton crashed his lips to hers taking her mouth in a long passionate kiss.

Rolling against the wall and a half naked woman, Colton reached over, flipping the switch and casting the room into total darkness once more.

Settling her head on his shoulder, they lay in silence as the time passed by. Even though the words hadn't formed, it was understood. He was spending the night.

Emma propped herself up on one elbow, deciding to end all pretenses of her being a typical girl. "Just so you know, I'm gonna have to eat at some point."

Colton shook with laughter. He knew that he'd very much enjoy getting to know her.

As disappointed as she was that the night had not gone as expected, Emma was never so happy to drift off to sleep in the arms of a man who made her heart beat a little faster.

CHAPTER 14

*W*hile getting dressed for an early work day, Cat realized that the shoes she wanted to wear were missing. Missing clothes at her house always meant one thing – Emma had been "shopping." That's why she was now driving the winding drive that led to Dillingham Manor.

She had two favorite pair of boots; unfortunately for her, they were also Emma's favorites. *I'd loan the child anything she wanted. I just wish she'd return it from time to time!* Cat laughed as she stepped from her truck.

Surveying the cars in the lot, her eyes instantly fell on the black and chrome motorcycle parked in the last parking space. *Emma said Colton has a bike.* Cat halfheartedly dismissed the thought, but the eyebrow that remained hitched proved that she didn't dismiss it altogether. The butterflies in her stomach rapidly multiplied as she wondered about her cousin's evening.

Cat glanced at her watch and frowned. She knew Emma would still be sleeping at this hour. She'd still be sleeping herself if she didn't have to go in for an early delivery.

As usual, the main entrance that led into Dillingham Manor was unlocked. Cat pushed through the door and headed down the dark hallway toward Emma's room. Pressing her ear to the door and not hearing any sounds of life, she eased her key into the lock and slowly opened the door.

The gentle hum of a floor fan broke the silence.

Cathryn Morgan hadn't been shocked speechless too many times in her life, but what she saw before her left her mute.

Briefly ignoring the elephant in the room, she took in the scene before her. Emma's normally tidy room now more closely resembled a college dorm. Near the foot of the bed, clothing lay heaped in a pile, littering the faded wood floor. Some of the articles Cat recognized as belonging to her, but she bit back a smile when she saw Colton's clothing in the mix. Her gaze traveled up to the single bed with the double occupancy. Colton lay against the wall with Emma's leg and left arm draped across him. She wore a pair of cotton shorts with the words *"good girl"* scrawled across her bottom and a maroon sweatshirt. *Sure am glad she brought out her sexy lingerie for the occasion. Poor thing probably doesn't have any lingerie!* Cat rolled her eyes at the pitiful observation.

Continuing to assess the room, she spotted pop cans sitting atop a pizza box on the desk and came to the conclusion that they hadn't even made it out the door once Colton showed up. *When Saint Emma said she had a date, I had no idea this is what she had in mind.* A smile tugged at Cat's lips. *She knocked out all the firsts in one night!*

Redirecting her focus, she spotted her black boots by the closet door. She quietly retrieved them.

As she turned to leave, she looked back over her shoulder. Seeing Emma's head resting on Colton's chest made her smile. It made her heart smile. She was so happy for her cousin.

Cat realized that the mere fact that Colton was allowed to visit could be the start of something big. *You go, Emma SINclaire,* she thought to herself, easing out the door.

Cat was about to burst and had to tell someone. She called Hayden. He was a guy. He wouldn't get it, but he was also *her* guy and would have to learn to love these reports. When he didn't answer, she knew he must be working on a case, so she left a message. "Hey babe, you'll never believe what I've just discovered about Saint Emma! Well, we can't call her that *anymore!*" She laughed. "Anyway, call me when you can. Or better yet, come see me."

~

Cat was glad that she had a light day because the second she noticed Emma's blinds open at work, she *would* be calling. The morning had already dragged on. The shipment had been delivered, inventoried, and she'd already received a morning cancellation. Just as well. It gave her more time to pace the floor and wait for Emma.

She peered across the street. The blinds were still closed. *Damn.*

~

Gentle kisses fluttered from her cheek to her lips to her neck. Emma smiled and stretched, but her eyes remained closed.

"Good morning, beautiful. Are you going to wake up?"

"Uh huh."

"Then why are your eyes still closed?"

"I'm afraid this is a dream and when I open my eyes, you

153

won't really be here." Emma snuggled deeper against his side. "Never in my life have I woken up with someone - a man - in my bed. I'm just enjoying the moment."

Colton's arms engulfed her. "Emma, if I have my way, you'll know this feeling often."

She opened her eyes and smiled.

The tender kiss that fell on her lips lingered there. Another followed, slower this time, more deliberate. Losing herself to his efforts, Emma's hands clasped against Colton's neck, pulling him closer. She automatically moved against his body.

With a groan, he slowly pulled away. "Emma, even if we could, we *can't* because I don't have protection. I don't know what I was thinking last night."

"We don't need protection. I've been on birth control for years."

At his curious glance she elaborated, "I didn't lie, Colton. I am a virgin. One that has to be on birth control to regulate my periods."

"I see."

Nothing like the "P" word to kill the mood . . .

Emma exhaled a frustrated breath. Then it hit her. *Oh God! I have morning breath!* Attempting a smooth move, she turned on her side with the intention of scurrying away, but was stopped short.

"Now, just where do you think you're going, Miss Saint-Claire?" Colton turned her on her back, sliding on top of her and pinning her to the bed under his weight. Sweet kisses rained down on her.

"Just gonna run to the bathroom and brush my teeth and maybe fix my makeup, or what's left of it."

"You're beautiful, Emma. You don't need to change a

thing." A light kiss fell on her nose. "But regrettably, I do have to get going. I want to see your friend at the courts. Kimberly, is it?"

"Yes. She gets there at nine."

Colton glanced at the clock. "Then I'm late. I wanted to see her first thing."

First thing? What time is it? Emma propped herself up to look, nearly bucking Colton onto the floor when she discovered that it was nearly ten o'clock. She was on her feet in a flash.

"I'm guessing you're late?"

"Very! I forgot to set my clock last night. We were supposed to discuss the winners this morning during the staff meeting."

Emma rummaged through her dresser for something to wear.

"How can I help?"

"Just let Cat know I might not make it for lunch."

"I will. May I see you later?"

"I certainly hope so, but I'll have to call you after I see what my day looks like. I have no idea what time I'll be able to leave."

Colton reached his hand out, placing it on her shoulder. Emma looked back. "Emma, I know last night didn't end up the way we wanted-"

"Not for the lack of trying on my part," she interrupted dryly.

His cocked eyebrow mocked hers, "But I promise that I'll make it up to you and soon." Tapping on her calendar, Colton made his intentions clear. "Try to pencil me in for this weekend."

Colton pulled her into his arms. Cradling her face in his hands, he lowered his head, kissing her goodbye. "The entire weekend, luv," he winked and walked out the door.

Emma hastily gathered a bathroom bag and made a mad dash for the shower. However, she was stopped by Nancy who berated her for having an unapproved guest over all night and the late night pizza delivery. Before she could tack on more charges, Emma protested.

"Look," Emma said as she held a hand up to stop the tirade, "I am tired of walking on egg shells around you. I'm tired of you poking your nose in my business. And I'm tired of you acting like my damn mother!"

"Your mother?" Nancy huffed with a look of disgust, "No unwed child of mine would have a strange man in her room all night, and-"

Loretta's words came back to Emma. With every fiber of her being she wanted to tell her hypocritical landlady what she knew, but instead, she simply interrupted her.

"You know what? You may as well get used to it, and I'll tell you why. He's gonna be in my room and in my bed anytime I see fit. Deal with it! Now if you don't mind, I'm late for work and frankly not a morning person, so you need to step back!"

Nancy stood there dumbfounded as Emma brushed past her. No tenant had ever spoken to her like that before. Her clicky little shoes echoed through the hall as she sulked back to her room.

Emma got ready in record time. Even though she was late, she arrived in time for the staff meeting where she applied her makeup. Phil didn't try to hide the fact that he was upset that she was late. She promised him that she'd make it up to him. The evil smile that spread across his face let her know that he had been waiting for such a declaration.

"I'm glad to hear you say that, Emma. As it turns out, Mr. Cooper needs someone to come and talk to the students in his class about a career in journalism."

"Seriously? I know I messed up, but don't make me go to the school. Middle Schoolers scare me! Please send Laura."

"Laura called in sick this morning. That's why we need someone else to fill her spot."

Uh huh. I just bet she was sick.

With the staff meeting over and Phil appeased, Emma found herself standing outside the classroom. She mentally ran through her speech as she affixed the tag labeled *"visitor"* to her shirt. Peeking through the long rectangular window in the door, she took in her audience and groaned inwardly. They looked as enthused as she felt. But they seemed to have one thing in common, this was the last place on earth that any of them wanted to be. Emma knew before she started where this would go. She would spend her time trying to sound excited about a career in journalism, and the kids would spend their time staring at her like she had three heads. *Awesome.* She would pause for questions, not that there would be any. *May as well get the "cricket app" for my phone. That way I can fill the awkward silence myself!*

Here goes nothing, she thought as she gently rapped on the door while peeking through the window. The teacher motioned her inside.

At the front of the class, centered in front of a white board, Mr. Cooper stood beside a lonesome wooden podium. Emma walked to his side. Once she'd been introduced to the class, she thanked him for the opportunity. *I'm such a liar. No way am I thankful to be here!* She turned to face the students, giving her best smile - which mirrored no one's.

Inhaling deeply, she began. "Well, as Mr. Cooper said, my name is Emma Saint-Claire. I work at the Brookfield Journal as a journalist and photographer . . ." As she gave the basics about her job, Emma scanned the room for anyone who seemed remotely interested in what she had to say. Even the teacher didn't pretend to be interested in her speech. He sat to her right by the window with his nose stuck in a newspaper. *Seriously?*

Turning her focus back on the students, she categorized them. Emma could tell by looking at them those who wished to be invisible. She made a mental note to not call on them. Having been that type of student herself once, she knew the panic that arose in these situations. She easily pegged her trouble makers and know-it-all's right away, too.

Her spiel was short and now it was time for the interactive portion. Emma tried to make small talk with the students, asking them what their future aspirations were, who they most admired . . . *Chime the crickets.* She was failing miserably at engaging this class.

The rattle of a newspaper broke the silence when Mr. Cooper shook the pages, then folded it. When he looked up, Emma's eyes were on him.

The students laughed. *Awesome.*

"You're in the Lexington Herald this morning, Emma," Mr. Cooper exclaimed as he held up the rectangle, pointing to an article.

With all my rushing around this morning, I forgot about the article being printed by today. This gave Emma a delightful idea. She had one of the students read the article aloud. That actually opened the door for a discussion about Dillingham Manor and the history of Brookfield. The students were given an assignment by Mr. Cooper to research interesting facts about their city, and he was promised an invitation to the ball by Emma.

~

In a suburb of Louisville, Dr. Derrick Wells opened the newspaper as he drank his morning coffee. This mediocre existence had become his daily ritual since the separation. Gone were the days of kissing his wife good morning, helping prepare sack lunches, or even driving his kids to school. They were gone. He'd lost it all – the children he loved, the home he'd worked hard to build, and the trust of the one person who meant the most to him, his wife.

With his red sharpie in hand, he turned straight to the want ads, tossing the news headlines aside. Even though he already had a job as a psychologist, he was always on the lookout for a higher paying one. Child support for two kids wasn't cheap.

He scanned the page, but nothing generated much interest. As he brought his drink to his lips, a passing siren sounded outside his window, blaring a wailing alarm and startling him.

"Son of a bitch!" he yelled, coffee drenching his dress shirt and trailing across his want ads.

Undressing as he went, Derrick tossed his soiled laundry into the hamper that sat in the corner of the bedroom. He pulled a fresh undershirt from the dresser drawer and glanced in the mirror as he dressed. Defined muscles pressed against the fabric, a visual reward for his dedication to fitness. His mixed heritage had provided him with intriguing features - caramel skin, wiry hair, and piercing eyes that were a combined hue of blue and gray. He smiled, finding smug satisfaction in the fact that he was a damn good looking man. The smile quickly faded when his gaze settled on the crescent shaped scar on his cheek and the memory of the bitch who put it there. He traced his finger down the grooved flesh.

After cleaning himself up, Derrick returned to his ruined newspaper. He cleaned it up and then sat down to read the remainder. Propping his feet up on the desk, he crossed one ankle over the other. As he reared back in his chair and gently rocked, he opened up the sports section and cursed out loud when he saw the scores. After checking out the rest of the sports page, he turned his attention to the main headlines.

Derrick shot up in his seat, his feet hitting the floor. He pulled the paper closer to his icy eyes while an evil smile sprawled across his face. "Well, hello, Amanda Taylor . . . We meet again."

Blinded by memories, his gaze grew distant and unfocused as images flashed through his mind - he and Jazmine turning to greet the guests on their wedding day, their upscale home, carving pumpkins with his son and daughter, a weekend rendezvous with his sexy new colleague, the betrayal, his sobbing wife . . . Running his fingers through his hair, he sighed, shaking away the feelings. He'd fucked up. That much was true. But had it not been for the article his wife read, the advice Amanda gave, Jaz would have forgiven him. He narrowed his eyes, redirecting the memories. No longer was he seeing the wife and kids he loved and the lover he missed. He saw *her*. A sinister smile tugged at his lips. He saw fear in her eyes, watched the tears, heard the screams, recalled the pleasure he derived as the blade sliced into her . .

. His eyes slid shut for a moment, the thrill of remembrance coursing through his veins.

Derrick spent the next few minutes staring at the article. Laying the paper on his desk, he lazily drew a red circle around the featured piece. As he pressed the sharpie down, he noticed how the ink bled. *This is your blood, Amanda. This time, I will succeed.* He read and re-read the article and then saw the caption that listed her as, "Emma Saint-Claire."

"Gotcha," Derrick said to himself as a sinister smile crossed his face.

He called his office stating that a family emergency would require some time off, possibly a leave of absence. But he would be back as the situation allowed.

CHAPTER 15

*C*olton strolled down the steps of the courthouse, tucking a copy of the deed to Dillingham Manor in his coat pocket. After Kimberly had given him the copy, she pointed out that all he had to do now was to prove that he, in fact, was a Dillingham heir and the rightful owner.

Due to the unfortunate condition of the home, Colton felt no urgency to act. Before staking his claim to the manor and uprooting Nancy, he first wanted to investigate by whom and why she was being blackmailed.

Colton disconnected the call in frustration. He'd called Cat three times now, and all he'd got was a busy signal. He needed to let her know that Emma wouldn't be able to make their lunch date. After trying one last time, unsuccessfully, he shoved his phone in his pocket and decided to walk the short distance to deliver the message in person.

Turning the knob, he furrowed his brows in frustration when he found the door locked. Colton peeked through the window. The lights were on inside indicating that she was open. He could hear the faint pulse of music as it echoed through the empty shop, but he didn't see her anywhere. As he looked on, his gaze traveled over the wall to the right. Black framed photos lined every inch, the art within revealing sample tattoos of all sorts. They ranged from angels to demons, butterflies to dragons, flowers to lyrics, and everything in between. Black leather chairs were laid out in an "L" formation underneath the pictures and edged around the other side below where he looked in.

To his left, a brushed chrome receptionist's counter with a rounded front caught his attention. It sat catty-cornered to the door and had the word *Inked* scrawled across the center in red paint-stroke letters. It was vacant with the exception of a black vintage telephone which sat atop the high counter and lay with the receiver resting on its side, clearly off the hook. Colton shook his head. He wondered how she ran a successful business with practices such as these.

Turning to walk away, he heard a noise inside. Colton turned back toward the plate glass window just in time to see a police officer coming out of a back room buttoning his shirt. Cat followed behind, adjusting her own clothing.

Colton recognized the officer as the man named Hayden that he'd met briefly at the diner. He laughed to himself when he realized why the phone had been busy and the door remained locked in the middle of a work day. *It would appear that there's more than tattooing going on in there.*

As Hayden exited the shop, he nodded to Colton, who went inside to deliver his message.

Cat turned when she heard his voice. "Well, hello, Colton. I trust your day's going well." She smiled a knowing smile.

Her cop friend certainly has made her happy today. "Hello, Cat. The reason I stopped by is because Emma asked me to call you-"

"Did she, now? Something you need to *tell* me?" Again, she laughed.

Colton narrowed his eyes. *Why the hell does she keep smiling at me like that?* "Right. She wanted me to tell you that she couldn't make your lunch date because she's tied up at work. I tried to call, but . . ." He pointed to the disjoined phone as he trailed off.

"Oh, you surely you aren't going to chastise me for doing the very thing you were?"

"Pardon? I-"

"Don't worry yourself, stud. Your secret's safe with me."

Secret? What secret? Frustrated with her game, Colton exhaled a forceful breath.

"Tell you what, big guy. I think you and I need to have that lunch date. There's a few things I want to know - and maybe a few things that you do. Do you know where the park is? It's a gorgeous day and my schedule is light, so let's meet down there."

Colton fought hard not to narrow his eyes. This woman was rather confusing the way she almost sang her responses. She clearly thought she knew something. But what, he had no idea. He smiled a tight smile. "Why can't we talk now?"

"Because I have to interview a receptionist in a few minutes. Now scooch," Cat said as she made a sweeping motion with her hands.

Colton eyed her carefully. Knowing that meeting with her was the only way to clear up whatever misconception she had, he obliged. "Right. I'm sure I'll have no problem finding the park. I'll see you soon."

∾

Colton spent a bit of time looking around Brookfield. He went to some local shops, including a stop at the glass-smiths where he made a few purchases.

He pondered his meeting with Cat. He'd met her several times now, but she was a bit odd today. Some people were socially awkward at times, so he tried to not carry that over to their lunch.

∾

As soon as he entered the park, he saw her. Cat was sitting on a park bench that backed up to the walking trail. She was chatting with Hayden. When Colton approached them, Hayden stood to greet him. The two men shook hands, then Hayden excused himself.

"Can your friend not stay?" Colton asked as he took a seat beside her.

"No. He just stopped since he was in the area." She opened her purse, pulling out chips and a pop.

"Is there a reason you wanted to meet in the park?"

Cat nodded her head as she popped a potato chip into her mouth, "Yes, too many listening ears at the diner. Want some?" she asked as she aimed the chip bag in his direction. When he shook his head, she continued. "Plus, it's a gorgeous day, so why be inside? Sooo Colton, we have much to discuss! I hope you have some time to set aside for me."

"What's this about, Cat? You've been acting strangely today."

"Well, I'll give you this, Mister. You're tight lipped. I *know* what happened."

Her innuendos were beginning to irritate him. Colton

165

threw his hand in the air and shook his head. "Cat, what is it that you think you know?"

"About you and Saint Emma. What else would I be talking about?"

"What about Emma and me?"

Cat reached out and shook his shoulders. "Good Lord, man! You don't make this easy, do you? I saw you two."

"Who did you see? What is it that you think I've done?"

"I think you've made my little Emma a very happy girl."

Colton smiled at the declaration, but still had no idea where she was going with this.

Laying her hand on his, she continued, "I know this because I saw you two this morning."

"When did we see you?"

"Oh, you two didn't see me, but I sure saw you - *in bed* - when I ran by Emma's room this morning."

Now things were making sense. Colton realized that Cat thought that he and Emma had slept together. "I'm glad to have that cleared up because I was beginning to that think that you surely were on drugs."

"What? Why would you think that?"

Colton laughed, "Well, you were acting so strangely and saying the oddest things. I thought you were either on drugs or worse," he tapped his temple and smiled. "But before you get ahead of yourself, Cat, you're mistaken. Yes, you may have seen Emma and me in bed together *asleep*, but it's not what you think."

Cat swatted her hand as if pushing the statement away, "Colton, honey, I've been around long enough to know that when people say, 'It's not what you think,' it's *exactly* what you think. So congratulations, stud, on deflowering Saint Emma."

Colton held his hand up, "Normally I wouldn't discuss these things."

"Not one to kiss and tell, huh?" She winked.

"Actually, I'm not. I respect Emma. I like her, and I find myself growing increasingly captivated with her the more time we spend together. She has me intrigued. When I found out that she was a virgin, it could go no further."

Cat gave him a deadpan stare. "You turned her down *because* she was a virgin? Do you realize how badly you must have hurt her? Way to go, asshole!"

Colton ignored the stinging insult. "I postponed. I wanted her first time to be something that she would want to remember. Something that would be as special to her as she's becoming to me."

Cat thought that just maybe he was redeeming himself.

"I asked her to clear her calendar for the weekend. I'll plan something romantic. I haven't worked the details out yet, but some wine, flowers-"

Cat shook her head. "Hold up, big boy! If you have any hopes of succeeding with Emma, I think we need to have a little chat, and I usually don't do this."

"Do what?"

"I usually don't break the girl-code."

The girl-code? Here we go again. "And that is?"

"Girl code is two things: never revealing secrets and never dating someone our girlfriends have dated. I get good vibes from you, and I know she likes you a lot. I want you to stick around and not mess up right off the bat, so I'm gonna help."

"What did I do?" *I barely said two words.* "I just want everything to be perfect for her, starting with her favorite flowers. Does she like roses, maybe yellow ones or-"

"Colton," Cat interrupted, "trust me when I say that I mean this in the nicest way possible, but you need to shut up and listen to me right about now. Don't do any of this planning without talking to me. Before you object, let me just stop you by saying that Emma hates flowers. Well, she hates roses. See? You'd of screwed up right from the start. And before you ask, there's a story behind this."

Colton waited patiently as Cat found her words to begin.

"Emma moved away earlier this year. I don't know if she told you, but our grandparents passed away last year in a house fire. She'd always been so close to them, and in her mind, the only way to cope with them not being here was for her to not be here.

Colton placed his hand on her forearm, squeezing gently. "I'm sorry to hear about your grandparents, Cat. What an unimaginable tragedy."

She smiled weakly, "Thanks. Like I was saying, Emma thought the big city was just the distraction she needed. I don't know what she was thinking. The only place she's ever lived was right here in Brookfield. Anyway, she worked for a paper in Louisville. They promised her the moon, gave her a sign-on bonus, travel allowances, and a pretty hefty salary. Everything sounded great, and it was at first. Among other duties, they wanted Emma to write an advice column, using a grass roots approach. She would focus on work and family. Emma was so happy to have the opportunity to help others. Her love for the column changed when a man wrote in asking her advice on his marriage."

"What was the issue with his marriage?"

"His wife was cheating on him. He needed advice as what to do and how to move forward. He said that his wife had cheated three times now in their seven year marriage and was currently cheating. They had one child who was five years old."

Colton turned toward her, wondering where the story was going. "So what happened?"

"Emma advised him that if he'd been trying to make it work with his wife for six years and she continued to cheat, that she didn't want to stop. She said the best thing for him to do was get out and stop letting that dysfunction be the only life that his daughter would deem as normal."

"That seems like sound advice to me. Did he not take that suggestion well?"

"Oh, he wasn't the problem. He sent a follow up letter to the paper informing Emma that he and his wife began counseling when he told her that he was leaving. As far as we know, Emma's advice to leave saved that marriage."

"Then how was the advice a problem?"

"She ended up with a stalker. He wrote her threatening letters and sent them to the newspaper office. He said that her advice had caused his wife to leave him. That it had shattered his perfect family, leaving their two children without a mother and father in a united family. Along with his letters, he always attached the article of Emma telling the man to leave his wife."

"So in his case, he was the one who cheated. But his situation didn't work out so well."

"Right. But he didn't stop at letters. When he found out what she drove, he burst her windshield and slashed her tires. He'd wait her out. Each time she repaired one thing, he'd strike again. One day he poured acid on her car hood, and it ate through the paint. He left a note under her windshield wiper saying that next time it would be her face, but only half of it. He wanted her to grieve for the beauty she would never have again, like he would never have his family. He tormented her."

Colton closed his eyes and swallowed, consciously unclenching his teeth. *How could anyone hurt her?* "What did the authorities do to him, and how did her employer handle it?"

"The authorities did nothing. And the paper loved the

attention all this behavior was garnering, so they made her keep the advice column going."

"I can't believe they'd place her in danger like that. And the authorities, how could they do nothing? Did Emma not press charges?"

"She would have, had she known who he was. But Colton, I'm still not finished. He hurt her, physically. One night when she was leaving work, he approached her with a package. She thought he was a courier from the florist. She said it wasn't until he said, 'For you, Amanda,' that she realized who he was."

"Amanda? Her given name."

"Yes, her birth name. I didn't know she'd told you about that, but it makes me telling you this seem right. So, like I was saying, he handed her the box. She described his menacing stare as soulless. When she tried to move past him, he grabbed her arm. She said he dragged her down the stairs and tossed her onto a bench before beating her." Cat looked away, lowering her voice almost to a whisper. "She had bruises for weeks."

Colton felt anger soaring through his veins. "Did she fight back?"

"The rest of the details are sketchy, but I know she tried because they found blood under her nails that didn't belong to her. She remembers putting her hands up, seeing the blade, then nothing else."

"Which explains her scarred wrist." Imagining her struggle, Colton's fists drew tightly together.

Cat nodded. "She's blocked his face and most of the encounter from her memory. All she can recall are his cruel eyes. Sometimes trauma victims do that, and for her sake, I'm glad she can't *see* him in her mind."

"That could be a blessing or a curse. What happened next?"

"She just remembers struggling with him. Nothing in detail, really."

"How'd she get away from him?"

"Someone overheard the altercation and followed the sounds of the struggle until he found her by the water's edge. He told police that a man was on top of Emma, beating her. But once he told him he had called the police, the stalker ran off. He said Emma was weak, and he feared he'd gotten there too late." Cat wiped a stray tear from her cheek.

Rage. He was filled with undeniable rage as he listened to the account of that fateful night. When Colton saw the tear roll down Cat's cheek, he laid his hand on hers to comfort her. "How can they be certain that it was the same man who was stalking her, Cat?"

"The article. It was near the box."

"So he left his calling card. He wanted Emma to know who was responsible."

"Exactly. He's truly a psycho!"

"I can't believe this. I had no idea she had endured something so . . ." Colton trailed off. There didn't seem to be an appropriate word for what she'd endured. He exhaled a forceful breath. "I was going to ask how she'd been lucky enough to escape him, but actually, I think I know."

"I'm sure you can guess by now that Emma used a pen name for the column, Amanda Taylor. He hasn't found her because he doesn't know her real name, and the authorities haven't found him because they don't know his. It's scary to think that Emma's a sitting duck."

"Damn," Colton pinched the bridge of his nose and shook his head as he tried to process everything she'd told him. Looking over at her, he continued. "When I saw her wrist, she knew what I thought. She told me someone else was responsible, but I had no idea such a frightening tale accompanied her scars. I imagine that she's constantly looking over her shoulder."

"It's certainly in the back of her mind."

"And now? How is she doing now after all this happened?"

"So fast forward a bit. Emma lived with me for a while when she came back to Brookfield. Night after night, I would run to her when her dreams proved too much and her screams spilled out. She's a tough girl, Colton, and never shows her fear - when she's in control. But as nighttime takes over, her mind and her defenses go down. She's vulnerable, and he's there living in the shadows. He's there day and night. But I'll tell you this. Since you've came to town, she has something to focus on, and I know that you'll help her through this. My little Emmabear needs you here for the distraction. Who knows?" She tilted her head, "Maybe it'll be for longer than the time you've set aside to visit." She smiled. "I can see things. I know when people click and when they don't. I think you just may work, might just be a perfect fit for her. One more thing, Colton. There's three people in Brookfield who know exactly what happened in Louisville - Emma, me, and now, you. We're gonna keep it that way. Do you understand?"

"I'll never share this with anyone. But I will say that some people already know that something occured."

"Some people like who? Who knows?"

"Peggy does. She told me that something bad had happened to Emma, but she didn't know specific details."

"Well, hell! She'll tell Uncle Daniel, and Emma will never get a moment's rest."

"According to Peggy, she isn't telling him because she said the same thing. She said that Emma doesn't need him crowding her. She's being respectful of her privacy."

"Well, that's a relief. Besides, there's no way she could

piece all that together. I mean that stalker guy is a messed-up whack job! Now, aren't you glad that I stopped you from making a monumental mistake with the roses?"

Colton exhaled a thankful breath. "Yes, Cat. I appreciate you sharing this with me. I would hate to think that I would be responsible for causing her fear. I'm thankful I didn't bring her roses last night. The only reason I didn't is because I was on my bike." Colton thought for a moment, "This brings me to the next thing I need help with."

CHAPTER 16

"What's that?" Cat asked. "What do you need help with?"

"I told you that I've asked Emma to go away with me for the weekend. The reservation is made, but I need your help."

"Oooh, where are you taking her?"

"I can't tell you that. I want her to be the first to know about it, but I could use your help with packing for her."

A smirk turned into a devious laugh. This was the moment she'd been waiting for all her life. Emma would kill her for some of the choices she would likely make, but Cat couldn't wait to throw a weekend bag together for her cousin. "Tell me this, stud, am I packing for a cold or warm climate?"

"It'll be cold. Quite cold, I imagine, so she'll need warm clothing. After the misunderstanding this morning, it's evident that you have a key to her room. Now we just have to plan a distraction to get you there without her knowing."

"That won't be a problem!" *And I won't be using many of her clothes, anyway.* "I love to play dress-up, so this will be fun for me. Also, she loves my taste- I mean, I know what she likes to wear." *Have you noticed we have similar tastes in fashion, stud muffin? As in, the exact same style?*

With Cat's help, Colton knew that he could orchestrate a weekend that Emma would never forget. "While I have your undivided attention, I wonder if there's anything else I need to know about Emma?"

"Oh, you mean besides the fact that I'll pump your carotid artery full of tattoo ink if you hurt her?" She glanced at her fingernails nonchalantly, "There may be a thing or two I can tell you."

Cat gave a coy smile, but somehow, he knew she'd follow that threat up with action should the need arise.

Colton laughed. "Dually noted. Is this the advice you give to all her suitors?"

"This is the exact advice I'd give if she'd ever give anyone the time of day." At his questioning look, Cat continued. "Emma rarely dates."

"Why is that?"

"She has this idea in her head that she's plain and that no one is truly interested in her. Although Hayden's brother, Troy, has been asking about her for a while." *Doesn't hurt to let him know that there's some competition.* "She doesn't believe anyone when they tell her she's beautiful. You may have noticed that she doesn't exactly know how to accept a compliment, bless her heart. It's her only personality flaw that I can point out to you. She works, reads, and eats. That's about it."

"How can she not see what everyone else sees?"

"Who knows? That's how my little Emma has always been, though. I guess you'd have to write it across the sky to make her believe it."

Cat thought for a moment. "You seriously aren't gonna tell me where you're taking her?"

"I'm *seriously* not," Colton teased.

"Let's see . . . cold weather gear. Is it Vermont? Oooh, or maybe Canada?" Cat searched his eyes for any signs of a hint. "I'll tell you this, Romeo, Emma loves the snow. Will you *at least* tell me if I'm in the general area with my guesses?" Again, she looked at him with pleading eyes.

Colton was tight lipped. He smiled, but said nothing.

Cat was overjoyed that Emma was dating someone who appeared to be planning to sweep her off her feet. *It's about time, and I'm so happy that she's letting him. She usually looks for their flaws and sets them free. I have a feeling that Colton doesn't have any plans of going anywhere anytime soon.* Switching gears, she thought she'd give him a break from her information overload. "Hey, Hayden and I are going out on Thursday since he has the night off. Would you and Emma like to join us? Actually, that would be a great time for me to sneak away early and go to the Dillingham to pack for her. You know, while she's all over *you* on the dance floor!"

Colton chuckled at her description. "I can ask and see what she has planned. I'd like to get to know Hayden. I don't know *any* men in this town. I could be on estrogen overload." They both laughed at his description.

Emma slid inside her car as she drew the door shut with a hefty slam. She closed her eyes behind her black sunglasses for just a moment, basking in the solitude. No loud voices. No scuffing sneakers. No eyes rolling in her direction, and no spoiled little rich kids staring at her like she had the loch ness monster on her back. It was peaceful inside her warm car. The worn seat conformed to her body, welcoming her as the faint smell of strawberries filled her senses. She glanced at the vents and made a mental note to change to her clip-on air fresheners soon.

She thought about Geoffrey Cooper and the invitation she had promised him. She had every hope that he wouldn't want to sit with her at the ball. He was kind of strange in the loner sort of way, and Emma had no plans of entertaining the teacher. She'd never been to a ball and may never have the chance to go to one again, so she was planning to have fun while she was there.

Heading back to town, her thoughts drifted back to the green gown that Colton had requested she wear. *It's a good thing I like green.*

She continued on the lonely highway, only passing a handful of cars on the peaceful trip. Southern rock spilled from her speakers, her drumming fingers on the steering wheel keeping time with the music. She sang loud, and she sang proud in the isolation of her car.

Rounding the bend on Park River Road, Emma thought she caught a glimpse of Cat and Colton sitting on a bench near the running trails.

Images of the night before immediately flooded her mind sending butterflies soaring through her stomach. She couldn't help the smile that lit up her face.

Even though she needed to return to work, Emma found herself making the right turn into the park district.

She parked her car in the upper lot. Walking down the gravel path as she approached them, Emma noticed how

Cat's red, flowing hair caught every ray of sunshine. Thoughts of her cousin were quickly diverted when she heard Colton's deep, sexy accent. Her heart skipped a beat. She didn't know what it was about him, but whatever it was, she wanted it. No one else had ever affected her the way he did.

"Two of my favorite people in the same place," Emma exclaimed happily, "It's my lucky day!"

Colton turned, flashing a killer smile in her direction. She couldn't help but mirror it. Damn if he didn't make her heart beat . . . everywhere.

Crossing the space between them, he met her with a lingering hug. With their arms folded around each other, Emma pressed her cheek against his chest, inhaling his delicious masculine scent. Colton dropped a kiss to the top of her head, then to her lips when she brought her gaze up.

They walked hand in hand, settling in beside Cat.

"Hi, Saint Emma," Cat said with a hug. "What brings you to the park district in the middle of a work day?"

Nodding at Colton, "The same thing that's brought you here, I would imagine." They both laughed.

"So, what are you two talking about?" Emma asked, looking back and forth between Colton and Cat.

"If we told you that, it would ruin the surprise," Colton chided, nudging her shoulder.

Emma remembered that he had asked her to clear the weekend for him, so she suspected that's what they were discussing. She could always tell when Cat was up to something, and right now, she was up to something big!

Hoping to sway the topic away from their trip, Colton redirected the conversation by asking how they were related.

"Our mothers are sisters. Even though they came from a big family, they each only had one child, so Cat and I grew up more like sisters than cousins. I was always at her house, and she was always at mine. Aunt Chloe was a saint for putting up with me."

"That's true," Cat said. "Anything you want to know about *Emmabear*, you just ask me. I've known her forever and know it all," she winked, "but Aunt Claire was the one who was the saint."

A snapping twig drew their attention behind them as they watched joggers pass by. "Emma, I go for a run on the river road every morning. Would you like to join me tomorrow? Maybe we could even run these trails," Colton thumbed behind him.

"Why on God's green earth would I do that?"

"Because Miss Saint-Claire, it's good for you."

"Colton, honey, the only way I'm running is if someone's chasing me!" They all laughed. He'd soon learn that Emma was not a fan of exercise in any form. "But I would be willing to meet you when you're finished."

"Speaking of chasing," Cat held the attention of her cousin, "I ran by your place this morning before I went to work."

"Oh? What time were you there?"

"What time? Oh, just early enough to see that you had an overnight visitor . . . and early enough to keep me staring out the shop window all damn morning waiting for your blinds to open, which they never did! Where have you been all day?"

"Sorry about that!" Emma went on to explain how she'd come about visiting the school. "But I'm sure you were tied up in knots at what you *thought* you saw!" Emma teased and leaned back on Colton who gladly accepted her weight, welcoming her by wrapping his arms around her waist.

Cat couldn't help the joy that filled her heart as she watched them. They seemed so familiar with each other, moving as one although only a few days earlier they had been total strangers. She looked on. Emma's laugher permeated the air around them. She had taken up half the bench with her back against Colton's chest and her feet brushing Cat's thighs. She was truly at peace, and it had been a long time since she'd been that way. The joy radiating from Emma as she leaned back to capture a kiss from her new beau made Cat realize how important Colton was becoming to her cousin.

She stood, nodding her head in approval. "Now *this* is a sight I like seeing!" Emma and Colton both smiled. "Ok, kids, I need to get back to work. I have a consult in twenty minutes. Colton, don't forget to ask about Thursday." With a wave, she was gone.

Emma knew that she should probably sit up now that Cat was gone, but she loved being wrapped in Colton's arms. She reluctantly started to pull away and smiled when he tightened his grip.

"Just where do you think you're going? I like you just like this."

Emma settled back against his chest. "Now see? That's why we work so well together. I like this, too."

Colton pressed a kiss to her neck.

"By the way, I promised another invitation today."

"Oh?"

"Yeah, I gave one to Geoffrey, the teacher whose class I

had to endure. It seemed like a good idea at the time." She giggled. "Oh, and our article ran today."

"We'll have to get a copy of it then."

Has being referred to as "we" ever been so comforting?

They sat in silence for some time. Emma's eyelids slid shut as she basked in the warmth of the sun and the feel of his strong arms surrounding her.

"May I ask you something?" Colton asked after a few moments. "Something personal about last night?"

Opening her eyes, Emma responded without turning. "I'm sure I can guess the question, but go for it."

As suspected, she was correct. Of course he would ask. It was a reasonable question, after all. Why would someone still be a virgin at the age of twenty-seven? He asked it more eloquently that that, of course, but to her it was like a band-aid over an irrational wound. May as well just rip it off and get it over with.

With a long sigh, Emma began the short explanation. "Well, it's a little embarrassing to admit your shortcomings, but it is what it is. I was awkward." She shrugged her shoulders. "I wasn't as pretty as my friends and certainly wasn't a hit with the boys. By the time guys began to notice me in college, I had my mind made up that I wouldn't settle for just anybody to be my first." Emma pulled Colton's arms tighter around her, "And I'm glad I waited."

He echoed her thoughts, "I'm glad you waited, too."

"So to sum it up, I was inadequate and awkward and that's why I've remained unbedded all this time. How's *that* for a winning combination?"

Shaking his head, Colton's words fluttered past her ear,

"Then there's something inherently wrong with the chaps in this town, luv, because there is nothing inadequate about you. Nothing at all."

Emma turned toward his touch when his lips brushed her right cheek.

Colton grasped her chin. "You are beautiful," he whispered, holding her gaze. The sentiments continued, "And you're perfect. You are perfect, Emma." She started to speak, but he silenced her with a kiss.

The sting of her confession faded away in his embrace. No longer did it matter why she was a virgin. She did feel perfect, felt certain that the words he uttered were true - at least to him. She was a virgin, but Colton would change that. Yes, that in itself was perfect.

More time passed as she sat nestled in her cocoon. They chatted about the nature that surrounded them. The river was still rushing from yesterday's rains. Its raging waters provided the perfect backdrop, both visually and audibly. As they listened to the birds sing, Emma shared a story from her childhood. "When I was a little girl waiting for the bus in the mornings, sometimes I would hear a bird sing something that sounded like, 'you're pretty, you're pretty, you're pretty,' but I could never see it. I just called it the 'you're pretty' bird."

"See Emma. Even the birds of the sky are shouting out to you what everyone around you sees and knows to be true."

Emma smiled, but said nothing. She knew that someday she would have to thank the makers of "Google" for bringing Colton Graves into her life. *He's very good for me.* "So, what's this about Thursday?"

"Cat and Hayden are going out and asked that we come along. Would you like to?"

"Would *you* like to? I'm always up for hanging out with Cat, but I want you to feel comfortable."

Colton tightened his arms around her once again, whispering in her ear, "Emma, as long as I'm with you, I don't care what we do."

For a brief second, she basked in the feeling, holding on to the moment as she lay her cheek against his arm. "Alrighty then, I'll tell her it's a double date. Do you know where we're going?"

"I'm not sure, but I think dancing will be involved. Does that give you any clue as to where we're going?"

"Not so much. But remember, I can't dance."

"I don't believe that, Emma. The other night at the Lewis estate when you didn't realize you were dancing, you did a fine job."

"That's because I was on a natural high being elated over almost just being kissed by the most interesting man I've ever known. I wasn't myself. My feet were just- they were just following your lead."

"That's what dancing is, luv, just following along."

"I need to learn to dance before the ball, so I say yes. You know, so I can get some practice. But there's no other reason, Mr. Graves. I mean, I don't want to be held close to your body, smelling your intoxicating scent, feeling your arms around me, and swaying for hours. And for the love of God, you don't need to kiss me. Okay?"

He loved hearing the playfulness in her voice.

Colton slid her back, lifting her easily onto his lap while wrapping his strong arms around her back and waist. He leaned down and placed a passionate kiss upon her lips. "Like that, luv? No kisses like that?"

Breathlessly, Emma responded, "No, don't even dare

repeat a kiss like that." And, of course, he did, just as she had hoped. Still sitting in his lap with her legs resting on the bench, Emma laid her head on his chest. She placed her ear to his heart and could feel his warmth as she listened to the drumming of his heartbeat. She knew that the sound of her own had an equally elevated rhythm.

"Emma, do you think that we can go away this weekend? Did you get a chance to check your schedule at work?"

"I didn't get the chance to look, but I know I can. I can't wait to go away with you. Will you give me a hint about where we're going?" She looked up to catch his answer.

He shook his head. "I rather fancy the idea of keeping you guessing."

"How will I know what to pack, then?"

Colton provided no hints, just continued holding her. "Is there anything else that you pretend you don't want me to do on our upcoming date? We've already covered the no holding you tight and certainly no kissing. Any other demands?"

"Oh yes, I have a few things in mind, but none of which can happen on this bench in broad daylight. Since you have broken all the other rules, I better keep it to myself."

Colton groaned, "Emma, you just may be insatiable. Good thing you set aside the whole weekend for me." He wiggled his eyebrows then his expression turned serious. "It's about more than that, though. I enjoy spending time with you," he brushed his lips against hers tenderly, "and I want to know you better. Want *us* to know each other better."

Emma smiled. "And that's why it's a good thing you've set aside the whole weekend for me." This time she pulled him into a kiss.

Being that she was already in trouble with the boss, they reluctantly parted ways in the parking lot. Sitting in her car,

Emma watched as Colton rode away on his quest to discover more about Dillingham Manor.

She pulled her phone from her bag. Knowing that Cat had a customer, she shot her a text consisting of the condensed version of her night and upcoming weekend. Something this monumental was never something they would discuss in a text message, but with the day that Emma had been dealt, that was the best she could do.

CHAPTER 17

*C*olton parked his bike street-side in one of the three spots marked *Brookfield Historical Society visitor*. He latched his helmet to the handle bars and dismounted.

Walking up the stone steps, he gazed ahead at the multi-level, light blue Victorian style home that served as the office. Colton noted its tall, rectangular windows with wide white trim and the high-pitched gables overtop them. *It looks like a doll house.* He smiled at the craftsmanship.

As he ascended the stairs to the wide porch, he noted the white wicker furniture with generous pillows and the ferns that spilled over plant stands that were positioned on each side of the crimson door.

Now that he was at the Brookfield Historical Society, Colton didn't know what he would find or who he'd speak with. He just thought he'd see where that led. A plaque beside the door read *Welcome to Eastbourne Court*. As he entered, he saw a pale, thin woman with gray hair and blue eyes sitting behind a desk. She was well dressed and from the one-sided conversation he overheard, obviously educated. One look at her name tag revealed that she was Natosha Couch, volunteer.

While he waited, Colton noticed the paintings that hung all around the room. They were massive in size, some as large as six feet tall. Some were portraits of a physician and a clinic, many portrayed a nurse on horseback, and others were enlarged documents. *Rather eclectic collection of memorabilia.*

When she had helped the caller, Natosha pushed her glasses up on her nose and turned her attention to him. "Well, hello there. What brings you to the historical society today?" She had a pleasant demeanor and an inviting smile.

"Hello, Ms. Couch. My name is Colton Graves. I'm an engineer and new in town. I'm just looking to pass some time. I've noticed a lot of nice homes in the area, such as this one, and am curious if there are any other historic homes, monuments, or notable structures you can tell me about."

"Nice to meet you, Mr. Graves," she said warmly. "First let me say that we are delighted to have you in Brookfield. You've come to the right place if architecture is what interests you. Our town is billowing over with treasures, so to speak. Are you just visiting or have you set up permanent residency?"

"Visiting for now, but I'm keeping an open mind." *And that's the truth. I have more than one thing that has piqued my interest in this town.*

"Your accent is just delightful. British?" She asked as she clasped her hands to her chest, beaming. When he nodded that her guess was correct, she continued. "Where are you staying, if you don't mind me asking?"

"I'm staying at the Jacobson Bed & Breakfast for the duration of my stay."

"Oh, that's a lovely place and one of our historic sites. The home itself was built in the early nineteen hundreds. If you notice, there's a rock wall on the grounds that's being restored and preserved. It was a stone fence that surrounded what was thought to be the first church of Brookfield . . ."

As Natosha went into the history of the Jacobson house, Colton knew that he had found the person he was looking for. He was certain that she'd have a wealth of information on Dillingham Manor, too.

"...Miss Francine runs the bed and breakfast now and insisted that the wall be placed on the registry. We didn't know it wasn't on there. It's easy, even for us to overlook things, I suppose. All the qualifying homes in Brookfield haven't been placed yet and, of course, the bed and breakfast is not on the list because it isn't the original home. It was built when the parishioner's home burned to the ground when the church did, leaving only a portion of the stone fence after everything was cleaned up."

"That's interesting about the rock wall, Ms. Couch. I'll have to look when I go back tonight. I noticed it the other day, but didn't have a chance to really inspect it." Colton motioned around him, "You mentioned that this home is on the historic registry. It's a gorgeous place. What might its history entail?"

"Eastbourne Court was constructed in the late eighteen hundreds. It has served as many things for the town, most notably, the local infirmary. For generations, everyone in town came here for their healthcare. The clinic operated here on the lower level and the upstairs rooms were reserved for the doctor at the time and his family. The house is also rumored to be haunted, but I've never seen anything," she made a motion with her hand as if she were batting away the idea.

"This house has quite the history then. You said that all homes aren't listed on the registry. Why would that be?"

"Here in Brookfield, we only place homes on the registry

if the owners request it. The homes or structures do have to be at least fifty years old to qualify. That's our number one rule. Then, of course, something notable had to occur in the home or on the site. And finally, the owner has to request it be placed on a waiting list for approval. It's really a simple process. Some homeowners are under the assumption that we would place outlandish restrictions on their remodeling materials or open it up like a museum. That's simply not the case."

"Do you have any other notable structures and homes that I might have seen?"

"Yes, there's Williams' bridge on the main road out of town. It's a swinging bridge. Make sure to see it soon, though. The city has made plans to tear it down and disassemble it. They'll sell some of the slats. Others will come here. I'm not sure what we'll make out of them, though. It needed to be taken down years ago. More generations than I care to count have crossed that bridge."

Natosha opened her desk drawer, riffling through file folders until she found what she was looking for. Handing him some paperwork, she continued, "I hope you have the chance to view as many of these as possible before you return home, Mr. Graves."

Colton flipped through the alphabetical listing of historic sites. "I appreciate that. I'll enjoy seeing as many as I can. This is quite a list, though." Colton laughed as he turned page after page in the thick packet. He thought they must have included everything from dog houses to outhouses in the collection.

"I know that that list can be a bit overwhelming if you're not familiar with the area. Did you have any specific questions?"

Just for show, he searched through the pages. "There is one home that I'm curious about, but I don't see it in this listing. I saw it yesterday. Dillingham Manor, I believe it was called. I remember it because it has a stately name."

"Dillingham Manor was a stately home at one time, but now it just sits, deteriorating."

"It appears quite old. Is it?"

"Yes, it's older than the Jacobson place and has such a rich history. They once had grand balls there. There also have been rumors of hidden passages," she laughed and waved off the notion as foolish. "But it's been my experience that none of these old homes have hidden passages. It's good for folklore though." She winked. "It's just an old treasure."

"Then why is it not on the registry, Ms. Couch?"

"Because no one's suggested it be placed there. It's quite sad. To someone like myself who marvels at these old homes, Dillingham Manor is a source of sadness."

"Do you know who the owners are?"

"We should. We conducted a census of historic homes three years ago. We made a note of the owners whose homes weren't on our list. Just let me pull it up." Her fingers flew over the keyboard. With a final click, she leaned back and pulled her glasses down her nose, examining the data. "Hmm." Natosha looked perplexed. "Not only do we have no record of the owners, but we have no mention of Dillingham Manor, whatsoever. That's rather odd. I need to leave a message for Martin."

"Martin?"

"Yes, Mr. Sanchez may know why this is. I could have sworn that I entered this into the files myself because that's the area of town that I was responsible for."

"Maybe someone else covered it. You seem very organized and responsible."

"Thank you, Mr. Graves. But there are only Martin and myself who work here now that he let the others go some time ago. But I really think it was my route. That's just so odd," she seemed to say the last more to herself than to Colton.

Very interesting indeed. I think I may have just found Nancy's blackmailer. It's one of the two, and my money's on Martin.

"You're very inquisitive, Mr. Graves. I love that some little boys never grow up!" She said with a twinkle in her eye.

He filed this knowledge away in his head for future use. Colton suspected that he could easily acquire any additional information needed with the mere mention of having a love of history.

When his phone began to ring, he took it as his opportunity to plan a return visit. He looked at the caller ID and saw that it was Emma.

"Please excuse me, I need to take this," Ms. Couch nodded pleasantly and returned her attention to her computer.

"Hello?"

"Hey, are you busy?"

"If you could hold just a moment, I'll get that information for you." Placing his phone to his chest, Colton addressed Natosha. "Ms. Couch, I have to excuse myself. I would enjoy chatting with you again. Will you be here any other day this week?"

"Yes, but Mr. Sanchez works on Tuesdays and Thursdays, and he could help you if it's a day that I'm not here."

"Maybe I'll see you in a few days then. You've been quite helpful."

Exiting the building, Colton apologized to Emma for making her hold.

"What was all that about? Where are you?" she asked.

"I'm at the historical society. I may be on to something. Do you know Martin Sanchez?"

Emma made a sickly sound. "Yes, and he's a total sleaze-bag! That's not who you're meeting in few days is it?"

"No, I don't know if I'll come back this week or not. However, I think he may be Nancy's blackmailer, but I'll explain more later."

CHAPTER 18

The autumn rays shone brightly through the sunroof, its warmth pouring down on Cat as she drove. "When did I become the 'meet the parents' kind of girl?" she asked herself. She simply wasn't the type of person to hang around long enough to reach that point in a relationship – not anymore, anyway. Experience had calloused her, teaching her a hard lesson that you get out before things become complicated.

A weekend, maybe two. That's as much as she was willing to give any man. Or at least that's the way it had been. So why was she still here a month and a half later? It seemed that things might be changing.

"Maybe *I'm* changing." Cat thought about that for a moment and the handsome police officer who could be responsible for that transformation. There was no arguing he was sexy with his tall, muscular frame, sandy blonde hair, and cobalt eyes. Damn sexy. And the sex – the sex was phenomenal. But it was more than that. When had they become comfortable enough with each other that Hayden would think it was ok to volunteer her artistic services? And more to the point, why was she ok with it? Cat exhaled a breath and smiled. Laying her hand on her stomach to calm the butterflies, she laughed. "I think my biological clock's buzzing!"

Whatever the reason for her agreeing to do this, her SUV carried her closer to the McAllister estate at Cross Creek.

An image of Hayden's parents popped in her head. Rebecca with her snooty upper class attitude and Hampton who was as genuine as the day was long. They seemed like a very unlikely pair. Cat wasn't sure what Hamp had in mind for a birthday present, but she was certain that his wife wouldn't like it. Her personality assured that.

Her gaze fell on the sprawling estate to the right. The perfectly groomed lawn with mature trees and sculpted shrubs played host to a massive two story home encased in brick. A narrow brook ran along the property's edge and underneath the small bridge that led to the McAllister's. Wording on the stone pillars just before the bridge clearly identified the neighborhood as *Cross Creek*.

As she approached, Cat saw Hampton near the three car garage talking to Rebecca, who was getting into her car. He was a ruggedly handsome man with short, dark brown hair. She had no doubt where the McAllister boys ended up with their good looks. She noticed his casual approach to fashion. He wore a flannel shirt, jeans, and boots. Rebecca McAllister was beautiful, too, if you were strictly talking physical beauty. She was tall and slim, her blonde hair piled loosely atop her Cambridge educated head. She was well dressed, as always, and wore movie star sunglasses. Cat laughed at the contradiction between the two and wondered how they ever got together and stayed together. They were polar opposites. Hampton was a kind, hard-working, and generous man with a smile that reached all the way up to his soulful eyes. Rebecca was snide, demeaning, and could be quite rude. She was born into old money - old money that had afforded her the learned behavior of being a demanding hag. Cat wondered what Hampton saw in her that caused him to love her still.

Parking the truck, she waved to the pair. Rebecca acknowledged her with a weak unfolding of her fingers disguised as a wave.

"Hello, Cathryn," Hampton called out. "Hayden'll be here shortly. Go on in and make yourself at home."

Genuine hospitality, that's what he had. "Sure thing, Mr. McAllister. Have a good trip, Mrs. McAllister." Rebecca looked her direction, but didn't speak. *Lovely.*

Cat entered the house and went straight out the back door to a rather impressive workshop. It more closely resembled a small do-it-yourself store with all the woodworking, electrical, and mechanical tools.

Before long, she heard the door behind her close. Turning to face him, she nodded her head in awareness. "Mr. McAllister."

He chuckled. "We can drop the act, *Cathryn*. She's gone."

"Thank heavens! If I had to hear you call me '*Cathryn*' one more time, I think I'd scream. That name's reserved for my mother and when I've been naughty."

He found Cat's personality to be a welcome change from his stodgy wife.

"Why on earth does she insist we be so formal?"

"It's her upbringing, Cat. She's a woman of tradition.

Everyone was addressed by their given names. She thinks it garners more respect."

"Where's she going, anyway?"

"Louisville. She'll be home day after tomorrow. She's going shopping with her sisters. So this gives us time to figure out a gift."

Cat quizzed him about things that she enjoyed and tried hard not to add any comments of her own. It appeared that Rebecca McAllister didn't like much of anything and had no real hobbies. *Forget getting the gift for someone who has everything, which she does, but what do I make for the person who likes nothing except for her family?* At that moment, Cat had a "light bulb moment."

"Alright, Hamp, I think I'm onto something. If part one goes over well, we can think more about part two for a Christmas present."

She let out a nervous laugh. Hamp gave her a sideways look and she continued. "Look, I know that Hayden and I haven't been seeing each other that long, but don't worry. Even if it doesn't work out, I'll still help you."

He laid his hand on hers, giving it a gentle squeeze. "We'll just hope it is going to work out, Cat. It'll be fun having you around here. I can tell that you have a free spirit and a lot of spunk. Not to mention that you are truly beautiful. There's no denying what Hayden sees in you. Now that you have my stamp of approval, what's your idea for part one of Becca's present?"

"Becca, huh? What happened to all that 'she's traditional' jazz?"

"I can get away with it," he winked.

Cat shook her head and laughed.

When she was creating, she was in her element. Drawing was second nature to her. She was a masterful artist who had a steady hand, patience to see the job through, and an imagination that led to creations that had amassed many accolades over the years. Hayden was correct in assuming that if anyone could come up with a design to please his displeasing mother, it was Cat.

"Ok, so I was thinking that family is very important to Mrs. McAllister, as is tradition. What if we start a history wall?" She could tell by his cocked eyebrow that Hamp did not follow her line of thinking, so she re-phrased.

"I was thinking that we could have a wall where the pictures tell your family's story. I can help you look through albums if you need help selecting the pictures. I personally think long, rectangular frames would look best. It would be a beautiful tribute to your family. Each frame would hold two picture sketches, one on top of the other. What would you think of finding some photos for me? Maybe your engagement photo, first home, and kid's baby pictures? Are you with me still?" She laughed as Hamp made a dizzy, stumbling motion, but then he nodded urging her to continue.

"We can take your engagement photo, and I would sketch it, as I would all the photos. It would be the top picture in the frame and a drawing of your first home would be the bottom. The next frame could be Hayden's baby picture and one of him now, maybe in his uniform. We'd follow on down the line with Bryce and Troy, baby pictures on top and current ones below. The final frame would be a current picture of you and Mrs. McAllister and a beautiful sketch of the house here at Cross Creek below. I would do all the sketching and you could make the frames here in your workshop. There's not a person alive who wouldn't want that. I promise that she will love it." Cat thought for a moment. "As you have grandkids, you could continue the McAllister family wall. Does anything like that interest you?"

Hamp nodded his head enthusiastically, "Yes, that sounds like the perfect idea, Cat. I don't know how you came up with it, but I'm sure happy to pass it off as my own idea."

Cat laughed and swatted his arm at his mischievous declaration.

When they heard the door close, they turned to find Hayden clearly amused with the comfort level that his father and new girlfriend had established.

"I take it she came up with the perfect idea?"

"Yes, she did. And one that even your mother can't find fault with."

Hayden's warm arms enveloped her, tugging her to his side. "That's my Cathryn."

She smiled.

"Hey, why does he get to call you that, and I don't?" Hamp asked playfully.

Because I plan on being very naughty with him very soon! Bad Cat. Bad, bad . . . "What can I say, Hamp?" "I like him a little bit, and he gets away with a whole lot!" She lifted her gaze to smile at Hayden and was shocked when he bent down and kissed her in front of his father. *Establishing intent. This would normally be the time that I would bolt. I think I like it, though.*

Cat peeked around Hayden in time to see the smirk on Hamp's face. She mirrored it as pink tinted her cheeks.

"I told you she was good," Hayden squeezed her closer. "Somebody gonna tell me what you two came up with?"

Hamp saw his chance to bow out, and he took it. "I'll let Cat fill you in on that while I drag out some photo albums."

As she watched Hamp leave, Cat returned her focus to Hayden. "I'm glad you could make it. When you called, you said you may have to go back. Any idea how long you can stay?"

"None. When they locate the suspect, I have to be present for his interview."

Cat pouted and straightened his skewed collar.

"Now, tell me how my girl saved the day by coming up with the perfect birthday gift." Hayden listened as Cat explained about the sketches.

He loved watching her, loved watching the excitement in her gestures as she went into detail about his mother's gift. Hayden could tell that she'd enjoy working on the project that she'd deemed "Operation Impossible."

"Oh, and you know what else?" She didn't wait for a reply. "I'm gonna enlist Emma's help."

"Oh?" Hayden asked curiously, wondering how Emma possibly fit into the equation.

"Absolutely. She's great at coming up with heartfelt sentiments. So I'll ask her to write a little story about your family. We'll frame it and place it alongside the sketches. I'll quiz Hamp for some details later." Cat thought about the frames. "Also, I think I'd like to have a one word description on each of your pictures. For example, 'Courageous' would be the label at the bottom of your sketch. 'Craftsman' under Bryce's and maybe 'Asshole' under Troy's drawing." She laughed when Hayden bit back a smile. "*Perhaps* I'll think on Troy's a bit more."

"Don't alter it on my account," Hayden laughed. "But, do you think she'll have time? You said Emma's doing a lot with Colton."

"Oh, she's doing plenty with Colton." Her eyebrow arched up to emphasize that most of it wasn't wholesome. "But like I said, she's really good. She could have something written in no time at all." *Besides, the more she has to do, the less time she has to think about the stalker.*

"What are your thoughts on this new boyfriend of hers?" Hayden asked, drawing her to his chest.

"I think he's good for her and good to her. She's truly happy. What more could I ask for?"

"Then I'm ok with him, too." Hayden tipped her chin up, placing a kiss on her lips. "And I think having Emma help is a great idea. Is there anything I can do?"

"You can help gather photos."

Cat and Hayden walked back to the main house, hand in hand. When they crossed into the breezeway, he pulled her into the shadows, pressing her against the cool brick. She loved the feel of his strong, hard body leaning into her, dominating her. He started to speak when she wound her fingers around his neck, pulling him into a kiss. His body pressed hard against hers as his kiss became more demanding. *Damn, he's a good kisser.*

"Come back to my apartment," he urged, breaking their connection.

"I can't, I-"

He didn't let her finish before his lips crashed against hers once more, leaving her breathless. Hayden's mouth trailed from her lips to her neck. Cat captured his gaze as his fingers walked down her chest, freeing a button. "You can come back to my apartment," swift hands released two more buttons, "or I fuck you right here." He pulled her bra down, allowing her breasts to fall free. "Right now," his mouth closed over her nipple briefly, "for anyone to see."

Cat's moan echoed all around them.

"It's your call," Hayden said, his tongue teasing against her aching flesh over and over.

She held his head tight, encouraging him, enjoying his attention. Before she could give her answer, his phone rang.

"Fuck," he groaned, pulling himself away. Hayden buried his face against her neck, pressing a delicate kiss before straightening and pulling the phone from his pocket.

I'm sorry, he mouthed as he took the call.

Cat adjusted her clothing while listening to him talk to the Chief. The suspect had been located and interview scheduled, which meant Hayden had to leave. Leaving her in a state that a woman should never be left in!

She didn't have time to wallow in self-pity, though. Hamp was waiting. She still had albums to go through and photos to select.

CHAPTER 19

*A*fter leaving Cross Creek, selected photos to be sketched in tote, Cat met up with Emma for an impromptu shopping trip at Vintage – a trendy clothing store. Not only was she spending time with her favorite person, but it gave her the opportunity to pick up a few things for Emma's trip.

Linking arms, the girls chatted as they entered the shop then slowly drifted apart as each perused their own sections.

Cat made a beeline for the lingerie. She thumbed through the racks only stopping when her fingers glided over a black, satin robe. She held it up to herself noting the mid-thigh length. A delighted smile tugged at her lips when she saw the matching accessories which consisted of a garter belt and pair of stockings. *And these will be going on the trip.* Even though she thought it unnecessary, she also included a spaghetti strap gown.

The clanking of hangers drew her attention. She looked up in time to see Emma scoot past her. In one arm she held a pile of clothing, the other clutched a long shoebox to her chest.

"Let me see when you get them on," Cat called as her cousin entered the dressing room.

Minutes ticked by.

Cat rapped her knuckles down the louvered fitting room door. "Quit trying things on and tossing them without letting me see!"

Emma laughed knowing the waiting was driving Cat crazy.

After what seemed like forever, the lock assembly clicked and the door opened - just a crack. A single leg peeked through the slit revealing a hand tooled brown cowboy boot. It wasn't a thigh-high hooker boot. There was no stiletto heel and no wild colors. In no way was it flashy, but it was exactly perfect for Emma and her casual style.

"Oooh, I likey," Cat cooed out her approval.

Emma stepped the rest of the way out wearing a short, denim skirt with frayed edges. It complemented her tanned skin as did the boots and rust colored top she'd paired together.

"Not too crazy about this shirt," Emma said, plucking at the collar.

Even though she looked beautiful, Cat knew that outfit wouldn't be going to Canada or whatever cold climate Colton had in mind for their weekend destination. But, she thought it would make a perfect outfit for dancing when they all went out on Thursday.

Once Emma disappeared back through the fitting room door, Cat thrust her hand above it. "Gimme," She requested. "All the ones you plan to keep."

Emma tossed the clothing over and kicked the boxed boots through the opening at the bottom of the door. Cat took them to the register and placed them in a "want pile."

She also grabbed a few things for herself and for Hayden.

When Emma resumed shopping, she spotted Cat's

purchases. "How can you just pick something and know it's his size?"

"Because, Saint Emma, I've stripped him enough to know what size he is."

They both sighed then moved on to the sale table in the center of the store.

As they dug through stacks of underwear, Emma revealed details of her evening. "If I hadn't been a virgin last night," she whispered, "well, I wouldn't be virgin right now! This is worse than the scarlet letter . . . only I'm wearing a scarlet V for *virgin!*"

"Not for long," Cat almost sang out.

"Do you know where he's taking me?"

"That I don't. He wouldn't budge. And I tried." Cat turned to face Emma and smiled, "I think he really likes you."

"I know, and it feels so good to finally have someone notice me."

Looking over the undies Emma had in her stack, Cat pinned her with a stare. "Okay, Em, it's time we had *the talk.*"

"Thanks, Mom, but my friend Cat explained how this works *long* ago." Their laughter erupted over the music, earning them the "side eye" from the clerk.

"Not *that* talk, babe. I'm referring to your undergarments."

Oh brother! Here we go.

"Quit rolling your eyes, Emma. No man wants to see those giant granny panties of yours or that," she faux yawned, "boring white bra you're sporting. It's time you stepped into your 'big girl' panties and made Alley Cat proud."

Cat held up a pink set with leopard print. "This is both tasteful and whoreish, the perfect combination, if you ask me."

The bra was fine. Emma thought it might actually cover both boobs – halfway - but the panties had barely enough fabric to make out the triangle patch in the front. The thin fabric stretching around the back revealed even less material.

"I can't wear those," Emma protested.

"And why the hell not? They're perfectly stylish. As a matter of fact, I own this set and the green one, too."

Pulling Cat closer, Emma elaborated, "When I say I *can't*, I mean exactly that!" She pointed to the triangle. "It'll show every hair I have."

Cat burst out laughing, and Emma's cheeks turned a deep crimson when everyone turned to look in their direction.

"Emma, Emma, Emma . . . Where do I begin with this conversation?" She looked up at the ceiling and bit her lip while she composed herself. "Grab something, *anything*. This requires privacy."

Emma yanked a shirt off the hanger as they walked by a rack and followed Cat to the fitting room.

"Ok, we're in private." Emma fell onto the padded stool with the shirt dangling between her knees. She knew instinctively that whatever Cat had dragged her into the fitting room for was just one more tick on her *I suck at being a girl* chart.

"So, you wear those horrid granny panties because they cover your *nether hair*?"

"Yes, otherwise-"

Cat held up her hand, interrupting. "Oh Emma, you have so very much to learn and do before your trip. Have you heard the saying, 'The drapes match the rug?'" Emma gave her a blank stare. Tugging on her hair, Cat repeated, "The *drapes* match-"

"Yes, I know what you're saying. But we're good. My *drapes do* match my *rug*."

"Emmabear, no one has *rugs* anymore."

Emma could tell by the smile that crept across Cat's face that she would not like where the rest of this conversation went, but she asked anyway. "What do they have?"

"Hardwood, baby! Sometimes they have 'runners' but no one has *rugs.* And no one besides *you* wears granny panties - except actual grannies! Do you see where I'm going with this?"

Emma gave an exasperated growl, "Just wipe that smile off your face, and make the damn appointment!" She couldn't help but laugh herself. "Now, if you'll excuse me, apparently, I have more shopping to do!" She stood and walked out the fitting room door.

When Emma went back into the fitting room to try on a few more items, Cat rushed to the sales counter and gave them a wad of bills. She knew how Emma operated. She'd choose clothes, say they were too expensive, place them in layaway, and never return for them. She was predictable, but today, Cat had a plan of her own. She made plans beforehand to purchase all of Emma's "want pile." She'd pick them up later, add what was appropriate to her weekend bag and come Friday, Emma would be set.

CHAPTER 20

S tanding at the window of her office, Emma watched as a slip of paper rode the current of a gentle breeze, finally coming to a rest on the sidewalk. Even it was unhurried. She knew with certainty that this would be the longest week of her life. She couldn't wait for the weekend to have uninterrupted alone time with Colton. She smiled. The more time she spent with him, the more she wanted.

Their time spent together played out in her head. Even though they hadn't known each other long, she recalled how their affection towards one another had intensified with each passing day. The kisses were deeper, the embraces longer, and the simple touches more tender. *I like him.* She nibbled her lip. Emma looked down at her stomach when it did that weird flippy thing. *I really like him and want to know more about him.*

She turned back toward her desk and settled in behind it. Flipping open her calendar, her finger ran over the entries from the first three days of the week. With deadlines to be met, she'd started the week off running but now found herself stuck on the hump of the mid-week slump.

Even though she'd received text messages and phone calls, she hadn't seen Colton since Monday. He'd been tied up with conference calls and video chats. Unexpectedly running a business from an offsite location had presented challenges, but he assured her everything would iron itself out.

Emma pulled the file from her desk drawer labeled *Entry Winners*. She thumbed through the stories from the elementary schools, pleased with the results. "The Naming of Brookfield" won first place followed by "Little Victoria and the Music Notes." Caleb's story, "Dragon's Academy" took third place which segued nicely into Parker's story, "The Chocolate Mines," where chocolate milk was piped into the school and distributed through the water fountain. "The Magical Shoe Store" about shoes that always fit perfectly and never pinched your toes took the fifth and final spot.

A grin tugged at her lips as she straightened the pages. Emma thought that the little minds that created those scenarios had a wonderful sense of adventure.

Returning the file to the drawer, her eyes drifted to the time on the computer monitor. She sighed.

Emma reached down to retrieve her camera from the messenger bag beside her desk. The poor sack made her chuckle. Its brown leather was weathered and worn. On second thought, she concluded, it was tattered and torn but she hadn't had the heart to replace it. It had been a gift from her parents years ago when she'd hired on as an entry level journalist at the Journal. The bag her parents had intended for important documents that would one day win her an esteemed award in journalism was now more of a multipurpose bag carrying everything from documents to the candy bar she'd just spotted in the bottom.

Returning her focus to the original quest, she retrieved her camera. Settling back in her chair, she reviewed the images from the day before. On slow days when she was between projects, Emma liked to walk around town and capture candid shots. She was rarely a fan of posed pictures, preferring natural ones.

She thought of the people she had photographed. She was eager for Phil to see the pictures and couldn't wait for his feedback. She loved the one she took of the elderly couple walking in front of her. She had snapped a picture of them and then zoomed in on their joined hands. Emma thought that the roadmap of lines in their aging hands, coupled with their interlaced fingers, told the story of how their paths had crossed and forever brought them together. She liked the angle that she held the camera at when she captured the kindness in the lady's baby blue eyes. She also snapped photos of the twins at ice cream parlor – one with his head thrown back laughing, the other pouting as ice cream dripped from his chin. She was particularly proud of the image she stole at the park when the mother lifted her toddler in the air. The mom was smiling at the baby and the baby with deep dimples was smiling at Emma.

Everyone loved when she showed up with her camera because they knew at some point that one of the shots would show up in the paper. *I wish Phil was here; I want him to see these pictures so bad!*

Emma thought about Dillingham Manor and the vision that Colton had shared about it. He was considering turning it into a bed and breakfast, leaving the ballroom for grand events. She had no doubt that he could do it, and she couldn't help hoping she was right by his side throughout it all. She knew that working long distance had to be a strain on him. But she felt he was staying because of her and that made her very happy.

Remembering that she had failed to return Mr. Sizemore's call, she phoned him to see about the details for the chili cook-off and was happy to discover that he wanted her to be a judge. "I can do that with no problem!" She exclaimed happily before she ended the call. Emma knew if she was judging, then Laura would have to play photographer, or, at least, that's how she hoped it would work.

She glanced at her watch. "Time to rock some photos!"

Emma arrived at the ribbon cutting ceremony for the new fire department. Glancing at the natural back drop, she knew the photos would turn out beautifully with all the bright colors and the gorgeous firemen.

She made her way through the crowd and chatted briefly with the mayor before stepping back as they lined up for the photo. She brought her camera up and adjusted her lens until the image showed crystal clear.

Four of the most sculpted firefighters in the department lined up beside Mayor Penny Joseph, two on each side. Each of the men wore yellow pants and no shirts. The ones closet to the mayor held weathered axes with marred red blades slung carefully over their shoulders. The men were all buff and tanned, their muscles rippling under a shimmery glaze, which caught the camera's eye as well as the operator's. Mayor Joseph, who looked like a Barbie doll with her slight, svelte figure and blonde hair, wore a tasteful black dress and was wielding an enormous pair of silver scissors to cut the ribbon.

The five of them were arranged in a straight line in front of the fire house. The glass doors behind them reflected the crowd behind Emma. She liked that the casted shadows had allowed her to capture everyone in one picture. *But it's not like anyone will be looking at the reflection when they have these tasty morsels to feast their eyes upon!* Snapping a test shot, she pulled the camera away to view the image. Emma couldn't help the sentiments of appreciation that slowly spilled from her lips. *Lordy mercy!* Yes, it appeared that her test subjects were mighty fine. So much so, she continued her efforts.

The ceremony began with Alexander Miller, the slightly rounded fire chief of Station One, taking the podium to the right of the ribbon cutting area. Through the camera's lens, Emma watched as a trickle of sweat spiraled down his temple. With the temperature being pleasantly cool, she attributed his perspiration to the navy dress uniform he'd donned.

He paid honor to the brotherhood of firefighters and gave a touching tribute to those who had fallen in the line of duty. That, of course, brought to mind Emma's own tragic loss of her grandparents, but even that was getting easier as time went on. She felt relief and guilt all at the same time over that fact.

When he had finished his speech, Chief Miller joined the

lineup coming to stand to the left of the mayor and among the other firefighters who were now fully dressed. Emma steadied her camera. Her lenses shuttered in succession as two dozen images were captured. An unseen voice began a countdown. *Five, Four, Three, Two, One.* The swooshing sound of metal sliding against metal filled the air. In two sections, the red ribbon fluttered to the ground as a deafening applause echoed all around them.

"Welcome to BFD Station One," Chief Miller called out then led the way inside the new fire house.

Emma dropped back and waited a moment. She took photos of everyone piling past her in twin swells as they poured into the building. Once everyone was inside, she stepped further back to get a panoramic view. Two shiny red fire trucks were parked outside the station. They were angled on an inward diagonal at each side of the structure. The three glass bays of the garage were encased with pillars of stacked stone that created a beautiful, rustic wall. Lowering her camera, she smiled at the images she'd captured. As suspected, the colors popped against each other, leaving her with amazing shots.

Once inside, Emma snapped photos of the entryway. A photo wall left no doubt as to the pecking order of the BFD city employees. They ranged from a single picture at the top of the wall, belonging to Chief Miller, and expanding down into a pyramid that ended with the most recent hires. All were proudly photographed wearing their formal dress uniforms and caps. Even the station pet made the lineup. Emma nodded in appreciation as she read the albino pup's bio. A mixed breed canine, Blaze had found a permanent home when he'd been rescued from the local humane society by the Chief. *Blaze,* Emma thought to herself, *appropriately suited name for the fire house pup.*

Moving further into the structure, Emma saw seven coats on hooks with boots lined up below. She knew this would look great in black and white. She made a note to come back sometime and have a fireman pose, soot on his face, while kneeling at this same location. She thought he'd have one hand on his bowed head. She knew that she could create a calendar starring the sexy studs of BFD Station One, and she knew that the ladies of Brookfield would love it very much. But she thought this was not the day to present that idea.

She watched as the station mascot trotted happily through the crowd, weaving in and out from one person to the next. His little white tail wagged enthusiastically. Emma bent down on one knee, patting her thigh as she called the pup over. She brought her camera up to snap some shots as he came barreling toward her with his tongue dancing wildly out the side of his mouth. *That's how to live your life,* she thought with a smile. *Living for the moment and giving it all you got!* Satisfied with the images she'd captured, Emma lowered her camera, letting it hang loosely around her neck by its strap. Blaze came to a sliding halt beside her. "Look at you, pretty boy," she said, reaching her hand out to run her fingers through his fur and scratching his head. He showed his appreciation by slurping a wet tongue up the side of her cheek. Emma threw her head back and shrieked in laughter at the unexpected moment.

"Now that would've made a nice shot," the tenor of a deep voice sounded beside her.

Emma looked up, catching the amused look on a handsome firefighter's face. Closer inspection of the name stitched on his black shirt indicated he was Grey. Grey, she thought, had the most flawless chocolate skin tone she'd ever seen and was abso-freakin-lutley gorgeous!

"Thanks."

"But then again, any picture with you in it would make a nice shot."

Emma's cheeks shot crimson, which was her cue to hit the road.

With the firehouse properly welcomed by the citizens of Brookfield and sufficiently documented by her, she made her way to the next assignment.

≈

Emma pulled up in front of Restoration, a garage specializing mainly in classic cars. By the time she'd grabbed her camera and notepad and stepped from the car, she was greeted by their lead mechanic. Bryce McAllister wore faded jeans, a long sleeved black t-shirt, and his black ball cap on backwards. Looking around, she could see all the guys that worked there were dressed like that. A modern day uniform. She liked it.

"It's Shelby," he said enthusiastically, as if he were greeting his long lost friend. "You know I'd gladly buy her from you, even though she's in poor condition. Or at the very least, I could fix her for you."

"Yeah? Well, I'm in pretty poor condition, too. So, I can't afford the insurance on a newer car."

He nodded in understanding. Doing the man thing, he circled her car like a vulture. Glancing at the tires, he shook his head.

"I know," Emma offered before Bryce even had the chance to point out their worn state.

His gaze fixed on the splotches. "What on earth happened to this hood?"

"It found itself in a losing battle with acid and a lunatic. Long story."

Bryce was a gentleman and didn't ask any more questions. He was a kind man, like his father, Hampton. As she listened to him talk, she realized just how much he looked like Hayden. She'd known them both for a long time. Why had she never noticed that?

Emma felt like something inside her had been reawakened, and she was seeing everything with a new appreciation. She knew that was partly the fault of Colton Graves. Since the moment she spoke to him on the phone, separated by thousands of miles, it seemed the atoms realigned in her body, and she burst into someone who found detail even in minuscule things – like the fact that Bryce had Lisa's number written on his hand. *Wait, what?* "Bryce, I couldn't help but notice that you have a number written on your hand."

He smiled up at her, his blue eyes twinkling. "Noticed that, did you?"

"Yes, I did. And I know exactly who that number belongs to."

"Just a girl who gave me her number."

"Are you seeing my friend, Lisa?"

"If she has her way, I'm seeing her tomorrow night. We're going out with Cat and Hayden."

"And me."

"What? You want to date me, too?" He winked.

"No, you baboon! Colton and I are going with them, too." They both laughed at his playfulness. "I'll have the best time ever hanging out with Cat and Lisa. I just hope you and Hayden like Colton."

"If he likes beer and football, I think we'll get along just fine."

They chatted some more about her car and Bryce told her that he could fix the hood and repaint her car fairly cheap. She made a mental note to talk to him when she had more money. Emma wanted as few questions as possible about her car.

Once the chit chat had ended, she and Bryce went around back to see the project that had brought Emma to the auto shop in the first place. The guys were working on a 1930 Roadster convertible. It currently had a shell and an engine, and that was it. No seats, no floor. It looked like a heap of junk to her, but she'd seen their work before and knew that it would be a vision of beauty in just a short time.

"Alright, let's get some pictures of you and the guys working on the car. You can tell me anything that you want me to print, and I'll be on my way. I'm meeting Cat when I leave here. And suddenly, I have the urge to call Lisa." Getting Bryce's attention, Emma said, "And I'll see you tomorrow when we go on our triple date!"

CHAPTER 21

It's now or never, Emma thought as she reluctantly placed her hand on the handle to the spa. Laughing to herself, she unclenched the legs that she'd subconsciously squeezed together. The words 'Revitalize Day Spa' were sprawled across the double doors in front of her with the slogan, 'Pamper her like a princess' written below.

"Funny, having the hair ripped from your hoo-ha sounds neither pampering nor revitalizing." Emma blew out a breath and pushed through the door for her scheduled mini-facial and "gentle evacuation of body hair."

She didn't hear any shrieks of agony, which was comforting, so she took a moment to look around the open space. Plush sofas in soft green flanked cream colored walls with magazines neatly displayed on the accent table between them. Low music played in the background. "Welcome to Revitalize," a pleasant voice called out, cutting Emma's assessment short. "My name's Erin." Emma took in Erin's features as she rose behind the receptionist desk.

She was tall, as tall as Emma, with red hair styled in a swing bob and clad in black from head to toe. Erin looked rather surprised to see her even though Cat had scheduled an appointment. Emma thought that the more she talked, the more the lady would relax. Then she realized that Erin couldn't relax – her eyebrows were arched high.

Locating her name on the appointment book, Erin showed Emma to the *Oasis Room*. It was dimly lit with a medicinal looking bench table in the center. A small table sat next to it. The sound of waves crashing in the distance filled the air.

"Relax," Erin instructed, "and let your worries be forgotten." She scooped up a folded robe off the bench and handed it to Emma along with a wide, terrycloth headband. She directed Emma to undress completely and place the headband so that it pulled her hair away from her face. "Your therapy specialist will be with you momentarily. Would you like a glass of wine while you wait?"

The biggest freakin' glass you have, preferably. "Yes, please," Emma answered with a smile. She was nervous, but refused to let it show.

The door clicked shut behind her. Emma quickly slipped out of her clothes, placing them onto a corner chair. Then she pulled on the thick, white robe.

She stretched out on the table, trying to get comfortable. She thought the crinkle paper disrupted her paradise a bit, but the lighting and ocean sounds helped move her toward relaxation. Emma was just getting settled when the receptionist returned with a tray that held a glass of wine and the bottle it came from.

Emma sat forward and reached for the half full goblet of

wine. She drank it as fast as she could while holding up a finger, signaling Erin to wait a moment. She drained every last drop from the glass. "Gimme another," Emma choked out. Erin looked surprised. *Oh, never mind. I forgot she can't help but look like that! I'm gonna make this bikini waxing as easy as possible on me. A few glasses of wine will make me mellow as can be.* Erin filled it halfway. Emma shook her head. "Keep it coming," she instructed. Erin did as she asked then left.

Emma had just knocked back the final gulp when her phone rang. She knew instantly that it was her mother because of the "Kasbah" ringtone. Leaping off the bed, she dug the phone out of her jeans pocket. "Hey, Mom."

"Emma, where have you been? You haven't called in a week. Your father's worried."

"Sorry, Mom," she said as she laid back on the table, "I've been really busy at work. I'm actually in the middle of getting a facial now. I'll have to call later. Love you guys." Ending the call, Emma slipped the phone into the pocket of the robe. *And now that song will be stuck in my head for the rest of the day.*

She rocked the empty wine glass back and forth, keeping time with the tune in her head. Singing to herself, Emma crooned, *"Sharie don't like it, bom bom bom, rocking the Kasbah, rocking the Kasbah . . ."* She lay there on the table enjoying her own little nirvana while she could. Her eyes slid shut and she felt the warmth in the pit of her stomach from the chugged wine. As her legs relaxed, her feet danced from side to side, the "Kasbah" song still echoing through her head.

Her peaceful buzz was interrupted by a conversation in the hallway. Apparently someone had not only been placed in the wrong room, but they were about to be worked on by the new girl, Jamie, who was receiving last minute coaching. It came as no surprise to Emma when she heard the door creak open. *Just my luck.* She peeked open one eye and saw a small oriental woman pushing a compact cart.

"Ha-low, my na Jaa-me. I hep you."

Both eyes popped open now. "Jamie? Your name is Jamie?" Emma asked doubtfully as she cocked one eyebrow higher than the other, looking half as surprised as the receptionist.

"Oh, yah. I maar-can."

I think not! But I really don't care. "My name's Emma. Nice to meet you."

"A-mee?"

"Emma." Emma corrected.

"A-mee?"

"Yeah, sure," Emma nodded her head. She just wanted to get this over with.

"A-mee buful na. I ma you fee goo."

You'll make me feel . . . good? Oh, Holy hell! I've heard of these places! At the top of her lungs, Emma screamed, "Wine guuurl, get in here!" Jamie was startled, but began anyway by placing warm compresses on Emma's face.

Erin entered. "Would you like more wine, Emma?" Emma shot forward, compresses falling to her lap, glass extended. When it was filled halfway, Emma looked at her with one eye brow cocked in warning, and Erin filled the glass to the brim.

"Leave the bottle."

"I can't leave the bottle. I-"

"I. Said. Leave. The. Bottle!" Emma repeated. Erin did as she was told. Once again, Emma chugged the contents of the goblet and lay back. It was cheap wine, weak wine, but would suffice.

Jamie applied fresh compresses and massaged Emma's jaw line then started for the décolletage area. "Hey, hey! Get out of there!" Emma protested as she drew the neck of her robe tighter together.

"Sawy, A-mee. Wro pa-ege."

Damn straight, wrong package!

When Emma determined that she might be safe from molestation, she eased back down on the table and placed the warm towels back on her own face.

Once cooled, they were removed and Jamie placed an exfoliating cream on her face and gently massaged. It did feel good. After several more steps, Emma laughed out loud envisioning Colton seeing her in her mud mask and cucumber slices on her eyes.

"Yu fee goo, A-mee?" Jamie asked.

Oh brother! She's back to trying to make me "fee goo."

"I'm good," Emma said.

After a few more steps, her mini facial was complete and Jamie had bid her farewell.

Deciding to relax further, Emma reached for the wine bottle. Placing the rim to her glass, she turned it up. "That bitch!" she whispered in frustration when only a few ounces came out.

Instead of calling Erin back in and showing her the error of her ways, Emma waited for the next person to enter who would gently evacuate the hair on her lower body.

With the previous wine still flowing through her system and "Kasbah" still stuck in her head, Emma found herself singing, "A-mee don't like it . . . waxing the hoo-ha, waxing the hoo-ha. A-mee don't like it . . . waxing the hoo-ha, waxing the hoo-ha." She snorted out a laugh at her play on words.

Once again, the door opened and her next therapy specialist entered.

"Ha-low, ageen."

Oh Lord.

Jamie asked Emma to open the bottom half of her robe and tug it up past her hips so that she wasn't sitting on it. When she did, Jamie reacted. "Oh no, haar evewher. Tha no sexxxy. *Jaa-me* ma yu sexxxy."

"I *know* that's not sexy, *Jamie!* That's why I'm here!"

"Tha okay. *Jaa-me ma yu buful. I geev yu Brazilian waax.*"

Emma didn't know what that meant but assumed it was what Cat had instructed when she'd scheduled the appointment.

Jamie alternated between trimming and smoothing, all pre-wax preparations, she advised.

If she pets me one more time, I'm gonna punch her in the face!

"Theese be lil werm."

Emma clinched her eyes shut as she felt the warm wax being applied. Jamie placed the cloth strip over the wax and pressed down.

"Lil sti,"

A little what? "Holy freakin' hell!" Emma screamed through gritted teeth as the strip was yanked from her skin. Red hot fire shot to her loins. *Cat said it wasn't too bad. One side down, one to go till I walk my waxed ass out of here and kill her!*

"Grin and bear it" became a phrase Emma familiarized herself with as Jamie took care of the other side. There was a thin strip left in the middle. "Leave it!" Emma ordered.

Jamie muttered something about the "landing strip" not being part of the package, but Emma didn't care! She looked down at herself. She looked better than she had when she came in. Ok, fine. It looked good. Relieved her ordeal was over, she lay there spread eagle staring at the ceiling. She couldn't believe her senses when she felt hot wax hit again. "What are you doing?" She screamed the question.

"Jaa-me ma yu buful and sexxy. Las ti."

"Last time?" Emma quickly realized that the crinkle paper

was stuck to her rear from the rustling that occurred when the warm wax hit where she hadn't even thought about having hair. *Dead. I will kill her dead!*

What else could she do? She had to let her finish.

Emma dressed in a hurry. The slide of her panties across her mound was mildly arousing, which made no sense because she had a cousin to kill! She left the spa feeling anything but revitalized. *All that drinking and screaming and trying to figure out what the hell Jaa-me was trying to say was exhausting!*

Not wanting Cat to miss this special moment, Emma snapped a selfie sporting her meanest scowl. "See this face? This is the last person you want to see right about now!" Pleased with the image and message, she texted it.

Cat got the message as she pulled up to the spa. She knew how Emma would react to that first waxing and had purposely showed up late. In retrospect, she thought she should have met her there then made plans to leave early so she wouldn't have to face the wrath of Emma.

Cat saw her walking down the sidewalk near the coffee shop.

"Hey, Emma. Wait up," she called out.

Emma turned and narrowed her eyes. "Well, hello, kitty Cat," she slurred dryly.

"Em, are you drunk?"

Emma laughed. "It's quite likely. I had *a lot* of wine and then there was Jamie the "maar-can" and surprised Erin, the wine girl. Oh, and did you *know* that you have hair between your-"

"Okay, Emmabear," Cat interrupted as she dropped her arm across Emma's shoulder. "Let's stop in here and grab you some coffee."

"-butt cheeks? 'Cause I didn't 'till my *ass* was *stuck* to the *table*!" Emma threw her head back laughing. "I was gonna run out of there, but I knew the paper would just keep rolling!" She giggled. "Can you imagine that, kitty Cat?" Her laughing continued as her balance began to fail.

"And food. We'll get you some food, too."

CHAPTER 22

With the effects of the wine finally waning, Emma called Colton to see if he was free. To her delight, he was. She gave him directions to Cat's house, which she knew would be easy to find in a town the size of Brookfield.

A quick shower and trip to her favorite boutique, Cat's closet, had her presentable for their impromptu date. Glancing at herself in the mirror, she nodded in appreciation at the outfit she'd chosen. She wore a taupe hooded sweater dress that reached almost to her knees and paired that with over-the-calf chocolate boots. The dress hugged her curves perfectly and showed just enough of her tanned legs to drive Colton crazy or at least she hoped it would have that effect. Emma knew it wasn't appropriate for motorcycle riding, should they go somewhere, but she didn't care. She thought that just might drive him crazy, too. And that pleased her greatly.

Colton's bike roared up onto the driveway, and she walked

out on the porch. Emma watched as he walked across the drive and up the steps. She swung her right hand loosely around the support beam as she balanced her body on her right foot, the left one locked behind. "Miss me?" She asked playfully, her hair falling across her shoulders.

Colton gave her an assessing nod, his gaze raking slowly over her body. She heard the low growl just before he shot his arms around her waist, lifting her off her feet. He hugged her tight and then let her slide *slowly* down his long, hard body to the feet that she couldn't feel. When Emma staggered, he helped support her by backing her up to the wall. He lowered his lips to hers, and she plunged her fingers through his wavy locks, holding him in place. He placed a hungry kiss upon her waiting lips. It was when Colton's hips pressed her to the wall that she felt the outline. Clearly, they were both appreciating the moment. He kissed her passionately then lowered his attention to her neck, raining kisses up the delicate column before returning to her lips. "Very much," he said between slow, controlled kisses. "I missed you very much, luv."

"And I missed you." Emma wondered if he could hear the genuineness in her statement. She had missed him. She felt like every minute away from him seemed like an eternity. She also suspected that he felt the same torture. "Let's get out of here," Emma said.

As they moved toward his bike, he glanced at her attire. When he stopped walking, Emma just knew he was going to object, but he didn't. Instead, he turned to face her. Eyeing the long silver chain that hung between her breasts, Colton reached out, grasping its heavy black pendant. He ran his thumb over the rounded tear drop onyx and smiled at an unspoken thought. Rather than dropping it back in place, he carefully lowered it back down, his knuckles brushing her breasts. The brief touch made her pulse quicken.

Colton walked ahead and mounted the bike first, steadying it for her. She wrapped an arm around his shoulder and then slid on behind him. "Emma," he said as he looked over his shoulder, "do you know what you're doing to me? Having you sit behind me like that with nothing between–" He didn't seem to have the composure to finish his thoughts. "How will you keep your dress down?"

Emma smiled at the control she was wielding over her brute. "I'll pull my dress under me like this in the back," she said as she tucked the tail of her dress underneath her, the motion making her breasts more pronounced, "and then of course my front will be pressed against you like this." She wrapped her arms around his waist and pulled her body flush against his. She couldn't suppress the smile that crept across her face when she saw the tick in his jaw.

"The death of me. You'll be the death of me."

Emma laughed. It seemed that perhaps she could be Colton Graves' kryptonite. She wiggled even closer.

When they turned onto Park River Road, she thought maybe they were going to the park, but he continued to drive out of town toward the bed and breakfast. Emma didn't care where they went. She was simply happy to spend some time with Colton. She rested her cheek on his back and appreciated being able to wrap her arms around him for whatever length of time their destination afforded her. She thought back to the scene from earlier. Colton wore faded jeans with holes in them, biker boots, and a black t-shirt that gripped his perfect abs and strong shoulders. The thoughts of their earlier exchange coupled with his scent had Emma inadvertently rocking her hips against his back side. Embarrassed, she stopped as soon as she realized she was doing it. He was flying down the road, so keeping her dress in place was more difficult than she had thought. Emma realized that the harder she pressed herself to him, the faster he drove. She couldn't help but chuckle.

The uneven pavement onto the dirt road signaled the end of the ride.

Colton shut the engine off, kicked down the stand, and slid off the bike first. Then, to Emma's surprise, he sat back on the bike backwards, pinning her with a heated gaze. Without pause, he began a tender massage of her open thighs.

Emma felt the warm slide of his hands, his calloused fingers tracing lazy patterns on her legs. With the hem of her dress already breached, it was difficult to focus on anything else. Still, she had to stop that line of thinking. "Would you like to check out that vacant house?" Emma asked as she gently turned his head in its direction. Nestled in the woods, off in the distance, a two story white house peeked out of the foliage. A lonesome light spilled from the second floor window.

"There's a light on. Are you sure its vacant?"

Emma nodded. "Yeah. No one has lived there for years. We must've left the light on the other day when I was asked to take some photos of it. I have the realtor's key code."

"You have a knack for breaking and entering," he grinned his sexy grin.

"Guilty as charged," Emma smiled. "But I know the heirs well. I promise they won't mind."

"Before we go, just let me say that your actions had me coming unglued on the ride over here." Colton grabbed her hips and pulled her legs over his.

Emma had no doubt as to what *actions* he was referring to. "I didn't mean to do that," she smiled shyly at his disbelieving look. "I didn't. As soon as I realized what I was doing, I stopped. But you have no room to talk, Mister!"

"No?" He asked through half closed eyes, still massaging her thighs.

"Don't think I failed to notice the *package* that you greeted me with on Cat's porch."

"This package?" Colton asked as he dragged her straight onto his lap.

With her hands cupping his face, Emma leaned down and kissed him. When she felt his hard ridge between her legs, her body - mindfully this time - ground against him.

"Not much longer, luv," Colton said, setting her to the ground.

They walked hand in hand into the woods. The wind picked up, and they watched lightning dance across the night sky in the distance. The warm breeze made the evening comfortable. As they walked, they didn't feel the need to fill the space with mindless chatter. They just enjoyed being able to be together. Emma thought the only thing that could make the night more perfect would have been a million twinkling stars shining bright, but the cloud cover made that fantasy impossible.

When they were several hundred feet from the vacant home, the wind shifted and the heavens unleashed their fury. As the storm intensified, they watched as the single light was snuffed out. Still, they ran for the shelter of the dark house. Colton accessed the flashlight app from his phone while

Emma entered the code into the realtor's key box. Rain driving against their backs, they spilled through the doorway, breathless and laughing.

A single beam of light lit the space from his phone. With the exception of a couch that sat against the far wall and the staircase to the left, it was empty inside. Colton shone his light upward through the cavity, illuminating the stairway. "I'm afraid the tour will have to wait another day. We'll bloody well kill ourselves if we miss a step in the dark."

"That's ok. I'm drenched anyway," Emma added as she plucked the clinging dress away from her chest.

"Let's get these rain soaked clothes off," Colton suggested.

Getting him naked was something she wouldn't dare scoff at. "Perfect," she said a little too eagerly.

"Emma, I vowed that your first time would be special, and I meant it. I promise you that two nights from now, about this time, you *will* be mine. I'll give you what we've both been wanting."

Emma checked her imaginary watch and gave him sad eyes to show her disapproval. "That's much too long," she said, pouting.

"It'll have to do, luv. I don't go back on my promises." Colton could hear the rain driving against the windows. "From the sound of it, we'll be here quite a while." Glancing at his phone, he noticed the battery symbol. Thirteen percent. Knowing that the flashlight would quickly drain the remainder of the charge, he switched his phone off, casting the room in total darkness.

Emma gasped.

"Sorry, luv. Conserving the battery. Now, let's get these clothes off."

"Can I at least undress you?"

Laying the phone on the staircase, he smiled. "That can be arranged." Colton appreciated her determination.

Emma moved toward the sound of his voice. When he was within reach, she began inching his shirt up. Ever so slowly, she pushed it up over his rock hard abs and then over his head. He kicked off his boots, and they each went for the button of his jeans.

"That's my job," she reminded, gently. She unbuttoned his pants then tugged them slowly down. He stepped out of the wet denim, and she trailed the jeans and his shirt over the railing. Turning, she closed the distance between them and captured his lips. He responded, eagerly.

As she reached for the band of his underwear, Colton's hand stilled her efforts. "These stay put, luv."

Thunder rumbled outside, causing Emma to jump at the unexpected sound. A flash of light filled the room from the windows around them. She could see the outline of Colton's sculpted body. Another strike. His gaze was commanding. He pulled her closer, his lips finding hers. "My turn," he whispered. Colton reached down to the hem of her dress, caressing her legs. As he bunched the material in his hands, he slowly pulled her closer to him. He dug his knuckles into her hips as he rocked against her.

Colton lifted his arms and pulled the dress over her head. Just as she'd done, he draped the material over the railing.

Pulses of light cast her image before him. Wearing sexy lingerie, her boots, and that damn necklace that called to him, it was becoming too much. "Leave them on," he called gruffly when she bent to remove her boots. Emma did as he commanded, her fingers trailing up her legs as she slowly stood. *Vixen.* She stepped closer, pressing her body against him. A low curse spilled from his lips as he ran his hand down her thigh, hooking her leg around him. She clung to him as he delivered a bruising kiss, his resolve quickly fading.

Releasing her, he moved behind her. She could feel the

hard press of his body against her back, could feel his breath on her neck before he feathered a kiss across it. Colton's hands cupped her breasts firmly through her bra, the wet fabric clinging to her hardening nipples. He ran his thumbs across them. Emma's moan echoed all around them, and her head fell back against his shoulder.

"You're so fucking sexy, Emma."

His illicit words excited her, causing the dull ache between her thighs to intensify. As if sensing her need, one hand trailed down her leg then across to the juncture of her thighs. His finger traced lightly across her panties, inching underneath them. She leaned into his touch.

Thunder rocked the house, jolting him back into awareness. Colton sucked in a breath, opening his eyes. Guided by lust, he was seconds away from breaking his vow. "I'm sorry," he whispered.

"I'm not," Emma replied then turned to face him.

Taking her by the hand, Colton moved toward the couch. When he was seated, Emma stepped into the space between his open thighs. Colton reached up, grasping the pendent, then pulled her slowly into a kiss. She crawled into his lap, chest to chest. His kisses trailed down to her neck as his hands found and kneaded her breasts, drawing her nipples to tight peaks beneath her bra. When lightning lit up the room again, Colton saw Emma's head thrown back as she pressed herself against him. He leaned his head forward and sucked her taut breast through the thin fabric.

"Oh God!" she exclaimed, raising her chest and pressing herself further into his mouth.

Lost in passion, he sucked harder, drawing on the peak with his teeth. Just as he was considering breaking his vow, a voice sounded behind them as a flashlight lit the room.

Emma scrambled off his lap, and he stood protectively in front of her.

"Police. Who's in here?"

"We're just riding out the storm, mate. We'll leave when the rain lets up," Colton offered.

Emma watched as the flashlight blasted Colton then turned its steady beam on her.

"Emma?" The voice questioned.

"Yes?" she answered curiously.

When masculine laughter filled the room, she had no doubt who'd caught their interlude. "Hello, Hayden."

"Well, I would ask what you're doing out here, but the scene I saw as I came through the door leaves no doubt what you were doing," he glanced at their scantily clad bodies, "or were about to do."

Emma felt the need to explain. "We were walking when the rain hit. Our clothes were soaking wet, so we stripped them so they'd dry faster and-"

Hayden's radio sounded requesting his location and status. "Maggard house on East eighty, code twelve."

Emma didn't know a lot of police lingo, but she did know what a code twelve meant. He'd reported that everything was fine. And being that she technically didn't have permission to be in there at that exact moment, that was a huge relief.

"That your bike off the river road?" Hayden directed his question to Colton.

"It is."

"Ok. You two get dressed, and I'll take you back up there. I'm parked on the upper road."

When Hayden stepped outside, they pulled their damp

clothes back on. "Well, that was embarrassing," Emma said. "But at least it was Hayden, and we're not going to jail in our skivvies."

"It would make for interesting mug shots, though," Colton joked.

As Emma started to leave, Colton grabbed for her hand, pulling her back and pressing her against the doorframe. "Stay with me tonight," he whispered as his lips feathered across hers.

She smiled, "I'd love nothing more."

CHAPTER 23

*E*mma was relieved when the conversation on the ride back centered around Colton's visit to Brookfield and not on the fact that Hayden had caught them in a rather compromising position. She silently cursed his sucky timing, but realized that had he shown up a few minutes later, he might have seen more than any of them would've preferred. Darkness hid the crimson wave slowly creeping up her cheeks.

Arriving back, they thanked Hayden and exited the jeep. Colton walked ahead while the police sergeant chatted with Emma through his open door, the light illuminating her figure. He gave her a once over. "Seriously, Emma? *That's* what you chose to wear for a motorcycle ride?" He shook his head and laughed. She knew within reason that Cat would know all the details of her night before she had the chance to utter a single word.

Bidding Hayden goodbye, she joined Colton.

Colton folded Emma into his arms as they watched the jeep's

red taillights fade into the distance. Humidity hung heavy in the air, reminding them that the lull in the storm would be short lived.

"I still had fun tonight," Emma said as she wrapped her arms tighter around his waist. "I just like being with you no matter what we're doing."

Colton tipped her chin up so she was looking at him. He held her like that for a moment. Whether he was searching for a hint of silhouette or for the right words to say, she wasn't sure. His touch was tender, his caress unhurried as he stroked his thumb across her skin. He started to speak, but dropped a lingering kiss to her lips instead.

The sincerity of the moment overwhelmed her. Masked by darkness, the tears that stung her eyes remained unseen. He kissed her again.

Colton steadied the bike for her to slide on behind him. With the kick of his foot, the motorcycle roared to life and they set off for their night together. An innocent one, albeit, but one that would be spent in each other's arms. She'd take it. A content sigh escaped her as she laid her cheek against his back.

Before the Jacobson House was in sight, the rain started again. It was harder this time and stung their exposed skin like an army of tiny bees. Colton drove as fast as he safely could, but the rain slickened roads slowed the Harley to a meandering crawl. The clothes that hadn't even dried from the earlier storm were completely drenched once again.

Miss Francine stood at the window watching tree branches eclipse the lamp post as they dipped and swayed in the wind. A single light crawling up the road drew her attention. She suspected it was her favorite customer. A smile tugged at her lips. She knew he'd track water all the way to his room, but she was okay with that. She liked to feel needed. Walking to the linen closet, she retrieved an armful of plush towels. She planned to just toss them down after him to sop up whatever mess he made.

She was prepared and ready when thunderous laughter erupted outside and a stampede of footsteps sounded on the porch. He wasn't alone.

Wind gushed through the door as Colton and Emma came barreling through it. They were both soaked to the core, water dripping off their hair and noses.

Miss Francine calmly handed them each a towel, then she threw her head back and laughed. They were a sight. "Get these wet clothes off quickly," she said, shaking her head. "Just leave them outside your door, and I'll come get them and put them in the wash. Now get." She motioned them away.

"Thank you," they both said, moving toward the stairs.

Colton's room was the first door on the right at the top of the steps.

Once inside, Emma quickly surveyed the cozy surroundings. A large bed, with a patchwork quilt in hues of soft blue and cream, sat prominently to the left of the room. To the right, a trio of windows faced the road. Straight ahead, situated underneath another row of windows, was a chair and matching wooden desk which, from the laptop and printer atop it, she knew was Colton's work area. An unlit corner fireplace hugged both walls giving the space a rustic, homey feel.

Emma followed Colton through a doorway between the bed and the desk that led to the bathroom.

Reaching into the shower, he adjusted the knobs, tweaking them until the water ran warm over his hand. He turned with the intention of telling Emma that she could change the temperature to her liking, but words escaped him when he saw her drag her dress over her head. She tossed it in the sink with a wet smack.

Standing before him in only her underwear, boots, and the necklace that rested between the twin swells of her breasts, she was gorgeous. His gaze poured over her. *Bloody hell.*

Emma appreciated the way he appraised her near naked body. Smiling, she unclasped her bra. Pulling it down her arms, she let it fall from her fingertips, joining the formless dress in the sink. Try as she may, there just wasn't a way to remove sopping wet boots in a sexy manner. Still, she tried.

"You know, there was a time, not that long ago, that you wouldn't have bared yourself to me for anything. Not that I'm complaining, of course," Colton smiled a crooked grin. "Just curious what happened to that girl?"

"That girl decided she's comfortable with who she is," Emma smiled, easing her panties over her hips and down her legs. "This is who I am. You either like the way I look or you don't. There's nothing I can do about it at this point." She bent to retrieve her underwear then pressed them into his hand as she stepped past.

"Will you be joining me?" She asked hopefully.

"Not if I plan to remain a man of my word," Colton answered, watching her step into the shower.

"That's too bad," she pouted playfully over her shoulder. "Could've been fun."

She closed the curtain. The showerhead rained down glorious warmth over her chilled body.

Colton shed his wet clothing, adding them to the pile in the sink. He scooped up the drenched articles and deposited them into a wastebasket. Walking nude through the bedroom, he cracked the door just enough to push the laundry into the hallway.

He entered the bathroom, closing the door a bit more firmly than intended. Resting his back against it, he watched steam rise above the shower.

When Emma heard the door close, she pulled the curtain back, poking her head out. "Sure you won't change your mind?"

Despite his noble intentions, he found his resolve crumbling.

"Come on," she prodded as a delicious smile crept across her face. "I'll be good."

"You being good is a given, Miss Saint-Claire. You behaving is another matter entirely." As if his body were betraying him, he started toward the opening curtain, climbing into the shower with her.

The water crashing over his chest was warm and soothing. Colton stretched his arms out, bracing them on the wall. He dipped his head and closed his eyes, basking in the feel of the warmth seeping into his body.

He slid one hand over Emma's when she formed her body to his, wrapping her arms around his waist. She pressed light kisses to his back. Colton didn't fail to notice what else was pressed to his back.

Emma generously poured liquid soap onto a sponge, working it into a rich lather. She ran it along his shoulders and watched as the suds ran down his sculpted back, over his backside, and down his legs. She let the soapy sponge trace the path of the bubbles, enjoying her work very much. She turned him so that the jets from the shower rinsed him clean. Starting at his neck, she began the pursuit of his front side. Focused on her work, she missed the weight of his stare. He held her back at arm's length allowing his gaze to pour over her body. "You're truly beautiful, Emma," he said as he stroked her hair. "You're stunning." He pulled her into a tender embrace before moving her into the stream of water.

With his chest to her back, Colton slowly worked shampoo then conditioner into her long locks, massaging as he went. There was something decidedly erotic about the way he continued to hold her, exploring her body. When his hands fell on her hips, she couldn't help but smile. They were rough and gentle at the same. The hold he had on her body was strong, not an inch separating them, but the lift of his hips was subtle. They contradicted each other. A struggle, she imagined, that mirrored the one going on in his mind. Emma wanted nothing more than to bend over and finally ease the ache that had been building between her thighs all night. That's what she wanted. But that's not what she did. "Careful there," she said over her shoulder. "There's only one of us trying to protect my virtue." She wiggled her ass, which Colton promptly swatted.

"Time for us to get out of here, while I still can," he said, having come back to his usual composure.

Stepping out of the shower, Colton wrapped her in a towel and then grabbed one for himself.

"I hope you're always this determined, luv."

"You say that like you plan on sticking around," she laughed, but quickly looked away to hide the hurt. More than anything in this world, she hoped he'd stay but knew that in a few weeks, he'd be gone.

"Emma, look at me. I'm not going anywhere." When her eyes searched his for meaning, he continued. "You're a hard woman to say no to, which I don't like doing, by the way," he nodded toward the shower. "But I love that you're so determined. I love your spirit, and I-" He hesitated as he struggled with what to say next. Instead, he pulled her into his arms and hugged her tight. *And I think I love you. I'm falling in love with you. Would she think I were mad if I told her that?* He leaned down and kissed her lips before walking into the bedroom.

What was that? Emma thought to herself as she fell back against the wall. *Am I crazy to think that he almost told me he loves me? That's crazy, right?*

"You coming, luv?" Colton called out from the bedroom.

"You can wear that to sleep in," he motioned to the shirt on the bed. Emma slipped into his long sleeve t-shirt before dropping her towel. "What? *Now you're bashful?*" He laughed as he fell back on the bed wearing a pair of dark blue boxer brief underwear.

"Not bashful, just trying to help you stay a good man. I've been relentless. I'll be the first to admit that," Emma smiled sincerely. "But I want you to know that I want more from you than just that." Thinking that she was sounding like one of those needy women that she despised, Emma corrected. "I want you to know that I enjoy spending time with you. I think you're smart and funny, not to mention you have an accent that still puts me in a fog when I hear you speak." She shook her head. "None of this is coming out right, Colton. But I like you, everything about you. And I really would like it, if after the 'first time,' you're around *all* the time. But we live thousands of miles apart, and I don't know how that could be." Emma exhaled when she said this. Pulling the edge of her bottom lip in, she bit down nervously as she shot him an unsure glance.

Colton rose to his feet to stand in front of her. He placed his fingertips under her chin, gently guiding her focus up to his eyes. "I'm not going anywhere, luv." He brushed a light kiss across her lips.

The sound of her growling stomach interrupted the tender moment and the kiss. "Except maybe to get you some food. I will do that," he laughed.

Emma told him that she'd go herself. She wanted to see if Miss Francine had any hot chocolate, too.

Still holding on to her hand, Colton raised it to his lips and kissed it before he let her go. Emma did a quick glance in the mirror. Deciding that his shirt covered almost as much as the dress she wore earlier, she headed downstairs.

Remembering something he needed to check for the upcoming board meeting, Colton scooted his chair up to the desk and flipped his notepad open. He worked until he heard her return. When he turned away from his notes, he saw that Emma held a tray containing two mugs, a couple pops, and sandwiches. "I take it we're really hungry?" he asked, amused.

Handing him his drink, she ignored his jab at her constant plight for food. "I brought you some hot tea," Emma beamed proudly.

Biting back a smile, Colton accepted the mug, but promptly sat it and the tray on the desk. He drew her into his lap. "Emma, I think it's time for full disclosure." At her puzzled look, he continued, "I truly hate tea. The only thing worse than hot tea would be iced tea." He glanced at the cup. "I find it to be positively dreadful."

Emma burst out laughing at his revelation.

"Why on earth have you been drinking the cup after cup that I've been pushing on you?"

"Because you troubled yourself enough to do it, luv. With me 'sticking around,' as you put it, I want to be honest with you. But I'd gladly share your hot chocolate."

"It's tea, too." She frowned. "Miss Francine was out of hot chocolate, but was adamant I'd like her tea. How could I refuse?" Emma glanced at the cup, pursing her lips.

Colton laughed at the expression. It was clear she wasn't about to try the beverage.

When they'd finished their sandwiches and drinks, Emma asked to borrow his phone so she could text Lisa.

"Everything okay?" Colton questioned.

"Yes. I just need her to bring some essentials to work in the morning."

With the text sent, Emma stood at the window watching the storm in the distance.

"Emma, are you ready to come to bed?" Colton asked, pulling the covers back for her to join him.

As she snuggled down, enjoying the warmth that enveloped her, she knew for certain that she'd never been so happy. She also knew that the time had come to reveal a painful secret.

"Colton, in light of full disclosure, there's something that I want to tell you."

By the seriousness of her tone, he knew what she'd likely say. He found himself at a crossroads. Did he tell her what he knew, risking her getting angry with Cat? Or did he listen, knowing the painful reminders she'd relive? He knew that revisiting one's past could, often times, be therapeutic. So he decided to keep mum.

"You awake?"

"Yes, luv. And I'd love to hear anything you'd like to share."

"I want to tell you about my scars and what happened. It's hard for me to talk about, but I want you to know." Emma lay in his arms as she shared her story, the part she could remember, anyway.

Colton hugged her and kissed away her tears as they fell, offering silent support.

"So that's it," she finally said. "That's the story. He truly is crazy. I can't help but wonder if he'll ever find me again and if he does . . ." she trailed off, unable to finish.

"I'll be here to protect you, Emma, for as long as you'll allow me to."

Emma glanced up at him. "How about forever?"

Colton smiled. "That might just be long enough," he said as he lowered his head to kiss her.

Snuggling closer to his chest, the steady rhythm of his heart helped her drift off to sleep.

Emma ran down dimly lit alleyways, lost in a city that she didn't recognize. She passed dumpsters, stacks of discarded newspapers, and boarded up store fronts in her plight to reach the safety of the church she could see in the distance. His footsteps grew louder, and she knew it was only a matter of time before he caught her. Again, she veered off the intended path, despairing that every turn led her further away from the cathedral. Glancing behind her, she caught the glimmer of his blade as she stumbled into what she thought was an escape. She was wrong. Surrounded by a trio of brick walls, Emma was trapped. Knowing she was cornered, she turned to face him with a confidence she didn't truly possess.

"Hello, Amanda," he said after a few moments. Eerie laughter filled the night as he raised the knife, twisting it menacingly. He struck without warning, sending lancing heat erupting across her shoulder. A crimson stain quickly spread across her white blouse, but she had little time to notice it. The force of his attack caused him to stumble, allowing her the chance to flee.

Injured and terrified, she ran. The stillness of the night amplified the sound of her foot fall against the cobblestone street. Would he hear? She was afraid to look back. If she did, would he be there? Be close enough to touch? She imagined a phantom hand tightening in her hair. Her heart thundered in her chest, and she cried out.

Keep going.

Run.

Emma turned the corner and was immediately flooded with a sense of relief. Ahead in the distance through the misty fog, she saw the steeple. Tears stung her eyes.

She picked up speed and raced toward the church that would provide a safe haven for her. Running through the heavy wooden doors, Emma screamed for anyone who'd help her. She lowered the horizontal wooden plank in place, barring the doors. As she turned to dash headlong toward the altar, she crashed face first into a monk, clad in a brown hooded robe. "Thank God, Father. You have to help me. I'm wounded, and I'm scared."

"Is that so?" The ominous voice purred. When he lowered his hood, Emma was paralyzed with fear by familiar, cold eyes. She rasped out a sob. It wasn't possible, but somehow it was. He was here. He smiled cruelly, the crease in his cheek revealing a scar she hadn't noticed before. Without warning, his hand shot forward, settling around her neck in a crippling vice.

"No!" Emma screamed out and fought frantically to wake from her nightmare. "No."

"Wake up, Emma," Colton urged beside her. "Wake up," He shook her shoulder gently, to no avail. She shoved against his chest, and a muffled scream filled the room. When she gasped and tried to pull away, he realized she was awake. "I've got you, luv. It's Colton. I'm right here, and you're safe."

Emma lay crying in his arms. "It was terrible," she sobbed. "I was running from him, and he stabbed me, then I ran to a church, but he found me again and-"

"Shh, Emma. I'm here."

"I hate these nightmares," she sniffled. "Always a different scenario. Always a different appearance. The only thing that remains the same is how he makes me feel. Completely terrified." Emma cried.

She lay in silence, gathering her composure. "I'd like another shower, if you don't mind." What she needed now was to relax and to forget about her stalker. "They just help me unwind."

"Would you like some help?"

"No," she said as she raised up to kiss him. "I'll be out soon."

When she came back to bed, Emma snuggled back down into the cocoon of Colton's warm, strong arms. She rose up and kissed him tenderly and then rested her head against his chest where she drifted off to sleep once more. With sleep capturing his consciousness, Colton found peace having the woman he was falling in love with spread across his chest.

CHAPTER 24

"Good morning, beautiful," Colton whispered, his alluring voice drawing her from her slumber while he rained kisses on her forehead and cheek.

"Ten more minutes," she pleaded.

"Okay, I'll wake you in ten minutes."

"No, I mean I need ten more minutes of this treatment," she said, hugging him then turning over to catch more sleep.

Colton eased out of bed and into the shower. When he came back, he gently nudged her. After more direct prodding, Emma stumbled into the bathroom, grumbling.

I'm thinking my Emma is not a morning person. He smiled at the thought. Colton dressed and started downstairs for some coffee and her clothes, only to find that Francine had already left a breakfast tray and their freshly laundered clothing on the wooden bench outside his door.

He hung Emma's clothes on a hook attached to the bathroom door then crossed into the bedroom where he sat on the end of the bed. Memories of their evening rushed through his mind - flashes of her silhouette in the vacant house, her curvaceous body as jets of water washed over her in the shower, the feel of her warm skin pressed against his. When he looked up, Emma was standing before him wearing only her underwear. The revealing lace, coupled with the images in his mind, caused a hunger he couldn't curb. Her hair hung around her shoulders, still wet. As he appraised her, his eyes focused again on the charm that hung between her breasts. Colton's mind trailed back to the erotic scene from the night before, Emma's head thrown back in passion as she rocked against him. Releasing the covers he had inadvertently grasped in his hand, he tried to shake the thought from his head, all the while ignoring the suddenly too tight feel of his pants. "You have no idea what you do to me, Emma Saint-Claire." Colton drew her closer until she stood between his open legs. Laying his head on her stomach, he draped his arms around her hips, resting them on her backside. She gently pushed her fingers through his hair, caressing lightly. He thought back to her nightmare and before he realized what he was doing, he had her wrist in his hand, trying to kiss away the hurt. Emma was touched by the tender moment.

Hoping to break his focus from her story, she spoke. "You know, this is the position that started everything last night," she smirked. "And if you expect me to remain a virtuous woman, I suggest you release me before I crawl in your lap and have my way with you."

Desire stirred inside him. Colton reached up, grabbed the pendant and pulled her down into a passionate kiss. She pushed against his shoulders, shoving him onto the bed.

"Remind me to wear this necklace every day," Emma said breathlessly as she lay beside him, her leg thrown over his. She leaned over to kiss him and rested her hand on his abdomen, lower than she had planned. Having not objected to that, she trailed her fingers to the waistband of his jeans, fanning her fingers out. As the kiss deepened, so did her pursuit of his growing erection. He pulled against her leg, encouraging her to straddle him.

Feeling the ridge underneath her, Emma couldn't help but move against it, grinding down nice and slow. "Please, Colton," she whispered mindlessly. "Give me what I want."

"I can't give you what you want, Emma, but I'll give you what you need."

Colton placed his hands on her hips and directed her motions while dragging her core hard against his own. She reached behind her back, unfastening her bra. The sight of her breasts spilling out caused him to utter words she didn't recognize. Reaching up, he palmed each one, working the tips until they tightened into firm ends. Never slowing, Emma's cries became louder, and her actions more intense when Colton drew one of her hard nipples into his mouth. Hungrily, he flicked his tongue across it, again and again. When he sucked the peak, Emma's moans urged him on. He turned his attention to the other before laying back. Colton trailed his hand down her abdomen, the pad of his thumb dipping below the edge of her panties.

He gazed upon her face. Emma's eyes, heavy with desire, begged him to continue. He did. Slowly. Her breaths came in short pants, and she lifted her hips in an effort to push herself against him. When his thumb brushed against her slick clit, they both groaned. Feeling her arousal, pleased with how responsive she was, he gave her what she needed. With deliberate strokes, Colton continued to pleasure her, mercilessly. Emma threw her head back, moaning, and rode him hard.

Colton watched as the pendant bounced with the rise and fall of her breasts. Taking her nipple into his mouth, he sucked and licked, matching the rhythm of the strokes between her thighs. His lips tightened around her then his teeth grazed her sensitive tip, biting down a moment before ecstasy washed over her. Colton slid two fingers inside her. Even if he couldn't take his pleasure, he would delight in the feel of her pulsing around him. To his surprise, the contractions grew in intensity. Emma continued to move and screamed out a second orgasm, grinding down on him.

She fell onto his chest and lay there, out of breath.

Colton held her close, caressing her hair until their breathing returned to normal. Emma shifted to lay beside him. Propping herself up on her elbow, she looked into his eyes and began unfastening his belt.

Colton smiled and stilled her hand. Even though he was painfully aware of his need, he'd made a promise, and he intended to keep it.

"Let me help you," Emma urged.

"I don't think so, luv. But come tomorrow night, you can do anything you want to me, and I'll do everything I want to you. Believe me when I say I want to do a lot." He bent to kiss her lips then excused himself.

Emma was dressed when he came back into the room. "Are you mad?" She asked as she finished zipping up her boots.

"Why would I be mad?" Colton asked with a look of confusion.

She stood and walked over to him. "Well, I know that probably didn't happen the way you had planned. But now that I've-"

"Released some steam?" He provided the phrase, jokingly.

"Yes, now that I've released some steam, I should be entirely tolerable." She smiled sheepishly.

"Emma, I'm afraid I'm to blame for that. My mind revisited a scenario that wound me up."

"Oh, would you like to share?"

"No. Because I need to get you to work, and if I tell you, we'll be right back in the same position. But I will say that I want you to leave your necklace here today. I don't want any other man getting that image in his mind. And while we're at it, put these on." Colton turned to retrieve a pair of sweat pants from the laundry basket.

"The necklace I'll agree to, if you promise to tell me later about the fantasy, but Colton, these pants are huge. No offense. I can't exactly walk around and work in them."

"No, but you can keep people from catching a glimpse of these and wrecking into the river as we ride by." He ran his hand up her leg, underneath her dress, and rested it on her panties.

As he ran his finger inside the material that hugged her hip, Emma shuddered. "Seriously, if you want me to leave you alone, you *must* stop doing things like this!"

Colton offered the pants again. "Ok," she shrugged in defeat. "I'll put these barbaric man pants on, but only to save the people of Brookfield, and myself, from overtime. A multicar pile-up will only cause more work for me!" She laughed, reaching for the non-stylish grey sweats.

When Colton dropped her off at her car, she wiggled out of his pants and tossed them on the seat beside her. Looking up at him, she couldn't resist a witty jab. "Odd, I thought getting into your pants would be more . . . enjoyable. You're not leaving me satisfied, babe, maybe we can work on that," she winked.

Colton pulled her to a standing position, pressing his body flush with hers. "I plan on giving you more pleasure than you can handle, luv." The kiss he placed on her lips had her wishing she could freeze time. "See you tonight, Emma."

CHAPTER 25

*P*hil sat behind his desk, staring down at the stack of photos. He had pushed them aside some ten minutes ago in an effort to come to a sensible conclusion, but the feeling of unease only continued to mount the longer he pondered the situation. He replayed a conversation about Emma that he'd had with Peggy months ago. At the time, he'd dismissed it as embellished truths. But now, he had to wonder.

He lifted the phone to his ear, placing a call to his office assistant. "Lisa, is Emma in yet?"

"Emma?" Lisa hesitated for half a second before the lie automatically fell from her lips. "Yeah, she's here. But she's in the bathroom."

"That's just as well. Come to my office right away."

Lisa wondered what was wrong with Phil as she hung up the phone. The tone in his voice left little doubt that he was upset over something. It involved Emma, that much was clear. But she was the golden child in Phil's eyes, so it didn't make sense.

A knock sounded on his door. "Come in," Phil instructed. "And close the door behind you."

Lisa sat in the open chair on the other side of the desk feeling somewhat like a naughty child in the principal's office. She waited for him to speak. A multitude of scenarios flooded her mind, causing her pulse to quicken. She knew it was, in part, because she had lied. And now she'd have to tell another to cover that one, depending on how this went.

"Did you hear me, Lisa?" Phil asked, shoving the photos toward her. "Look at these pictures Emma took, and tell me what you see."

Nodding, she flipped through the stack. "Well, I see a kick-ass photographer. She really knows how to capture a shot. I love this one," she said, holding up the black and white version of the firefighter's jackets and boots. "Nope, it would be *this* one that I love," she pointed to the four half-naked firefighters. "Oh, and look at that cute puppy, Phil. Everyone *loves* a puppy!"

Phil shook his head. If he wasn't so concerned, he'd find humor in her efforts. He had to hand it to her. She was certainly trying to lessen the blow for her friend by building her up. "Lisa, she's not in trouble, so you don't have to sell her shots to me. There's a guy that's showing up in a lot of these photos."

Lisa tensed instantly. *Oh shit! She's taking Colton on assignment, and Phil's busted her.*

As he flipped through the photos, he tossed the ones he had earmarked onto the desk, leaving them to land in a haphazard pile. He blew out a frustrated breath. "I wouldn't think anything of it, but he's at multiple locations." Going through the stack again, the concern grew in his voice. "Look here," he said, turning the picture toward her and tapping the stranger in the image. "This is the man. I want to see if you can spot him in the others."

What is this? Where's fricken Waldo? Lisa glanced at the person in question. She saw a black man whose features were hidden by layers of clothing, sunglasses, and a hat. He just looked like a regular Joe. Relief flooded her system at the realization that it most definitely wasn't Colton. Both her demeanor and her voice relaxed. "Phil, it was the grand opening of the firehouse. The public always comes out in droves to these things for the freebies alone."

"That's true. But let's look at these according to the time stamp, and you'll see what I'm talking about." Again, they combed through the pile. They saw several shots of the crowd waiting for the grand opening. "If you look through these, he's not in them. Now look at the ribbon cutting photo."

"He's not in it either," she said happily, not really knowing where he was going with this anyway.

"Lisa, this is why I'm the editor, and you are not. Look at the reflection on the truck bays, then tell me what you see from there."

"Ok. I see the crowd, Emma, the firefighters, and Mayor Joseph." She paused a moment. "And him." Lisa glanced up at Phil. "I see him now. He's across the street, but the reflection clearly picks him up." Through the reflected images, they watched as the crowd dissipated, but the stranger still remained. Lisa brought her hand to her mouth. "Phil, this is odd. It's like he's watching her . . . studying her."

"Okay, now go to the ones of the car. I didn't think he was there until I got to this one," he said as he shoved a picture of the convertible toward her.

"I don't see him, Phil," she admitted, confused.

"Look in the rear view mirror, Lisa. He's there, too." They shared an anguished glance. "I want you to get on your computer and send me those pictures that she took on Tuesday, wherever she was. The ones from Monday, too."

254

"Phil, this is scaring me."

"We're going to err on the side of caution, for now. Don't tell anyone what we've seen, especially not your sister. I don't mean to hurt your feelings, but she's not-"

"Yeah, we've actually met." They both laughed nervously. "I know she's not exactly Fort Knox when it comes to information."

Pointing again to the stranger in the photos, Lisa couldn't help but ask the question they were likely both thinking. "Phil, do you think this is connected to Louisville? She's never told me in detail what happened, but I know it involved a man that hurt her."

"I don't know. Let's take this a step at a time. Forward me those photos."

Lisa exited Phil's office as Emma was coming in late. Emma gave a questioning glance towards Phil's closed door. "What's that about?"

"Oh, that's just him being a dick because I came in late this morning. He's been busting my chops for the last fifteen minutes! Anyway, I left your 'requested items' in the bathroom. When you come out of your long bathroom break, because that's where you've been, you know," she winked, "I expect the *complete* rundown on where you've really been!" Lisa flashed her best smile and hoped that Emma couldn't tell that she was worried. "Now go," she said, motioning Emma toward the bathroom.

Settling behind her computer, Lisa sent the requested files to Phil.

That was when Laura broke her silence. "I don't know

why you're covering for her. What's it to you if she gets in trouble?"

Lisa turned to face her sister's desk. "What's it to *you*, Laura? Could you please just look out for someone else, just once in your life? Let this go, please!"

Several minutes later, Emma left the bathroom and Lisa followed her into the office, necessities in tow. Without asking, she started brushing Emma's long hair. Pulling it over one shoulder, she casually styled it into a fishbone braid and secured it with a tie and hairspray. She held out a mirror, and Emma smiled gratefully. "Cat does fashion. You do hair. And all I can do is photography. Hey, I think I just discovered our next employment opportunity!"

"Before we discuss that, I want to hear all the wicked details from last night."

Emma gave her the cliff notes of the evening. "…and then he asked me to spend the night with him, so I did."

"And?"

"*And* I think I'll keep the rest to myself," she winked.

Sitting on the corner of the desk, Lisa looked her over with a disapproving grunt. "Well, how 'bout I fill in the blanks myself? You're able to walk today and can cross your legs without cringing. You're either still a virgin, *luv,* or had the worst sex imaginable. Maybe he's got a tiny tom." She shook her head and looked to the ceiling, fanning herself and feigning off fake tears. "Either way, my heart breaks for you, still." A playful smile tugged at her lips.

Emma laughed but said nothing.

"But seriously, guess who came by this morning?"

"Cat?"

"Tank! He just wanted to know how you've been. I swear Emma, that man's got it bad for you, and he never gets to see you now that you've got yourself a British stud. Tell me, how are the plans for the ball coming along?"

"First off, he assures me that he's hired the necessary people to pull it off. We sent out the invitations. Did you get yours?"

"Yes, I did. And I'm bringing Bryce."

"You're bringing him on our date tonight, too." At Lisa's strange look, Emma added, "Small town, babe."

The girls were deep in conversation when Phil called Emma's line and asked her to send Lisa to his office. He stated that their conversation was unfinished. Emma frowned as she hung up the phone. "He wants you back in there," she said apologetically.

Lisa arose, grumbling under her breath as she walked out, clearly putting on a show for Emma. Closing the door, she resisted the urge to break into a sprint as she hastily walked to Phil's office.

She closed the door behind her and watched as her boss looked up from his computer. "He's been watching her for two days."

Lisa walked around behind Phil's chair so she could look over his shoulder as he scrolled through the images.

"See this picture of Alice and Bill?" he asked, pointing to the elderly couple Emma had photographed a couple days before. "If you look back here at this store front," he tapped it with his pencil, "he's here, trying to blend in, but he's watching her out of the corner of his eye."

"This is a problem. I mean, maybe it's a problem. I don't know. If she didn't have this in her background, I wouldn't think much of it. I think I need to meet with Cat and Hayden and share our suspicions, but I'll need these pictures printed."

Phil nodded and in seconds, the selected images spilled

from the printer. "Lisa, for the digital copies, can you work your magic and make him disappear? Emma doesn't need to live in fear of the 'what ifs' unless we find out for sure that this is the guy from Louisville. She's finally becoming the old Emma again, only better. She laughs more, seems to be getting comfortable in her skin again, and her photography has actually never been better. She asks all the right questions when on assignment and is turning into a damn fine journalist. She doesn't need worry to cause a setback." Digging through his desk drawer, Phil retrieved an empty folder then slid the printed pictures inside before handing them to her. "Go to your desk and slip these in your bag. I'll come out, sending you off on an errand, and you go meet Cat and Hayden."

Lisa went back to her desk and busied herself on her computer. Phil came out into the office after a while and said he needed someone to go get him a print cartridge. Lisa said that she'd go since she needed one, too, before the supplier came back again. She grabbed her large bohemian purse, folder neatly tucked inside, and left as quickly as she could.

In disgust, Laura tossed the magazine that she'd been reading, knowing that it was a charade. *I'd question it if I cared enough to ask.*

Lisa called Inked. Cat had barely finished her greeting before Lisa dove into conversation. "I need you to clear your schedule for about an hour. Call Hayden and have him meet us at the park. And Cat, it involves Emma's safety, so do not tell her I called."

Cat felt dread building in the pit of her stomach. Through teary eyes, she called Hayden and instructed him to meet them. As she drove to the park district, she instinctively knew that the stalker that Emma had managed to evade for months had once again found her.

The trio arrived within minutes of each other.

"Cat, I need you to tell me what happened to Emma in Louisville," Lisa urged.

"Forget that! Why are we here, Lisa?" Cat's tone was controlled, but she clipped the words off just the same.

"Let me show you." Lisa laid out picture after picture, circling the mystery man's face with a red marker. She pointed out the time and date stamp on each photo. As she did, tears began to well up in Cat's eyes.

Lisa pinned Cat with a steady gaze. "I don't know what happened in Louisville, but I know you do. I also know that you and Emma are tight lipped about a lot of things. But this guy is here, Cat. He's in Brookfield, and he's following her. It's time you tell us what you know."

Feeling as if she were betraying Emma, but trying to protect her too, Cat did tell the story. Hayden offered support when her voice became thick with emotion. She broke down, recalling the terror that Emma went through, all alone in a strange city.

"This doesn't make sense," Hayden objected. "If she used a pen name, how could he possibly find her? It's not like Emma is a world renowned journalist."

"The article," Cat said as all the pieces came crashing into place. "The article for the ball ran in Monday's paper."

"What paper? Not the Journal," Lisa said.

"In the Lexington Herald . . . and it's statewide." Dread built in the pit of her stomach, and she felt bile rise into her throat. Cat dropped her head, holding it in her hands. "Hayden, her picture was there. And her name – her real name." She looked up at him and could see the concern on his face.

"It's okay, baby. We'll protect her. I'll assign trusted officers to her around the clock. We'll call Colton-"

"We will *not* call Colton," Cat implored. "He and Emma are going away for the weekend, so she won't be here, anyway. We'll be with her tonight. Lisa, you make sure that you and Emma come to my house after work, and we'll meet up with the guys together."

Lisa nodded. "She spent the night with him last night, so we'll plant the idea that she should do that again tonight. That gives us the weekend to come up with a plan."

Having agreed on the details, the girls went back to work and Hayden started his case against the mystery man. They all three were mindful of every stranger they passed in the city of Brookfield that day. Lisa grabbed the cartridges and headed back to the Journal where Laura was still complaining, Emma was still unaware, and Phil was mindfully scanning every picture that came across his desk.

CHAPTER 26

*F*eigning a fashion emergency, Lisa insisted that a trip to Cat's house was in order. Being a living and breathing glamour disaster herself, Emma understood the need and led the way to her cousin's, unaware that she was following a carefully laid out plan.

Lisa pulled into the drive behind Emma's car, and they both walked up the stairs together. Emma used her key that she was thankful to have. Turning to Lisa, she gave a confession. "Anytime in my life that I've looked halfway fashionable, this baby right here was the cause of it." She twisted the silver key between her fingers.

While Emma went to take a shower, Lisa sank down in one of the plush, chocolate brown leather sofas, making a mental note that she needed one. She liked the color pallet that Cat had selected for the common rooms in her house. The browns, beiges, blacks, and reds were welcoming with their warm, earthy feel. She admired the artwork that was tastefully displayed throughout the room. When she rose to look at the artist's signature, she was highly impressed to see that Cat herself was responsible for all the oil paintings and charcoal sketches. She walked over to the art desk and saw a work in progress. She picked it up to look at it.

"I'm almost finished with that one," the voice sounded from the entryway. Cat had arrived in time to catch Lisa riffling through her things.

"I'm sorry for looking at your sketch pad," Lisa apologized. "As I was admiring your artwork, I saw this project. You're really good."

"Thanks. It's something that I'm working on for Hayden's dad."

"Emma's in the shower. I faked a jewelry meltdown to get her over here early, so I'll just be on my way."

"Lisa, style is what I do. If you know what you're wearing tonight, we'll really try to match something up. Emma knows everything I own, and if you show up without it, she'll wonder why."

"I don't want to take something that you plan to wear."

"I know what Emma and I both will be wearing, so don't worry about that."

With jewelry in hand, Lisa left with plans to meet them in a few hours at the Tavern.

When Emma got out of the shower, she saw clothes laid out on the bed. "These for me?" she called out.

"Yes," Cat said, waiting for the shouts of glee. "Three, two . . ."

"Oh my God, Cat!"

"That's my girl. Predictable as always," Cat said to herself.

Emma dressed and walked from the bedroom in her black and tan leopard print bra, frayed denim skirt, and the cowboy boots she'd admired at Vintage.

"I cannot believe that you bought these for me. Thank you so much!"

"I cannot believe you *still* haven't told me about what happened at the Maggard house! Spill, already!" Cat's eyebrow shot up in warning.

"First let me say that I'd like to kill your boyfriend and his sucky timing!" They both snorted out a laugh then Emma filled her cousin in on the details.

Satisfied with what she'd heard, Cat prompted Emma again about the shirt.

"I had planned to wear my white tank top and peach shirt, but those are at my place. So, I'll take whatever you hand me."

They walked back into the bedroom and Cat gave her a skintight white tank and rust colored button down shirt. Then she capped a cowboy hat on her head. Emma twisted from side to side admiring her look.

"Emma, men can't resist a beautiful lady in a cowboy hat. If you wear it low like this," Cat said as she settled the hat further down on Emma's head, "they get that 'ride 'em cowgirl' image in their head, and it drives 'em wild!"

"Well, I was going to say that maybe that was too much for me to pull off, but *I'm up* for driving Colton crazy."

"He'll likely 'be up,' too!" They both laughed wickedly. Cat got dressed in a similar outfit. When they finished their hair and makeup, they stood side by side and did a final appraisal in the mirror. "We're gonna turn some heads tonight, babe." Cat turned and checked her backside in the mirror. "I'd do me," she said with a shrug. When Emma started laughing, Cat continued. "What? Gram gave us some good genes. Who are we to hide them?"

Riding together in Cat's SUV, the cousins arrived at the Tavern. As they parked and walked across the parking lot, the pulsing beat of drums reached out to greet them, growing louder as they got closer.

"Sounds like a good night already," Cat said with a wicked smile. "I can't wait to drag you on stage to sing!"

They pushed through the entrance and into a spirited crowd who were dancing and knocking back shots in celebration of the female karaoke singer on stage.

"Finally! I didn't think you two would ever get here," Lisa shouted, getting their attention. "The guys are back there," she said as she locked arms with them and steered them toward the billiard room.

As they approached the room, they saw Hayden and Colton standing side by side, holding pool cues and sharing a laugh. Bryce was bent over the pool table with his head hung low. The white cue ball rolling slowly toward the corner pocket told the story. He had scratched, and his friends weren't disappointed in the least.

"Give the poor boy a break," Emma said, wrapping her arms around Colton's waist.

"*Poor?*" Colton questioned with a raised eyebrow. "That chap's anything but poor tonight."

"That *poor guy* took us for fifty bucks in the last game," Hayden offered. "He's getting what he deserves."

"Whining like true losers," Bryce fired back over his shoulder, his eyes twinkling with amusement.

Colton gave Emma a hug and kiss. "You look beautiful tonight, luv."

They moved to a table where the six of them shared appetizers and a pitcher of beer. Emma looked around at her circle of friends, pleased that everyone was enjoying themselves.

After a round of dancing, the guys went off to throw a game of darts while the girls combed through the book of karaoke song choices. Cat was the only one who'd done this before. Lisa and Emma were going to be backup singers. Or "clear the house" singers. It could go either way since neither of them had ever sung karaoke before. With their selection made, they turned in their slip and waited their turn.

The singer on stage was wrapping up his set when he suddenly cut off, eyes wide in shock. Everyone turned to see a cluster of men shouting obscenities and bodies colliding in a growing scuffle. Emma, Cat, and Lisa were pushed through the crowd toward the commotion. They tried to retreat when Cat realized that their guys were in the middle of the barroom brawl.

"What the hell?" Cat yelled when she saw Hayden emerge.

"Change of plans," Hayden told her. "Take the girls outside. We need to leave. That's the only way the rest of these people will see any peace tonight."

"Okay, but maybe you could tell me why you guys have suddenly become public enemy number one?"

"I'll explain later. But right now, we need to leave. I'll get the guys."

Meeting up in the parking lot, Hayden gave a brief explanation. "It was just a local thug and his friends trying to cause trouble. I arrested his sister the other day, and he was trying to exact revenge. I don't want to deal with that shit tonight. That's why we're leaving."

"We can go back to my place," Cat offered.

"Let's go to the cabin instead," Hayden countered and was pleased when everyone agreed.

Emma and Colton piled on his bike, Emma directing every turn. Lisa and Bryce followed in his truck, and Hayden and Cat drove hers.

"I'm starting to think that all our dates will be interrupted," Emma said once they parked and she had retrieved her hat from the saddle bag.

"That's ok, luv. I wasn't too pleased with all the attention your long legs were garnering, anyway," he winked. "And you have no idea the thoughts I had when you walked in wearing *that*," he tapped her hat.

You may be surprised.

A blaze erupted to life with a loud whoosh off to the left of the dirt road. The teepee'd timbers of the bonfire glowed a bright orange, assisted by Hayden's use of something he called "girl scout juice." As they walked toward the others, Colton took in the fire lit scene. He scanned the wide wasteland that was void of any vegetation. "What is this place?" He asked.

"It used to be a logging road, but the company pulled out years ago. Hayden's mom owns the property, so the McAllister's got even richer on this endeavor. Their cabin is just before you get to that ridge," she pointed to a dim light off in the distance. "It'll be amusing to see which brother claims it first tonight," Emma joked but secretly wished she could claim it for Colton and herself.

Colton looked ahead. Roughly a dozen mammoth tree stumps fanned out a safe distance around the fire. He could imagine the loggers sitting on those stumps at one time while eating their lunches.

With his focus back on the clearing, he chose a stump to sit on. Emma sat leaned back against his chest, just as Cat was doing with Hayden and Lisa with Bryce.

With everyone gathered around, Hayden began telling his story, which was directed to Cat. "You know earlier in the week when you came out to help Dad and then I got called in to work to interview a suspect?" When she nodded, he continued. "When they brought him in, he had a large amount of cocaine in the trunk of his car. We kept tacking on more charges until he provided us with the name of the dealer. And in return, he earned himself a lighter sentence. It makes me sick, but that's how our system works – go easy on the bad guy so you can put away the worse guy. Anyway, we raided a warehouse near the East Street Bridge. That bust put away four men and a woman. The man at the bar tonight was her brother."

He turned his attention to Bryce and Colton. "I'm sorry that happened tonight. You two didn't deserve getting dragged into a battle that wasn't yours to fight. I appreciated the back-up, though." He laughed. "People are usually pretty cool in this town, but he was a no good thug looking for trouble."

"No worries, big brother. None of us are worse for the wear. Now that we know why we had to leave, let's get this party started," Bryce said as he started walking to his truck.

"Where you going?" Emma called out.

"Where else? To get the beer and music." His big truck roared to life and he pulled closer to the impromptu party. In just seconds, music spilled from the open windows. Bryce walked around to the back of his truck and unlocked the storage box which was doubling as a cooler tonight. Colton and Hayden came to help distribute drinks. When everyone had a beer, they all settled back around the fire.

"If I get disorderly, will you arrest me?" Cat asked Hayden as she clamped her wrists together and then pointed her fingers upward in a praying motion. "I think I've been a bad girl tonight."

Hayden smirked. "You're a bad girl every night, Cathryn."

Colton gently leaned Emma forward then backed off their seat. When she turned, he extended his hand to her. Without asking where they were going or what they were doing, she placed her hand in his and followed his lead. He pulled her close as they swayed to the music. Bryce and Lisa joined in. Colton ran his hands about Emma's back lazily, their hips rocking in time to the music. He felt the coolness of the night, the heat of the fire, and the desire that burned deep for the woman he held in his arms. Bryce and Lisa talked and laughed, but Colton and Emma swayed in silence as the music filled the only void between their bodies. He knew with certainty that he would spend his every tomorrow making sure that Emma was as relaxed and loved as she was at this moment. Colton leaned down and gently pulled her into a delicate kiss. He released her lips, but not her gaze. She raised up on her toes and captured his lips with tenderness.

"Let's go for a walk," Colton suggested as he led her away from the group.

Bryce called out after them. "Already flipped the coin. Cabin's mine tonight!" Cat let out a groan of disappointment while Emma looked over her shoulder playfully pouting.

Emma and Colton walked hand in hand down the moonlit

path. "I needed to pull you away for a moment," he said as he sat upon a large, flat boulder.

"Oh yeah? Why's that?" Emma asked moving toward him.

"Because of this." Colton pulled her into his lap and placed a passionate kiss upon her lips. "I want you to stay with me again tonight. I liked falling asleep with you in my arms, almost as much as I liked finding you there when I awoke."

"And you couldn't risk me saying 'yes' in front of them?"

"I didn't want to share the moment with them when I kissed you like I've wanted to kiss you all night. Like I'm about to kiss you again." As the smoldering kiss continued, Colton's hands explored the long legs that had wrapped around him. He pulled away briefly. "My only regret is that I can't see you better right now. Some images you just want in your head. With you sitting on me like this, flashbacks of this morning are coming back to me." While he spoke, his hands ran along and underneath the hem of her skirt. "Let's go back, stay a little while longer, and then get out of here."

"I'd like that," Emma agreed, eagerly.

They started walking back toward the group when Colton turned her in his arms. "And Emma, I really enjoyed myself this morning." At the glimpse of her smile, he lowered his mouth to hers.

Headlights blasted them. As they stepped aside, Bryce and Lisa drove past toward the cabin. "Have a great weekend, you two," Lisa yelled, her body leaned out the window.

Cat and Hayden weren't there when they returned. Colton sat back on a stump. Instead of Emma sitting down in front of him, she placed her hands on his shoulders and smiled. "What are you doing, luv?" he asked.

"Giving you that image," she said as she straddled him. She kissed him tenderly then laid her head on his chest.

Colton sat there enjoying the tranquil moment, enjoying the act of simply holding her. Cat and Hayden returned and sat on the stump across from them in the same position that they had been before. They were far enough away that whispers couldn't be heard.

"I think their groins are magnetized," Hayden said. "This is starting to become a common sight." Cat laughed at his joke, but she was happy for Emma.

After some time, Emma let out a sigh and Colton knew she was asleep. "I love you, Colt," she murmured against his chest, barely audible.

Even though he knew she was asleep and had no control over what she was saying, his heart filled with emotion. He couldn't help but close his eyes and whisper lightly, "I love you, too, Emma." He closed his eyes, breathing in the cool night air while still feeling the heat from the dwindling fire.

"Look at them," Hayden said. "They're falling asleep."

Cat opened her eyes and looked across the fire. She smiled. "No, baby, they're falling in love."

CHAPTER 27

"Seriously, Colt. There's no need to muffle my ears every time they make an announcement. If you truly understood my geographical abilities, you'd know why that is completely unnecessary." Emma looked around the terminal at all the other travelers. "I mean, if you said we were going to Montreal and we ended up in Montana, I'd have absolutely no idea that anything was off."

Colton gave her an amused grin. "I like it when you call me Colt."

"I didn't call you Colt . . ." *Did I?*

"You talk in your sleep and say things when you think no one's listening, Emma. This isn't the first time you've called me that." He gave her a moment to think that over. He hoped she meant the words she had uttered in her sleep the night before. "You'll find out soon enough where we're going."

Boarding the flight, they found their seats and were happy they had gotten the two-seater side of the plane rather than the three.

As the plane took off, Colton began a story. "Last year, on a flight to the States, I was seated beside an elderly lady. Seatmates either ramble on mindlessly or say nothing at all. I was knackered from the day I'd had, so I was hoping for the latter. When she pulled a novel from her handbag, I breathed a sigh of relief. I had just settled down into a peaceful slumber when she spoke. But she wasn't talking to me."

"Who was she talking to?" Emma asked.

"Miss Fluff," he laughed. "She was talking to her cat, Miss Fluff. Thinking I was asleep, she began to read her book 'How to Talk to Your Pet' aloud. Apparently, her feline had behavior issues. So she practiced the commands in a stern but loving voice, just as the author suggested. 'Now Miss Fluff, we don't shred paper. That was very naughty. These are our kitty toys.'"

Colton's rendition of an American woman talking to her cat had Emma quickly dissolving into giggles. They both had a good laugh about that as they shared a drink.

The heat from the alcohol, paired with the warmth of the airline blanket, soon had Emma nestling down against the wonderful man to her side. The smell of leather filled her senses, and her eyes grew heavy. She slid her arm around his waist.

"We won't be joining the mile high club - not this time around, anyway," Colton whispered with amusement.

"I'll behave," Emma answered with a tight hug. "This time around, anyway." The feel of Colton's fingers tracing a path against her back was the last memory she had before drifting off to sleep.

"Wake up, Emma. We're here."

They had landed somewhere, but she didn't know where "here" was. Colton had managed to keep the destination a secret by covering her ears every time anyone made an announcement. She raised her groggy head making a mental note to have a few of those little drinks every time they flew. As her eyes adjusted to the light and her ears to the noise of the fellow passengers eagerly rustling bags and un-clicking their seatbelts before they were allowed, Emma took a moment to clear her foggy head. Lifting the visor to look out the window of the plane while they taxied to a stop, she watched luggage carriers hastily moving bags onto a neighboring plane. Billows of steam blew out every time they spoke. Even though the sky was clear, a view of the landscape further in the distance revealed snow – lots of snow.

"Where are we?" Emma asked.

"Lé Marguerite - a small Canadian town near Quebec. You've been asleep practically the whole trip."

They exited the plane, gathered their bags, and were whisked away by a limo to an unknown destination.

Emma listened as Colton made a phone call to a caretaker of a cabin, assuring that the groceries had been gathered and fires started. As he finalized other details, she took in the scenery. The further they drove away from the airport, the more remote their route became. She saw a little village with quaint homes clustered together and could see children playing on a hillside in the snow.

It reminded her of her childhood with Cat. *Beautiful snow*, she thought. As long as she could remember, Emma had loved the snow. Thinking back to when she was a child, she recalled watching it fall from the kitchen window at her grandparents' house. She always felt as if a peaceful blanket had encompassed her as she watched the snowflakes dance gracefully toward the earth and spread into a soft carpet. Her grandmother would make hot chocolate after she and Cat came in from sprinkling bread crumbs on the railings for the birds. Emma thought how good a warm cup would feel in her hands right about now. Remembering the gloves in her pockets, she reached her hands inside to grab them. She felt paper, then heard it crinkle, as she pulled it from her pocket. Unfolding the sheet, she smiled when she scanned it.

Emmabear, I hope you have a wonderful weekend. I think you'll find that I packed everything you need and want . . . except for your beloved GP's.

Xoxo, Cat

Emma laughed knowing that "GP" stood for granny panties and for once, she was thankful that they had not been packed.

Ending his call, Colton turned his attention to her. "What's that?"

"Just a note from Cat assuring me that everything I need is packed." She pointed to the frozen land surrounding them. "This is gorgeous, Colton. Thank you for bringing me here."

"You're quite welcome." He raised her hand to his lips, placing a tender kiss on it. "Do you have any questions yet?"

"Let's see. First I have to think about what I know about Canada, and that ain't much!" He laughed at her honesty. "Why here?" she asked with a shrug of her shoulders. "You know that I'm a simple girl and would have been just as happy staying home."

Colton shook his head. "Emma, when will you ever realize what I see when I look at you? There's nothing simple about you, luv." He stroked her cheek. "Here," he motioned around him, "because there's something they have here that they don't have in Brookfield."

"Canadian Bacon? Cause that's disturbing to me. It's just ham!" She tried to keep a straight face, but failed miserably.

Colton laughed and pulled her closer, "Emma, I love-" he caught himself, "your sense of humor. You truly delight me."

She watched as the homes grew further apart.

A dim light shone in the distance. As they came closer, a two story log cabin came into focus. It was surrounded by a split-rail fence, and she could see a barn peeking out from the left corner of the property behind the home.

Emma realized the picturesque cabin was their destination as the limo pulled to a stop in front of a neatly shoveled walk. The driver opened Colton's door. He slid out and extended his hand to Emma to help her safely exit the car. Once the luggage was placed on the walk, Emma looked down at her three bags and wondered what her cousin had packed and how much of it she'd want to kill her for. She imagined jeans, boots, sweaters, and scanty underwear in the large suitcase, and bathroom essentials in the overnight bag. But she was curious what the garment bag held.

Colton spoke in hushed tones with the limo driver. She wondered what it was about, but decided to let him have his surprise. She'd never had anyone fuss over her like he had, and she found that she was enjoying it.

"Alexander and I will be back soon," the driver called out.

Colton nodded in acknowledgement and bent to pick up his bags. When Emma reached for hers, he shook his head. "I'll come back for those."

"I'm not helpless, Colton."

"And that's one of the things I adore about you, luv. Still, I hope you'll allow me to take care of you."

And how do you argue with reasoning like that? She didn't

275

even try. Emma raised up on her tip toes, pressing a kiss to his cheek before turning to lead the way.

"If you could open the door, I'll come back for the rest."

As she proceeded up the walk, Emma inhaled the cold evening air. The smell of wood smoke brought her gaze to the shadow of a chimney poking through the roof. Welcoming soft lights spilled from the windows below. Emma climbed the steps to the porch and reached for the door.

"I hope you like it," Colton said from behind her. "Hope it's not too rustic."

"I think it'll be just perfect." Emma opened the door. Warmth and the smell of wood burning in the fireplace greeted her.

Colton felt the twinges of his heart telling him this was right. It felt like coming home, though he had never been here. Any place Emma was, he was discovering, was where he wanted to be.

Her eyes swept the room. It was encased in hardwood. The floors, ceilings, and walls all were constructed of knotted pine. Emma stepped up to the back of one of the couches and ran her fingers across it, feeling its softness. The black over-sized leather sofas sat in an "L" formation and shared a sizable end table. A brushed bronze lamp sat atop it, casting a warm, yellow hue into the room from underneath the shade. The only thing sitting between the fireplace and the couches was a massive square ottoman that doubled as a coffee table and a large cream colored rug. Emma noticed the cream colored crushed velvet throws that were strewn about the couches and thought that they were a perfect contrast to the dark sofas.

She trained her eyes on the rock fireplace constructed of jagged stones. It was beautiful. Her gaze followed the pattern of stones to the ceiling where she spotted exposed log beams that ran across to the other wall behind her. As she turned to follow the direction of the beam, she was pleased to find Colton watching her. He had just packed in the last of the bags and closed the door. *I will never get used to seeing him look at me like I'm the only woman in the world.*

"So what do you think?"

"I think you're the most handsome man that I have ever met," Emma said as she closed the distance between them. She came up on her toes and placed a kiss on his lips.

Colton pulled her against him as he leaned back against the door. He kissed her softly then held her in a gentle embrace.

Emma rested her head on his chest, listening to the thrumming of his heart. This felt right.

He appreciated the workmanship before him. Smiling, he thought about her answer. "About the cabin, luv. What do you think about the cabin?"

"Oh, it's handsome, too," she joked. Turning in his arms, Emma pointed across the room. "Look at the stonework and that gorgeous grandfather clock." She pointed to the left of the fireplace. "I'm so happy I have my camera with me. I'll be taking lots of pictures."

Emma grabbed Colton's hand and pulled him behind her. "Let's look at the rest of the cabin." The area was small, but the open floor plan made it look bigger. The main floor consisted of a great room, a kitchen with a breakfast nook, and a small bathroom. The stairway that led upstairs was to the right of the fireplace. After they climbed the stairs, Emma saw two bedrooms and a large bathroom. The larger of the two bedrooms had a wall of windows unobstructed by curtains or shades and a fireplace with the same stonework as downstairs. A gentle blaze roared within.

As they walked further into the room, Colton led her to the windows. Chest to chest, they stood in an embrace gazing into the distance. "I have a surprise for you, one I think you'll be happy with."

"I guess that's what you and the limo driver were whispering about?"

He smiled, but said nothing more.

The blanket of snow provided contrast to a shadowy movement below. Emma narrowed her eyes, not quite believing what she saw. "Colton, is that-" she tilted her head to the side trying to make sense of what she saw. Looking up at him, she read his expression. "That's what I think it is?"

A smile spilled across his lips. "Indeed it is."

"Let's go!" Emma grabbed his hand and raced toward the staircase.

Colton couldn't help but share in her excitement. He knew this was a dream of hers, and he was more than happy to make it come true.

When they reached the front door, Emma turned and grabbed the throws off the couch before heading out.

The porch light filtered far enough into the yard for her to see that she wasn't just imagining a horse drawn sleigh. She approached with elation, Colton right on her heels.

Without pause or permission, she slowly ran her hand down the horse's silky black mane. He neighed in appreciation. He was gorgeous, and the cranberry sleigh that he pulled was perfect too. "Thank you," Emma said to Colton as she turned to hug him. "This is wonderful . . . something from a story book."

He tipped her chin up, dropping a lingering kiss to her lips. It was tender but full of promise.

Alexander's thickly accented voice broke the silence. "'e'll roam around the yard as long as you'll let 'im. Just tie 'im back up 'ere when you're done," he capped his gloved hand over the tethering post. "Tomorrow, we'll see about taking you for a longer ride." He untied the reins, handing them to Colton.

"After you, luv." Colton nodded toward the sleigh, offering his hand in support. Emma draped the covers over her arm and stepped up. He climbed in next.

"Do we even know how to do this?" she asked only half joking as she tucked the velvety throws around their laps.

"No, but I suspect the horse is smarter than I am and won't go where his instincts tell him not to." Colton quirked a crooked grin when Emma laughed.

As they rode, Emma snuggled down closer in the recess of Colton's body and the seat. She closed her eyes and felt the light breeze pass across her face and tickle her nose. When the sleigh would dip, her belly would do that fluttery flippy thing. Colton's must have done it, too, because he'd always chuckle at the same time. She felt like he was enjoying the ride as much as she was. She had mentioned days ago, in passing, that she'd always wanted to go on a horse drawn sleigh ride. That he'd paid attention made her smile. *I think I'm falling in love with him.* Now her belly was fluttering for a different reason. *Is that insane?* As she searched her thoughts, she pulled the covers more tightly around her.

"Are you cold, Emma? We can go back."

"No, I'm fine," she answered, not wanting this to end.

"Well, I'm a bit chilled and would like to warm up."

Emma replied using her best British accent, "Well then, perhaps I could put the kettle on to boil and serve you a delightful spot of tea. Then, perhaps, I could draw you a soothing bath." Colton barked out a laugh at her terrible accent.

"The tea sounds dreadful, luv. But the bath? The bath we can do."

That piqued her interest. "On second thought, I'm freezing! I think I'm ready to go back now."

~

The warmth of the cozy cabin greeted them once more. They sat on the rug in front of the gently roaring blaze and leaned back against the ottoman. Emma felt Colton's strong arms envelope her. Side by side, they watched the mesmerizing flames, her head resting on his shoulder. It was peaceful with Colton's fingers tracing up and down her arm.

The heat within her began to grow with every pass of his fingers.

Colton shifted slightly and gazed down at her. He brought his fingertips underneath her chin and tilted it slightly upwards. With Emma's head resting on the ottoman, his lips brushed against hers. Again and again, his mouth fell on hers, lingering there. As she responded, he gently lifted her into his lap then lowered her to the rug, following her down.

Colton cupped her cheek, pausing for just a moment. He was taken aback. She was beautiful with her hazel eyes searching his. Slowly he lowered his head, placing a delicate kiss to her mouth.

Emma's fingers wound firmly in his hair, holding him

close. He tugged her bottom lip, nipping it gently with his teeth. A soft noise escaped her throat, so he did it again. Tenderness forgotten, Colton took what he wanted. What they both wanted.

Even though they were both fully dressed, she felt his rigid length teasing her cruelly, full of promise. Emma wanted to touch him, for him to touch her, for their bodies to move together as one in a dance she'd never known. The steady rhythm that pulsed between her thighs now had become a throbbing ache. Every time Colton pressed his body against hers, it magnified the effect. She spread her legs wider, tilting against him. "I need you," she whispered.

He answered by pinning her hips to the floor with his own. Her hoarse admission was nearly his undoing. He needed her, too. And if she kept rubbing herself against him, he'd take her. Right here. Right now. On the floor. And it wouldn't be gentle.

Taking a deep breath, Colton coached himself to slow down. But he had to touch her. Sliding onto his left hip, he watched her reaction as his searching fingers dipped underneath the hem of her shirt. Eyes drifting shut, Emma clearly appreciated his warm hands as they slowly slid across her skin. They lingered only a moment before moving up her torso, finding first the lace of her bra, then the release of the front-side clasp. The moan that escaped her spurred him on when he palmed her breast. They both groaned when his fingers found the puckered tip of her nipple. Colton lowered his head, nipped it through her shirt, then came up to kiss her deeply.

Breaking away, he saw the longing in her eyes. "How about that bath, luv?"

Emma leaned against the doorway and watched as he moved about the room, lighting candles. The votives were short and placed in rounded glass tumblers. Low music played in the background. She watched as Colton brought a dozen small flames flickering to life. They were placed in a straight line, reflecting off the vanity mirror.

He moved to the left of the door and illuminated the ones on the shelf by the tub. *Would I have thought to do that?* No. Never would it have crossed her mind.

Emma was quickly learning that Colton held many surprises. Whether he was a romantic at heart, she wasn't sure. As long as his efforts were aimed at her, she didn't care.

Her thoughts were cut short as Colton shrugged his shirt off. He let it fall to the floor, revealing strong shoulders and corded abs. He was beautiful. He locked his eyes on hers and moved closer. Dropping a kiss to her lips, he flipped the light off. Colton walked back to the tub. The dancing flames of the candles cast the room in a romantic glow. The sound of water brought her focus back to him. Emma watched as steam billowed up from the sizeable claw foot tub he was filling. He poured a small amount of liquid from a cut crystal bottle into the bath and the smell of coconut oil immediately filled the room. Bubbles quickly formed into soft peaks.

He turned and seated himself in the vanity chair.

The request wasn't spoken. It didn't have to be. Emma slowly crossed the room, coming to stand just shy of his open legs. The passion in his eyes lowered her inhibitions. Seductively, she began to undress, peeling off layer after layer of clothing and letting them fall carelessly to the floor.

Colton watched, clearly pleased. Her body was shapely, perfect. She embodied everything that made a woman irresistible to him – intelligence, beauty, soft curves, and hungry eyes that had him locked in her sights.

In the heat of the moment, her nipples hardened instantly. She longed for his touch. She longed to touch him. Turning away slightly, her silhouette was cast in a sensual glow.

He saw what she wanted him to see. She was teasing him, inviting his touch. Colton stood in front of her. His lips descended on hers, then lowered to her breasts, which he grasped firmly in his calloused hands. This was what she wanted, what they both wanted. Her fingers threaded through his hair, pulling him closer. Emma threw her head back when the moist heat of his mouth teased her. She caught a glimpse of the erotic scene in the mirror. Colton's tongue flicked hungrily against the tip of her aching nipple before lavishing the other with the same delicious treatment.

"No", she cried out when he moved away to get a better look at her while he undressed fully.

The sight of his fully nude body caused an indescribable ache between her legs. Even though she had no experience, she knew he was everything a man should be. Strong and virile, he was capable of loving her slow and gentle or fast and hard. Her gaze dropped between his legs. Yes, *hard* was a rather fitting description.

Colton pulled her into his arms. Holding her tight, he fought every urge he had to push her up against the sink and fuck her hard, to wrap her legs around him and plunge into her until every inch of his cock was fully seated and fully sated. That's what he wanted, but she deserved better. This was her first time, he reminded himself, and he would take it slow. Or at least he'd attempt it.

Taking her by the hand, Colton slid into the warm water first then helped her in. He pulled Emma back against his chest and folded his arms around her waist, kissing her neck.

Emma closed her eyes. She reveled in the feel of the water, the warmth relaxing her. The peaceful embrace of Colton's arms comforted her and excited her all at the same time. *How can one man evoke so many emotions all at once?*

As he stretched out, Colton was glad the tub was long enough and spacious enough for the two of them. Colton generously filled a porous sponge with coconut bath gel. He washed her arms and neck, taking slow pains to avoid her breasts, which only heightened her anticipation. Emma leaned her head back, inviting a kiss. He eagerly accepted her plump lips. The angle thrust her breasts forward, exposing her more and demanding attention. Colton dropped the sponge low on her belly. Her breathing hitched, not knowing which direction his ministrations would go. He brought the sponge straight up through her generous cleavage and circled her breast firmly, then turned his attention to the other side. He tossed the sponge aside as he caressed both her breasts, slick with suds. Emma arched herself further into his hands. As he felt her nipples harden against his palms, Colton lowered his hands until the stiff points fell between his splayed fingers. Closing them, he tugged gently. Emma's hands fell on his, and she pushed his hands closer together, providing more pleasure for her. When she dropped her hands back to her sides, he rolled her pebbled nipples between his thumbs and fingers. Whispers of encouragement softly fell from her lips, urging him on.

His sweet torture continued. Colton let one hand drop

lower. As he fanned his fingers out, he ran them across her belly and smiled when he felt her quiver at his touch. He enjoyed the feel of her body and took his time palming water across her chest and belly until all traces of suds were washed away.

Laying his hand low on her belly again, he continued on his intended path until he traced her thin strip of curls. "So damn sexy," he whispered. She leaned up to kiss him again as he nudged her knees apart. Colton inched his finger lower, caressing her. She bucked her hips in response. He chuckled, "Eager?"

But he already knew the answer. As his finger lingered, he felt the steady pulse of her heartbeat on the tender flesh. A smile tugged at his lips. The slow tilt of her hips angled his finger farther down, aligning it with her entrance. Emma sucked in a breath when he slid in unhurriedly. Withdrawing, he repeated the action, delving deeper. Meeting no resistance, he easily added another finger. When she began rocking against his buried fingers, he could take no more.

Stepping from the bath, Emma wrapped herself in a plush yellow towel and padded toward the bedroom. Looking back at Colton who was extinguishing candles, she was overwhelmed with emotion that had nothing to do with sex. *I think I love him.* She knew what she felt in her soul, and it just felt right. *I know I love him.* Tonight she would give herself to him completely, body and soul, and sort out matters of the heart another time.

Walking into the bedroom by the light of the fire, Emma noticed how the flames' reflection danced across the wall of windows. Looking ahead at the image, she saw him approach behind her. He said nothing and moments passed before he even touched her. Colton's hands reached out to rest on her hips as his lips brushed a warm kiss to her neck. They swayed in silence.

Colton moved his hands up her sides and across her breasts, meeting at the knotted center of the towel. He released it, letting it fall to the floor. "You won't be needing this, luv." He turned her and swept her up in his arms. Gazing down at her, he bent to kiss her.

He carried her to the king-size bed that sat prominently in front of the windows. Lowering her down, he lay beside her, propping himself up on his elbow. Colton ran the backs of his fingers down her cheek when she turned to meet his gaze. She was lovely. He loved her. *Beyond a shadow of a doubt, I have fallen in love with her.* Colton searched her eyes. *But will she return my feelings?*

His inner struggle was cut short by Emma placing her left hand on his head and drawing him closer. Their lips hovered inches apart for only a moment before she pulled him into a kiss, the tenderness contradicted the hunger stirring within them both. As Emma's hands wove more tightly in his hair, the kiss became more passionate.

Running her fingers down his body and across his hip, she didn't stop until her hand wrapped around his thick base. She began a slow caress. Colton sucked in a sharp breath, lost in the sensation. Emma felt his hand tugging her knees apart as his lips captured her taut nipple. His tongue flicked mercilessly and his finger found her wet center once again, alternating between gentle caresses and deep penetration. He soon felt her tighten around him. Knowing she was on the verge of orgasm, he pulled away. Before he'd given her time to protest, Colton was between her legs, kissing her inner thighs. He brought his head up, gazing upon her. The light of the fire revealed her glistening sex. Emma cried out the moment his tongue brushed her overly sensitive flesh. She needed more, but he didn't allow it.

Colton reached beneath the pillow. Retrieving a condom he had placed there earlier, he rolled it on. The throbbing between his legs had become unbearable. He looked at her questioningly. The unspoken answer was given when she let her legs fall wide apart, beckoning him in. Lowering his body, he kissed her tenderly. With the tilt of her hips, he traced himself against her core until neither could wait another second. Inch by slow inch, he slid inside until he was fully seated. "Are you ok, luv? We'll stay like this as long as you need, until you get used to me."

Emma could feel Colton throbbing inside her. The strain on his face told her that it was taking all the control he could muster to allow her time to grow accustomed to his size. She tilted her hips again, encouraging him to move. It did hurt at first, but as Colton began rocking inside her, the pain quickly turned to pleasure. He found his rhythm, pulling out and sliding in over and over. Emma wrapped her legs around him and met him thrust for thrust. He bent forward, licking and sucking each tight nipple. He could see the shimmer off each breast as the dancing flames revealed the wet path he had created.

Emma wanted him to enjoy this moment to the fullest. "Lay back," she whispered. Colton didn't argue. He gave two hard thrusts, holding himself tight against her before he complied. Instead of rolling to the side, he fell to his back and pulled her forward until she straddled him. Emma smiled down at him, knowing the firelight behind his head would illuminate every motion she made atop him. She lowered her head and captured his lips then eased herself down on him. She pressed one breast into his mouth, then the other before leaning back. With her hands on his chest, they moved together, her hips meeting his. She felt his fingertips gripping the soft flesh of her ass as he dragged her against him. Seeing the rise and fall of her breasts fueled his desire, and he pounded into her relentlessly. The sensation of it all quickly became too much. Emma closed her eyes, grinding herself against him. Soft encouragement fell from her lips as she teetered on the edge of ecstasy. She didn't have to tell him when it happened. He knew. She tightened around him like a glove and threw her head back with abandon, riding out every last wave. Panting and out of breath, she collapsed against his chest.

"I want you to lie back the way you were, Emma." With the fire to his back once again, Colton pushed into her, deep. She let out a sexy moan. He continued his slow, deep thrusts, setting a rhythm that would bring them both ecstasy.

The flash of light in the sky caught his attention. He smiled. Leaning down, he kissed her lips tenderly then apologized just before he pulled out.

He couldn't help but chuckle. The look on Emma's face was murderous.

"What the-"

Colton placed his finger on her lips. "This is something you won't want to miss, luv, the reason we came here." He sat back on his knees, pulling her into his lap. With her back to him, he slid into her, holding her tight to his chest. Feeling her breasts bounce against his arm spurred him on more. He felt the telltale ripples pulsing around him and knew it wouldn't take much to push her over the edge. Colton reached his hand between her legs, caressing her. Emma wound her arm behind his neck and rocked against him.

With her eyes tightly closed, she focused on the feel of him, of the passion he had ignited within her.

"Open your eyes, luv."

She did so just as the sky lit up with the green and white streaks of the Aurora Borealis. Colton's ministrations increased. Just like the sky that couldn't contain the lights, her body could no longer contain the feelings of ecstasy coursing through it. Emma fell forward as her orgasm washed over her. Seconds later, Colton joined her. He rained kisses up her back and then turned her to lie beside him. Emma snuggled down next to him reliving the most wonderful evening she had ever had.

After a midnight snack, passion brought them together once more, their love making lasting into the early morning hours.

When Colton finally drifted off, he knew that he could easily spend forever falling asleep just like this with the woman he loved in his arms.

CHAPTER 28

*E*mma's eyes fluttered open. Like the rush of sunlight pouring into the room, memories of last night flooded her mind. She smiled a knowing smile. It was better than anything she had ever imaged. Fueled by passion and need, the way their bodies moved together, becoming one had been perfect. Stretching, she felt the evidence of the night's activities. She was a little sore, but it was well worth it, she determined with an unsuppressed smile.

Turning over, she reached out for Colton, but found the bed empty.

The aroma of freshly brewed coffee filled the air, leaving her with every hope that he hadn't poured a cup for her. *After all the tea he's choked down at my insistence, it would only serve me right.* She grimaced. Emma scooted up against the headboard, drawing the sheet tightly around her. It was then that she saw the black silky night gown and matching robe laid across the end of the bed.

She heard Colton speaking to someone from another room. She could tell by the details of the one sided conversation that he was on a business call.

Seeing her overnight bag in a chair beside the door, she seized the opportunity to freshen up before joining him.

With her shower and primping finished, Emma slipped into the only thing that she could find. The gown glided over her body like a ribbon of satin, hugging her curves perfectly. As she walked down the stairs, she drew the robe around her and secured the tie.

The smell of bacon made her stomach growl, and she realized how hungry she was. *Yep! That's the way to my heart,* she thought with a chuckle.

He was still on the phone, so she was silent as she walked into the room. The kitchen was small, but open and inviting. Morning sunlight poured through the window above the sink, illuminating the space around him. The curtains, the color of buttercups, added a cheery hue to the room.

Colton placed the phone on the counter, switching it to speaker while he riffled through some notes. The man on the other end of the line had the same delightful accent as his.

Emma leaned back against the counter and took in the sight before her. Colton wore a white shirt with the sleeves rolled up a few turns, dark jeans, and no shoes. He was the epitome of sexy. She imagined running her fingers through his unkempt hair. At the very least, she was going to hug him. She could do that quietly. As she moved toward him, he turned.

"Hold on, I see something that I need to take care of." He winked and quirked a sexy smile.

Laying the file down, his arms wound around her. "Good morning, beautiful. This feels nice," he whispered as his hands ran across her robe. Colton leaned down to kiss her as he pulled her to him. He groaned when Emma's hands reached inside his open shirt. She splayed them across his warm chest for a moment before sliding them around his waist. He dropped his hands lower, appreciating the feel of the silk as it moved against her bottom. He lifted her easily and sat her atop the counter, untying her robe. Nudging her thighs apart, he stood between them, his hands roaming up her legs and underneath the slip. "I see you found what I left for you." He kissed her neck. Pushing the robe down her arms, he lowered a strap of her gown, raining light kisses across her collar bone.

"You didn't leave me any panties," Emma teased.

"That's because you're not going to be needing them, luv." Colton grabbed her hips and pulled her to the edge of the counter, kneeling before her. He dropped his head, placing open mouth kisses on her inner thighs.

"Mmm, that feels good," Emma admitted, running her fingers through his hair to pull him closer.

"It's about to feel even better."

"Colton, you know I'm still holding the line, right?" The caller questioned as he laughed.

"Damn!" Colton said looking up at Emma. "I forgot about him, and we're right in the middle of finalizing a deal."

"Funny, I thought we were, too," she smirked, sliding to her feet. "I'll just get dressed. I wanted to take some photos anyway.

Colton kissed her then led her to the table. "Not before you eat, luv." Emma slid into the chair he pulled out for her. On the table before her was a breakfast spread of orange juice, toast, jam, and bacon. She gave an amused glance at the bacon.

"It's not that ham the Canadians try to pass off as bacon," Colton said in his best American accent.

She laughed so hard, her belly hurt.

While she ate, Colton disappeared upstairs with the

remainder of her luggage. Emma thought about their night together. She'd heard stories of all her friends' 'first times,' the ones who could remember them, anyway. She was positive that none of theirs could compare to hers. Inhaling deeply, she let out a loud, contented sigh.

"Are you happy, luv?" A sexy voice asked.

"Very," she said as she turned, only to find that Colton wasn't in the room. Her eyes darted about, searching for him. She furrowed her brows. *Did I imagine that?*

"What's your name?" The question came from the phone that still lay on the counter.

Not really feeling comfortable answering, but not wanting to be rude either, Emma rose from her seat and crossed the room. Leaning against the counter, she stared down at the phone then leaned closer. "Hello?"

"Finally, someone decides to talk to me," his laugh made her smile. "What happened to Colton?"

"Who *is* this?" Emma asked only because he sounded just like Colton.

"I'm Kane, the brother. What's your name, luv?"

Oh my God! Colton said that people had mistook them for twins, but they sound exactly alike, too. Composing herself, she continued, "Hi, Kane. I'm Emma."

"Emma," he said as if he were trying it out. "So Emma, where'd my brother disappear to?"

"I . . . he's upstairs, I think."

"That was a pretty loud sigh earlier, Emma. I trust my brother is treating you right?"

"The way your brother treats her is none of your bloody business, Kane," Colton barked into the phone as he snatched it from the counter.

"Put *Emma* back on. Her voice was much sexier," Kane requested.

Colton placed his hand over the receiver. "Your luggage is on the bed." He pulled her in for one final kiss before returning to the call that he had neglected.

Damn, Emma thought as she climbed the stairs. *Just damn.* Sometimes a man's character was captured in his looks and you knew instinctively if he was good or bad. Emma knew instinctively that Kane Graves was a bad boy just by listening to the seductive purr of his voice. Shaking that thought out of her head, she turned her attention to the task at hand. Before she rummaged through her bags to see what goodies they held, she opened the new purse that Cat had bought her and retrieved her phone. She had a very important message to send.

Good morning from snowy Canada!
Emma

She set the phone down and turned toward her bags. Her text tone immediately chirped, and she turned back to her phone.

Emma?

SINclaire, baby! Emma grinned broadly as she typed.

A huge smiley face appeared on the phone then Cat texted a single word. *Well?*

Like an Amtrak train trying to fit through a key hole! But it was absolutely amazing . . . and so was the time after that. And it almost was again at breakfast, but a phone call interrupted us!

Wow! You ho!

Guilty as charged, Emma replied with a smile then added a goodbye.

Emma inched a pair of "barely there" lacy panties over her hips, then slid into the matching white bra. They looked good against her tanned skin. She pulled a white sweater over her head then eased her legs into a faded pair of jeans. She paired those with beige Uggs with white fur lining and dangling puff balls, then topped the outfit with a camel colored jacket. She grabbed her camera and headed downstairs.

Colton was still talking to Kane and mouthed, "I'm sorry" as he kissed her.

Holding her camera in the air, he nodded and she set out on her mission. First stop, the split rail fence that caught her eye last night. The zigzag pattern was interesting and perfectly accented the logs of the rustic home. It was a gorgeous day, where the blue sky lured her out and the beauty of the day kept her there, despite the brisk air. As Emma walked, she followed the hoof tracks to the barn.

"You like horses?" Alexander asked, startling her.

She'd been so focused on the black horse she was petting that she hadn't seen the stable hand. "I do like horses. I thought I'd come down here and see if I could snap some photos of him."

"'e's a beauty, eh?" Alexander asked with pride.

"Very much so," Emma said, running her hand down his silky mane. "He's just gorgeous. What's his name?"

"Raven. 'e's not been exercised today. Would you like to ride 'im?"

Emma shook her head and laughed a nervous laugh, trying to think of a tactful way to explain that the last thing she needed to do was ride a horse after the night she'd had. "Oh, I don't know. I've not ridden in years. Maybe I'll just stay safely on the ground."

"Nonsense," Alexander replied.

Long ago, a wise friend had given Emma advice that if someone offers you something, you take it, so as not to hurt any feelings. "Maybe I could take him for a little walk. As long as you'll agree to take some pictures of us." And with that, she found herself handing over her camera and taking the reins. Raven was already saddled up.

Emma placed her foot in the stirrup. With a jump, she swung her leg over. *That wasn't so bad.* She felt like she was twenty feet tall. She knew how beautiful his deep black mane would look against the snow, so she was glad she'd asked Alexander to take photos.

As they left the stable, Raven decided that he wanted to trot. "Oww, Oww, Oww! No, No, No!" Emma muttered as she pulled back on the reins, slowing the pace.

Finishing up the business end of his call with Kane, Colton looked out the kitchen window and saw Emma riding the horse from last night. *She continues to surprise me. First photography, now horseback riding.* Colton watched as Emma's chestnut hair bounced all around her back and caught every ray of sunshine. She looked like a goddess with her locks revealing tones of flaming red.

"Colton, are you still with me?" Kane asked, but continued without waiting for his answer. "About Dillingham Manor, what have you discovered?"

"I have all the documentation now that I need to uproot everyone who's living there. But I'm holding off for a few reasons. There's a man who is blackmailing the landlady – who has no right to be there. It's a convoluted story, but he wants the house. I just need to determine why. My hunch tells me that there's something in the house that is valuable to him. If he simply wanted the house gone, it would have met with an 'accidental' inferno years ago. He needs in there, and I need to determine why before I proceed. I have plans to start on him this week."

"You've been there for weeks now, Colton. I don't understand what's taking you so long. Unless the lovely *Emma* is keeping you occupied," he laughed snidely, and Colton didn't like his tone.

"Kane, she's off limits. I don't even want you saying her name."

"Me thinks big brother doth protest too much," Kane said mockingly. "You act as though you're smitten." When Colton didn't reply, Kane did. "You can't be serious!"

When he saw Emma walking back toward the house, he ended his call. Kane always got under his skin when it came to personal matters. Professionally, he was a great ally to have. Personally, he was the cause of much distress and the reason Colton's last relationship didn't work out.

"I'm sorry I've been on the phone all morning," Colton said as Emma came through the door. They walked into the living room. "Regal Engineering was awarded the contract, so I'm yours for the rest of the time."

"Now, I like the sound of that," Emma said, rolling herself up in a throw and falling back on the sofa. Colton joined her, leaning in for a kiss. "What are our plans for the rest of the day?" Emma asked.

"We have plans this evening, but nothing else is set in stone. Is there anything that you'd like to do?" He stroked his fingers down her cheek.

"I'd like for you to get under this blanket with me and warm me up, Mr. Graves."

"That's an order that I'll gladly take, Miss Saint-Claire. Are you enjoying yourself?" He asked as he kissed her then held her in his arms. "We haven't had a chance to talk about last night."

"Last night," she murmured against his chest, "was absolutely wonderful." Emma glanced up, capturing his gaze. "It was perfect, Colton. You were perfect. I'm sorry I didn't have the chance to fully enjoy the Northern Lights. I was a little distracted by the gentle giant behind me." Colton's lips quirked into a crooked smile, and his gaze softened, letting Emma know that he had enjoyed it just as much as she had. But still, she wanted to hear him say the words. "Was it ok for you? Was I ok?"

Colton lowered his lips to hers and lightly brushed against them. "Emma, never has anyone pleased me more. I mean that in every aspect, not just in bed. You are a passionate, desirable, beautiful woman. You're talented and smart, and I'm so happy to have met you." He said this as his thumb brushed against her cheek, then to her lower lip. *And I love you.* Colton captured her lips in a lingering kiss.

Emma nestled herself closer. Tranquility capturing her, she drifted off to sleep in the strong arms of the man she had fallen in love with.

CHAPTER 29

*E*mma awoke to that delectable scent that was distinctly Colton. As she inhaled deeply, she was aware of the chill in the air, despite still being wrapped in his arms. She raised her head to discover that the fire had gone out. Thinking that she'd restart it, she began to rise when Colton stirred. "Don't go," he whispered.

"I'll just be a minute."

She turned to look back at him and knew the first thing she would do was grab her camera. He was propped up in the crook of the couch, shirt opened just enough to show his strong abs. His wavy locks fell to his shoulders and blended in with the midnight sofa. Emma retrieved the camera and took her first picture. "Gorgeous," she whispered. She took a few at different angles then zoomed in on his rippled center.

She lowered the camera to find his smoldering gaze locked on hers. The silent request was understood. She placed the camera on the ottoman. Colton sat up, and she lowered herself into his lap. Emma reached down, placing his beautiful face firmly in her hands, then lowered her lips to his. Colton's palm lightly brushed against her breast. "Let's get this off," he whispered.

Emma leaned back, pulling the sweater up and over her head. Her hair fanned out around her shoulders, then swept the swells of her breasts which nearly spilled from the lacy bra. His hands fell on them immediately. Caressing them, he closed the gap of her cleavage, which elicited cries of delight from Emma. She reached between her legs, her hand falling on him. She smiled. It was evident that he was as excited as she was. Colton unfastened her bra, tossing it to the side before capturing her nipple in his mouth. Emma's moans filled the silence, as did the clock that chimed five times. Colton groaned. "I'm sorry, luv. It's later than I realized, and the ride to town is lengthy. We have to postpone this just for now. I need to shower, but first, I'll show you what I want you to wear for the surprise."

"You're too good to me," Emma said as she leaned in for a kiss, not wanting this moment to end.

"And you can show me your appreciation later, but for now, let me show you your gown."

Gown? Where are we going?

Colton led Emma upstairs to the other bedroom. As she entered, she noticed a royal blue gown laid across the bed. Silver strappy high heels lay beside it. "It's beautiful," Emma whispered. She crossed the distance to the bed and gathered the dress in her arms. Walking to the full length mirror, she held it against her body as she admired the beautiful deep hue.

"You like it?" Colton asked, watching from behind. She nodded her head, and he leaned forward kissing and gently nipping the space between her shoulder and neck. "I'll be out soon." He disappeared into the bathroom.

"I'll call you when I'm ready. Don't come in here before I tell you, though," she snapped out the mock order.

"Yes, Ma'am," she heard him chuckle.

Emma styled her hair in an elegant up-do. With her make-up finished, she slid into the gown and strappy sandals. Once again, she was in front of the mirror. She twisted from side to side admiring the beautiful dress that, admittedly, looked striking on her. It sat off the shoulders and had a sterling silver oval that gathered the material to one side of her waist. She thought its intricate design accented her shoes perfectly and looked gorgeous. The long, flowing skirt had a slit up the side. Emma felt like a beautiful princess. She didn't know where they were going, and she didn't care. As long as Colton was by her side, that was the only detail she needed.

When she turned away from the mirror, she was ambushed by flashes of light. Colton had found her camera and had captured the moment. He looked so handsome and debonair in his black tux.

"You look absolutely stunning, Emma," he said as he gathered her in his arms and lowered his head to kiss her.

"Uh-uh," she protested. "You'll mess up my makeup. But on the way home, anything goes."

"Anything, luv?" He asked as he kissed her neck.

"Seriously, Colton. If you plan on leaving this cabin, we need to leave this conversation right where it is."

He laughed heartily. He loved her delightful sense of humor, especially when she was trying to hamper her needs.

Emma placed the camera on the dressing table and set the timer so they could get some photographs together.

From the upstairs window, she saw a limousine pull in front of the cabin. She looked at him questioningly.

"I think it only appropriate for us to show up to the opera in style," Colton replied.

"Limos, the opera. Where have you been all my life!" Emma reached forward to stroke his cheek, and he turned to place a tender kiss on her wrist.

"Ready to go, luv?" He asked as he led her to the stairs.

Once inside the limo, the conversation turned to Cat when Colton complimented Emma's new purse. She explained that she had gathered a "want pile" on their last shopping trip and that Cat had purchased every item for her.

"Her business is doing well, I take it."

"Yes, her business is thriving. She may have come to own it in an unconventional way, but she's worked hard to make it what it is."

Colton pondered that statement for a moment. "How did she come about owning it?"

"When she was married to Martin-"

"Cat's been married?" Colton interrupted.

"Yes, she was married and hopelessly in love. One night she came home early and found him in bed with someone. Remember Shelly Arnold from the printers?" When he nodded that he remembered, she continued. "Well, Cat caught them in bed together but was quick to keep her cool, slipping out before he knew what she had witnessed. Cat came to my old house, and she was devastated. But instead of planning to kill him or trying to make it work, she set a devious plan in motion to milk him of every dime he had. He wanted to have Cat and cheat on her, too. She made his life miserable. The only time she would make things harmonious at home is when he went along with her latest idea. She told him about her dream of owning a tattoo shop. Making her happy meant easy times for him, so he funded Inked. After a while, she said she might be getting bored with that business and thought that real estate property might satisfy her. So the 'rental' that she bought was twice as nice as the home that they owned. By the time he realized that she knew about his cheating ways, he knew he had lost her. He tried anything he could to change her mind. He gave her sole ownership of the businesses and the rental in a last ditch effort to get her to stay, which played into her plan perfectly. After the way he hurt her, she was never the same. And so, the 'love 'em and leave 'em' mentality was born. When I told you that Martin Sanchez was a sleazeball, I was speaking from personal experience. He treated her like a porcelain doll, sitting her on the shelf and taking her down only when he wanted to play with her. The problem was, he had a vast doll collection! But she got the last laugh. Her business is thriving, and he's basically penniless, working at the historical society." Emma laughed at his misfortune.

That's quite a story. "Do you think she still has feelings for him?"

"I don't think so. You can't rebound from a hurt like that. But I know he still loves her. She finally became the 'whore he always wanted,' and now she won't look his way. Sweet, sweet justice!"

Colton knew that Cat was Emma's best friend, so he was shocked to hear her be so crass. "That's harsh."

"I say that only because those were her parting words to him. 'Congratulations! I've finally became the whore you've always wanted, Martino. But never again for you . . . ' She left him groveling on his knees and never looked back. Those final months of the charade hardened her heart toward him and relationships, in general. She said that being faithful got her nowhere, so she'd try having fun. I hope you don't change your thoughts about her, Colton. She's really a good person. She's just 'good' to a lot more people, now." They both chuckled. "I get the feeling that she and Kane would make a good pair."

"Why do you say that?" Colton asked.

"Just a hunch, really."

"Kane," he said in an exasperated tone, "is someone that I tolerate solely because he's my sibling. He's a fierce businessman, but a lousy brother. He's always wanted what I have, and at times, has been successful in taking those things away."

"Why do I get the feeling you're not talking about business anymore?" Emma frowned.

"Because I'm not. I dated a woman several years ago. I thought we had something. And we did. We had my manipulating brother in the relationship with us, but only two of us were aware. Finally, my secretary, Eleanor, took pity and told me what was happening. I caught them together, and it was over. I didn't have to see her anymore. But, of course, I didn't have the same luxury with Kane. That's why when he was talking to you like he was today, it made my blood boil. I know him, Emma. When he heard your voice, he began looking at his next conquest."

"Colton, I promise you that no one will turn my attention away from you. Kane could never compare to you, I know this without even meeting him."

"Let's change the subject. My brother is *never* a topic that I like to discuss. Have you ever been to the opera before?"

"I haven't. But before yesterday, I wasn't accustomed to riding in limos, either." Emma quirked a smile looking around. "But it's looking pretty roomy for the ride home."

He laughed at her innuendo.

Once they were seated, Emma looked around at all the beautiful people. Everyone was dressed impeccably. *I'm so glad he laid out clothes for me. I would've been at the opera in my jeans and sweater thinking that I looked good. I have so much to learn!*

Colton studied her expression. "What has you amused, luv?"

"Oh, I was just thinking that I wished I was dressed a little more appropriately, like I was on my last date before I met you." When he looked bewildered, she motioned to her dress. "Hey, this wouldn't have worked at all for all you can eat ribs. You gotta look nice at a place like that!"

Colton chuckled. "Emma, you are the funniest person that I've ever met," he said as he pulled her close and kissed her cheek.

The house lights dimmed and voices turned to a whisper. It didn't take Emma long to discover that she was a fan of the opera. She liked the drama, the music, and the clothes. She noticed something during the end of the first act. It was Colton, and he was watching her. "Why are you watching me instead of the show?" Emma asked with blushed cheeks.

"Just seeing if you were enjoying yourself, luv."

"I like it. I don't understand some of it, but I like it. I like Carmen."

Waiting for the car after the show ended, Emma thought about the performance. "Did Carmen remind you of anyone we know?" When Colton nodded his head and smiled, she continued. "Cat could easily be a gypsy."

Once the car was in route to the cabin, Colton pulled a

chilled bottle of champagne from the chest. He poured each of them a glass and proposed a toast. "To tonight . . . May it mean as much to you as it will to me."

Emma raised her glass but had no idea what he was talking about.

"May I kiss you now, Emma? I couldn't smudge your makeup before, but-"

Before he could finish his question, she tossed back her champagne then lowered both their glasses to the floor. She wove her fingers through the lapels of his jacket, pulling him closer until her lips met his.

Colton responded by leading her down against the seat then gave her a gentle reminder as he kissed the delicate column of her neck. "I feel the need to refresh your memory, Emma. You said, 'anything goes,' when we talked about the ride back home." While he dropped broken kisses from her neck to her lips, he dipped his hand through the slit in her skirt, finding the lacy fabric beneath. "Well, the first thing I want to go are these panties."

Emma's eyes shot open, and she glanced toward the driver, thankful that the privacy window was up. "Anything goes," she echoed, pushing him away slightly so she could raise her hips in the air.

Colton slipped his fingers around the thin fabric and slowly pulled them down her legs. Lying beside her, his hand went up her dress once again, only this time, there was nothing there to prevent his touch. He pressed his finger to her entrance and let out a groan when he found her wet.

"Do you have protection?"

Without answering, Colton produced a shiny wrapper. And the night at the opera ended with a long, blissful ride back to the cabin.

CHAPTER 30

*B*ack at the cabin, they went upstairs to change into comfortable clothes. Emma lowered herself to the bed, removing her strappy sandals. She wiggled her toes and leaned down to caress her sore feet. The shoes were beautiful to look at, but brutal to wear. A tradeoff for looking fashionable, she thought. Movement redirected her attention. Looking up, she smiled when Colton appeared in the doorway. He wore black cotton pants and a white t-shirt. She decided he looked nice in white shirts, especially that one that hugged every muscle he had.

"Meet me downstairs when you've finished changing," he said with a wink.

Emma smiled. "I won't be long."

Colton disappeared into the dimly lit hallway while she crossed to the mirror, taking one last look at her dress. She truly felt like a princess tonight.

Finding her bag, Emma dug through it until she found what she wanted to wear. Even though she hated to take off her beautiful gown, she knew her apricot colored velour pants would feel much better. She paired those with a white spaghetti strap tank top. Emma thought her casual clothing looked cute with her elegant hair.

When she entered the great room, she saw that Colton had champagne chilling in a glass container filled with ice. The green bottle looked similar to the one they left in the limo. There were also two champagne flutes and two wrapped boxes spread out in front of the fire. As she walked closer, Emma noticed the sizes of the shiny red boxes. One was a large square, the other small. She wondered what could be in them.

"Champagne?" he asked.

She nodded her head. "What are these?" Emma asked as he took her hand and led her to the floor.

"One's for now and the other is for later. Maybe."

Maybe? "No way are you showing me a gift and not giving it to me, Buck-o!" Emma propped her hand on her hip and arched an eyebrow.

"Buck-o? I call you luv and you call me, Buck-o?" Colton grinned his crooked smile.

"I also call you Colt, *or so you say.*"

"That's true, luv. And I'd much rather be called Colt than Buck-o," he chuckled.

"Nevertheless, I'm getting that gift, *Colt.*"

He leaned forward and kissed her.

"I want you to open this one first," Colton said, handing her the large box.

Emma sat cross legged, placing the gift in her lap. "It's heavy." When she opened the box and looked inside, she saw a bowl full of plump strawberries. Some were covered with drizzles of white chocolate, some were not. "I love strawberries." She reached inside, pulling the container out. "And this bowl is gorgeous."

"Oh, it's not a bowl, Emma. It's a *wine glass*." Colton's lips quirked up into a smile.

When realization struck her, she looked at him bewildered. "You went back and got it? Is this the same one?"

"Oh, it is indeed, Miss Saint-Claire. This is the beautiful wine goblet that Michael and Tim were crafting on the first day I met you, the one that turned into a bowl on a pedestal."

Emma swatted at his arm. "I was trying to impress you because you found glassblowing so interesting. I pass those windows everyday, and I wanted you to think I was smart and interesting. How was I supposed to know that the glass would keep getting bigger and bigger?" she laughed. "I tried to tear you away from the window numerous times when it was apparent that the wine glass was *not*, but you wouldn't budge." Emma threw her hands up, remembering her dilemma.

"That's because I've seen the art enough to know the difference. I also wanted to see how you'd handle it when your goblet became a bowl." Colton reached for a juicy berry, pressing it to her mouth. When she bit down on it and a drop of juice ran down her lip, he leaned forward, kissing away the spill.

"I'm so happy you went back for this," Emma said, pointing to the bowl. "It really means more to me than you'll ever know."

Colton sat with his back resting against the ottoman, Emma between his open legs, leaning back on him. They watched the dancing flames and talked. It just felt right; they felt right.

"Emma, have you ever been in love?" The glowing embers of the fire reflected off the unopened box prompting his question.

"I think you need to date someone before you can fall in

love. We've established that I didn't really date before you. What about you?"

Colton hesitated for a moment before he answered. "Unequivocally."

"Tell me about her," Emma said before silently berating herself. *What the hell is wrong with me? I don't want to hear about him loving someone else. Any other stupid things you want to say, Emma?*

"Where do I begin? I hadn't known her long before we were involved. She certainly intrigued me, though. We spent as much time as we could together. She was beautiful, smart, talented, funny, passionate - very passionate," he added as he pulled Emma closer and kissed her neck.

She felt a stab of jealousy.

"And I found myself wanting to spend the rest of my life with her."

She sounds hideous! "She sounds wonderful . . . and like someone I could never compete with," Emma whispered. She closed her eyes and laid her head back against his chest, defeated. "How old were you when you fell in love?"

"Thirty-five."

Her eyes shot open, but she didn't turn. "You're thirty-five now."

Wrapping his arms tightly around her, Colton murmured in her ear, "Yes, Emma. I'm thirty-five now, and this lady that you could never compete with, as you put it, is you. I love *you*, Emma."

She turned to face him, not quite knowing how to process the information.

"Emma," Colton said as he stroked her cheek, "I know that this comes as a surprise to you, and I don't expect you to say it back. I can't explain it. I've tried to make sense out of how I could fall in love with someone so quickly. And I guess

311

I'm just going to have to understand that sometimes, you just know. This I know. I love you, Emma."

Emma came up on her knees in front of him and captured his face with her hands. As the tears rolled down her cheeks, she leaned down to kiss him – gently at first, but then passionately. Again and again, she brushed delicate kisses on his lips. Silently, she climbed into his lap and collapsed against his chest. "I've been struggling with how *you* make *me* feel. I've never been in love. Not even close, Colton. So I couldn't make my mind make sense of these feelings that I have for you. It seemed too rushed, but it felt right . . . feels right. I won't try to understand it anymore." Emma raised her head to capture his gaze. "I love you, too. So very much." Another tear spiraled down her cheek. When his smile mirrored her own, she kissed him again.

They had found themselves sitting this way many times before. But tonight their only intent was to press their hearts close enough for the other to feel - to feel the promise of a new love dawning. "You don't know how happy this makes me, Emma, to know that you share the same feelings." Colton pulled her close and kissed her. "I have another gift for you, but first I'd like to tell you the story behind it." She gave him a questioning glance. "You open it while I explain."

Emma sat beside him and tore the paper off the box. As she lifted the lid, her heart beat indentions into her ribs. Even though the box was larger than it needed to be to occupy such a tiny token, she knew what she would find - it would be a ring. They had pledged their love for one another, it was the natural progression. *Leather?* "What are they?" she asked, pulling two braided leather bands from the box.

"Do you have traditions in your family, Emma?"

"No, not really. Is this a tradition that you have in your family?" she asked as she held the bands in her hand. *Is your tradition to confuse the hell out of the woman you're proposing to?*

"Yes, this is a tradition that was passed down from my great-grandfather, Samuel. When he fell in love with my grandmother, Elizabeth, he didn't have money to buy a ring for her. He worked in a leather shop and wove together two identical bands. She wore one on her wrist and he wore the other on his. It was his pledge to her that they would be married one day. They vowed to never take them off until they were ready to marry or unless their intent changed. So Emma, this is my vow to you. I love you, and my intent is to marry you someday when you're ready. If you accept. No one has to know what they mean, unless you tell them." He placed his hand on top of hers.

Emma took a moment for the information to sink in. She looked at Colton and her eyes went teary when she saw the pleading in his eyes. "Yes. I say yes." Placing one band in his hand, she tied the other to his wrist.

Colton tied the bracelet to her left wrist as a means of masking the scars that monster had given her. "Emma, I'm placing this here so you'll be happy when you look at your wrist. I'll spend forever erasing what he did to you. I love you," he said as he gently tugged her chin and pulled her to him in a tender kiss. "I love you."

"I love you, too, Colt."

Colton drew her to his chest again and whispered in her ear. "That's the second time you've said those words to me."

Emma raised her head to think about it. "I thought I was dreaming. Did I say, 'I love you,' the night of the bonfire?"

"You did and I told you that I loved you. But you were asleep and didn't hear me. I've told you so many times in my head, but I was afraid to say it out loud."

"Say it again," she whispered.

He smiled. "I love you." Colton's arms tightened around her. "And I'll spend the rest of my life showing you how much."

Emma rose. "Dance with me," she offered, extending her hand to him.

Colton stood and drew her close. Silence filling the air, they swayed to the ticking of the clock and the cracking embers of the fire. Emma looked up as the firelight captured the features of his handsome face. She stroked his cheek. His profession of love, his perfect scent, and the feel of his strong arms rocking her in time fueled her desire. She drew his face closer to hers, placing a firm kiss on his lips. He responded eagerly pulling her closer to his body. Colton's hands slid down beneath her bottom and he lifted until he had her legs wrapped around his waist.

The passion that flowed between their kiss was unmistakable. "Now that you have me, what are you going to do with me?" Emma asked, breaking away from his crushing kiss.

"I'll show you." Colton walked toward the staircase. She placed tender kisses to his neck as he carried her. When she sucked his earlobe between her lips, lightly running her tongue across it, he groaned. "Emma, unless you want me to take you right here on the stairs, I really need you to stop that . . . just for a minute, luv."

She, of course, continued.

Colton carried her to the bedroom, lit only by the soft glow of the fireplace. He set her on her feet and she caught a devilish glint in his eyes. "You don't play nice," he said as he turned her in his arms until her back was to him. He swayed his hips, moving hers in a sensual rhythm from side to side, one hand on her hip. With the other, he lowered the thin strap of her top and ran his lips along her shoulder then to her neck.

Emma attempted to drop her hips back, but he put space between them, causing her to protest.

"Maybe I don't play nice, either," he whispered in her ear, tugging the lobe between his lips.

Emma's head fell back against his chest. Colton's hands slowly crept up her sides then trailed ever so lightly across her breasts. She thrust them forward, inviting further touch. Colton lowered his head to brush a lingering kiss on her neck. Chills raced down her arms at his touch. He lifted his hips, pressing their bodies together again. The corners of his mouth turned up into a grin when she called his name, pleading for more. He hooked his thumbs in the band of her soft pants and slowly tugged them past her hips, the slinky material sliding the rest of the way down on their own. Emma kicked them aside.

Colton held her against his chest, his hands easily exploring her body. She turned her head breathlessly when he tugged at her hardened nipples. He lowered the other strap, dropping her shirt enough so that her breasts spilled out. Slipping one hand lower, he slid his fingers downward and let out a groan when he found that her arousal matched his own. He took great pleasure from her slow torture, dipping his finger in and out, again and again. He caressed her until he was capturing her moans in his mouth.

Emma reached behind, stroking him through his pants. "Take them off," he instructed. She happily did as she was told. Kneeling before him, she tugged his pants and underwear down his muscular legs, slowly. He watched through eyes burning with desire when she didn't rise. As she took him in her hands, he groaned loudly. Throwing his head back, he closed his eyes, appreciating the feel of her soft hands as they moved around him. "Oh, fuck," the soft curse fell from his lips the moment her moist breath fell against his skin. Colton slid his hand around her cheek, the other resting lightly on the back of her head. "I don't think I can handle much more of that tonight, luv," he said, pulling her to her feet. As she searched his face, wondering if she had done something wrong, he whispered, "I want to make love to you, Emma. I'm slowing the pace because you deserve better than I've given you so far."

With a trail of clothing littering the path and an empty foil wrapper on the floor, he lowered her to the bed. Colton eased himself on top of her and kissed her gently. "I love you, Emma."

She broke away from his kiss. "I love you, too, Colton. I love you so much."

Sliding inside her, he silenced her profession. Their moans of pleasure mingled as he found the rhythm that she liked. As the feelings of ecstasy overtook her, Emma was aware of everything - their interlaced fingers, his leather bracelet pressed firmly on hers, the weight of his body pressing her into the mattress, and the feel of his lips stroking against her own. Tonight's love making was slow and steady, because that's what it was . . . making love. Their bodies had been entwined many times before, but it wasn't until now that Emma felt as if their souls were linked as well. As their orgasms ripped through them, they both whispered, "I love you."

CHAPTER 31

"*Roses are red*
            Violets are blue
I'm a whore
And so are you . . ."

Cat looked down at the poem she had written for Emma and giggled. Then she promptly wadded it up, shoving it into her purse. *No roses.* Even though she thought it was funny, she quickly realized the memories it would likely stir up.

She looked at her watch then drummed her fingers on the table. Keeping with tradition, Cat sat in their usual booth at the diner for their standing, Monday, lunch date. And also keeping with tradition, Emma was late.

Cat thought of the vague texts she'd received over the weekend. She couldn't wait to hear the details of the trip. It was crazy, but *she* had butterflies in *her* stomach. And the longer she waited, the more they multiplied.

A lot had changed for her cousin in the last year - some really good things like meeting Colton Graves - and some indescribably bad. The death of their grandparents had sent Emma's life into a tailspin and in a plight to escape that pain, she had moved hundreds of miles away, and directly into harm's way.

Cat's thoughts trailed back to the stack of photos that Lisa had. Even though Hayden was a police Sergeant, he couldn't arrest the man who simply appeared in pictures. No crime had been committed. But if the stranger in the background of those photos was the man from Louisville, Emma wasn't safe. Maybe it was him, but there was an even greater likelihood that it was not. For now, the only man she needed consuming her thoughts was Colton. So for now, no one would mention the mystery man.

The dinging of the door drew Cat's attention to the beautiful brunette entering the Diner. She wore a coral colored top that she paired with distressed jeans. Her boots matched the brown leather bag slung over her right shoulder.

Emma strolled toward her cousin with a megawatt smile. Cat slid out of the booth and within seconds, the two were hugging like it had been years since they'd seen each other, rather than days.

"Look at that smile," Cat said, holding Emma at arms' length. "You look good, babe. And we have lots of catching up to do."

They had barely gotten settled into the booth before the curly haired waitress popped to their side.

"Girls, I was about to put your faces on a milk carton!

Where have you been?" In usual Bonny style, she didn't give them the chance to answer before she continued. "I've missed seeing you two and Sal has missed preparing your specials for you. Right Sal?" she called over her shoulder. They looked to the kitchen and saw him give a spatula wave. "So, what'll it be?"

Bonny seamlessly blended nonstop chatter with her specials of the day. She seemed truly happy to see them. They didn't feel like they were seeing much of each other lately, either. Tucking a loose curl behind her ear, she continued jotting down the order. Emma had always been envious of Bonny's perfect blonde hair that looked good no matter how she styled it.

When she turned to leave, the girls drew their heads closer together.

"Sooo, tell me about Canada and your super stud," Cat encouraged.

Emma's hazel eyes lit up. "Gosh, where do I begin? We went to Lé Marguerite, Quebec."

"Sounds fancy."

"It wasn't. And that's what made it absolutely perfect. It was gorgeous, though, with snow as far as the eye could see. I saw some kids' sleigh riding on a hillside and thought about the times you and I did that."

Cat smiled, remembering.

"We stayed in a rustic little cabin and went for a horse drawn sleigh ride. I saw the Northern Lights for the first time. I went horseback riding – which was *not* planned. I took some great pictures that I can't wait to show you." Emma patted her bag containing her camera. "We went to the Opera . . . It was a wonderful time."

"*You had a little sex . . .*" Cat urged her to continue.

"No, we had *a lot* of sex," Emma interjected enthusiastically then laughed. "And this is the part that you're gonna freak over." Cat looked skeptically at her ring finger. "He told me he loved me, and I told him I loved him, too."

Cat sat back, appraising her cousin. "Well, you may be surprised to know that I saw *that* coming days ago!" Cat smiled at her correct intuition.

"Well, you probably didn't see this coming, Alley Cat. He said he wants to marry me someday, and I agreed."

Cat dropped her head several inches and gave Emma a blank stare. "Just one question, Emmabear. You do know that bucket lists don't have to be completed in the course of a weekend. Correct? You're supposed to leisurely check them off one by one. Not with an ink stamp slammed down over the whole page boldly proclaiming, '*Done!*'"

"I know." A sheepish grin spread across Emma's face. "He just planned this amazing weekend for us. Could you imagine listening to that accent everyday for the rest of your life, Cat? I can't wait to start. I feel like a school girl who's totally smitten and like a grown woman, at the same time, who has fallen completely in love with him." Emma let out a content sigh as her head dropped back against the booth.

Cat caught sight of the leather band. "Cute bracelet, by the way."

"Thanks." Emma lazily spun it around her wrist. "It looks simple, but has a *big* meaning."

Cat couldn't wait to hear the story.

"First, I-"

"Here's your food, girls." Bonny sat a platter in front of each of them then sat another to the right of Emma. "Sal knew I was happy to have you back, so he let me have a little break, too. So scoot yourself over, Emma, and let's catch up." The cousins shot amused glances toward each other over her bad timing. *They* were just catching up on Saint Emma's amazing weekend. But that would have to wait. "So Cat, you and Hayden, huh? Could it be that the infamous Cat Morgan is settling down?"

"Yeah, I'm not really a 'forever' kind of girl, you know? But for now, he's pretty damn fine!"

The, "oh yeah!" and "uh huhs!" that rang out signified they were all in agreement.

Bonny turned her attention to Emma.

"And you, young lady. Where have you been?"

"Most recently?" Emma asked with a guilty grin, "Canada."

"And I'm guessing from the look on your face that you weren't alone. Would a certain Brit have accompanied you?" Bonny loved to hear about everyone's relationships. She had played the "Dear Abby" part for most everyone in town at some point.

"Yes. Colton and I went away for the weekend," Emma said as she twirled the bracelet on her wrist that rested in her lap.

"And what do we think about this Colton?" Bonny asked, gently nudging her shoulder.

Emma inhaled and exhaled as joy filled her heart and spilled out in the form of a genuine smile. "*We* think we like him . . . a whole lot."

Cat glanced toward her cousin, trying to suppress a grin.

"I'm glad to hear it, luv. I rather fancy you, too." Kneeling in the booth behind her, Colton darted his head between her and Bonny to kiss Emma on the cheek before moving around to the vacant seat.

Cat watched as they glanced across the table at each other noting how everyone else seemed to fade from their awareness. She could clearly see the love dance between their gazes and noticed how the smile played across their lips when he reached for Emma's hand. As if there had been any question before, she knew for sure that Emma had fallen hard for Colton Graves and he for her.

"Would it be too much of an intrusion if I joined you ladies for lunch?" He questioned before grabbing a fry off Emma's plate. Of course everyone welcomed him.

Bonny checked her watch. "Ok, kids. Looks like my break's over." She pouted. "Those ten minutes sure passed fast." Directing her attention at Colton, she continued. "Next time, I'll find out more about you."

With Bonny back to work, Colton moved to sit beside Emma. She gladly welcomed him with a hug then spooned in her first mouthful of chocolate milkshake. "Mmm. That was so worth the wait!" The Diner was known for their thick milkshakes topped with several inches of whipped cream.

"Em, you got something right here," Cat said as she tapped the corner of her own mouth.

Colton turned Emma's face toward him, rubbing his thumb across the smidgen of whipped cream. When he brought his thumb to his own mouth, his leather band caught Cat's eye.

"Anyone care to explain to me what these matching bracelets symbolize?"

Emma smiled. "That's what I was about to tell you before Bonny decided to have lunch with us." She looked at Colton who seemed to be beaming from ear to ear that Emma had chose to share their news.

"Would you allow me to tell her?" Colton asked. When Emma nodded, he began the story about his Grandparents. He explained that his grandfather was quite poor and didn't have anything to give his Grandmother except that that he could make with his own hands. He explained how the tradition had passed down through his family, despite their wealth. "I love this beautiful lady," he said as he gently tugged her chin and lifted her lips to meet his own. "And I'll spend my life buying her expensive things, but I wanted to give her a gift that was from my heart for the very first one."

"Actually, these were the second gift," Emma chided jokingly.

"That's true, luv. The first gift was the 'wine glass.'"

"A single wine glass?" Cat questioned.

They told her the story of the beautiful bowl on a pedestal. Cat looked at them in disbelief. "That is so romantic. I mean, the bracelets are too, don't get me wrong, but the fact that you went back and bought the bowl is great. I'm so happy for you two. Do you have a brother?" She asked, knowing the answer already. *Hayden's such an ass. He never does anything romantic!*

Emma shot Colton an anguished glance and he quipped, "Indeed I do. But you'd do well to stay far away from the likes of Kane."

"Oh, Colton! Of all the things you could have said to my free loving, bad boy seeking friend, that's the worst. Now he's on her radar!" Emma and Cat laughed, but Colton remained silent.

When they'd finished eating, Emma said she had to get back to work. Cat was happy that Colton would accompany her. She watched as they walked hip to hip, arms wrapped around each other. As they faded into the distance, her smile did as well. She called Hayden and Lisa and they came to join her.

～

"Cat, I've had officers looking for this creep all weekend,"

Hayden said as he studied the picture. "He's simply gone. The Chief won't allow any more resources to be spent since not a single officer has seen him. He thinks that I'm overreacting and is chalking this up to an isolated incident. If this mystery man doesn't show up soon, and for Emma's sake, I hope he doesn't, the department can't help look for him." He could tell that she wasn't happy with his answer. He continued, "*I've* not seen him, have you all?" They both shook their heads. "Then it could just be a coincidence and even if it isn't, we really don't have much to go on besides his coat, hat, and sunglasses. He's African American. That's the only given in this equation. I'm sorry, Cat," he said, reaching for her hand. "It's just not much to go on. I'm glad we didn't scare Emma by telling her. The Chief did say that if he does turn up, we'll question him. That's the best I can do."

Cat left in a huff, Lisa waited for Bryce to show up for lunch, and Hayden went back to work wondering why *he* had suddenly become the bad guy in his girlfriend's eyes.

Derrick arrived at work. He planned to make today no different than any other day - completely snow the fools in his life. The first person he'd have to deal with was his much too chipper assistant of three years, Jillian Walters.

"Oh, good morning, Dr. Wells," the receptionist called out excitedly when he stepped off the elevator. "I didn't know to expect you back today, so all your appointments have been moved."

"Thank you, Jill," Derrick delivered a syrupy smile. "Grandfather seemed to be having a good day today, so I thought I'd come in. You know I *always* have plenty of paperwork to catch up on, so I welcome the reprieve." Jill laughed because she knew how much Dr. Wells hated to do paper-work and always had a stack on his desk.

"I passed your message along to your clients about your Grandfather. They were all so sad that they couldn't see you last week. Mrs. Collins even brought you some danishes today hoping that you'd stop by the office."

"That was very kind of her. Unless my family calls again with more bad news, I guess I'll plan to see clients all week. I know how much they need their therapy sessions, and it just brings happiness to me to be able to help them. Alright Jillian, I'm off to make a dent in Mount Saint-paper stack."

She chuckled at his joke as she watched him disappear through his office doors. *"He's such a kind man and so caring for his clients,"* Jill said to herself.

Derrick tossed his briefcase in the leather high-back chair followed by his trench coat. *"Idiot!"* He said to himself as he strolled to look out the rain soaked window. "She's a fool and so are those nut jobs that I pretend to care about. I knew that by her passing along my message about 'poor grandfather,' I'd garner sympathy and that my missed appointments would go unreported."

Derrick thought back over his past week. It started when he saw the article about Amanda. A sinister pull tugged at his lips. *But, of course, I know now that that's not her real name.* He thought back to when he saw Emma in Brookfield, Kentucky. *She's so smug walking around without a care in the world. Soon she'll realize what fear truly is . . .*

Looking out into the rapidly filling parking lot, he watched the people who were piling out of their cars. A tall redhead caught his attention. *She looks like Jaz.* An emptiness settled into his soul when he remembered the day that

Jazmine had found out about his affair. He recalled the hurt in her eyes. All his pleading hadn't helped and she'd asked him to leave. It was one thing to leave her, but to leave his kids was asking too much. In the months following the discovery, he thought he was making headway with her and insinuating himself back in their lives. *Then Amanda Taylor blew everything all to hell! Her article ruined my life. Why the hell was Jaz reading that nonsense anyway?*

His attention was drawn to a rain drop that slid down the window in front of him. *Like tears. They fall down like tears. And Amanda, your tears are going to rival these.* He traced abundant streams of raindrops down the window. *You'll watch your family move on and forget you like I've watched mine, but not before your blood is shed, you bitch!* The stinging in his palms drew his attention to his hands and he realized he'd clenched his fists so tight, that his nails had pierced his skin. *That's another lick you'll take, Amanda. You've caused me too much pain.*

Jill interrupted his thoughts with the intercom. "Dr. Wells, Jazmine is on line one."

The smile dropped from his lips. *Much too much pain, Amanda . . .*

CHAPTER 32

*C*olton went out for an early morning run in the park, and against her better judgment, Emma went with him.

"Come on, Emma, keep up," he joked as he raced ahead.

"*Why* are we doing this, again?" she protested.

He looked back over his shoulder. "Because luv, it's good for us."

Lagging behind and stopping for a break, she rested her hands on her knees while catching her breath. A weak laugh spilled from her lips. "This thing between us, I don't think it's gonna work out. You love exercise, and I love to eat. And sleep! *Why* are we here so early?" she groaned.

Colton walked back to join her, shaking his head the whole way.

"I mean, you *know* I'm just gonna undo all this healthiness later when I have a meal of my choosing."

Colton chuckled. "Tell you what. If we walk the rest of

the trail and I give you a checkpoint kiss every time we reach a quarter mile, will that make it work for us?" He dipped his head. Just as she thought he'd kiss her lips, he gave her a peck on the cheek, instead.

"Hey!" Emma protested but continued with her speech. "Yes, if we walk the trail, we *might* work this out." He hugged her and kissed her nose. "That's still not a proper kiss, you know," she urged.

"We've still not walked a proper distance, you know," Colton reminded with that accent she loved. She gave him an incredulous grin, but fell in step beside him.

As they continued on, Emma took in the scene that nature had painted for them on this gorgeous autumn morning. She looked around at the beautiful trees that framed their running trail - the foliage was vibrant and thick despite the impending winter. An overnight rain caused fog to roll deep and was lifting off the trail by day break. She glanced up the hill toward Park River Road and noted that she could barely see the passing cars through the veil of fog. *I really do like coming to the park, just on my own terms . . .*

A kiss fell hard on her lips and she realized that she'd gotten to her first checkpoint and had received her first reward. The smile that crossed her lips made Colton know that she had a devious idea.

So, it was no surprise to him as she ran ahead. Colton knew that she was trying to reach the next checkpoint faster. Anticipation fueled her stride when she heard the footsteps coming up behind her as she passed the green marker without stopping. Strong arms grabbed her around the waist and hauled her off her feet before tackling her, gently, to the leaf cushioned ground. Emma let out a shriek of delight, but

Colton silenced her by placing a hungry kiss on her lips as he pressed his weight down on her.

"I've been waiting for you to pull a stunt like that," he said, kissing her again.

"I told you I didn't want to exercise to begin with! I would've gladly broken the rules upfront to receive this wonderful punishment." Emma captured his lips with her own. Breaking away, she added, "It's a good thing I love you."

"And why's that?" Colton asked, lowering his focus to trail kisses along her neck.

"Because I wouldn't take kindly to a gorgeous brute wrestling me to the ground. But then again, on second thought . . ."

"I love you, too, Emma, but I'd better be the only brute wrestling you to the ground." He chuckled as he pushed himself off her, extending his hand.

Raised voices caught their attention. "That sounds like Miss Nancy," Emma whispered. Colton pulled her to her feet. As they walked closer, they were thankful for the recent rainfall that made the leaves not give away their approach. Emma peeked through the break in a thick shrub. She motioned for Colton to look. They spoke in hushed tones. "I was right," she whispered, "and that's Martin Sanchez with her."

Colton gave Emma a doubtful look. "*That's* Martin Sanchez?"

She nodded.

"When you called him a 'little weasel,' I was picturing someone who looked, well, a little more like Tank."

"When did you meet Tank?"

"Last week when you were at the school. I was walking in town and heard someone call his name. When he turned around and I caught a glimpse of him, I must admit that I was relieved that your 'betrothed' was, ummm, not as refined as me. I don't really know how to say it without sounding smug." Emma grinned at his tactfulness. "But Martin is not at all as I expected."

Martin is gorgeous, Emma thought, *until you get to know him!* To her, he would always be a weasel. The voices started again. Through the camouflage of the trees, they could see the two of them arguing on the park bench.

"Look, I'm tired of doing your bidding, Martin," Nancy barked. "I've turned down three renters this month. Don't you think they wonder why I have available rooms and not renting them once a tenant leaves? To me, that would seem suspicious."

"You'd do well to do as you're told," Martin reminded her. "I only need five more years of that heap of junk going unclaimed and that fortune is mine!" When Nancy cleared her throat, he corrected. "You know what I mean. You'll get a cut of it."

"Martin, what makes you so certain there *is* a fortune? I've been taking orders from you for years now with no proof. It was just advantageous to us that Mrs. Flannery died without a will, leaving me to live there with no objections from anyone. I've been slowly running the renters off ever since. No one questioned my authority – they just assumed that old Mrs. Flannery had willed it that way. It was going well until Natosha was at Dillingham Manor the day Emma asked for a room. I couldn't turn her down leaving her to ask questions. Natosha may just be a volunteer at the historical society, but she could turn stones we don't need disturbed. This is getting to be too much. The way I see it, I deserve a hefty reward for my service - if there even is a fortune!" Her demeaning tone made it clear that she was beginning to doubt the claim.

"The fortune is real. *But the way I see it*, you're in no position to place demands. Your ladies would love to get their hands on the juicy information about you and Oliver all those years ago," Martin taunted. "I was very lucky to be provided that tidbit from my grandfather. It was a genius move to supply me with that leverage. He knew exactly how to make this work. Of course, if you want your ladies group to find out . . ." he trailed off.

"Stop it, Martin, I'm an old woman. I'm starting to think that my time will come before that house is torn to shreds. Until then, in order to keep me quiet, I want to see it."

"See what?" He snapped.

"I want to see the letter from your grandfather."

"You will."

"Now! I want to see it now."

"Nancy, you know that it's locked up in my safety deposit box." He motioned around to the dawn that had just recently broke, "I can't get it for you now - the bank doesn't open for hours still."

Colton drew Emma close and whispered in her ear. "We can't leave until they do, even if this makes you late for work. But when we do leave, we need to pull in a favor from Cat. I want that letter."

Movement from the park bench refocused their attention. Showing a defiance that shocked Colton, Emma, and Martin, Nancy rose, giving one final ultimatum. "You will tell me what the letter says now, or we are finished."

Knowing that if Nancy walked, the chances of him ever getting his hands on the fortune were slim, he conceded temporary defeat and recalled his grandfather's letter that was passed to him with the shaking hands of a dying man. Martin began to tell Nancy what the letter said. He had read it enough to know it verbatim:

Martino,

I'm sorry I won't be here to watch you grow older and raise the children that you'll have some day. I won't be there to physically help you out, but I have a secret that I've been guarding for years that will help you, financially. Your father is too weak of a man to carry this out, but I think you and I are cut from the same cloth, Martino. I think you will find a way.

When my father was a young man, he had plans to marry Leah Dillingham. Her mother, Elizabeth, disapproved of the union because of his age. They had plans to runaway together. He wanted to give her the life she was accustomed to, but that took money – money that he didn't possess. Leah began stashing money and hid it her bedroom so they would be able to live comfortably and run away together someday. She told him that she had managed to squander over ten thousand dollars, gold bonds, and silver certificates from her parents.

Days before they planned to leave, she suffered a terrible fall when she was thrown from her horse. Her injuries were severe and she didn't survive the accident. The only people that knew about the amassed fortune were Leah and my father. He passed a letter on to me. Of course, I never had the opportunity to get into Dillingham Manor, so I am bestowing this unclaimed fortune on to you. It won't guarantee financial freedom, but it will help you get started.

Good luck, son. Make me proud.

Grandpa

"Did you know about Leah? Is this true?" Emma whispered.

"What he says is true. But, of course, none of us were aware of the hidden fortune.

According to her journals, my grandmother, Elizabeth, was so distraught after Leah's death, that her room was sealed shut. If the claim is true," Colton shrugged, "then it's plausible that the money's still there today."

Nancy seemed eager to leave and Martin seemed determined to make sure she didn't do anything stupid like try to claim the fortune for herself.

"Nancy, do I need to remind you that tearing up a house looking for a hidden treasure is quite noisy? We can't do that until all the renters are gone. I trust you will work on making that happen faster?" Martin felt like his plan was falling into place with an unclaimed fortune within his grasp. With Nancy appeased, they both left.

"Well that was an enlightening encounter," Colton quipped. "And they're fools if they think for one second that they're dismantling my house to find it. Oh, bloody hell," he said through seething teeth.

"What's wrong?" Emma asked.

"Kane. My sincere hope was that he'd lose interest. But now that this has come to light-"

"You don't have to tell him," Emma interrupted. She said this knowing that the gentleman before her would never stoop to that deceit.

"Emma, I can't do that." His crooked grin lit up his face.

"I know you can't. You're an honest man, and that's why I love you. Just presenting the possibilities." Emma gave him a sheepish grin. Colton leaned down, dropping a quick kiss to her lips. His longing gaze made her know that he loved her, too. She was happy that they had heard the contents of the supposed letter.

"So, when do you pick him up?" Emma asked.

"Kane? I'm not picking him up," Colton scoffed. "I told him he could take a cab just like I did when I arrived in town. I can promise you this. He won't take a cab and will show up in the flashiest car he can get his hands on. That's just his style. He arrives tonight and Miss Francine has a room waiting for him. I wanted to object, but how would that look – me not wanting my own brother here?"

"But she's always booked. That's what you could've said."

"That's what I *did* say. She overheard our conversation and interrupted, providing that she'd happily prepare a room for my brother. She knows I know about the extra room she always keeps in reserve." Colton let out an exasperated sigh. "It was bloody retched timing that she overheard that conversation."

With a renewed interest in their workout, Colton took a grumbling Emma by the hand, leading her back to the trail.

Since she was working late the next few days, Emma's work day started later than the usual eight o'clock. She and Colton went back to his place and discussed how and when he planned to take over Dillingham Manor. She told him that only four rooms were rented now and they belonged to two police officers, herself, and Nancy. "The officers can stay until I decide what we're doing with the house, but Nancy's out of there," Colton said.

"What about me?" Emma laughed.

"I'd like your time to be spent with me, if you agree." He tapped her chin, playfully.

"I do agree; I very much agree," Emma beamed as she kissed him. "But that still doesn't mean that I'm not gonna be happy when Nancy Reardon gets the boot!" She smiled.

Emma went to work with plans to meet Colton back at his place that night. Since the Canada trip, they had basically been inseparable and spent every night together. She loved waking up in his arms . . . and he made the going to sleep part enjoyable, too.

CHAPTER 33

Colton ended the call without turning to face her. "He'll arrive any moment now," he said as he let out an exasperated sigh while pulling his sweater down over his head. When Emma started to follow, he told her that he wanted to greet Kane alone. "I need him concentrating on what I'm saying, luv, not on you." He gave a wink and headed out the door.

Emma crossed the distance of his bedroom to the trio of windows that framed the wall. Pulling the curtains back, she glanced out into the night and watched as car lights wound up the road toward the Jacobson house. The butterflies in her stomach told her it was Kane. She inhaled and exhaled, trying to steady her nerves and not even understanding why his arrival was affecting her like it was. Sure, Colton had reason to dread his visit, but he was cool and collected. *I think it's the way he spoke on the phone to me. So alluring . . .* The chance conversation had been brief, but days later, it proved memorable.

The car snaked up the hill and into the drive, coming to a stop beside Colton's bike.

Just as he'd predicted, it was not a cab that dropped his brother off. When a carbon copy of Colton Graves stepped out of the silver, two door sports car, Emma exhaled the breath she didn't realize she'd been holding. Kane was dressed similar to Colton. Both wore dark pants, sweaters, and boots. Each had that wavy, black hair that fell to just above their shoulders and made them look more like movie stars than regular men. *"He looks just like Colton."* Emma watched as the brothers exchanged a handshake, and she wondered what they were discussing. She saw Colton shake his head then point toward the house. When Kane's gaze fell on her, she felt a knot in the pit of her stomach. A wide smile spread across his face as he lifted his hand to wave. Emma suddenly felt like prey with his gaze raking down her body, or at least that's how it seemed. *"What is wrong with me? I'm just overreacting,"* Emma said to herself as she waved back to him and smiled. Colton turned his attention to the window, and Emma felt the need to back away. He'd warned her about Kane, so she was probably accurate in her assessment of him. Still, she couldn't help but feel drawn to the site of them. *Beautiful specimens of towering perfection.* When Colton motioned for her to come down, she nodded her head in agreement and let the gauzy curtains fall shut behind her. Emma walked to the mirror and checked to see that she looked ok. She wore black from head to toe, which gave her an heir of elegance, she felt. She opted for slacks rather than the skirts that she preferred to wear around Colton. She was hoping to make this initial meeting with Kane as painless as possible for Colton and the showing of legs wasn't the way to go. She gave her hair a final toss and was pleased at the way it fell around her shoulders.

Emma exited the door onto the porch, and Colton extended

his hand to her as she descended the stairs. He hugged her to his side as they walked toward Kane. She watched as Kane took in the scene before him and hadn't failed to notice that Colton never once received a passing glance.

"Kane, this is Emma. Emma, this is Kane," Colton said as he made the proper introduction.

"Nice to meet you, Kane." Emma said as casually as she could. She tried to show no emotion as she extended her hand because the smile that spread across Kane's face was enough to cause Colton to come unglued, she was afraid.

Kane reached for her hand and brought it to his mouth, rather than shaking it. "Like wise," Kane rumbled across her hand, pressing a kiss to it. Emma noticed the way he gently squeezed it before reluctantly letting it drop. "As beautiful as your voice, and a cute accent, too."

A bad boy disguised a British gentleman. Emma thought to herself.

Clearing his throat, Colton broke up the awkward moment. "Kane has been traveling all day and not had the chance to eat. Would you like to go with us as we catch up?" Knowing that that's exactly what Colton wanted, she agreed. Kane slid his long legs into his car, and Emma and Colton walked toward his bike. Wanting to make her allegiance clear, Emma pulled Colton into a lingering kiss. As Kane's car roared to life, and he backed out, she was certain he had caught the moment.

Just in case he didn't, Emma thought, *I'll make sure now that his lights are shined on us that he does see it.* So she deepened the kiss.

"We can stay here, if you're feeling the need, luv." Colton joked as he held her tight.

"Just giving you a preview of dessert," Emma teased.

Colton and Kane spoke in hushed tones anytime someone was close enough to hear about their plans for Dillingham Manor. Kane seemed receptive and respectful and let Colton take the lead. *If they continue to act like this, they may get along just fine on his trip.* Emma thought. Colton excused himself to make a call, but Emma suspected it was to see how Kane acted when he thought no one was watching. To her surprise, she and her future brother-in-law got along fine in Colton's absence. Kane was on his best behavior with none of the awkwardness of their initial introduction. He politely asked her about her background. He wanted to know about her college studies, where she worked, what she drove, the size of her family . . . just normal 'getting to know you' stuff. She thought that maybe she had misjudged him, or at the very least, over judged him. As he talked, she thought he sounded so much like Colton. He even called her 'luv,' but she was quick to realize that he only did it in Colton's absence. She took in his features. He was so similar to Colton. She couldn't help but smile at that thought. Emma decided that the only discernible difference between he and Colton was that Kane had brown eyes, where Colton's were green.

Emma felt like Kane watched her wrist, and she wondered if he had caught sight of their bracelets. *He would know what they symbolize since it's their family's tradition.*

After making his calls, Colton returned in time to overhear Emma and Kane talking about the Festival.

"It truly is one of my favorite things about Brookfield. And it all begins tomorrow," Emma finished up.

Thinking ahead to some of the booths, she couldn't help but wonder what Kane's reaction to apple bobbing would be. She knew that Colton found it to be odd, but amusing.

Emma wondered where the similarities ended between the brothers. Physically, they were nearly carbon copies of each other. She found herself enjoying the sight.

When they had all finished eating, Emma and Colton went back to the Jacobson house while Kane went to purchase a few forgotten items for his stay.

~

"That wasn't so bad, was it?" Emma asked as they dressed for bed.

"No, he seems to be trying. I would say maybe I've been dreading his visit for nothing, but I know him, Emma."

Emma walked to the window and pulled the curtains open. Looking out at the stars, she pointed to the sky. "Colton, do you know any of the constellations?" she asked, urging him to change gears mentally. He crossed the distance of the room, the dim firelight illuminating the space. Emma smiled when his arms slid around her waist. "You always smell so good," she said, dropping her head back against his chest and inhaling deeply.

Colton untied her robe, tugged it down, and watched as it fell to the floor. He dropped his head to her exposed neck and ran open mouth kisses along her shoulder and collar bone. "See that cluster of stars right there?" he pointed, never looking up or slowing his pursuit. "That's the Big Dipper."

Colton gathered her hair off her neck and swung it over the other shoulder he had been trailing kisses down. "And see that cluster of stars there?" he said as he lowered the strap of her gown, "that's Orion's Belt." The shower of kisses continued.

"Oh, really?" Emma asked, amused.

VANISHED

"Absolutely," Colton proclaimed as he lowered the other strap of her gown.

"I only question, because you pointed to the same cluster of stars. I'm thinking that you aren't focused on the job at hand, Mr. Graves." Emma accused, jokingly.

"No, luv," Colton said as he turned her in his arms. "*You're* not focused on the job at hand. You promised me dessert when we got home and I'm collecting." He pulled her flush with his body then placed a demanding kiss upon her lips. As he let the gown slide down her body, he stepped back appreciating the perfect silhouette that was cast on the wall.

He stood there watching her, but not saying a word. "What are you doing?" Emma giggled as she asked the obvious question.

Colton extended his hand and pulled Emma toward the bed.

Kane grumbled to himself, stepping from the shadows of the driveway. *That was quite a show. Bloody shame big brother is on the other side of that window with the lovely Emma Saint-Claire, instead of me . . .*

341

CHAPTER 34

"I'm sorry, Hayden. You know that, right?" Cat whispered as she lay in his arms feeling his strong chest against her cheek.

"I know, angel, it's ok." He leaned down, placing a gentle kiss to the top of her head.

"I was just scared - scared for Emma. I know that you can't help it if the Chief won't agree to provide resources. And maybe we all *were* overreacting. I mean, I've not seen this guy at all. Hopefully he was just someone that was trying to get the nerve to ask her out. Can you imagine? Me getting the police involved because someone wanted to date my Emma?" They both chuckled. "She would've killed me!"

"No, I know you had reason to be concerned, Cat. But, I think it's nothing." *At least I hope it's nothing. Something doesn't feel right about this, but I'm not scaring her until I have something to go on.*

And now for something that's equally as frightening as a stalker - Mom's birthday party. "Get some sleep, Cat," Hayden urged with an encouraging voice. "I don't need you crabby and cranky tomorrow. We need you on your best behavior."

"Now Hayden," Cat interrupted, "I have it on good authority that you *never* want me on my best behavior." She drew the sheet around her and propped up on one elbow, giving a playful look.

"Very true, Cathryn. But tomorrow for Mom's birthday lunch, I need you to be good. Just for a little while, angel, and then I'll reward you greatly." Hayden held her gaze before pulling her into a hungry kiss. Cat always liked to get her rewards upfront - and afterwards, too - so she turned her attention from sleeping to collecting on his promise.

Sleep evading him, Kane thought about his day. The trip from Shanburg was exhausting, but it was good to see Colton and to meet his new girlfriend, Emma. *Emma.*

He thought back to days ago when Colton was in Canada. From the moment he had heard Emma's sweet voice when he was on the phone with Colton, he couldn't get her out of his mind. "Why do I always do this?" He scrubbed his hands down his face trying to make sense of things. He knew it was wrong to pursue his brother's girlfriend. *Knowing it and stopping it are two different things. I'm trying to be a better man . . . it's just so damn hard.*

Kane recalled how Emma's eyes lit up when she smiled and her delightful sense of humor. *Did I see that right? Did she wear the band on her wrist? With her and Colton both wearing long sleeves, it was hard to tell, but I thought I caught a glimpse of it.* Kane made up his mind that he would only back off if they both wore the bands. If, indeed, it was what he saw, his pursuit would stop and Emma would think he was nothing more than a flirt.

Once they had straightened out the mystery with Dillingham Manor, he would go back to England never knowing the feel of her lips against his own or anything else. *That's the plan tonight. We'll see if I can follow through once I see her again . . .*

CHAPTER 35

*E*mma awoke to the bright morning sun assaulting her eyes. She scrunched up her nose in protest and groaned. *Curse you flimsy curtains and giant sun ball too early in the morning!* She stopped short of pumping her fist in the air. The massive windows at her feet made it like trying to sleep in the yard because the sun shone straight in her eyes. She turned on her left side but was distracted by Colton pecking away on the computer. She tried laying on her right side, but the noise from the hallway filtered into the room from other guests mulling about the Jacobson house.

Deciding that she wasn't going down without a fight - meaning she wasn't getting up before her alarm went off - she did the only thing she could do. She wound herself in the blankets and covered her head with Colton's pillow.

"Good morning, luv," his sultry voice called out.

"Not yet," Emma replied.

"Not yet?"

"It's too *early*," she groaned.

Colton could hear the pout in her voice and her adorable southern drawl. He watched as she nestled down further into

345

the soft mattress. Laughing to himself, he wondered how *he* being a morning person, and his Emma *not* being one, would work out for them. *It'll be fun to figure out,* he thought with a glimmer in his eye.

He turned his focus back on his work. While he was already sending messages to Eleanor about Regal Engineering, Colton also gave her some ideas about Emma's gown for the ball. He knew he could ask Cat, but he wanted Emma to be the first to see what he had in mind for her to wear. She had seemed to love the style and fit of the dress that Eleanor had picked out for the Opera, so he was certain that she would like the new one, too.

Emma stirred under the covers and growled loudly when the alarm went off. With all the finesse of a baby giraffe, she smacked at the bedside table with flailing arms and fists until the clock stopped alarming.

"Well, she's either managed to hit the snooze button or has bludgeoned the poor thing to death." Colton bit back a smile as he gazed upon his grumpy love. His eyes then fell on her hand that was draped across the clock . . . and to the bracelet that was tied around her wrist. His heart swelled with pride thinking about the beautiful woman stretched out before him.

The 'ding' of the computer had Colton spinning back around to check his instant message from Eleanor.

"Mr. Graves, are you available for a video chat with a new client?"

Colton glanced back at Emma before replying.

Thinking of how she'd treated the clock, Colton was careful to hold a pillow over his face when he bent to talk to her. "Emma?" He shook her arm gently. "Emma, can you wake up?"

She stirred beneath the covers. Thinking he'd take his chances, Colton lowered the pillow and pulled the blanket back. He placed a kiss to the top of her head. "I need you to wake up, sweetheart."

She inhaled and stretched, opening only one eye. "Good morning," Emma smiled.

"Good morning, luv. I'm sorry to wake you, but I have a video chat in ten minutes." Colton glanced back at his laptop – which would have a direct line of sight to the bed. "Having a beautiful woman stretched across my bed behind me is something my prospective new client may not appreciate." Colton winked and smiled at her.

"I'm going," Emma said as she reluctantly rose and shuffled off to the bathroom.

Stepping from the shower, she found an outfit of clothing hanging on the door. She deducted that his conference had already began.

Emma got dressed quickly and clamped her hair in a loose style on top her head. Once her makeup was on, she poked her head out of the bathroom and whispered Colton's name. When he turned to look at her, he nodded his head when she asked if she could run past.

With Emma out the door, the smell of bacon directed her steps to the dining room. Mounds of fruit, eggs, bacon, biscuits, gravy, and assorted jellies lined the buffet table. She grabbed a plate and scooped up an assortment of each before moving outside. As she sat on the swing in the yard overlooking the river, her peaceful stupor was interrupted by a sexy voice.

"Mind if I join you?"

"Not at all." Emma called as she scooted over for Colton to join her. When she looked over, she was surprised to see Kane settling in beside her. *Just as well. This will give me the opportunity to see if I imagined things last night. He'll be himself with Colton not here. Wait.* "Kane, shouldn't you be video chatting with Colton? He's having a meeting right now."

"No, we do this in stages. Colton snags them with the initial meeting, and I work my magic after we've committed them to working with us. We make a bloody good team." Kane gazed down at her tray.

"Have you had breakfast?" Emma asked.

He shook his head. "No, I don't particularly care for breakfast food. But I can clearly see that you do." Kane snickered at the portion size that Emma had on her plate.

"Hey! What are you getting at?" She joked.

"Oh, nothing, luv. Just making an observation," he winked.

Luv . . . hmm. I don't like it when he calls me that. Time to make some things clear. "So Kane, tell me about yourself."

"Not much to tell, really. I'm thirty-three, single, and work as an engineer in the family business."

"Single as in 'not married' or 'not dating'?"

"Why do you ask, luv?" He questioned as he wiggled his eyebrows.

"Just getting to know you, Kane. Good Lord! I'm not trying to hook you up with one of my friends or anything." *Although Cat would loooove you!*

"Do you have any friends who are available?"

"Single – yes. Available – no." At his questioning look, she continued. "I have a lot of gorgeous friends . . . with a lot of gorgeous boyfriends."

"So they *are* available," Kane teased.

"They are *not*. Committed relationships are as good as marriage, Kane."

"How about you, Emma? Are you in a committed relationship with my brother?" Emma noticed how he furrowed his brows while waiting for her response.

"I'm in love with Colton, Kane," Emma said as she placed her hand to her chest. "And he loves me."

Kane stared at the unity bracelet that encircled her left wrist.

So he does. "You've only known each other a short while, Emma. It seems a bit rushed; don't you think?"

"Trust me. It took us both by surprise. But I am in love with him. I've never met anyone like him before. He's-" she sighed, "well, he's simply amazing."

Kane watched as the smile lit up her beautiful hazel eyes.

"I'm happy for you." He reached forward to stroke her cheek, then thought better of it. "I'm happy for him, too," Kane said dryly as he listened to the words that fell like a foreign language from his lips. *Am I happy for them?* Kane questioned himself. *No, I'm not. I want Emma for myself. But I made a vow and I'll try to keep it.* "He's a lucky man to have found someone like you, Emma." *Very lucky, indeed.* Kane shifted uncomfortably and turned his focus back toward the river.

"Do you like riding his bike?" Kane asked, making idle chit chat.

"Yeah, it's fun. I hadn't ridden one in years. He's taking it back later today, though, because he's going to lease another vehicle."

"I see. What time do you have to be in to work today?"

"Not until afternoon. Colton and I were gonna go on a walk, but his unscheduled meeting changed our plans."

"Oh, well I can take you to work if he's delayed longer."

"Thanks, but my car's here," Emma pointed to the black car in the driveway.

Kane barked out a laugh. "A bloody awful mess, that one!" A stab of regret washed over him instantly when he saw the hurt in her eyes.

"Well, it may be old," Emma acknowledged, "but it means something to me. My Grandpa gave it to me as my first car. I'll repaint it someday when I have some extra money." She shrugged her shoulders, "But you know what? Even if I could afford another car, I wouldn't want it."

"I apologize, Emma," I speak without thinking sometimes," Kane admitted, truthfully.

She nodded her head in agreement. He felt it was more of an acknowledgement that he was an ass than an acceptance of his apology.

"I hope you're able to restore it one day."

When his text alert rang out, Kane took that as his opportunity to excuse himself before he said anything else that was stupid and hurtful. He was usually suave and smooth around the ladies. And he usually didn't care if he hurt someone's feelings. He was finding that a lot of stuff was off about him today.

He thought about Emma's bracelet. *For once in your life, Kane, do the right thing. Stay away from this one!* He gave himself a silent pep talk as he walked back to the house for the video conference. He had every hope that his charms would work better on the customer than they had on Emma.

Colton closed his laptop and pondered the interaction he'd just had with his brother. For the first time, he could see that

Kane was trying to change. *If it will last, that's anyone's guess. History tells me that it won't. I can't believe he congratulated me about mine and Emma's commitment. That's certainly out of character for him.*

Peering out the window, Colton saw Emma sitting on the swing. He made his way outside to spend time with her before she left for work.

"Mind if I join you?" Colton asked, dropping a kiss to her cheek, startling her.

They sat on the swing and discussed the day ahead.

"I have to go to work for a while," Emma pouted, playfully. "But I have such a surprise for you." She was clearly beaming about something.

"What would the surprise be, luv?"

"Now Colton, if I told you, it wouldn't be a surprise. You'll just have to wait."

Even though he had no clue what it could be, she'd certainly piqued his curiosity. Colton was finding she was good at that on many levels.

CHAPTER 36

*H*ayden had always heard the phrase 'sweating like a whore in church' and for the first time, he truly knew what that meant. He was on his way to pick up Cat for his mother's birthday party at the Brookfield Country Club.

The two ladies had never actually had a confrontation, but he knew them both well enough to know that they wouldn't get along for very long. He had insisted on picking Cat up so they would have only one car. He'd recruited his buddies from the station to assure that they had to bolt early. Brent was to call at one twenty-five and Brian was on slate for one thirty. Back to back calls would suggest an emergency, which would give Hayden and Cat a way out of the party.

Pulling up in front of her shop, Hayden patiently waited for his feisty beauty to appear. He thought if Cat had one thing that would be pleasing to his mother it was the fact that she didn't have visible tattoos. She had a tattoo, but the only member of the McAllister family that was privy to its location was him. Hayden smiled at that thought.

He drummed his fingers on the dash as he waited for her to finish up with her client.

Hayden's mind drifted to Emma and the man that may or may not be her stalker. With the festival upon them, he knew his fears were echoed by all who knew that someone was watching Emma. With that thought, his eyes searched every passing person. Town was more populated than usual with patrons visiting the booths.

A glimmer from the sun reflected onto his windshield drawing his attention away from the crowd. Looking up, he saw Cat exiting her shop. He caught his breath. She looked beautiful in her royal blue top with her hair falling all around her shoulders in a thick fiery mane. She was dressed in her normal work clothes, but for someone like Cat, that meant she was decked out to the fullest. She stopped to talk to a man near the door of her shop. Passing him her business card, she spoke with him briefly and then walked away. Hayden didn't like the way the man watched her. He could imagine his thoughts and definitely saw his eyes as they settled on her rounded bottom and long legs that were fitted nicely into a pair of dark slacks.

"Hey, babe!" Cat said as she bound across the seat to plant a kiss on his lips. Hayden liked the way she could always make him forget about everything. When she continued the kiss, and it became more passionate, he realized what she was doing.

"As much as I'm loving this, Cathryn, we still have to go to Mom's party."

"Are you sure? Because I could think of about sixty-nine ways to change your mind." Her tone was inviting as she captured his lips again.

With a low groan in his throat, he pulled away from the kiss. "We really have to go, baby, but Brian and Brent are calling to get us out of staying."

Cat and Hayden arrived at the country club that sat high on a hill. The drive was nestled between endless rows of maples. "I guess when they built snob knob, they made sure they would look down on the whole damn town!" Cat said.

"I thought Dad was the only who called this place 'snob knob.'"

"Well, in all fairness, he is the one who named it that. I'm just the one who decided that it fit." Hayden shot her an amused glance.

"T minus twenty-five," Hayden said as he glanced at his watch. They walked through the doors and found the other party goers.

"Hello, Cathryn," Rebecca fawned faux excitement to see her. You look lovely, dear.

"Thank you, Mrs. McAllister. I hope you are having a good birthday so far." *I'm pretty sure vodka would help the rest of us enjoy it a bit more.*

Rebecca turned her attention on Hayden. "And Hayden, darling, you look so handsome in your uniform."

"You say that every time you see me, Mom," Hayden said as he leaned in to kiss her cheek.

"That's because it's true," Rebecca beamed.

They ordered their food. As they waited for it to arrive, Rebecca opened her gifts. Troy gave her an obnoxious stone sculpture that looked like a blob of a person. It was utterly ridiculous and Hayden wondered what the hell Troy was thinking when he picked it out. A questioning glance in his direction told the story. Troy looked bewildered at the mass as if it were the first time he were seeing it, too. Obviously their Mother had bought her own gift. When the brothers' made eye contact, Troy had a 'what the heck?' look, too. Hayden suppressed a chuckle.

Rebecca opened Bryce's gift next. It was the spa day that he and Troy had bought for her. Bryce appeared nervous because he knew if the first gift was from Troy, then she must have a monstrosity planned as a gift from him as well. She opened up the gift that Bryce had never seen. "A genuine ostrich briefcase," she exclaimed loudly.

Hayden knew that a gift like that would cost thousands of dollars. *No wonder she screamed it across the room.* She came to Hayden's gift next, which again, was something he had never seen.

"Why don't you buy me a fancy ass watch like that?" Cat whispered, clearly amused. The roll of Hayden's eyes had him looking at his own watch.

"She's crazy, Cat," Hayden said in hushed tones. "You know that, right?" They both giggled.

When they came to the real gift that Hayden had purchased, a sapphire and diamond pendant set in white gold, she seemed to enjoy it for a fleeting moment.

She then turned her attention to Hampton's gifts. Pulling Cat close, Hayden whispered, "I bet it's a dancing monkey."

Rebecca opened an envelope containing Broadway tickets. They were to the Phantom of the Opera and Wicked. *Wicked is about right!* Hayden thought to himself as he checked his watch again. *Why haven't they called, it's one thirty-seven?*

Rebecca reached for the bundle that contained five rectangular packages. As she began to tear the paper away, Hampton revealed that the gifts were something that he and Cat had collaborated on. It was evident that she liked the sketches that Cat had made of the boys, Rebecca and Hampton, and their homes. Cat watched as tears filled her eyes and streamed down her face. It was apparent to all in attendance that the gifts were truly appreciated.

"These are beautiful," she said to Hampton. "You made the frames?"

"I made the frames," he said, proudly. "And Cathryn did the rest." Rebecca turned to Cat and thanked her, thanked them all as their food arrived.

Hayden couldn't imagine why Brian and Brent hadn't called, but he was coming up with creative ideas to remind them to never disobey a direct order. *Making me stay in this stuffy place a second longer than necessary is reason enough to bring them both in front of a firing squad.*

Hayden's phone rang. At his mother's disapproving glance, he patted his badge and reminded her that he was on duty. He pulled Cat close and kissed her head as he excused himself to take the call. A look at the caller ID revealed that it was Brent - just as he expected - only about thirty minutes late.

Hayden walked past all the blue hairs having their tea and stepped outside. "What the hell, man? I told you to call me at one twenty-five."

"He's here," Brent said.

"You can drop the act. I'm outside, but seriously dude. Why did you wait so long? I had to endure the entire-"

"Hayden!" Brent barked into the phone. "The guy from the picture, he's here. Reynolds saw him on Maple Street, but lost sight of him in the crowd." Silence fell upon the line. "Hayden, did you hear-"

"Yeah, no." Hayden ran his hand over his face. "I heard you. I'm just thinking."

"We're combing the street over."

"That's good. Call me back when you find him."

Hayden ended his call and joined the guests back in the dining room. He made polite conversation. Brent's words echoed through his mind, "He's here." *I knew this didn't feel right.*

Hayden reached his fork to his plate and wondered how he could have polished off his entire meal without ever recalling taking a bite? The fullness he felt made him know he had eaten, but he didn't recall it. He'd been so lost in thought that he was running on auto pilot.

"You ok, babe?" Cat whispered.

"Yeah, just thinking about the case they just called about."

When Cat gave him an amused glance, he whispered, "Seriously, that's why they were late calling."

Hayden and Cat left the party. He was relieved that all had gone well between his mother and his girlfriend. He couldn't help but wonder if things would continue to go well for Emma. He couldn't shake the feeling of unease that continued to eat away at him.

CHAPTER 37

*W*ith her late workday drawing near, Emma, Colton, and Kane left the Jacobson house for separate locations.

Since it was apparent that Colton would be in Brookfield for much longer than anticipated, he went to exchange the bike for a truck.

Kane made his way to Dillingham Manor to get his first look at the house that brought his brother to town.

And Emma went to take pictures in the town square.

CHAPTER 38

The One Hundredth Annual Brookfield Harvest Festival was in full swing. Emma had many booths and people she wanted to visit. Even though Brookfield was a small town, there were some people that she only saw once a year.

This was another reason that autumn was her favorite season. When the cool winds of October began to blow, everyone seemed to be nicer as if the warmth that they covered their bodies with spilled out in their actions.

This day was a cloudless fifty degrees. The warm hues of orange, yellow, and red leaves littered the streets and brought a smile to Emma's face.

Various bands were slated to take the stage throughout the day. Photographing local talent was one thing that Emma enjoyed and was always a big hit with the residents of Brookfield when the pictures were printed in the paper.

Emma steadied her camera to capture a shot when she saw Cat weaving her way through the crowd toward her. "Hey, babe," Cat called out moments before pulling her into a hug.

The cousins chatted about Evan, the singer onstage, and her very fine boyfriend who looked on. "There's a picture for you!" Cat quirked an eyebrow at the site of Gage.

"For real!" Emma agreed. "Ok, babe, I gotta run. If Phil sees me standing around chit chatting, he'll hang me out to dry. Do you want to meet up at the carnival later?" Emma asked.

"You know I do, but I'm not carrying your twenty bags of cotton candy around this year - no matter how many pictures you have to take!" They both giggled at the memory from last year's festival.

Emma snapped pictures as she walked to the craft booths and was amazed at the workmanship that went into each item. A beautiful quilt caught her eye. She photographed it with Orlena, the little lady who crafted it.

She paused at the still shot that came into view on her camera and was taken aback - not only at the magnificent heirloom - but by the creator herself. The little lady had gray hair that she spun into a bun on the back of her head. Her blues eyes were like sparkling diamonds glimmering in the sun. Her hands were riddled with age, and Emma could see her calloused fingers that told the story of a life of hard work.

Emma imagined Orlena raising a large family and working in the fields when she was younger. The kindness in the lady's face and gentleness of her smile made Emma want to cry, and she had no idea why.

Refocusing before she burst into tears, Emma learned

about the quilt. It was called 'Star in Commons' and sold for six hundred and fifty dollars. Even though she loved it, Emma knew she couldn't afford anything like that, even though it was truly lovely with its diamond blocks of blues, pinks, purples, and grays. She thanked Orlena for showing her the lovely quilt, wished her luck in winning top spot in the competition, and hastily left before she choked on the lump in her throat. *She reminds me of Granny.*

Scanning the exhibits, her eyes locked onto a makeshift shack. The sign outside proclaimed, "Fortune Teller." Emma entered the first section of a dark room and felt a chill fall upon her instantly. When goose bumps popped up on her arms, she turned to make a hasty retreat but stopped when she heard a booming voice command, "Enter!" Emma laughed at her uneasiness and walked through the door.

"Hey, I'm Emma. I'm just taking some photos for the paper."

"I know why you are here, Emma. We know everything," the gypsy looking fortune teller whispered in an eerie voice as she pointed to her crystal ball. She had black hair that was partially covered by a swath of Egyptian silk that was laced in sequins and beads. Her wrists were adorned with bangle bracelets that clanked together when she moved her arms. "You seek answers," she said as she waved her hands wildly over a crystal ball.

I think you should seek out some Prozac! "Yeah, I don't think so," Emma shook her head. I can take your picture if you'd like and then I'll just scoot on out of here so you can see someone else."

"You search for answers, Emma, but you are skeptical."

Got that right!

The gypsy lady motioned to the seat across from her, "Sit."

Emma did as she was instructed. *This should be funny – and I'm pretty sure I can predict what she'll say. I can see her now flickering her fingers over this clear bowling ball, eyelids narrowing, focusing and relaxing, focusing and relaxing with the ghostly sounds of whoooo, whooooo . . . I see great fortune in your future, you'll find love, you'll save a lot of money by switching to g-*

"I see danger."

"What?" *That didn't go as I predicted.*

She looked directly into Emma's eyes. Furrowing her brow, she repeated her revelation. "I see danger, Emma."

And I'm sure if I pay you, you'll tell me what the danger is! Emma smiled, stood, thanked her for her time, turned, and walked away.

Ok, thank you Miss Crazy Gypsy Lady. I'm outta here! I should've gone with my gut instinct and hightailed it back out the door the second I got the heebeegeebee's! Emma thought as she made her way back to the exit and the sanity of the town square.

Taking a moment to refocus, Emma stood back from the crowd and watched as people buzzed from one booth to the other. She tapped her foot along to some Bluegrass music. That's one thing she liked about Brookfield, the music was as eclectic as the people.

"There she is," a delicious voice called out behind her as mighty arms circled her waist.

"Tank, is that you?" Emma joked as she turned to seize the lips that were already closing in on hers.

"These lips," Colton said as he lightly brushed them with his thumb, "belong on mine and no one else's, luv." He captured her lips again. Emma hoped that the flutter she felt in her stomach when he was near would never subside.

"Ready for your surprise?" Emma asked. "It won't be much longer."

"I'll admit you do have me curious," Colton replied.

As they meandered through the square, Colton seemed to be thoroughly enjoying the festivities. "Is Shanburg a large city in England? I was afraid that you wouldn't enjoy our little festival if it is."

"No, it's a small village – quite a bit larger than Brook-field, but still small.

Emma saw the food vendors up ahead. This was what she waited for from year to year. She grabbed Colton by the hand and took off through the crowd. "Where are we going in such a hurry?" He laughed.

"You, Mr. Graves, are about to discover a little piece of Heaven." Emma pulled him along, weaving in and out of scores of people. She took mercy on him allowing him to stop at the wood working bench. "You can shop, and I'll be right back," Emma said as she happily placed a kiss to his cheek and made her way to the line that had formed.

A few minutes passed when Colton saw her making her way back to him. His eyes dragged from the plate to her smiling face, plate to her smiling face, over and over. "What *is* it?" He asked with a perplexed look on his face. He could tell by the grease laden plate that it wasn't healthy.

"As promised, a little slice of Heaven," Emma raised the

food up to him as if presenting an offering. "This, Mr. Graves, is a funnel cake."

Colton furrowed his brow and looked at the heap of rubbish on the plate. It was a round, puffed batter thing that had been deep fried and smothered in powdered sugar. "It looks positively dreadful, Miss Saint-Claire." He laughed, but then tore a bite off and popped it in his mouth. Emma did the same. "It's not repulsive, but I think I'd prefer you to finish it," Colton said in his usual refined approach.

"Suit yourself, snooty pants," Emma teased as she plopped another bite in her mouth, leaving a trail of powdered sugar on her chin. Colton ignored her verbal jab and kissed her, tipping her head to press a kiss to her chin. "How about we grab some hotdogs and pops and go to the park for a while? I need to get out of the square before Phil finds something else for me to do."

They found an empty spot near a tree and sat down for their impromptu lunch. The day was perfect with the sun shining down, warming them. When they'd finished eating, Emma sat back between Colton's legs and rested her back to his chest. His back rested on the tree. They could hear the band playing. A man with a velvet voice sang a country love song about a woman who was everything to him.

Emma couldn't help but notice how Colton held her tighter when those lyrics sounded out. She understood because he was everything to her. She watched as he lazily spun his bracelet.

Emma laid back against his chest, closed her eyes and listened to the song that played in the distance.

"Do you want to have children someday, Emma?" Her peaceful slumber was interrupted by Colton's question and the gentle kiss he pressed to her neck.

She opened her eyes and thought about his question. "I do; I want four boys," Emma smiled. "Don't ask me why -

that's just the magic number in my head. And I want them to look just like you."

"We might have girls, too," he teased.

"We could have at least one of each. Colette and Emerson . . . and a dog named Betty," Emma giggled.

"You're never going to forget the 'Betty thing,' are you?" Colton joked.

"I love this," Emma said as she turned in his arms. "And I love you. I love talking with you about anything." She settled back against his chest. "I love the fact that you make me feel small. I was always the kid who was too tall and then the woman who was too tall. But beside you, I feel perfectly small, and I love it."

"I love you, too, Emma," Colton said as he tilted her head back to kiss her.

Emma's phone rang. The caller ID signaled that Phil was on the other line. Emma looked up at Colton regrettably and answered.

"Hey, Phil. What's up?"

"The East Street Warehouse is on fire. I need you to go down there and cover the story."

"On my way," Emma replied, ending the call.

"Everything ok, luv?" Colton asked as he watched Emma lurch to her feet hastily.

"Duty calls," Emma reported with a pout. "I'm off to cover a fire at the East Street Warehouse. Walk me to my car?"

"Of course."

As they walked, Emma told him what she had planned. "Ok, I wanted to be here when you got your surprise, but that's not happening. Michael and Tim have agreed to let you work with them today. I told them how much you loved watching glasssmiths and the story of our 'wine glass.' They're expecting you within the hour."

From the smile on his face, she could tell that Colton was pleased to be able to try his hand at a craft he had only observed.

On that note, Emma left and Colton went to the shop for his lesson.

CHAPTER 39

*S*wiping her camera off the passenger's seat, Emma hastily stepped from the car. Sirens wailed as emergency vehicles continued to pour into the parking lot. She took in the destruction that played out before her. It was horrific and mesmerizing all at the same time. The East Street Warehouse - an old, glass panel building - sat fully intact, but fading fast. Inside, she could see burning beams falling from the upper levels.

Raising her camera, Emma captured images of the red and orange flames licking at the sky. The heat rippling off the fully engulfed warehouse distorted its surroundings, as did billows of black smoke that spilled into the heavens. She continued to photograph the fire, oblivious to the fact that she was being watched . . .

For Emma, being on the scene of a fire was always a painful reminder of her Grandparents' deaths, her move to Louis-ville, and the stalker she gained while in the city.

Fires destroyed everything in their paths and ruined lives,

and for that reason, she hated them. But the pictures that came from them were vivid and powerful. This fire wasn't destroying homes, lives, or valuable keepsakes, so Emma relaxed and let her creativity take over as she successfully captured a succession of perfect shots.

Movement caught her attention. Through a haze of smoke, she gazed towards East Street Bridge. She saw a man standing there. His ominous presence anchored her for a moment, rendering her useless. A cold chill encompassed her body, despite the heat from the flames. Even from a distance, she could sense the danger.

Raising her camera, she zoomed in on the figure. Heat and smoke from the blaze caused the focus to waver, producing a grainy image. She tried again. Locking on to a crystal clear likeness, the photo she captured was not of the man.

With temperatures inside the structure rising and becoming too much for the building to contain, the windows in the warehouse exploded, raining down glass shards like drops of water.

Emma faintly registered the warning behind her but chose to ignore the officer calling for the crowd to get back. Zooming in on the bridge again, she continued her plight. But he was gone. *Or was he really even there? Maybe I just imagined him.* She looked again.

A firm hand fell on her shoulder, startling her to the point she almost screamed.

"Emma!" The male voice growled out.

Emma jerked her body out of his grasp, spinning around to see who had her. A weak laugh spilled from her lips. "Oh, hey, Hayden," she squeaked out the greeting. "You scared me to death grabbing ahold of me like that!"

"Don't 'Hey, Hayden' me," he said with a huff. "It's not safe for you to be here - at least not this close. Now go!"

Emma made another sweep of the area before agreeing to Hayden's request. The mystery man had simply disappeared. Or maybe he only existed in her mind. She decided that the heat from the flames had affected her noggin. *Maybe that crazy ass gypsy lady planted that seed in my head.* Emma shook her head as if trying to force the 'danger' comment out of it.

As she walked to her car, she questioned Hayden about his knowledge of the fire. He, of course, was tight lipped. All talk of the fire seemed to go by the wayside when both their gazes fell on her flat as a pancake back tire.

Emma sighed. "Seriously?"

Without another word, she moved to the back of the car. Opening the trunk, she was relieved to find that the spare wasn't buried under a ton of stuff . Grabbing the tool bag her daddy had provided her with years ago, Emma dropped it to the ground, then reached in to heft the tire out.

"Don't even think about it," Hayden said smoothly as he took over the task.

She gladly accepted. "Thanks, Hayden," Emma said, stepping out of his way. "I appreciate you helping me. It's been awhile, but I think I could do it."

As Hayden worked, Emma stood back and couldn't help but admire his beautiful form. She'd always thought he was handsome, and now he was in uniform. *Just something about a man in uniform. Cat's one lucky lady!*

Emma put her phone on silent and snapped a picture of her unknowing subject. She forwarded the photo to Cat with the caption, "Brookfield's finest - going above and beyond."

Emma received a reply right away.

"Quit ogling my man's ass!"

Emma replied with a smiley face.

"Emma," Hayden's voice pulled her from her message, "the spare's as bad as the tire it's replacing!"

She slumped her shoulders. "I know, but I can't afford new ones right now, so it'll have to do. Besides, they were used when I bought them," she said regretfully.

When Hayden finished and had given her a warning about the hazards of bald tires, Emma thanked him and headed back to town.

When the railroad tracks came into view, Emma glanced at her watch. As if on que, the alarm sounded. A smile tugged at her lips at her correct assumption. She liked the predictability of small town living. She pulled to a stop as the railway lights began to flash red. Moments later, the gates lowered. "Like clockwork."

Emma felt the vibrations rumbling beneath her and knew it wouldn't take long. She couldn't see it, but knew the train was coming. Looking to the right, it came into view just as the train horn sounded. She glanced in her rearview mirror at the cars and trucks that were lining up behind her. Again, she looked in the direction that the train was approaching. When she saw that there was no end in sight, she cranked up the radio, and sang along as she drummed her fingers on her lap.

"What was that?" Emma asked herself as she sat up a little straighter peering ahead at the break in train cars. On the other side of the train, the man from the bridge stood watching her. He was smiling. He wore a hat, sunglasses, brown plaid jacket, jeans, and boots. The only thing that was apparent about him was that he was African American. Emma felt panic set in. She knew that she couldn't remember what the stalker looked like, but she sensed it could be him. *It doesn't make sense. Why now? Why would I see him now? And how could he find me? Ok, Emma, think. Come up with a plan and don't panic.* She was the proverbial sitting duck. The car behind her was inches from her bumper and, of course, a train blocked the only other way out. With every break in train cars, he stood there, smiling and waving his hand from side to side.

"Oh, God!" Emma cried out. Her heart drummed in her chest and her palms began to sweat. Every pull of breath felt weighted, constricted. Her stomach began to churn and tears stung her eyes. She considered running, just leaving her car and fleeing. But she thought better of it. If she was in her car, at least she had some protection. She'd run his ass over if he stepped in front of her.

When the caboose finally dragged by, the gates remained in place. "Oh, God! No, no, no!" Emma cried out as her body quaked with fear. Her vision began to tunnel. The man stepped forward, walking toward her. She had to get away. The man turned his head. A long scar adorned one cheek. She gripped the gear shift. If the gates didn't go up, she'd bust through them.

She watched him through the right side of the windshield. He walked past the front of the car. She looked at the passenger's door. It was unlocked. With a harsh thud, she brought her arm over and slammed the button down to securely lock the door as the stranger walked passed. Emma's foot slipped off the clutch and the engine died. "*Shit!*" He didn't give her a second glance. He didn't even slow his pace. She watched in her rearview mirror as he walked down the road behind her, past the line of cars, never turning to look her direction. When the car horns behind her sounded, she realized the gates had risen. She started her car and drove on.

When she was a safe distance away, Emma pulled to the side of the road, opened her car door, and tried to throw up. Only dry heaves. She started to wonder if everything about her was an overreaction. Once she was fully back inside, she relaxed in her seat, leaned her head against the headrest, and cried. The man was obviously no one. "He's no threat, no danger, and no *fucking* reason to get so tore up!" She hit the steering wheel in frustration. She was angry at herself for being so stupid. She thought about Louisville. "It's in my past. And so is he!"

When Colton finished working with Michael and Tim, he drove to Dillingham Manor to meet Kane. As he drove his big truck through the open gates, he wondered if Emma would ever have positive thoughts about the house that lie ahead, around the bend. It was important to him to restore the home, and he had every hope that she would enjoy the project as much as he would.

He pulled up beside Kane's car and took in the house before him. *I know everyone can't see what I do when I look at it, but I know with hard work, it can be spectacular.*

As Colton stepped from his truck, Kane appeared on the porch.

"Well, brother, what are your initial thoughts?" Colton asked.

"Just as I expected, Colton – a heap of rubbish," Kane barked with the shake of his head. "But I can see that it would be something that would interest you. If anyone can restore this place to its glory, it's you," Kane complimented.

They walked around the property taking notes and checking the condition of the house and grounds. "What are the odds that you'd hook up with some American girl who lives in our grandparents' former home?" Kane chuckled at the irony of the whole situation.

"We both know that she's more than just "some girl," Kane. She's my future wife. Maybe we'll even live here one day; I don't know."

"Right, but that whole 'falling in love' with the lovely Emma seems too rushed."

Words weren't necessary as Colton's warning glance told the story.

Kane threw his hands up in surrender, "I'm sorry. I'll let it go." He backed away to prove his point.

They walked to the side of the house, discussing the structure.

"This is private property, gentlemen," Nancy chastised them. "I suggest you leave. We have two officers who live here, and I'll have you escorted off the property if you don't go immediately." Nancy turned to walk back toward the porch, Colton and Kane right on her heels.

"Go ahead," Colton said as his eyes narrowed and a sinister smile spread across his face. "While you're at it, phone your friend, Martin, at the historical society."

Nancy stopped in her tracks.

"We have lots to discuss, and the officers who live here just may be interested in what we have to say - how the two of you have been stealing from our family for years. Go ahead," Colton said, "we'll wait."

Kane shot Colton a smug grin, then they both trained their eyes on Nancy.

"That's absurd! I don't know what you're talking about," she began to stammer. "I don't know anything about anyone stealing. I'm calling the police."

She walked until she reached the front stoop - the handsome brothers right behind her.

"And Nancy," Colton twisted his phone in front of her when she turned to look at him. "They'll find it bloody interesting, this recording I made in the park a few mornings back. I have it all on tape about the hidden fortune, the blackmail - do I need to go into detail about the blackmail?"

Nancy glared at him, but didn't challenge him further.

Colton grinned a triumphant smile. "As I imagined. Now, while you call the police - and your friend, Martin, and anyone else you think might help you - my brother and I are going inside to have a look around *our* house."

"You will not," Nancy ordered. "You can't."

"We can, and we will," Kane said with smug confidence as he pushed past her.

Colton pulled the deed from his jacket pocket and held it in front of Nancy. Realization washed over her. "I'll have your things shipped to the Brookfield Police Department," Colton barked out as he followed his brother inside.

Once the door closed, Kane turned to Colton. "I gather this recording is nothing more than a ruse?"

"Just a sham, mate, but she doesn't know that."

With the brothers entering the house and securing the lock behind them, Nancy knew her time here was up. She didn't know if Colton possessed the recording he claimed to, but he clearly knew too much. She had done Martin's dirty work for far too long and she knew that given the chance, he'd lay sole blame on her.

With one last glance at the house, she walked away before things could get worse.

CHAPTER 40

*C*olton and Kane searched the upstairs bedrooms. All were either empty entirely or sparsely furnished.

"It's baffling," Kane said. "We've looked in all these rooms. Wasn't Leah's room to be sealed off?"

"Yes, according to the journals, Grandmother was so distraught that she left her room as it was on the day of Leah's death and had it sealed. If her room was up here," Colton said as he motioned around the hallway, "then it's been opened and emptied." But chances are that it's on one of the lower floors. Perhaps we need another look at Grandmother's journals and albums. That's our best starting point."

"I agree. But Colton, have you ever stopped to think that maybe the grandfather was wrong, or quite simply lied? Or, it's feasible that Martin fabricated the story himself in order to get Nancy to do his bidding - for whatever reason. Anyone could write a letter to provide 'proof.' Hell, I could write a note pretending to be his grandfather."

Colton thought about this for a moment and then agreed that it was plausible.

With a glance at his watch, he knew this would have to wait, though. He'd be meeting Emma soon.

~

With the One Hundredth Annual Brookfield Harvest Festival in full swing, music and laughter echoed into every corner of the quaint Kentucky town. The round twinkling lights strung throughout town square lit up the night sky, a nostalgic nod to small town America of yesteryear.

Colton watched as children darted through the crowd, eager to move from game to game. There were more people in Brookfield that night than he'd seen the entire time he'd been there - hundreds, he imagined. As he searched for Emma, he took the time to stop by each booth and marvel at the exhibits.

He barked out a laugh when he caught sight of two brothers whose egg toss game had gone terribly awry. He knew they were brothers because they looked just alike with their sandy hair and freckled cheeks.

"You made us lose," the boy with egg on his shirt spat to the other before wrestling him to the ground.

Colton moved along. He spotted a half dozen squirming youngsters bent over a large, oval shaped metal basin. They were bobbing for apples. Laughter erupted from bystanders when splashing water sloshed out. From their repeated attempts, it was harder than it looked, he imagined, though he'd never been presented the opportunity as a child. Colton felt a stab of regret at the things his life of privilege had denied him. He promised himself that wouldn't be the case for the children he and Emma would have someday.

Shrieks of laughter drew his attention, as did encouragement of the sweet voice he'd come to love. Colton smiled. He quickly scanned the crowd, moving her direction when he spotted her.

"You're almost there! Keep going," she cheered, running alongside them.

Colton watched as five determined children neared the finish line of the sack race. It would be a close call. Suddenly, Emma fell out of step with them. He looked on as her clipboard tumbled to the ground, scattering its contents everywhere. A smile tugged at his lips. She put on a show of hurriedness, gathering the dropped items before she stood. The shocked expressions of bewildered racers stared back at her. They had already crossed the finish line. Grumbles began to form instantly.

"How do you know who won?" Someone shouted.

A handsome grin spread across Colton's face as he reached for his wallet. He pulled out five – fifty dollar bills and handed them to Emma. She quirked a brow and pursed her lips to keep from smiling.

"I don't," she admitted. "So I guess they're all winners." The children cheered when Emma gave them each a crisp cash prize. They scattered out in opposite directions, off to spend their hard earned reward.

Emma turned to Colton. "Mr. Graves, I didn't promise them anything except having the winning title. I was simply going to give them these," she lifted the flap on a manila envelope containing five platinum pendants that hung from red, white, and blue ribbons.

He nodded. "You've tipped your hand, Miss Saint-Claire," Colton chided.

"How so?" She asked, placing her hand to her heart, feigning innocence.

"Because, luv, they're all first place medallions. One might think that the clipboard falling from your hands at the last second was no accident at all."

"Oh, well, I can see how one *might* be confused and think that," Emma smiled a sheepish grin. "But it was a *total* coincidence."

"Mmm hmm," Colton winked, pulling her to his side and resisting the urge to kiss her in front of everyone.

With her duties finished, Colton took Emma by the hand as he weaved them further into the darkness toward the tree line. Her phone sounded in her pocket, but she ignored it – just as she had the earlier calls and texts.

"Do you need to take that?" Colton asked.

Emma shook her head. "Nope. Plausible deniability," she grinned. "If I don't look at the text or see who called, I can't be held accountable for not doing whatever it is that Phil is trying to pawn off on me – and I'm sure it's him. Besides, it's awfully noisy here. I'm sure I really haven't heard some." It was dishonest, but at the moment, she didn't care.

Once they were a safe distance away, Colton backed Emma up to an Oak, then raised his hand to caress her check. "I've missed you today, luv," Colton whispered across her lips before brushing a kiss to them. What was meant to be a simple caress as his hands fell on her hips, turned into searching need as he pulled their bodies flush, hauling her against him. Emma clutched his shirt, mingling their body heat.

"Have I told you today that I love you?" She asked.

"Not recently," Colton answered, placing a gentle kiss on her lips.

"Well, I love you, Colton Graves," Emma threaded her

fingers through his hair, holding him in place. "I wish we could leave, but I told Cat I'd meet her at the carnival."

Colton lightly nipped her bottom lip, kissed her passionately, then broke away. "I love you, too, Emma Saint-Claire. So damn much." There was no denying that he wished they could leave as well.

"You're doing it, again," Colton whispered as he stilled her hips. Emma laughed when she realized she was tilting herself into his hips like Colton said she always did when she was getting aroused.

"I've gotta get out of this dark corner with you, Colton, or we'll both be in jail. But first, just one more kiss, please."

He willingly obliged.

"How did your glassblowing lesson go today with Michael and Tim?" Emma asked as she stood in his embrace.

"As it turns out, I'm not very good at it," Colton chuckled. "I tried, and they tried to show me, but I broke every piece of glass I tried to create. It appears much easier than it actually is. It also appears that I need to leave it up to them!" Emma giggled at his admission.

Emma took his hand. They stepped from the darkness, immersing themselves back into the crowd. Her head snapped from side to side, her gaze darting from booth to booth.

"What are you looking for?" Colton asked.

"It has to be here somewhere," Emma joked as she pretended to look around frantically. "I just can't find it."

Colton smiled. "What does? What are you doing?"

"I'm looking for my booth," she smiled at him. "I told you it would be beside the two headed chicken exhibit."

Colton thought back to the only night that he had spent with her at Dillingham Manor. "Right. But Emma," he took her chin and tilted it so her eyes met his, "you can no longer honestly operate the 'last remaining virgin of Brookfield' booth. And I, for one, am bloody thrilled about that." Colton dropped a quick kiss to her lips.

As they walked back to the confines of the crowd, they spotted Kane.

"There's Kane - looking as if Mum dressed us as twins this morning," Colton said, furrowing his brow. "And that reminds me, I have something to tell you." Emma turned to face him. "I slayed the dragon for you, today."

"You mean-"

"Indeed," Colton interrupted with a smile. "I mean, we showed Nancy the paperwork. She's gone." Emma hugged him and kissed him as she squealed with excitement that Nancy had finally gotten what was coming to her.

Kane watched as Emma threw her arms around Colton's neck. He picked her up and spun her around with one arm around her waist. She kissed him then tossed her head back laughing. He wished he knew what had made her so happy . . . and his biggest wish was that he could switch places with his brother. He knew it wasn't right, but he couldn't fight his attraction to her.

Kane approached them.

"I thought you were staying at the house in case Martin came back," Colton said.

"I was until I talked to the officers who live there. I hired them to watch the place since you said they were trustworthy. And that reminds me; the tall one had a question for you. I said you'd call him."

Kane focused his attention on Emma once Colton had stepped away to make the call. "What's the cause of that beautiful smile, Emma?"

"Colton is. He got rid of Miss Nancy," Emma beamed.

"I had a hand in that, too, luv," Kane corrected. "Don't I get a hug and kiss like I saw you give my big brother as I approached?"

"You don't get a hug or a kiss, Kane! And you don't have the right to call me 'luv.' You need to stop that," Emma implored.

"Right," Kane agreed with cocky arrogance. What *shall* I call you, then?"

"How about *Emma!*" Emma suggested, sternly.

"Emma *is* a lovely name, but that's so impersonal . . . *luv*," Kane chided.

"Kane, *we* are impersonal! Seriously, you cannot call me that."

"I can't?" Kane asked as he tapped his thumb to his chin. "It's like renaming a pet. I have to come up with a new pet name for you. I think I'll call you . . . pet," Kane joked.

Emma shot him an irritated glance. The corners of his mouth turned up into a sinister grin. Had she not reacted at all, he might have moved on, but she knew now what her name would be to him.

"Everything lined out?" Kane asked, straightening his stance as Colton approached.

"Yes, they just needed our numbers and where we were staying if Martin or Nancy returned - something they said you had already provided them with."

"Must have slipped my mind," Kane responded as if he were searching his memory for the conversation.

Emma, Colton, and Kane walked away from town square, down the hill, toward the carnival. Leaving Kane to fend for himself, Emma explained that the first ride of the night always belonged to the Ferris Wheel.

"No rocking the car," Emma implored with a pointed finger as she stepped on the ride. Colton crossed his heart in agreement before settling in beside her. The ride attendant was gracious, giving them many go arounds.

"It's customary to place a kiss on the lips of your date when your car stops at the very top," Emma advised.

Colton chuckled at her inability to tell the truth. "That's the third time your story has changed, Emma."

"Are you complaining?" She asked as she came in for another kiss.

"Not at all, luv, not at all."

When the ride came to an end, they stepped off, and headed toward their next destination.

A spooky crooked sign, tacked up on a wooden plank, pointed the way to the haunted house. "Charming," Colton said as he gazed ahead at the illuminated structure just down the path. By the broad smile that lit up his eyes, Emma could tell his interest had been piqued.

"It's an old country store, long out of commission," she answered the unasked question without prompt. "The copper roof and the wheelchair ramps have been added, but nearly everything else is original."

Colton looked ahead at the rectangular building with the slanted roof covering the porch. The patina of the metal was just beginning to reveal its wonderful green hue. The exterior of the building was covered in brownish-gray planks that showed the distress that age and elements had marred it with.

"The old girl has character," Colton exclaimed.

Emma smiled. She supposed that was true.

The line snaked around the path leading up to the old store. It was just as well. It gave Colton longer to look at all the vintage memorabilia attached to the walls.

Inch by inch, they moved forward until they were inside. With the windows covered, very little light penetrated the room. A curtain separated them from the screams of despair beyond. Emma's phone sounded. She decided to check this time. A text from Lisa.

"I've tried to call you a dozen times," she wrote. "So has Phil. The taste testing for the chili cook-off has already started. They needed a judge. I'm here."

For a moment, Emma was elated thinking she had gotten out of the extra duty. Then it hit her. If Lisa was covering her booth-

"Everything ok, Luv?" Colton asked, dragging her from her horrific realization.

"Just work. Everything's fine," she lied and put on a fake smile. Dread churned like a hurricane inside her gut. If Lisa was the chili taster, that meant Emma would have to cover the kissing booth. No way was she telling Colton. As fate would have it, their group was summoned in just as Emma got another text. She glanced at her phone.

"So, you know what that means . . ." Lisa wrote.

"You go," Emma feigned what could pass for a smile. "I'll catch up to protect you after I check in with Lisa." They both laughed at her show of bravery. Her phone dinged again. She didn't have the courage to look at it until she was outside.

"Pucker up, baby!" Lisa ended the text with two red kissy lip emojis.

Emma's deadpan glare and deafening sigh told the story her lips had yet to form. She was so screwed.

She could only imagine how far the line of eager men would stretch who were waiting to kiss her gorgeous friend. "Maybe they'll see me there and just leave on their own," she thought. "Or, I'll just close it." *Yes*, she thought. *That's exactly what I'll do. I'm a genius!*

As Emma approached the stand, she was surprised to see that there were no lines whatsoever. She breathed a sigh of relief. Until her phone rang. She glanced at it. The screen revealed it was Phil. It rang again. Her finger hovered over the ignore button. Knowing that wasn't a wise move, she reluctantly answered.

He began his spiel the moment she answered. "I'm just calling to remind you that the money you raise at the booth tonight will be used to purchase Christmas gifts for disadvantaged children. I'm simply reminding you of this in case you had an idea to, oh, say, close the booth altogether."

Emma sighed. "No, Phil. That never crossed my mind." Of course it had crossed her mind. That was plan A.

"We have to do this. We've already lost profits," he ended the call with that guilt trip.

We? We? Uggg. 'We' aren't the one who will be pressing my lips to every hobo in town!

Her phone beeped once, indicating a low battery, then bleeped into darkness. "Great!"

Pocketing her phone, Emma stood before the exhibit she'd been guilted into running. It was nothing fancy, basically just a sturdy box with an overhead frame. Hanging from the frame was a jagged wooden sign. In black, wood burnt letters, the words "Kissing Booth" were scrawled across the plank along with Lisa's name. Emma's gaze settled on the dollar amount - five dollars. *Five Dollars? I'm doing this for five dollars per kiss!* Her mind quickly raced to recall the balance of her last bank statement. Her shoulders automatically slumped. Who was she kidding? She didn't have enough extra money to help anyone. She had to do this.

Finding supplies near the collection box atop the counter, she jotted down her name on a scrap of poster board, placing tape dots on the back. With the makeshift sign in hand, she climbed up on the platform. Emma pressed the paper in place, covering Lisa's name with her own. She could hear people approaching below her, but didn't have the stomach to look to see how many had already lined up. As she turned to climb back down, strong arms wrapped around her calves, guiding her to the ground. *Shit.* She thought to herself. *I'll have to tell him now.*

When she looked up to thank her familiar rescuer, she found herself in the capable, warm arms of Kane Graves.

"Little pet, what are you doing?" He asked as he quirked a brow at the words, "Kissing Booth."

Emma scurried out of his grasp, trying to put some distance between them, and trying to shake the velvety sound of his voice out of her head. He sounded so much like Colton, and damn it if he wasn't already calling her 'pet!'

"I'm doing my job. Well, it wasn't supposed to be my job, but I'm doing it anyway." She peeked around him and couldn't believe the crowd that had already formed. "I can't do this," Emma said more to herself than Kane.

Kane looked at her with sympathetic eyes. He could hear the despair in her voice. He didn't want her to do it, either. Seeing her kiss his brother was bad enough. He'd be damned if he'd watch her kiss anyone else. He'd beat them to a bloody pulp if they even attempted it. He turned to face the crowd. "The booth is closed," he warned.

Grumbles began to form instantly.

"The money collected here goes to charity," one man said.

"You can't just close the booth just because you don't want someone kissing your girlfriend!"

Kane smiled, wishing the words were true. "Move along, gentlemen. This booth is now closed."

"Kane?"

He turned when Emma spoke.

"I can't close it. I don't want to do it, but I have to. I have to collect money for the children. It goes for Christmas presents for them."

Kane reached for his wallet, pulling out a wad of bills. "This should help," he said as he poked the money in the collection slot.

"I can't take that," Emma protested.

Kane studied her eyes. He took her face in his hands and lowered his head.

Oh, God! Emma's heart fell into her stomach like a ten ton weight, anchoring her to the spot. Her pulse sped up and her mouth went dry. "Kane, what are you doing?"

He paused. "Little pet, I just paid three hundred dollars for a kiss . . . and I intend to collect on it." Kane stared at her mouth and ran his thumb across her plump lips. Emma stood paralyzed not believing that this was happening. Again, he closed the distance between them. Emma's breath hitched when she felt warm lips land firmly and precisely against her forehead. She opened the eyes that she didn't realize had fallen shut in anticipation of his kiss. Kane pulled back, winked at her, and walked away without another word.

CHAPTER 41

*W*ith her pulse racing and emotions on a collision course, she watched him disappear into the crowd. Emma tried to process what just happened – more specifically, why she did nothing to stop it when Kane could have easily kissed her. She brushed her fingers where his lips had been. *What the hell is wrong with me? Why would I allow him to kiss me?* Her eyes slid shut for a moment. She knew the answer. Right or wrong, she was attracted to him, though she'd never admit it to anyone.

I need Colton, Emma thought to herself, trying to regain her focus. Turning back toward the booth, she flipped the latch on the collection box, scooped out the money, poked it in her pocket, then went on a mission to find him.

She weaved through the crowd, making her way back to where she'd originally started. When she approached the Ferris Wheel, a loud commotion from an upper car drew her attention. Long, fiery red hair flipped about. Emma smiled. She knew within reason who was causing such a ruckus. For as long as she could remember, she and Cat had always gone to the carnival together. It was their thing, their tradition. But tonight, they were there with the men in their lives. Hayden waved to Emma and she waved back.

The car approached the ground, Cat shouting out something.

"What?" Emma yelled.

Again, the ride did another loop, and again, Cat repeated the same garbled message. Emma shrugged her shoulders, threw her hands out, and shook her head. Instead of trying to verbalize it, Cat repeatedly jabbed her finger in the direction of the Haunted House.

"Ah," she said with a nod of her head, realizing Cat must have seen Colton at the Haunted House. Emma gave two thumbs up before mouthing "thank you," then went in search of him.

Walking up the ramp, Emma pushed open the door to the haunted house. A flood of relief washed over her when she saw Colton standing where he was before. He was alone in the room. She moved toward him before the sliver of light faded away from the closing door. "There he is," she squeaked out, trying to sound more cheerful than she felt.

"Emma?"

"The one and only," she whispered as she laid her head on his back. Thoughts of Kane swirled around her, as did feelings of guilt for something she hadn't actually done.

Almost as if he could sense her despair, Colton turned and cupped her chin, lifting it. She felt his forehead press against hers as if he were savoring the moment. Emma leaned into him, brushing her lips across his. He gripped her upper arms and held her away.

"Emma, I'm not-"

"Colton," she interrupted. "You're not what? Into haunted houses, waiting any longer . . . *Not in the mood*?" She whispered the tease. "Well, I can change that." Without another word, Emma pressed her body to his, pulling his head toward her until their lips crashed together briefly.

"Emma," she heard him whisper, his words feathering across her lips.

With a hunger that sent a steady pulse between her thighs, he responded to her kiss, hauling her against him, then against the wall.

Kane knew he was a bastard for not stopping her the second her arms wrapped around him, for not stopping her the moment her tender lips brushed against his, and for not stopping her now as her tongue danced with his own. He knew he didn't have the right to run his down her back, to deepen the kiss with every echo of pleasure that slipped from her mouth. He knew he shouldn't grasp her hips and pull her close, and he knew he had to stop her searching hands that had just released the button on his jeans. He also knew that he'd never have this opportunity again once he said his next words. But as much as he wanted this, wanted her, he pulled away.

"Hey-"

The second the words formed, Kane seized her lips, silencing the protest. He again placed his forehead to hers, basking in the moments of togetherness they had left.

As if no time at all had passed, Emma continued her inquiry. "So, what is it that you're not, Mr. Graves?"

Kane kissed her tenderly one final time then broke away. "I'm not Colton, little pet."

If the room had been lit, he knew he would have found Emma's questioning eyes searching as she tried to make sense of his last words. *I'm not Colton.*

And even though he knew this, he-

"What the fuck?" Kane shouted a second after her hard

fist connected with his jaw. He clutched his throbbing cheek. "What the hell is wrong with you, Emma?"

"With me? You have the nerve to ask what's wrong with *me*? Damn you, Kane!" A tear streamed down her face. "You knew I thought you were Colton. You knew that," she whispered. "What the hell is wrong with *you?*"

Kane knew he ran the risk of a black eye or busted nose, but he couldn't stand to hear her cry and he especially couldn't stand the thought that he had been the cause of it. He moved forward and tried to comfort her as she flung her arms wildly.

"Get away from me," she demanded, trying to move passed him.

"Emma, you're not going anywhere until we talk about this. I tried to be noble tonight. That's not easy for a man like me. I tried to tell you several times that I wasn't him, even after you brushed your lips against mine."

Emma kicked in his direction but the wall took the brunt of her anger.

"You missed," Kane said smugly.

"And that's too bad - I was aiming for your balls!" She scrubbed her hand down her face. "I can't believe you, Kane. How far would you have let it go?"

"Emma, you can't kiss a man like that and expect him – his body not to react."

"I thought you were Colton," Emma screamed as she swung and missed. He caught her and held her in an embrace – her back to his chest. She struggled to break free, but he held her tight.

"I'm not blaming you for this. But Emma, you responded to *my* touch, my kiss. Mine. Not his. Your mind may have wanted Colton, but your body wanted me."

She pulled out of his arms. "I will *never* want you, Kane," Emma spat.

"Keep telling yourself that, sweetheart."

Kane stormed out. As the door fell shut behind him, he heard her broken cry.

Instantly, regret inched in. Remorse was something Kane was unfamiliar with. He had always done what felt right at the moment, never thinking about the aftermath, and never looking back. He did want Emma, but he didn't want to hurt Colton.

He stepped back inside. "Emma, we can make this ok."

"It's too late for that, Kane."

He could tell by the direction of her voice that she was kneeling near the floor.

He could hear her sobs and they drove daggers into his heart. "Please, hear me out." When she said nothing, he continued as he crouched in front of her. "I'm sorry that I tricked you, Emma, that I let you believe I was Colton. It wasn't my intent - not in the beginning, anyway. I just finally had you in my arms and I wanted to hold you, nothing more. That's all I had planned to do until you kissed me."

"I thought-"

"I know," Kane replied, softening his tone. "You thought I was him." The similarities between he and Colton passed through his own mind. *Why would she have thought anything else? Bloody hell, I am a bastard!* "I just wanted to be near you. I should have pulled away, but instead, I let you believe I was him. I'm sorry. Let me be clear about this. I do want you, but not at the risk of hurting my brother. I won't do that again. So I'm asking you not to tell him what happened. You have my word that I won't tell. I know my word probably doesn't mean much to you, Emma. This was my fault. You are blameless."

"I kissed you," Emma said, her voice thick with despair.

"I allowed you to think I was him. If you tell him, I'll say that I forced myself on you. As much as I don't want to hurt Colton, I want to hurt you even less."

Kane reached his hands forward grasping her shoulders and gently tugged her to her feet. When he brushed his thumb across her cheek, she recoiled. "Just go, Kane," Emma whispered.

The lump that had risen in his throat ensured that he walked away without another word.

CHAPTER 42

From her vantage point, high atop the ride, Cat watched as Colton emerged from the trail leading away from the haunted house. He was alone. A sinking feeling settled into her gut. "There's Colton," she said, her brows drawing tightly together. "Wonder where Emma is?"

As he walked closer, and the shadows fell away, one part of the puzzle became perfectly clear. "I'm not used to two of them being here," Hayden replied. "That's not Colton."

Cat took a double take. She recalled sending Emma toward the haunted house. If she'd gone there thinking it was Colton . . . "Signal for the ride to stop," she pleaded.

"What's wrong?" Hayden asked.

She looked at him and pointed at Kane. "*That's* what's wrong! You may not know Emma very well, but I certainly do." Again, she pointed to Kane. "And that one is trouble for her!"

With the ride ending, Cat bolted toward the haunted house

as quickly as she could without drawing attention to her haste. A thousand scenarios raced through her mind – none of which gave her any peace. Had Emma been alone with Kane? Had she thought he was Colton? Had Colton came back and found them together?

"Hey."

Emma's voice pulled Cat from her thoughts. She was walking up the trail toward her cousin. Emma didn't look forlorn or distraught. More aloof than anything. Just when Cat was beginning to think that maybe Emma hadn't been alone with Kane at all, the words tumbled from her lips.

"I kissed him," Emma blurted out without the first nudge from Cat.

Oh shit! "On purpose?"

Emma shrugged her shoulders. "Yeah, I kissed him on purpose because I was expecting to find my boyfriend when I entered that building."

"I'm sorry, Em," Cat drew her cousin into a quick embrace. "I'm so sorry. I saw him and thought he was Colton."

"So did I," tears stung her eyes at the revelation. "But you have nothing to be sorry for. If anyone should know the difference between the two, it's me."

"I was down there earlier, Emma. I know how dark the room was. You don't need to beat yourself up."

Emma ignored her efforts. "Maybe that's true. But earlier, when I knew perfectly well I was with Kane, I did nothing to stop it when he tried to kiss me," Emma looked away.

"Oh," Cat's eyes grew wide. "You-" she regrouped. "He what? And you didn't tell me?"

Emma pulled her phone from her pocket, twisting it from side to side. "It's dead. And so am I when I tell Colton."

Cat held her hands out in front of her. "Whoa, girl. Let's think this through."

"Ok, he didn't actually kiss me the first time, only on the forehead. But still yet, I did nothing to stop it if he had."

"Then there's nothing to confess." Cat took her by the shoulders and pinned her with a stare. "Listen to what I'm saying to you. If you think the right thing to do is unburden yourself with this confession, you're wrong. All you're managing to do is cause Colton heartache. You won't feel better – neither will he. You don't want that."

Emma shook her head. "No! I don't want that."

"You didn't enter into this purposely, Em. Take my advice and let this one go."

"I don't know," Emma replied with a sigh. "Maybe you're right. I think I'll sleep on it and decide in the morning."

"That's my girl," Cat smiled, proudly. "Now, I'm gonna text your man to meet us and take you home."

"Thank you," Emma whispered. She was emotionally and physically drained. Avoiding her problems may not have been the best plan, but at the moment, it was the only one she could focus on.

CHAPTER 43

*D*espite the uncertainties she faced, a new day had dawned. Warm sunshine spilled through the curtains while the melody of a joyful bird rang out on the mountainside. If the day could begin anew as if nothing had changed, maybe she could, too. Emma thought about Kane. Nothing about the kiss was intentional on her part. That much was true. She refused to hurt Colton with a confession she was an innocent party to. With a deep exhale, she momentarily pushed away any feelings of guilt.

Emma stretched, reaching her hand behind her. A sense of dread settled into her stomach when she found the bed cold and empty. Had Kane told him after all? Urgency guided her motion as she flipped over. A note rested on his pillow. Emma pulled herself up in the bed, reaching for it.

"Working from the terrace, Colton."

She breathed a sigh of relief. "Is this how it will always be? Will every side step in usual behavior make me fear the worst?" Emma didn't like this feeling, but remembered Cat's words. She folded the letter, then placed it on the nightstand before getting out of bed. The deep baritone of laughter drew her curiosity to the window. Emma pulled the curtain aside and peeked out into the yard. Movement below caught her attention. It was Kane. Before she could shy away, their gazes met. With a wink and a smile, he acknowledged her presence. She allowed the fabric to fall slowly back in place, blurring out his existence. Had she made a deal with the devil? Only time would tell . . .

CHAPTER 44

*M*orning turned into evening in the quaint town of Brookfield. With Colton working from the terrace for most of the day, Emma had made a quick trip into work to download pictures. Those intended few minutes had turned into several hours.

Pulling up to the Jacobson House, she shut off the engine. She glanced up at their room. A subtle glow spilled out from the vintage window. She loved that the crank out panels had been preserved and not replaced with more modern choices. It lent a charming quality to the bed and breakfast.

Emma slipped through the front door, then made her way upstairs. A delightful aroma wafted outside their room causing her belly to grumble instantly. She closed her eyes and inhaled as a smile tugged at her lips. *What's he up to?*

She inched the door open. Soft candlelight flickered off the walls, casting a romantic glow. A small round table sat on the far side of the room near the fireplace, its white table-cloth skirting the floor. Emma's attention was drawn to Colton who was pouring wine into two goblets. He placed the glasses next to each plate on the impeccably set table.

"What's all this?" Emma asked, closing the door.

Colton turned and smiled. "It's a date, luv."

Emma looked down at the clothes she was wearing, an airy dress with a jean jacket over top. "Am I dressed properly?" She smiled.

"Overdressed, actually. But I can assist you with that matter," he raised a suggestive brow.

"You're incorrigible," Emma giggled.

With the meal finished, they moved to the bed to talk. Emma settled in beside Colton, laying her head on his chest.

"Emma," Colton said, stroking her cheek. "Do you like living in Brookfield?"

"Yeah, I do," she answered. "It's small, and not very exciting, but I like it here."

"What do you like specifically?"

"Oh," Emma began to tick things off on her fingers. "I love the people – they're laid back and friendly. I love the mountains and the park. I love the river and the nature trails. I love the old architecture we have here and the town's rich history."

"Does that include Dillingham Manor?"

She thought for a moment before she answered. "Hmm. Well, I thought I hated it for the longest time. Now I realize it wasn't the home at all. It was Nancy. I have a renewed appreciation for it now."

"Could you see yourself ever wanting to live there?" Colton asked.

Emma pulled herself up to face him. His expression was unreadable. "Why are you asking me these things, Colton?"

"Because I want you to be happy, luv. It doesn't matter to me where we live. I can work from anywhere; I could even start up a new business here in Brookfield," Colton studied her reaction as meaning set in.

"Do you mean that *you* want to stay here?"

He smiled. "Anywhere you are, Emma, is where I want to be. You said you like it here, right?"

"As in 'here' at the Jacobson house? Are you buying it?" She was puzzled because she'd never heard Miss Francine mention selling it.

Colton reached underneath the bed, pulling out a stack of gifts. Switching on the bedside lamp, he handed her a small package wrapped in shimmering teal paper. A matching opaque bow topped it. "To answer your question, no, I have no intentions of purchasing this house."

"What on Earth are all these gifts for?"

"An early birthday present," he nudged the box closer into her hands. "Open it."

Emma unwrapped the small, rectangular box. She bit her lip to keep from laughing. "It's a pencil," she said, looking up at him.

"Very good, Emma," he smiled.

She had known him long enough to discover that any simple gift he offered had great meaning. "What shall I do with it?" Emma asked as she glanced toward the other packages.

Colton handed her a tubular package. She popped the top off the end, tapping out the rolled up papers inside. She flattened them out.

"Do you know what they are, Emma?"

"I think they're blueprints - but they're blank."

"'They're blank' because they need a design."

"What are we designing?" She asked.

"Absolutely anything your heart desires," Colton placed a kiss on her lips before reaching for the third package. It was the size of a legal document. He instructed her to open it. Tearing away the paper, she found the deed for the property at Dillingham Manor. "I'm giving you free reign to re-design the house of our dreams, Emma. I love you, and I want you to be happy."

The handwritten names on the document caused her to pause. Her gaze slowly rose to meet his. "This says, 'Colton and Emma Graves.'"

He shrugged one shoulder, "A bit presumptuous on my part, luv. I apologize." Colton pushed himself off the bed, lowering down to one knee.

Emma threw her hand over her mouth as her eyes filled with tears.

"Emma, I've spent my whole life searching for the one person whom I could share my every tomorrow with, the one who could make my heart skip a beat at the mere sound of her voice, one who is talented, respectable, hardworking, and funny, someone that I feel unbridled passion with, and above all else, someone whom I could fall deeply and madly in love with. I'm fortunate to have found that person in you, Emma. When I visualize my future, what I see is you. You're the one I want to start a family with, to grow old with, and the only one that I will ever love. My heart fills with pride every time that I glance at your wrist and see the unity bracelet that signifies our love. But it's time this was replaced." Colton turned her wrist and untied the bracelet, catching it as it fell. He placed it beside her.

Emma exhaled a shaky breath.

Colton held her gaze as he reached in his pocket and pulled out a tiny box encased in black velvet. The creaking hinges drew Emma's attention to an emerald cut diamond solitaire encased in a halo of smaller stones. A platinum band surrounded the gems.

Overwhelmed by the moment, tears streamed down her face.

"The jeweler suggested we start with a one carat. If it's not big enough, we can exchange it."

Emma shook her head, "No, it's beautiful, Colton. It's perfect."

"Emma Saint-Claire, would you do me the extraordinary honor of making me the happiest man in this world by becoming my wife?"

Delicate teardrops fell onto her cheeks as she tried to speak past the lump in her throat. "Yes, Colton," she managed to whisper, "Yes, I'll marry you!"

With a smile tearing across his face, Colton placed the ring on her finger. In a swift motion, he stood, pulling her to her feet then into a kiss. Holding her in an embrace, he whispered, "Thank you. You've made me a very happy man."

She stepped back. "No," Emma said, "It's you that's made me happy - ecstatic, actually!"

Colton brushed away a tear from her cheek. "You tend to cry a lot for someone who's ecstatic," he winked as he delivered the jab.

Emma giggled at his playfulness. "Yeah, I guess so."

Her gaze fell to his lips. "But I am happy. I love you, Colton."

"And I love you." He dropped a gentle kiss to her lips. The tender moment quickly turned passionate when Colton deepened their embrace, leading Emma down against the bed.

She felt the boxes crush beneath her at the same time Colton heard them. Emma tilted up, attempting to sweep them aside.

"Wait," Colton instructed.

Emma's eyes popped open, "No," she protested, pulling him back against her.

"Just one more gift."

"Colton, I don't need any more gifts. This is what I need," she ground herself against him, continuing the kiss.

Colton groaned. He propped himself up on his elbows, looking down at her. "This one is more for me, luv," a smile tugged at his lips. At her questioning glance, he elaborated. "When you came home tonight, I said you were overdressed. You still are. This last gift will remedy that."

Emma quirked a brow at his suggestive tone. Colton placed a kiss on her neck then pushed himself off her.

Reaching for the last box, Emma eased the lid off. She peeled back the tissue to reveal the contents – a pair of thigh high stockings, the color of midnight, and her onyx pendent on a long silver chain. That was it. A seductive aura came over her when their eyes met.

Emma stood and slowly let her jacket fall to the floor. Turning her back to him, she glanced over her shoulder. "A little help?" She requested when her gathered hair revealed a neckline fastener.

Colton was against her in a second, his lips tracing the delicate column of her neck. He loosened the button and quickly freed her of the dress. In a moment, his hands were everywhere – between her legs, against her breasts, and against her throat as he eased her head back on his chest. He whispered something in her ear causing a chill to run down her spine. Emma was so turned on. The throbbing between her legs intensified, making it impossible to concentrate on the task at hand.

She turned in his arms, turning the tables on this seduction. She pushed against his chest. He obliged, lowering himself to the bed. Emma stood before him in nothing but a black lacy bra and matching panties. She walked toward the bed, slowly, leaning in toward Colton. Her lips barely brushed against his. He tried to pull her closer when she stepped back, the contents of the box in hand.

"Vixen."

She smiled. Emma walked slowly across the room and retrieved a straight back chair from their impromptu dinner. She sat it close to the bed. Propping one foot on the edge of the chair, she rolled on a sheer thigh high, making sure to caress her leg as she went. She held his gaze before repeating the step on the other side. Emma slid the pendant over her head then slid into the chair backwards. She placed her elbows on the chair back and propped her chin on her folded hands. "Enjoying the show?" she asked with a voice she barely recognized.

Colton's gaze traveled her body, appreciating her curves and open legs that taunted him. "Indeed," he growled out.

"It's about to get better," Emma countered. She reached her hands behind her back, releasing her bra. Slowly, she slid off one strap then the other. He watched as the material was tossed aside. Emma caressed her breasts, pushing them together. A low curse fell from his lips when he witnessed her nipples harden at her own touch. "Like what you see?"

"I can't take much more of this, Emma. Take your panties off and come here." Colton's tone made it clear that it wasn't a request.

"Yes, Sir." Emma stood, easing her panties down her legs. She moved toward him with unhurried prowess.

Colton stood when she reached the bed. Drawing her to him, he kissed her hard. Unyielding. She knew she had pushed him too far. She also knew she'd reap the rewards of that. Colton inched her back on the bed. He traced his fingers down each link of the necklace and then the pendant that hung between her breasts. A chill raced through her at his touch. His pursuit continued as he traced his finger down her stomach to the juncture of her thighs. Emma's breath hitched in her throat. "Good girl," he praised. "Don't move."

Colton leaned over and switched the lamp off. Rising from the bed, he made his way about the room snuffing out candles. With only one remaining, Emma watched as he came back to the bed. "We won't be needing this," he said, casting the room in total darkness. It excited her to rely on her senses of sound and touch only. In the darkness, she heard the ticking of the clock and his breathing. Anticipation surged through her body when she felt Colton's warm hands on her inner thighs, pushing them outward.

"Spread your legs, luv."

Satisfied with the results, Kane scrawled her name across the envelope, then laid the pen aside. It was done. For the better part of the evening, a jumble of ideas stared back at him. With every attempt, a new thought took shape causing him to tear away the words, discarding them. Balled up wads of paper littered the floor around him, a testament to the effort he'd made. A battle raged within him, playing tug of war with his emotions. He knew what he wanted to say. He also knew the ramifications of that. What he wanted to say is that he loved her. As his time in Brookfield drew to a close, the straining of his heart made that evident. Kane glanced across the room at his bags; he knew it was now or never.

Having finally garnered the courage to say goodbye, Kane inhaled deeply and walked down the hall giving himself a pep talk the entire way. He still didn't know if he'd talk to her or simply slide the letter under the door. He raised his hand to knock, but pulled away to gather his thoughts. Allowing himself a minute more to gain his composure had proven to be a grave mistake. From the other side of the door, Kane heard her. He had heard her many times - her laughter, her happiness, her anger, her sorrow - but what Kane had never had to endure was overhearing Emma call out his brother's name in the throes of passion. He closed his eyes to the pain. Reality branded his heart, driving home the fact that the woman he loved didn't need his words, his letter . . . or him. Crumpling the envelope in his hand, he walked away.

CHAPTER 45

"Colton, I'm gonna run down to my car and get my new shampoo that I keep forgetting to bring up," Emma called out through the open bathroom door where he was taking a shower.

She pulled her hair up in a messy ponytail, slipped on his black button down shirt from the night before and a pair of flip flops. As she walked toward the door, she caught sight of her discarded hosiery lying on the floor, riddled with holes. She laughed to herself and nibbled her thumbnail as images of the previous night danced through her head. Emma let out a content sigh and continued out the door. She eased down the steps toward the main hall and was pleased that the floor didn't creak like the ones at Dillingham Manor.

It was just after dawn. Emma was confident that she'd be able to slip down to the car and back without being detected since the house guests usually didn't mull about in the wee hours of the morning.

As she stepped out the front door, a blanket of fog greeted her. The early morning air encircled her legs, the frosty nip reminding her that winter was just around the bend. Emma pulled her arms tightly around her body and hurriedly walked to her car.

She rummaged through the trunk, hefting out a sack of hair products. The handle on the plastic bag snapped in half under the weight, sending a heavy bottle careening toward the ground. Emma bent to retrieve it at the same time another hand reached for it. She shuffled away then shot to her feet in an instant, her flight response seconds from causing her to soar. "Jesus, Kane! You scared me to death!" Emma shouted as she peered down on him. Clutching her shirt to her heart, she took a moment to catch her breath. The rise and fall of her breasts drew his eyes upward and upon her. She felt the scrutiny of his gaze. Kane rose to stand beside her, towering over her. He wore a light blue pullover that clung to his muscled chest and spilled onto dark denim jeans. The scruff on his face invited a touch, but she wouldn't dare.

If she were to be totally honest with herself, she was attracted to him. And being a fiercely loyal person, she hated herself for it. If he wasn't her soon to be brother-in-law, she might have appreciated his beautiful form. She didn't. She wouldn't. *I won't.*

"What are you doing out here so early?" Emma finally managed to say.

"I'm leaving."

"Leaving?" Before she had the chance to question him further, she spotted the bags beside his car. "You're going back to England?" Emma asked as she furrowed her brow, confused by her reaction.

"My time here is finished, Emma," he said as a look of regret crossed his face.

She thought back to the night of the festival. Trying to block out what happened between them, she recalled Kane's words: *Let me be clear about this. I do want you, but not at the risk of hurting my brother.*

"I think that's for the best," Emma said, looking away. Kane confused her. She had always considered herself to be level headed, but she decided that Kane Graves was the proverbial monkey wrench in an equation she didn't need. Things were going fine for her until he showed up clouding her mind with intrigue and doubt – not that she doubted her feelings for Colton - Kane just muddled her thoughts altogether!

She thought about the ball. "Do you still plan to come back with your mom for the ball?"

Kane crossed his arms over his wide chest and looked out toward the river, obviously collecting his thoughts before he spoke. Bringing his focus back on Emma, he answered. "I'm not sure. She doesn't like to fly alone. My hope is that Eleanor will come back with her. And if not Eleanor, then someone."

Emma could fill in the blanks of what he wasn't saying - he was hoping anyone but he would accompany his mother back to the States.

Kane reached forward and tucked a stray strand of hair behind her ear letting the backs of his fingertips caress her cheek for just a moment. His gaze locked on hers. "I don't need to come back here, Emma."

She didn't understand the butterflies she felt in her stomach – or was it a knot - or maybe both?

"Emma, I want you to know that I'm truly sorry for what happened between us; I never meant to hurt you." Kane hung his head. His gaze fell on the hand that she held on her hip. He lifted it, his focus falling on her engagement ring – a ring he'd never seen her wear before. He forced a smile. "I hope my brother makes you happy, Emma." He pressed a kiss to her forehead.

She should've pulled away, should've refused his embrace, but she couldn't.

"Goodbye, little pet," he whispered across her skin as he clutched the back of her head.

He started to walk away, then turned back. "I came to tell you goodbye last night, but-."

"But what?" Emma asked.

"You were . . . *occupied.*" As much as he didn't want to continue with his statement, he knew Emma wouldn't let it go. "I came to your room last night. I thought you were sleeping because the lights were off. Then I heard you."

"What did I say?" She asked.

He hitched a brow, "Something that thin walls can't contain."

Emma's eyes grew big, "Oh, God!"

Kane exhaled loudly. "You said that, too."

Emma threw her hand over her mouth as a crimson hue raced up her cheeks. Kane smiled a sincere smile. She had no idea how much he appreciated her genuine show of emotions - never pretentious, always sassy, and always perfect.

He looked at his watch as the corners of his mouth fell. "I have to arrive at the airport soon." He thought for a moment. "I likely won't see you again before the wedding. It was a pleasure and an honor to meet you, Emma."

Kane inched closer, wanting to take her in an embrace, but stopped himself. He studied her face, memorizing every detail.

She watched as the anguished look crossed his features.

"Je t'aime, little pet," he said softly.

"What does that mean?" Emma asked.

It means I love you. If only I could say that. Kane cocked his head and gave a gorgeous sideways smile before turning to walk away without saying another word.

Emma watched as he loaded his bags. She couldn't understand the stab of regret that she felt as she watched him pull away. He hesitated for only a moment then disappeared into the fog on the winding river road.

~

As she topped the steps, just outside their room, Miss Francine called out to her.

"Emma, I was cleaning Mr. Kane's room when I found this letter addressed to you." She pulled an envelope from the pocket of her white apron. It was folded in half and badly crumpled."

"Where did you find this?" Emma questioned because it looked as if it had been trampled on.

"It was in the trash can. I'm sure it was an accident that he threw it away. His room was rented for three more days. He left in a hurry. He probably accidentally knocked it off his desk."

"Thank you," Emma responded, taking the letter from her hand.

Miss Francine headed down the stairs with a basket of laundry tucked under her arm.

Emma ducked inside the room. She tossed the bag beside her, then lowered herself to the edge of the bed, ripping the letter open. She had to make sure he hadn't mentioned the kiss.

She pulled the letter from the envelope, wondering why Kane hadn't given it to her or even mentioned that he'd written it. He'd already told her he was sorry and she believed him. Emma quickly scanned the contents. Beautiful penmanship revealed general well wishes, a revelation that he was leaving, and an appreciation of meeting her. The last line of the letter, the portion right above his name, was written in French. It sounded like what he had just said to her. She made a mental note to go online and find a French to English translation when she got to work. She didn't want to use Colton's computer in case it was something inappropriate - and knowing Kane, that was a great possibility.

Colton's phone rang. She placed the letter on the bed before crossing the room to retrieve it. She rushed into the bathroom.

"Colton," she called out pulling the shower curtain aside. "You have a phone call. Do you need to answer it?"

Emma turned the phone toward him so he could read the screen.

He shook his head. "What I need is for you to get in this shower," he responded with a sly grin.

Emma laid the phone on the sink and pulled her hair free of the tie. She slowly released the buttons on the shirt, letting it fall to the floor. "When a sexy man makes a request such as that, what's a girl to do?" Emma countered as she climbed in to join him . . .

Colton entered the room with their breakfast tray, balancing it against his body as he lightly kicked the door shut. The shower was still running, so he placed the tray on the nightstand. The overhead fan caused a paper to flutter, drawing his attention to the bed. Colton saw an open face letter addressed to Emma. The word "Kane" in the closing line stood out to him. His usual rule to respect the privacy of another disappeared. Colton snatched up the letter as his hands tightened around the note. He quickly scanned it. He read the last line, then he read it again, translated, out loud: "'I love you, little pet?' What the bloody hell?" He wadded up the letter and threw it against the wall. Walking over to stare out the window, he placed his palms on the desk, gripping the edge as he tried to control his anger. Thoughts of Kane's profession multiplied his rage. He pushed off the desk and reached for his phone. Dialing Kane's number, he waited to unleash his fury. The call went to voicemail. "You have a lot of nerve, Kane! I better never lay eyes on you again, *brother*, because if I do, I'll rip your *fucking* throat out!" Colton barked the threat into the receiver.

As she stepped from the shower, Emma heard Colton's raised voice. Profanity echoed through the open door as she tried to make sense of what she heard. She jerked on his black shirt and bolted out of the bathroom. There was only one thing - only one person - who had ever made Colton this mad, and that was Kane. Emma thought that he had come back and that they were fighting. Relief washed over her to find that they were alone, but one look at his sideways glance made his wrath apparent.

Immediately, she feared he knew about the kiss. "Colton, what's the matter?" Emma asked as she hurried over to stand by his side, placing her hand on his arm.

"Kane, Emma. Kane is the matter. He has a lot of fucking nerve writing you a letter professing his love!"

Emma could clearly see that Colton was livid, but Kane hadn't said he loved her. She didn't know what he was talking about. Still, it was apparent he knew nothing of the kiss. "Colton, you need to calm down."

He shot her a look that reminded her of a feral animal. "You are mine, Emma, and Kane is dead if he so much as looks at you ever again."

She had to defuse the situation, but she didn't know how to calm him down. "Colton, listen to me." He looked ahead staring out the window. "Look at me - please," she urged.

Colton turned toward her.

"I don't know what has you so angry, but all Kane said

was that he was happy to have met me, he was leaving, and that he hoped you made me happy."

"And that he loves you," Colton seethed.

She was about at her wit's end with this conversation. "Colton, he never once said he loved me!"

"Do you speak French, Emma?"

Emma shook her head.

"Well, I do. And believe me when I say he said it," Colton growled.

"Oh," Emma whispered as she realized the last words that Kane had said to her at her car and in his letter.

Peering out onto the foggy river, Colton continued. "And why the bloody hell is he calling you 'little pet'?"

Emma thought it best not to tell Colton that Kane had called her that for days now and she certainly wasn't going to tell him that he'd called her 'luv' from the beginning. She absolutely wasn't going to tell him that Kane had kissed her on the forehead and that she'd let it happen twice now, and he'd never hear her confess that she'd accidentally kissed Kane with all the passion she could pour into a kiss thinking he was Colton. Cat was right. Some things really were best left unsaid.

"Look, I don't know why he does half the stuff he does, Colton. But he's gone now and we don't have to see him, don't have to think about him, and we don't have to talk about him - anymore." She grasped his shoulders and turned him to face her. "*You* are the one *I* love. *You* are the one *I* want. *You* are the one *I* need. And *you, Colton Graves,* are the one *I* plan to marry. *You* - not him!" Emma demonstrated each point with a finger to his chest. "And Kane is nothing to me." She wrapped her arms around him, relived that his anger was visibly subsiding.

He exhaled as if pushing out all the anger. "I'm sorry, Emma," Colton said as he sat in the chair beside him, pulling her down with him. She instinctively curled herself against his chest. He kissed the top of her head as her wet hair fanned across his shirt. "He just makes me so angry. When I read what he wrote, it infuriated me. I'm so sorry, luv. I should've been more in control. Please know that I'm not angry with you." He tipped her chin up so he held her attention. "I'm not angry with you – never with you." Colton leaned into a reassuring kiss.

CHAPTER 46

*D*errick drove into the lot and parked in the spot reserved solely for him. He nudged his designer sunglasses lower and smiled ahead at the sign that told the world he was important – *Reserved for Dr. Derrick Wells*. He stepped from his car, running his fingertips gently down the side as he went. The sleek design reminded anyone who saw the foreign sports car that he was wealthy. His reflection bounced back at him from his glass constructed office building. He noted his sharp dress, fine car, and tall build. A sinister smile tugged at his lips. "I have it all."

Derrick opened the trunk to retrieve his briefcase. When he lifted the brown plaid jacket that lay on top, a knife fell out, marring the bag. He looked around to make sure no one saw it. Thoughts of Amanda Taylor caused his previous smile to turn downward into an ominous scowl. *I would have had it all. Soon she'll realize the pain of losing everyone she ever loved, too.* Derrick's fingers curled painfully into his palms at the thought.

He stepped onto the crowded elevator and looked at the array of lit up numbers, his stop being one of them. His office sat atop the fourteenth floor, so he amused himself while he waited for the doors to open. Derrick pulled his phone from his pocket and flipped through image after image of Amanda, her tall companion, and a red headed friend. He'd have fun toying with them, he thought.

Derrick thought back to the fire he had set at the warehouse. He thought he would get the journalist then by flattening her tire, but the officer that showed up to assist her halted that plan. He remembered the fear in Amanda's eyes when she saw him at the railroad track - the terror rolling off her was nearly palatable when the engine to her car died. Yes, the little rabbit wanted to run, thought she'd recognized him – he was certain of it. He loved how he'd played it so cool by walking past her time and time again. He wanted her spooked, wanted her to suspect that he was coming for her – never knowing when he'd strike. That was half the fun.

"Dr. Wells, this is your stop," an elderly man called out, pulling Derrick from his nirvana.

"Thank you, Tony. I was lost in my research and didn't realize I was here already." Derrick nodded to the gentleman and stepped into the open office space where Jillian greeted him – much too chipper, as always.

"Oh, good morning Dr. Wells," she beamed with excitement.

He silently compared her to a human Jack Russel. "Good morning, Ms. Walters," he forced a smile. He knew that questions about his dear dying grandfather would bombard him any second.

"How was your hunting trip?" She asked.

He was surprised that she had skipped the usual sick granddaddy questions. "It was entirely enjoyable; thank you for asking. I'm going again this weekend."

A squeamish look crossed Jillian's face.

"What's troubling you, Ms. Walters?"

"Oh, I don't know, Dr. Wells. I don't think I could kill anything. And I certainly don't think I could do it two weekends in a row."

He laughed as genuine joy billowed out of him. "This past weekend was just scouting, Jillian," he said as a smile lit up his face. "The actual kill is coming up." Derrick wondered if his eyes revealed the excitement his soul felt. Thoughts of torturing then killing Amanda caused his pulse to race and his eyes to dilate. He wasn't experienced at delving out pain, but he could be a quick and eager study . . .

Entering numbers on the spreadsheet, Cat heard the dinging of the door chime. *Damnit.* Her appointment was early. "Be with you in just a sec," she called out without looking up.

"Take your time," the familiar voice called out.

Cat perked up instantly, rising from behind the desk. "Saint Emma," she smiled, "to what do I owe the pleasure?"

Emma held up a bag of doughnuts and a drink carrier that held two pops. "We need a little girl time and grub." Even though she smiled as she said it, a troublesome expression weighed heavy on her features.

Cat circled around the counter. "I'm always up for some girl time and grub," she said as she pulled her cousin into a quick hug.

"I had to come this morning in case Colton joined us for lunch."

"And that would be a problem because . . ."

"Because we have good *and* bad to discuss," Emma answered.

Cat gave an understanding nod, "I see."

They each took a seat, the food and drinks on the seat between them.

"You didn't tell him about the kiss did you?"

Emma sighed. "No. And now, more than ever, I'm glad I didn't." At Cat's questioning glance, Emma waved her left hand excitedly between their faces.

"Oh, my God!" Cat squealed. She grabbed Emma's hand and investigated the beautiful solitaire on her finger. "It's gorgeous! Is this an engagement ring?" She asked, already knowing the answer.

"It is indeed," Emma sang back. "It was so unexpected and romantic." Emma explained how an ordinary evening had turned into the best one of her life.

Cat enjoyed hearing the recap of the previous night. She watched as Emma tucked her hair behind ear and giggled over the pencil gift. She told her about the deed and the proposal. Emma was practically glowing. Colton had been good for her, coming into Emma's life at a time that she needed him most.

"Ok, so we've covered the good news. What's the bad - that you have to live in that mausoleum?" As far as she could tell, Emma was ok with Dillingham Manor now, but maybe she was mistaken.

Emma shook her head, finishing her bite of doughnut. "The bad," Emma said, "has nothing to do with Dillingham Manor. It's Kane."

"Isn't it always?"

"Yeah, but you'll never believe this." She closed her eyes, pinching the bridge of her nose as she gathered her thoughts.

Cat listened intently as Emma recounted her early morning chance encounter with Kane, the letter, and about Colton finding it. Then she dropped the final bombshell.

"He loves you?" Cat questioned, her eyes big as saucers. "Holy shit!"

"I guess," Emma answered, shaking her head. "I mean, I don't think he ever intended for me to see the letter. You should see how crumpled up it was."

"And why am I *not* seeing it?"

"Think about it. If I took the letter, Colton would have seen that in a completely different light. I'm having to tread very carefully here."

Cat nodded her head.

"So, like I said, I don't think he ever intended for me to see that letter even though he came to the room with it."

"Yeah, overhearing you *loving* on his brother was probably a mind changer," Cat burst out laughing.

Emma gave her a half amused smirk. "You're loving this."

"Hell, yes, I'm loving this!" She pinned Emma with a stare, "And if you were completely honest with yourself, you'd admit that part of you is loving it, too."

Emma shrugged her shoulders and stood to leave. "All I know is that it'll be easier with only one of them here – the one I love."

"Fair enough," Cat replied as she drew Emma into a hug. "See you in a few hours for lunch."

"See you there," Emma said as she walked out the doors of the tattoo shop.

CHAPTER 47

*E*mma strolled down the street enjoying the sunshine on her face. The chill of the morning had given way to a gorgeous day. She knew that the warm autumn days were drawing to a close, so she planned to enjoy every last one she could.

She called out to Michael and Tim as she passed their shop. It looked like they were working on a long neck vase whose opening was impossibly small for a flower to pass into. *It's likely a canon.* Emma said to herself and giggled. History had proven that she wasn't very good at gauging what they were crafting.

As she neared the Diner, she saw two elderly men on a bench enjoying the day as well. Emma stopped in front of them to chat. She roared with laughter when the younger of the two decided to tell a very inappropriate joke. She shook her head and wagged her finger in front of his face. They all had a good laugh at the mock scolding.

Colton looked up when he heard her. He'd know her infectious laughter anywhere; it was one of the first things that he noticed about her from the beginning.

He leaned against the brick wall wearing a white button down shirt and dark jeans. Of all the women who passed by admiring his presence, he was only interested in the one whom he'd just locked eyes with - Emma. He waited patiently as she approached. The sunlight danced through her hair revealing fiery highlights of auburn red. She sat her mouth to the side and narrowed her eyes as she always did when she was contemplating something.

Emma stopped when she stood toe to toe with him. He snaked his arms around her and hauled her off her feet, eliciting a squeal of delight. Colton's mouth crushed against hers quickly before setting her back down.

"Well, I was going to ask what you were thinking about so intently, Mr. Graves, but maybe that was my answer." Emma grabbed each side of his collar and pulled him into another kiss.

The pecking on the window drew their attention to Cat. With a phone perched between her ear and shoulder, she tossed her arms up in a "what the heck?" gesture, then pointed to some children in an adjoining booth. They were making smoochy faces at each other. Emma muffled a laugh with her hand and they walked into the Diner to join her cousin.

"*Sorry*," she mouthed to the mother as she passed by.

Emma and Colton slid into one side of the booth, Cat on the other, still on the phone. From the end of the conversation they overheard, Hayden's original plan to join them fell through. Just as the call ended, Bonny bounced out to take their order.

Before they had even had the chance to ask for drinks, she jumped straight into gossip mode. "I sure am happy to see you kids. The rumor mill has been swirling!"

Emma playfully bumped Colton's shoulder. He gave her a sideways glance and that gorgeous crooked smile. They assumed someone had already told her about their engagement. After all, it was the *only* topic of conversation once Emma had got to work.

Bonny continued, "Is it true that you kicked Nancy out of the boarding house? I can't believe that she and Martin were working together." She flipped a pencil between her fingers as she excitedly waited for the answer. Brookfield wasn't known for mystery and intrigue, so this news was clearly buzz worthy - and Bonny was happy to help spread it around.

"Yes, it's true," Colton said. "They were in search of a fortune that simply isn't there." He wasn't sure if it was there or not, but he wanted that rumor to circulate as well.

Bonny held up her finger in a 'hold that thought' gesture. She took their orders and rushed away.

"So, there's no money stashed away?" Cat asked.

"I simply don't know," Colton answered. "I wish to preserve as much of the house as possible, so I'm not overly eager to rip it apart in search of a pipe dream by a likely senile man. I do know that the account of where the grandfather said Leah's room was - and my Grandmother's story - don't line up. I think it's safe to assume that a hidden fortune simply does not exist in Dillingham Manor."

"You know, Colton," Cat said, "I would hate for your house to be torn apart, but I like imagining Martin working hard all these years only to find absolutely nothing!" She laughed at the thought. "That would have been sweet justice to watch him suffer!" She looked off in the distance with a pleased look on her face. It was at this moment that she saw Martin pass by the window. Her mouth gaped open. "Why on earth is he not in jail?"

Colton glanced the direction she was facing, then turned

back. "Because we can't prove wrong doing. They said it was hearsay. At this point, they have nothing to hold him on. Nancy, either."

Knowing that Colton was frustrated that Nancy and Martin would likely walk away from charges, Emma changed the subject to a more pleasant conversation. "I thought Bonny had heard about our engagement when she said the rumor mill was buzzing."

"Engagement?" Bonny shrieked from behind them. She slid in beside Cat then reached across the table for Emma's hand. As she looked the ring over, she became teary eyed. "I just love romance!"

"Order up," Sal called out. Bonny rose to her feet and tucked a loose curl behind her ear. As she bounced away to get their food, Emma could tell that she was excited to have another bit of gossip to spread. She suspected that once their food was dropped off that they wouldn't see their slim waitress again – as she had many people to inform of the latest news.

Once the food was delivered, Bonny quickly scurried away and stayed away.

"What's the matter, babe?" Emma asked, sensing something was wrong with Cat.

"It's Hayden, as if you had to ask. He's been busy with work and has been working on a case that he won't talk about," she furrowed her brow. "Or at least that's what he *says* is keeping him busy. Maybe he's just losing interest," Cat said, shrugging her shoulders as if she didn't care. But the tiny nibble on her lip as a look of despair crossed her face gave her away.

"Cat, I know he's crazy about you – everyone can see that. Why can't you?"

"Well *that's* the pot calling the kettle black!" Cat said with a snort. She reminded Emma of all the times that she had pointed out that very same fact to her.

"This is different. He's in love with you. I can see it and if you'd quit being so stubborn, you'd see it, too!"

As the cousins traded barbs about who wasn't listening to whom, Colton sat quietly eating his lunch. He was a smart man and knew when to keep his opinions to himself. He, too, thought that Hayden cared deeply for Cat and could see that she was immensely fond of him as well. He also realized that it wasn't manly to make such an observation and it certainly wasn't wise to oppose Emma or Cat when it came to matters of the heart. So, he did as any good fiancé would do – smiled and nodded, saying nothing.

CHAPTER 48

*H*er last assignment of the day had taken her to a corn maze out in the county. While she was thrilled with the images she'd captured, a misstep on the farm had sent Emma careening to the ground. Now her left leg and arm were covered in drying mud while dirt streaked down her face. Even though it wasn't her most flattering look, she had someone snap her picture. She thought it would be funny to include in her collection of photos for the paper.

Returning home, she couldn't wait to see Colton's reaction to her new look. Emma inched the door open to find him shrugging his shirt off. Unaware of his audience, Colton stared out the window, lost in thought.

"Looks like I'm home just in time," Emma joked, closing the door.

Colton turned. His broad smile grew even bigger when he saw her. "You look positively lovely," he bit back a smile.

Emma recounted her unfortunate fall.

"You missed a spot, luv," Colton said as he dropped a quick kiss to the only clean surface on her face.

"I'm glad you find this so amusing," Emma teased.

Colton slid his pants down his legs.

"Heeey," Emma replied.

"Dirty, Harriet," he said with the shake of his head, "it's time we get back to exercising. That's what I was doing when you came home."

Emma pointed to the dirt and mud that covered most of her body. "I *have* exercised."

"Come on," Colton urged.

"You come on; I'm taking a shower!" She walked into the bathroom knowing he wouldn't follow. Colton was much more into fitness than she was. Emma showered, blotted her hair dry, then wrapped herself in the plush blue towel. She returned to find him doing push-ups.

Emma walked across the room and stood with her feet between his hands. She watched as the sweat rolled across the corded muscles of his back and shoulders. Even though she disliked exercise immensely, she found it rather arousing to watch his muscles flexing with each up and down motion.

She was pulled from her reverie when a kiss landed on her toe. With every downward motion of his push-up, Colton placed gentle kisses on each of her toes until he had effectively nipped them all.

"Well that was nice," Emma said as she wiggled her zebra stripped toenails.

Having abandoned his exercise, Colton brushed his lips along the sensitive skin of her inner ankles. The gentle caress of his lips then landed on each of her calves as his hands massaged her legs.

Colton sat up on his knees and looked up into her eyes as he purposely tugged the towel until it inched toward the floor, surrounding her feet. He raised his hands to cup each breast, placing a kiss upon her stomach. As his thumbs danced across her nipples, she let out a low moan – arching into his touch. Emma laced her fingers through his hair, steadying herself for his pursuit. His arms slid down her body until she felt his hands pressing outward against her inner thighs. When she widened her stance, she was rewarded with a long and lingering kiss appropriately placed on the throbbing flesh between her legs. Emma's head dropped back as she basked in the desire he stirred within her.

He kneaded her backside as his open-mouthed caress continued against her core. As if a switch had been flipped, he pulled away.

"No," Emma protested, trying to pull his head closer

Colton stood, kissed her hard, then sat her on the bed. "Wait for me."

Emma gave him a murderous glance. "You cannot be serious!"

"Oh, I'm serious," Colton grinned at her over his shoulder as he disappeared through the bathroom door. In minutes, he returned fresh from the shower and very much naked.

Emma sat on the edge of the bed, eyes heavy with desire as she watched him approach. He stepped between her open thighs. His eyes slid shut at the feel of her warm hands moving around him. He pushed himself further into her tight grip. She worked him faster as low curses fell from his lips. Colton sucked in a sharp breath when he felt her mouth close around him like a vise.

The gentle rock of his hips increased as his passion was ignited. He fisted the hair at the nape of her neck when she swirled her tongue against him. The pull of her cheeks closing in on him caused him to thrust harder. He roared with need, but stilled himself and her.

Colton pulled away and pushed her back against the bed.

His hard body covered hers and he took her mouth with his own until her lips were red and swollen. His thick flesh pressed against her most sensitive area, never entering, despite her pleas. He ravished her mouth and then her breasts. Her nipples were responsive as his tongue flicked against them sending jolts of need straight to her core.

"Colton, please," Emma whispered.

Without warning, he placed her bended legs in the crook of his arms and dragged her down to the edge of the bed. He pressed his palms to the back of her thighs, pushing her legs back while pulling her knees apart. The glistening folds that greeted him elicited a low growl and almost feral look from him.

A shiver of delight ran through her and was only heightened as he traced his finger down the thin strip of curls. Emma bucked her hips.

"Easy, luv," he murmured as he dropped to his knees, settling himself between her legs.

The slow, deliberate strokes of his fingers pushed her closer and closer to ecstasy while keeping it just out of her reach at the same time. He circled and pressed against her, occasionally thrusting a finger, then two, deep inside, keeping her arousal high. When she felt his moist breath against her inner thighs, she wound her hands into his hair and pulled him straight on as she moved against his mouth. Colton obliged, snaking his tongue out to deliver sweet torture. The combination of the scruff against her delicate thighs, his dancing tongue, and delving fingers resulted in tremors racing through her trembling legs. When Emma dug her heels into the bed and thrust herself harder against his mouth, he pulled back.

She strung together an array of oddly joined curse words. Colton chuckled at her reaction.

Colton moved over her body until his hips aligned with

hers. The feel of his weight pressing against her heightened her arousal, sending a flood of moisture between her legs. One nudge was all it would take to push her over the edge and into the bliss she craved. Colton settled his forearms at each side of her head and just perched there, watching her, but not moving. Emma tried to raise her hips in invitation as her nails pressed into his back, but he simply bore more weight on her - pinning her to the bed. She waited for the fullness that only he could provide. Nothing. Her eyes shot open.

"What are you doing?" She asked in an almost irritated tone. She wanted him, needed him inside her, but he just smiled.

"You're quite beautiful and determined when you're striving for a goal, luv," he said as he brushed a kiss against her lips.

So close, but so far away. Again, she tried to raise her hips. She planned to wrap her legs around him, digging her heels into his bottom, and pulling him to her - the angle assuring that she'd get what she needed. Again, the mass that pressed her into the bed guaranteed that she failed.

"Why are you torturing me?"

Colton pressed his fingers between her legs, her arousal removing any barrier that would prevent them from penetrating. Over and over he drove them deeper, harder until her cries echoed through the room and she teetered on the brink of release. He pulled back , providing the answer that her hard stare demanded.

"Because, luv, it's supposed to make it so much stronger the longer you wait."

Emma let out a pitiful groan. She stared into his eyes that were filled with laughter. "I don't know why I love you!"

Colton nudged forward, entering her ever so slightly. "I can think of a reason." He pushed in again, "Or maybe two."

AMELIA BLAKE

Emma's fingers dug into his backside as she raised her hips to the fullness he was finally providing. He pushed in twice as far. "Maybe four reasons." He stilled himself, halfway in, and looked at the beautiful woman writhing under his body, begging for more – reaching for completion. He grabbed her hips and settled himself with such a force that her ass slapped against his thighs. He hammered into her again and again.

"Eight reasons. I can think of at least eight reasons you love me." With a throaty moan, her orgasm rolled through her body sending jolts of pleasure straight to her toes. Spasms danced through her as her folds pulsed around him. Colton bent to take her mouth hard.

"Up on your knees, luv."

He settled himself behind her. Grasping her hips, he pushed in deep. When her moans of approval spilled from her throat, his thrusts increased and he pumped into her unyielding. Emma quickly felt the pressure building again and pressed her chest closer to bed. With her hips high, she was more anchored and open to the angle that would push her over the edge. The sounds of flesh meeting flesh coupled with their cries of passion as every nerve in her body exploded. She lay there panting for moments as he continued to move inside her drawing out every last wave of pleasure.

Colton lay back and Emma turned to seat herself on him. She bent to kiss him. "Thank you," she whispered across his lips before setting back. His hands fell on her breasts, reawakening her desire. She arched into his hands as his fingertips traced each nipple, pinching them. Emma threw her head back and rocked hard against him. The spasms that still quivered through her inner walls danced across him. Colton fisted the sheets as he thrust harder into her. Her rhythmic motions and moans of pleasure drove him higher, closer to completion. He grabbed her hips and pulled her

432

across him as he thrust deep and hard - her hips meeting every motion. With a roar, lightning shot through him and he pumped into her merciless as he reached his release.

Emma collapsed on his chest letting out a sigh of a well sated woman.

~

Emma awoke to the feel of gentle kisses being placed on her neck and to the feel of a hard ridge against her backside.

"Well, good morning to you, too!" she said over her shoulder.

"I think it could be," Colton said as he nudged himself closer, closing his lips over hers.

Emma raised up to look at the clock. "Do you think you can work your magic in fifteen minutes?"

Colton chuckled. "I'll do my best."

Emma wasn't one of those gals who could hop straight to "business" first thing in the morning, so a quick trip to the bathroom shaved off one minute of their time. As she settled back in bed, he nudged her thighs apart with his knees. Colton pressed himself against her center as he kneaded her breasts. Her arousal quickly matched his own. Setting the pace he knew she liked, he began to move in a familiar rhythm. His breathing became elevated as his thrusts came faster and harder.

Emma ran her hands up his back, holding him tightly to her.

"Oh God," Colton called out.

Emma's eyes grew big. "What? NO!" She whimpered.

Colton buried his face in the recess of her neck and shoulder and let out a loud groan as he thrust hard inside her one final time.

She glanced at the clock. "Are you *freaking* kidding me?

Three minutes? *Three.* I pulled my panties down for three minutes of sexy time?" Emma felt him shake on top of her almost like he was *laughing*. "Are you *laughing*?" She asked with an emphasis on *fing*.

Colton raised his head to look down in her eyes. "I'm sorry, luv. I had to see what your reaction would be." He moved inside her, making her realize he was anything but finished.

"I'm gonna kill you," Emma said as she kissed him.

"Can you wait until we're finished?" He glanced at the clock, "Technically, I still have about ten minutes to 'work my magic'." And he did.

Emma thought that it just might be possible for her to become a morning person after all if waking up with him was like this forever.

CHAPTER 49

*W*ith winter right around the corner, Emma and Colton went for a drive to see the last of the fall foliage. Colton drove down the narrow road, barely large enough for two cars. Emma stole sideways glances at him when the darting sun drew her attention as it passed through the trees. Her fiancé, with his shoulder length hair and dark sunglasses, was more handsome than any Hollywood actor. His yellow shirt popped against his dark jeans and black leather jacket. *He's beautiful.* A smile lit up her face at the thought.

Emma placed her hand on his that rested on the seat between them, caressing it with her thumb. He rewarded her by bringing her hand up to his mouth, kissing it tenderly. Emma leaned across the seat to kiss his cheek then rested her head on his shoulder. "I love you," she said as she returned her focus to their leisurely ride. The gentle double squeeze against her knee was his way of saying, "and I love you," but he said it as well.

The music played lightly in the background as they

turned off the main road onto Oakland Hills Road. "Where are we going?" Emma asked as she straightened in the seat.

"There's a house I saw listed in the paper this morning. I wanted to see if it was something we'd be interested in calling about. Regardless, we're moving somewhere until Dillingham Manor is ready."

Emma was all too familiar with this route. She looked ahead into the distance at the familiar surroundings and wished she could pull into the drive just one more time. Oakland Hills is where she lived before leaving Brookfield.

The single lane road was peaceful with the canopy of tree branches overhead. Colton could see why she had loved it. While the streets of Brookfield certainly would never be considered a metropolis, they were bustling compared to the leaf ridden path before them. He looked forward to the isolation as it was something he wasn't accustomed to.

As Colton sat engrossed in his thoughts, Emma did the same.

She remembered swimming in the pond on hot days after work, the feel of the cool water rushing over her skin as the stress of the day fell away. There was so much about her old stomping grounds that she vividly remembered. She noted the missing bark from the giant Oak tree they passed and recalled the day when the icy road left her in a losing battle with the timber.

A smile even tugged at her lips when she looked around the mountains peppered with trees and remembered her attempt at hiking. Hiking made her hot and sweaty and it hadn't taken her long to realize she wasn't cut out for it!

She saw the polka dotted mailbox ahead and thought back to the day that she'd replaced the original. *Now someone else is using it. That's my mailbox!* Emma thought as a twinge of jealousy gnawed at her. "I used to-"

The clicking of the signal halted her words as Colton

made the turn to climb the gravel driveway. The gasp that escaped her throat was met with a proud smile from her handsome driver.

Her heartstrings strummed into action as butterflies soared through her belly. Colton was turning in to the driveway she knew all too well. As they drove up the incline and the house came into view, her eyes welled up with tears.

He shut the engine off and gave her a moment to process what was happening.

Emma had loved the little white house since the moment she had seen it five years ago. It perched high atop a hill overlooking the road below and a pond beyond that. Mature white Oaks surrounded the house and provided copious amounts of shade on hot summer days and beautiful fall foliage on crisp autumn mornings.

Just being here again was a comforting embrace where she found herself enveloped in tranquility.

She turned to him pushing past the lump in her throat. "Colton, how-"

"Welcome home, sweetheart." That's all he said before pulling her into his arms and capturing her lips with his own.

They exited the truck, Emma bounding around to Colton's side and into his arms. She kissed him firmly over and over again. Every time her lips left his, she said, "Thank you!"

They stood hand in hand as they looked at the quaint wood sided house with a covered porch. It was small with two long windows on either side of the matte black door. The four square windows that ran across the top of it were impossibly high to see out of, but added charm of the three panel door.

The red porch swing made slow, gentle passes in the breeze. Emma recalled countless days of doing the same as she wrapped herself in a throw while reading a novel.

Birds squawked noisily overhead, pulling her from her memory. "How did you know how to find it, Colton? I've never brought you out here."

"Peggy called saying it would be available in a couple weeks. She said she could work in a showing today and gave me the key code in case we got here first. She said you'd be happy and thought I would love it, too, with my 'penchant for fixin' things'." He shook his head and smiled.

Colton watched as Emma eagerly skipped ahead, her ponytail swinging back and forth. She drew her arms tightly around her waist, pulling her thin purple top closer against her body. As she waited at the door, she ran her palms over the thighs of her jeans in an attempt to warm up. "I told you you needed a jacket," Colton laughed as he walked toward her.

"You can warm me up once we're inside," Emma replied, blowing warm air into her hands.

Colton punched in the key code and pushed the door open. "After you, luv."

Boxes and packaging papers littered the wooden floor in the near vacant living room that used to be hers. Several pictures hung askew on the beige walls as if they'd been knocked sideways in the careless retreat of movers. To her right, a single kitchen chair with a busted out straw bottom lay overturned near the fireplace. Emma imagined it happened in an effort to remove a clock that had likely hung above the oak mantle like hers once had. And even though she was surrounded by trash and someone else's things, it felt like coming home. The house held a special place in her heart and she was happy that she had been given the opportunity to share it with Colton.

Walking a few steps across the room, Emma motioned to a column. "This is where I used to hang my Christmas cards every year – even the ones I got from family that I didn't like." She heard Colton chuckle as she ran her hands along the smooth column that divided the living room and dining room.

The living room backed into the dining room which sat adjacent to the kitchen.

They walked from room to room which didn't take long. The two bedroom one bath home was tiny. And it was perfect.

Emma threw her hands out to the side. A smile crept across her face. "Hear that?" She asked. Colton drew his brows together and shook his head signaling that he hadn't heard anything. She pointed towards the kitchen. "*That* is the sound of a drippy kitchen sink."

Colton laughed, "Well, I can fix that."

"Can we wait awhile? That's one of the sounds that used to help me sleep at night."

Colton closed the distance between them as he backed her against the wall. He cupped her chin and held it firmly as his other hand slipped against her bottom, pulling her flush with his body. "Emma," he whispered across her lips, "I intend to thoroughly exhaust you every. Single. Night."

Colton's voice was raw with passion as he growled the last three words, punctuating them as he thrust his hips into hers. Emma's heart thrummed in her chest as she imagined the ways.

"We can keep it," Colton said, "but I can assure you that you won't need the lull of a drippy sink to help you sleep." Her fingers wove through his thick hair pulling him even closer as they became lost in a passionate kiss.

The door creaked opened behind them, Peggy calling out before she was fully inside. "Well kids, what's . . . *the verdict?*" Her voice trailed off with the sight of them entangled in a lover's embrace.

Colton pulled away slightly - eyes still transfixed on

Emma. "We'll take it." He caressed her cheek with his thumb when her smile matched his own.

"I just knew you'd love it, Colton. Emma always loved it out here. Now, we better get those gutters looked at. They probably need cleaned. I know you're the handy sort, so this house will be just perfect for you, Colton. Now . . ."

As Peggy rambled on and on about to-do lists, Colton drew Emma closer, "Lucky for you I'm the 'handy *sort*.'"

Emma swatted him away playfully. She was so happy to be in this house again, to be beginning her life with Colton.

The week had passed by much too quickly and now the weekend was upon them. It was Halloween day and also the day that half the town had been looking forward to, as many of them would attend their first masquerade ball.

The frantic knocking on the door jolted Emma out of a peaceful sleep. She threw the covers off and raised up in time to see Lisa sail past her, "Gotta pee."

Emma sat up in a semi reclined position, her palms planted firmly on the bed beside her hips. She tried to blink away the confusion as the elements of the morning assaulted her - bright light, conversation, and Lisa. *Why is Lisa here?* She cleared her throat to speak past the sleep in her voice. "You gotta pee? Why didn't you pee at your house?" Emma asked as she tried to make sense of the situation.

She heard all sorts of commotion coming from the bathroom - the rattling of a plastic bag, tearing of paper, or was it a plastic wrapper? Then she heard the undeniable sounds of tinkling.

"I've never had to pee so bad in all my life!" Lisa exclaimed. "I'm late," she yelled through the closed door.

Emma looked at the clock. "We don't have our manicures until after lunch. *Why* are you here so early, and what the heck are you doing in there?"

The door opened, and Lisa threw a box at Emma. "Read this - I can't focus."

Emma stared at the box as she wiped the sleep from her eyes. "Oh shit!"

"Where's Colton?" Lisa asked.

"I don't know. He probably went down to get some breakfast since the door was unlocked." Emma brought her attention back to the box. "Lisa, you think you're pregnant?"

"Just tell me what I'm looking for!"

Emma read the instructions and called them out. "Ok, it says two lines for pregnant, one line for not, and don't count a faint line. And that it takes three minutes to read."

"I can't believe this," she heard Lisa say, the despair in her voice evident.

Emma bolted into the bathroom, box in hand. "Does it say already?"

Lisa was sitting on the closed toilet lid. With her head held low, dark hair cascaded around her face, hiding her anguish. She brushed it back and grasped the long locks at the crown at the sound of the Emma's voice.

"No, I'm just scared. This can't be happening to me, Emma!" Lisa stared at her friend. "I couldn't do this alone; that's why I'm here."

"Is Bryce not home?"

Lisa gave her a deadpan stare. "If I am pregnant, you know the timing's not right for it to be Bryce's."

"Oh." Emma recalled the marine that Lisa had dated last. Her mouth drew into a hard grimace that mirrored Lisa's.

Emma walked across the room and sat on the edge of the

tub. "How about we find out together," she said as she placed a reassuring squeeze against Lisa's knee.

"This waiting is killing me!" Lisa said as she shot to her feet and began to pace with the pee stick in hand. "How long has it been, anyway?"

Emma glanced at her watch. "One minute." They both grimaced.

Hearing the door slam, Lisa realized that Colton had returned. She hadn't wrapped her head around the fact that she might be pregnant and wasn't ready to share the news with anyone other than Emma. She opened the closest drawer to her and tossed the evidence inside.

"Did you seriously just toss that on my tooth brush?" Emma laughed as she heard the drawer close.

"I can't take it with me – Bryce and I have always used condoms," she whispered. "If it's negative, I'm not ready to explain that Ron and I took stupid chances, you know? And anyway, the results haven't read yet. And I don't want to be alone when they do."

Lisa folded the box flat and stuck it in her waistband, pulling her shirt overtop to cover it. "I'll toss this before I get home." She opened the drawer again for one last look but it still hadn't read. Lisa turned to leave then turned back to face her. "Emma, if the result is positive, don't tell me over the phone, ok?" She hugged her goodbye. They exited the bathroom together much to the confusion of Colton.

Lisa flashed her dangle earrings. "Needed jewelry for tonight." She gave him her best smile then forced herself to calmly walk to the door.

CHAPTER 50

*I*n preparation for the ball, Cat and Emma met Lisa at the salon for mani-pedis.

While they waited for three chairs to open up, Lisa drew her friends closer in a semi huddle and spoke in whispered tones. She directed her question at Emma. "One or two?"

"What the hell are you talking about?" Cat questioned. "Are you Emma's potty police now?" She smirked at her own joke.

They both laughed at Cat's lack of couth.

Emma smiled a reassuring smile and reached across Cat's legs to place her hand on Lisa's. She squeezed gently. "One line, Lisa," she whispered. "You're not pregnant!"

A long drawn out, "Oh," was Cat's only response; that's all she could muster. She was just trying to be funny with the "potty police" comment. She had no idea that it was an actual part of the equation.

"Cat," Lisa said bringing her attention back, "please don't tell Hayden. And especially don't tell Bryce." At Cat's quizzical look, Lisa added, "Just do the math!" She drew in her bottom lip and exhaled loudly.

Cat nodded in acknowledgement as the memory of a very handsome, but rather asshole-ish marine came into her mind.

Emma redirected the awkward moment by pointing to a hair style in a fashion magazine.

"I like that up do. I'm gonna attempt it for tonight." As the girls discussed various hairstyles, a tall, slim man showed them to their chairs.

Emma sat in the middle with Cat to her left and Lisa to her right. As she read over the spa options, her friends suddenly burst out into laugher. Emma looked up in time to see a familiar face settle on the stool at her feet. The lady looked up, captured her gaze and said, "Oh, ha-low ageen, A-mee! Oops! I be ri ba." She stood and hastily retreated to a back room.

Emma sat her mouth to the side and exhaled forcefully as she closed her eyes. She drummed her fingers on her leg. After a few moments, she opened her eyes and looked straight ahead. She tried not to smile, tried not to react at all when she realized that *Jamie* "the maar-can" had a brand new job and would likely, once again, find a whole other way to torture her – much to her friends delight!

"It's ok, Emma," Lisa laughed. "She'll 'ma yu buful!"

"And what's even better," Cat rolled with laughter as she bounced her feet up and down in the waterless tub, "she'll make you 'fee goo'! You might even get another who-ha overhaul. Check the package. I bet it's on there!" Cat laughed until her side hurt.

Everyone turned to look at the friends who were clearly enjoying themselves – some more than others.

Emma slowly closed her eyes again and shook her head

lightly from side to side as a smile swept across her face. She couldn't help it. It *was* funny. And it wasn't, all at the same time!

Once her nails were done, Emma called Colton to tell him that she'd been abducted by her so called friends. She explained about seeing *Jamie* the 'maar-can' again and he laughed right along with her.

He didn't mind that the girls wanted to help each other with their hair. He was happy that Emma was having a good time. He told her that everything would be waiting for her at Victorian Gardens.

When Emma arrived, she saw Colton's truck parked in the circular drive in front of the mansion. It was hours still before guests would arrive, but Colton had to be there early in case the caterers, florist, valets, or any other hired hands had questions for him.

Having sent Lisa on her way, Emma walked up the steps and pushed her way through the glass doors. She stepped down into the ballroom and took in the scene before her. The room was abuzz with workers. Some arranged tables, others fussed with the dark table cloths, and a few placed completed floral centerpieces in the middle of each table.

She was pleased that the plump white hydrangeas didn't have an overpowering floral scent. *Flowers smell like death.* She frowned. Instinctively, she looked down, rubbing her wrist at the thought. Shaking the image of her marred flesh from her head, she instead noted the contrasting beauty of the white flowers rooted deep in crimson hued pebbles. They were gobbled up by short square vases and she thought the stark difference in colors against the dark table covers they sat upon was just perfect.

Not seeing Colton in the ballroom, Emma climbed the impressive staircase to the second floor, running her fingertips along the handrail as she went. The smooth mahogany was soft like satin under her touch.

The last time Emma visited Victorian Gardens, Mrs. Lewis had been less than hospitable, offering no tour whatsoever. She really wasn't certain where to find the dressing rooms that Colton had mentioned.

When she reached the top of the staircase, she wandered down the hall to the left in search of him.

She saw him through an open doorway near the end of the hall. He hadn't heard her approach. It reminded her of the only night he had spent with her at Dillingham Manor. He had found her room the same way, through the only open door.

Emma quietly observed from the corridor. Colton sat in the far corner of the bedroom in a walnut chair that matched the antique furniture of the room. Directly in front of him sat a vast bookcase that spanned the length of the wall. Novels of various sizes filled it to capacity. To his right was an arched fireplace that looked to be from another time, a restoration, she imagined. The marbled apricot hue of the frame, paired with the walnut mantel, blended well with the cream colored walls. On either side of the fireplace were long, wide windows with deep bench seating. *Perfect reading nooks*, Emma thought.

She brought her attention back to Colton. His dark hair shielded his face as he worked to adjust the strap on his mask. His plain gray t-shirt pulled just right, outlining his defined chest when his hands stretched behind his head. Her eyes fell on the corded muscles that clung to the thin fabric when he moved. Emma was immediately thankful for his dedication to fitness and was reminded of how a recent exercise regimen had fallen to the wayside in favor of the only *workout* she liked. A delicious smile played across her lips at the memory.

The mask that he worked on now rested in his denim clad lap.

Emma thought that most men would fall short of the mark with such basic clothing of jeans and a cotton shirt, but on her fiancé, they were positively gorgeous. *He* was gorgeous – inside and out.

She glanced at her watch, the plan falling into place as familiar feelings began to stir within her. Emma closed her eyes and inhaled. Exhaling louder than she intended, she opened them again only to find Colton now watching her and smiling a knowing smile.

"There he is," she called out in a voice just above a whisper as she entered the room. When he made the move to stand, Emma placed her hands out, palms forward as she instructed him to stay put. He smirked, but settled back in his seat.

Colton watched appreciatively as Emma entered the room. Her chestnut hair fell in loose curls around her shoulders, the darkness of her locks lovely against the soft buttercup top she wore. His gaze traced the necklace that dipped to her navel. As his appraisal continued down her body, his eyes rested on the white tips of her toes poking out under long dark jeans. He smiled when she wiggled them.

Grasping the door knob, she gently tugged the door toward her then backed up against it, bumping it closed with her backside. Emma dropped her bag on the floor and smiled at him as she reached her hand behind her back. In the thick silence of the room, the unmistakable click caught Colton's attention as the lock tumbled into position. He quirked a brow, but said not a word. Emma walked toward him slowly, his gaze steadily locked on hers.

She stopped just shy of his knees. Bending forward, her lips were only inches from his. He reached out to cup her cheek as she pulled away.

"Emma," he groaned when she stepped back and walked away, taking his mask with her.

She walked to the window seat. Glancing back at him over her shoulder, she answered the question he had yet to form. "I thought you'd need both your hands for more . . . *pressing matters,* Mr. Graves." Emma winked as she placed the item on the padded seat before returning to his side.

Hungry eyes met with a devilish smile as he reached for her, pulling her across his lap and deep into the kiss she had denied him. Emma turned to straddle his lap. "We have to do this my way."

"Is that right?" Colton asked, fingering the long strand of charcoal pearls she wore around her neck.

She weaved her hands through his thick hair, massaging lightly. "We can do this only if you agree to some rules."

"Rules," he repeated against the skin of her décolletage as he unbuttoned the shirt that posed the barrier he sought to breach.

"You're not listening," Emma sang as she exaggeratedly wiggled in his lap to get his attention.

Letting her top fall to the floor, Colton continued his trail of kisses. Cupping each breast, he pressed upwards and ran featherlike kisses upon the swell of both. The dipping of his tongue into her cleavage brought Emma back to her request.

She gently grabbed the back of his hair and tugged lightly until she brought his face up, capturing his gaze and his amusement.

"I'm a little busy, luv," Colton chuckled as he attempted to return to his previous path.

"We can't mess up my hair-"

"Why not?" Colton interrupted, "you're messing up mine," he smiled as he fumbled for the clasp of her bra.

"Colton!"

"Hair. Yes, it's lovely – can't mess it up," he laughed, dipping his head back down.

Another tug, "or my make-up."

"That might be a challenge," he said as the scruff from his trimmed beard brushed the delicate column of her neck when he nipped at her ear.

"And I can't get sweaty or this will all be for nothing," she motioned to her hair and makeup.

"And how do you propose that I do it right without you getting sweaty, hmm?" Colton freed her bra without waiting for her answer.

"I just can't move too much."

"You're bossy," he said as his gaze followed the same pursuit as his hands – straight to her chest, ignoring the necklace that now hung between her exposed breasts.

Emma cleared her throat. Colton's focus retrained on her face and the demands she had placed. "Let me get this straight." He pretended to think for a moment while he tapped his chin. He began to tick the points off on his fingers. "So, I can't mess up your make-up, or your hair, and you can't move too much because you don't want to sweat? Do I have the rules down?" Emma nodded. A devious smile spread across his lips. He leaned in close, "I can work with that."

"I'm almost afraid to ask how you'll work with that," Emma laughed.

"Is this new?" Colton asked as he tugged on the pearls, pulling her into a kiss.

Breaking free, she answered. "We had an idea to weave pearls through our hair for tonight, but couldn't make it work. Now I have no use for them."

Colton smiled. *I do . . .* He tugged the necklace over her head, tossing it on the bed before capturing a nipple in his mouth. He caressed her back as he held her tight. Echoes of desire filled the silence as Emma's passion was ignited. Colton turned his attention to the other breast, mirroring his previous efforts. Releasing her, he pulled her into a hungry kiss. "The rules. I forgot,." he nuzzled the tender area between her neck and shoulder.

With each passing moment, she was more than ready to abandon the rules.

Emma wrapped her legs around him when he stood. He kissed her gently. She didn't care that he was fully dressed while she clung to him naked from the waist up. He kissed her again then sat her to her feet.

Colton snaked his arms around her and pulled her close. He raked his palms across her backside and reveled in the fact that she tilted into him, her desire mounting and matching his own. One hand pulling her against him, he brought the other up to gently grasp her chin between his thumb and finger. He held her gaze longer than necessary as if he were drinking her in then tilted her mouth to his, capturing her lips once more. With every plunder of her mouth, he inched her closer to the bed until her knees caught the edge and she lost her balance, falling to her bottom.

Emma took advantage of their physical position and reached forward, unbuttoning his pants. Colton caught her hands in his and pulled her to her feet, turning her around.

"You make following the rules quite difficult, Emma. That will certainly mess up what's left of your lipstick," he growled against her ear. One arm crossed over her chest holding her tightly to his body, while the other gently caressed her hip. Colton slowly ran his fingertips across her neck, down her chest, brushing lightly over her nipples, then across her stomach until her torso trembled under his touch. He slid his hand inside her jeans, his failure to unfasten them only adding to the friction of his touch.

Emma's head fell back against his shoulder. She wrapped an arm around his neck and turned slightly, inviting a kiss. His tongue plunged into her mouth, his fingers refusing to mirror the pace. Instead, he gently teased her. She tried to arch further into his touch knowing that his hesitation stemmed from the fact that he was purposely prolonging the seduction.

"Colton, please," she groaned against his mouth, her hips lifting and receding of their own accord.

He kissed her hard, her grinding spurring him on. When he pulled out of the kiss, he saw her lips red and swollen, the roughness of his beard against her delicate face evident. He knew he'd already ruined her make-up. *One out of three's not bad . . .*

Colton inched her toward the bed again. Emma's approval was apparent when he pulled his hand from her jeans and slowly began working them down. She kicked them and her shoes to the side then hooked her thumbs under the edges of her pink panties.

"Maybe we'll do this my way," Colton whispered.

Emma shivered in anticipation. She had no idea what he

meant, but she was ready. Again she reached for her panties to tug them down. Colton's hand caught her wrists. She turned slightly to face him over her shoulder as his body pressed over her. Excitement coursed through her body.

She felt something slide across her wrist. Emma looked down and then back at the man who loomed at her backside. "Like my necklace?" She asked genuinely confused.

A seductive chuckle escaped his throat as he nipped her ear. "Yes, but I think it will look better as a bracelet or two – and it will keep you from 'moving too much'." He smiled as he reminded her of her own rules.

Emma's heart began to pound in her chest *in anticipation*. He kissed her tenderly as he delicately bound her wrists in front of her.

"They're very pretty," Colton whispered as he looked over her shoulders at her wrists.

Emma looked down at her hands that rested against her belly. The charcoal pearls enveloping both wrists were- Her thoughts were interrupted by the feel of Colton's splayed hand trailing down her back. It breached the fringe of her underwear. Jolts of need raced through her as he cupped her cheek then plunged two fingers deep inside her aching core, her desire abundantly evident.

He growled against her ear as he repeated the motion, "You liked having your wrists bound more than I thought you would." He continued his rhythmic plunder. "You do like that, don't you, Emma?"

She wanted to deny it, wanted to say no, but was afraid that he'd stop completely if she didn't answer, or lied altogether. *Only a whore would like having her wrists restrained, right?* But she *did* like it, liked everything he was doing, and didn't want him to stop. *I'm a shameless, shameless hussy.*

Emma knew when Colton pulled away that he thought he had crossed a line.

"Don't," she said barely audible.

"You don't like it?" Colton asked confused because her body gave every indication that she did like it *a lot*.

She hesitated only a moment glancing at her bound wrists. "I *do* like it very much. Don't stop," Emma said as she pushed back against him while bracing her knees on the bed.

She nearly cried out in need when she heard the pull of his zipper behind her.

Colton placed his palm on the small of her back gently pushing her forward until she rested on her forearms. He grasped her hips and tugged them upward, positioning her where he wanted. She felt his fingers skirt her folds as he pulled her panties to the side then slowly pushed in.

"Yes," Emma whispered, leaning further into him.

The knock at the door made her want to scream. Colton bent forward, laying his cheek against her back. "Bloody hell!" He murmured, but continued to move inside her hoping the unwanted person would leave. The knock sounded again. "Go away!" He shouted in an irritated tone.

"Delivery for Miss Saint-Claire," the announcement came.

"I was working on a delivery of my own," Colton said, nudging her forward. A soft curse escaped both their lips with a final rapt at the door.

"Just leave it," Colton instructed.

"I'm sorry, Sir. It requires Miss Saint-Claire's signature."

Emma buried her face in the soft quilt as she grumbled incoherent words and banged her outstretched wrists against the bed in protest. She pulled herself back up on her forearms. "Gimme a minute!" she yelled.

They both groaned when he withdrew. Colton stepped away zipping his pants as he moved to gather her clothes. Emma flipped over on the bed attempting to work her wrists free.

"Colton, we have a problem," her laughter let him know that it was nothing dire.

He turned to face her. She held her wrists up, rolling and flipping them toward each other in a show that let him know she couldn't free them herself, her efforts only causing them to bind tighter.

He walked to her, placing her clothes beside her on the bed. Colton worked to loosen the impossible knot, but had done such an efficient job, he couldn't get them unwound either.

"They're just costume jewelry. You're gonna have to break them," Emma said. She couldn't contain the giggle that spilled out of her at the predicament they found themselves in.

Colton knew she was right. The only way to free her was to rip the strand of pearls loose. Careful not to hurt her, he wound his fingers through the beads, hefting them apart. A cascade of charcoal beads exploded through the air. The sound of them clanking against the hardwood floor made it apparent to Emma that bondage was better left to crafty storytellers in novels than in the bedrooms of real people who had to deal with the fallout if things went awry.

"I'm so sorry," Colton said as he kissed and rubbed her wrists. Looking around at the aftermath, he pinched the bridge of his nose and shook his head in amused disbelief. "I foresaw that going, differently, smoother, in my head." He chuckled as he handed her her clothing.

Emma hastily pulled her jeans on then fumbled with the buttons of her shirt. She was sure that the messenger had no doubt what was going on behind the closed doors.

Carefully sidestepping the pearls that littered the floor, she smoothed wrinkles from her clothing that had lay piled in heaps. She attempted to arrange her hair in the mirror, but decided that was pointless. She took a deep breath, clutched the knob, and swung the door open.

The kid standing before her was young, maybe twenty years old. His sandy blonde hair looked as disheveled as hers, but she suspected *his* style was intentional. Ear bud headphones draped down his chest, the long string disappearing into the pocket of his khaki pants where she could see the outline of his phone. He wore a red striped polo that bore the same hue as his crimson cheeks.

She followed his gaze and wanted to hide when she caught sight of her plump nipples straining against the thin shirt. *No doubt at all what we were doing.* Emma smiled in embarrassment of her own at the thought. "I needed to sign something?"

"Yes," he said shoving a clip board and ink pen into her hands. He pointed to the line that required her signature, then handed her the square package.

Before she could reach for her purse to retrieve a tip, Colton provided one over her shoulder. The messenger grasped the money, thanked them, then left.

Emma looked at the gift in her hands. It was pink with a matching ribbon, two shades lighter than the box. She walked to the window nook, pulling the ribbon free and allowing it to fall beside her as she sat. She wiggled the lid off the box and removed a folded note. A cotton square concealed the contents. When she lifted it, three diamond studded hair pins were revealed. They were beautiful. A family heirloom, she suspected.

"Thank you," she said to Colton. "They're beautiful."

He knelt before her caressing her knees while peeking

into the box. "They are lovely, Emma." He captured her gaze, "But they're not from me.

She drew her brows together wondering who would know to send a gift to her at Victorian Gardens. Unfolding the creased letter, she scanned it quickly in search of the author. A gasp escaped her throat once the discovery was made. "The note is from your Mother. These were your grandmothers."

He smiled. "Indeed they were."

Emma continued to read. The long pewter hair pins were tipped with chiseled metal flowers surrounding diamond centers. They had belonged to Colton's great, great-grandmother, Elizabeth Dillingham. His mother wanted Emma to wear them tonight at the ball as her great-grandmother once had. "I can't believe she gave these to me," Emma whispered. "It will be an honor to wear them. I guess I'll be doing an up do after all. I want her to see how much I appreciate her generosity."

"As you know, she's been ill."

Emma nodded.

Colton inspected the contents of the box, picking up a long pin to investigate. "I received these earlier in the week. She mailed them in case she couldn't fly in for the ball."

"That was so sweet of her. But I don't understand how they ended up coming here by messenger."

"That's simple," Colton smiled a crooked grin. "I forgot to bring them with me and called Miss Francine. She found them on the bed and sent them over by messenger."

"You're too much," Emma said as she leaned down to kiss him. "Your Mom is something else, too."

"I'm eager for her to meet you because I know she will love you as much as I do," Colton reached forward, brushing the back of his fingertips down her cheek.

Emma smiled and nuzzled her face into his hand, kissing

his palm. "I hope she feels well enough to make the trip. Have you called to see if she made her plane?"

"No," Colton said. "But I checked online and saw the airfare charges, so the tickets I reserved have been used. Still yet, she may not feel well enough to attend tonight. Eleanor may, though."

Emma thought about Colton's mom. From what he had told her, his mother was very different from herself. His description made her seem stuffy and reserved, or maybe proper and classy would be better terms. Either way, Emma was the complete opposite. She was forevermore putting her foot in her mouth allowing her crude humor to shine through in times that it often shouldn't. *What if I say the totally wrong thing? I don't know the first thing about religion or geography. What if she thinks I'm stupid or rude?* Emma dropped her head, her gaze falling on her legs. *Or fashion impaired, fat, and just plain ugly.* She instinctively sucked her stomach in at the thought. "Colton, I'm nervous about meeting her."

"Emma," Colton tipped her chin up with a firm finger, "I know you well enough to know some of the scenarios that are likely playing out in your head. Don't try to be someone that you're not. Just be yourself. She'll like you. Trust me. You don't have to impress her. Just be you."

"Just be me? What if I say or do something stupid, Colton? She won't be so impressed then!"

"You tripped over a squirrel on the very day I met you, and I fell in love with you still." He smiled and she did too remembering that day.

Emma looked at the hair pins then glanced at her watch. "We still have hours before the ball begins. Cinderella has some transforming to do before she has any hopes of impressing the queen mother." She laughed and bunched her long hair in a cascade of flowing locks.

"Hours, huh?" He looked from Emma to the big door behind him that he wanted to press her up against. "I think it's time to pick up where we left off . . ."

CHAPTER 51

*A*s requested, the yellow cab pulled up just shy of the gates. The entrance to the lakeside estate was up ahead to the right. Derrick Wells shouldered his leather bag and held a fifty dollar bill in his hand – more than enough to cover the cab fare but not so generous that he would be memorable.

The chauffeur - short, tan, and round opened the door behind him after popping the trunk lid. His passenger stepped out, slipping the money into his waiting hand.

The plan was forming before Derrick's feet had even touched the pavement. He had been uncertain as to how he would secure the names he needed without raising suspicion, but the answer appeared right before him as the black car crawled passed. It un-assuredly approached the gates and then entered after hesitation. *This is promising,* Derrick thought to himself. He grabbed the black duffle bag from the trunk, and bid adieu to his cab driver as he entered the gates on foot, following the red taillights of the indecisive guest.

Derrick took advantage of a small labyrinth shrub just off the path of the driveway and easily concealed the heavy black bag. He knew that when he retrieved it at the end of the night, Amanda Taylor's fate would forever be altered.

The icy coldness that drove him offered no remorse for what he had planned.

Voices ahead brought his focus back to his task at hand.

He watched as the man exited the car for a valet dressed in a maroon uniform. Rather than walking up the steps and joining the other party goers, he crossed the path to the lake where he stood alone. The man held his head low, toeing something on the ground. *He can't even make the decision to go inside!* Derrick thought to himself and wondered how the loser had even garnered an invitation to begin with?

Dr. Wells had worked in the mental health field long enough to recognize the signs of a person struggling to fit in. And the man who stood at the edge of the lake appeared to have a hefty affliction with it, despite his debonair looks.

He took in the stranger's attributes as he thought of an excuse to approach him. The stranger stood tall, maybe six feet and was dressed like most of the other men there – black tux and white shirt. His black hair was cut short and styled neatly. The man glanced toward the house, began a slow gate forward, then stopped. He needed a purpose to nudge him through the doors, and the cruel stranger who watched him was about to provide one.

Derrick smiled at the thought and the realization that his mark was right in front of him. The plan was falling into place with fewer obstacles than originally perceived.

"Show time," Derrick said to himself as he approached the tall stranger. "Excuse me."

Startled, the man jumped. "Yes?"

"Hi, my name is Ben. I know we've met, but I can't recall your name."

"Geoffrey," the man provided as he tried to place Derrick.

"I apologize, Geoffrey. I'm fairly new in town and just can't keep everyone straight," Derrick lied.

"No problem," Geoffrey said placing his mask in the same hand that held his invitation. He extended his hand to greet the stranger who claimed to know him.

"I work for a messenger service that was hired to provide a twist to tonight's entertainment," Derrick said. He pointed to the taillights that were disappearing around the circular lake road. "And I left the most important part of my kit in the cab," he frowned.

"What type of twist are you providing?" Geoffrey asked with a hint of trepidation.

"A Halloween riddle," Derrick answered. He opened his bag to reveal five shimmering boxes. "The curator requested that we drop off these gifts to certain guests. The problem is that I was running late and didn't get the names on the packages. Now I'm here at the event and the names in question are lying on the car seat of the cab that dropped me off." Again, he pointed to the road and sighed exaggeratedly.

"I'm not sure that I can help you, Ben."

"Actually, you can," Derrick added. "You can help me with names. Two of them are friends with a journalist, Emma somebody."

"Emma Saint-Claire," Geoffrey provided with a smile.

Derrick had made a connection, made Geoffrey feel important and needed. The rest was smooth sailing. "Right, there's a redhead and a dark haired lady, but I don't know their names."

"The redhead is Emma's cousin. Her friends call her Cat, but her real name is Cathryn. Cathryn Morgan. The other friend is Lisa Hernandez."

"Yes, yes! That's it! Man, am I happy to have run into you. That's perfect!" Derrick said as he scribed their names on the envelopes and tucked them inside ribbons on the gifts. He wanted a "gift" to go to Colton, but since he was the one who supposedly hired the agency, that story wouldn't fly.

He had two more names to get and then the fun could begin. It didn't matter who received these, he just needed two more people to complete the scam. "Her," Derrick motioned to the random lady stepping from the car. "What's her name? She's one of the people that I'm supposed to give one to?"

Geoffrey looked to the lady who had just stepped from the white car, then looked back at the man he called Ben. "Her?" He questioned. He looked back at Mrs. Loretta with her poufy teased hair that was so black, it had a blue tinge to it. "Oh, the one in the white dress is Loretta Townsand. Are you sure she's on your list? She's a little crazy!" He laughed.

Derrick chuckled, "I don't question it, man, I just do my job. It pays the bills."

I'll allow three more cars, then choose the next person that gets out after that. "Aunt Jemima over there," Derrick pointed to the lady wearing the orange, black, and green dress.

"Aunt Jemima?" Geoffrey laughed and shook his head. Derrick nodded and was provided with her name, Francine Jones. He jotted her name on the envelope, placed the box back in the bag, and closed the flap.

Derrick nearly choked on his playfulness. He wasn't a playful person – he was vengeful and that fury would come out in spades on this night.

"Do you have them all now?" Geoffrey asked as he looked at his watch realizing they were late.

"Yes, shall we?" Derrick asked, making an 'after you' motion with his hand.

The pair proceeded down the cobblestone path away from the lake. "Geoffrey, do you think you could do me one more favor? It's an easy task; I just need you to call out the names at the appropriate time. That will leave me available to assist our recipients without them knowing that I'm part of the game."

Geoffrey agreed and the plan was set in motion. At the predetermined time, he would announce the recipients without giving Derrick away as an accomplice - allowing him to kill two birds with one stone, so to speak.

Geoffrey had no idea that he was making a deal with the devil, for there was nothing kind about the man he had struck up a friendship with.

"Damn it!" Derrick spat through gritted teeth.

Geoffrey looked over at him as they approached the steps. "Now what's the matter?"

"Not only did I leave my list in the cab, but I left my invitation, too. I'm going to get fired if I don't make it inside."

"I can get you inside," Geoffrey nodded toward the man at the top of the stairs who was checking the invitations, "I know him."

Derrick knocked the contents from Geoffrey's hands when he excitedly shouldered his bag again. "Gosh! I'm so sorry," he said as he bent to pick up the items: a mask, an invitation, and the valet tag to Geoffrey's car.

He placed the mask in Geoffrey's hand and the invitation in the doorman's. Conversation ensued immediately and no one noticed when the valet tag was slipped into Derrick's own pocket.

His charismatic demeanor put the doorman at ease as he explained his predicament. The bag of gifts along with Geoffrey's friendship with the man granted him entry.

He had been very convincing . . . which was about to prove devastation for Emma.

With the first few obstacles hurdled, Derrick lowered his mask and strode through the doors with arrogant self-assurance. He smiled at how easily he slipped in uninvited. *Idiots never cease to amaze me.*

He stepped down into the massive ballroom. Adrenaline raced through him as his gaze swept the room for her. "Who are you looking for?" Geoffrey asked, having popped to his side like an eager to please pup.

Derrick closed his eyes and inhaled sharply at the unwelcomed intrusion. His new friend wanted to be joined at the hip.

"I need to step over here and make a call. If the curator sees me hanging around talking, he'll report me to the boss. I'll catch up with you later."

Having successfully ditched his tag-a-long, Derrick leaned against a smooth ivory column and took in the scene before him. Round tables draped in elegant black cloths lined the perimeter of the room. Behind them, to the left, massive windows framed the walls and were wrapped in crimson and crème flowing curtains. Throughout the rest of the room, well placed wall niches housed expensive lighted statues and floral arrangements. *Not a black rose in sight; such a pity . . .*

High-pitched laughter redirected his focus to the guests. With everyone wearing masks, Derrick knew that finding Amanda would be more challenging, but over the last few months, predatory urges had arisen in him, readying him for the hunt.

Spotting his new friend, he was relieved that Geoffrey bought his story about getting in trouble.

As he continued to sweep the room, Derrick noted the

lack of women on the ballroom floor. He counted. *One, two . . . ten.* The announcer's voice shattered his concentration. An evil smile crept across his face when his attention was diverted. He realized that all the ladies were being announced, individually. *Unless her name has already been called, my chances of finding her have just improved.*

In the center of the room, a vast staircase spilled out onto the mahogany floor. The Belle's of the ball lined the stairs and the railings beyond that led to it. They stood in a T formation. Alternating, they single-filed downward as their names were called.

A masked speaker stood at a podium on the floor to the left of the staircase. He took great pride in making sure that each lady had ample time to maneuver the stairs where she would join her date and then be led onto the dance floor. One by one, they paired up until there was one female guest left to announce.

The final guest approached the staircase. She hesitated before descending. Her emerald green dress with its tight bodice was accentuated by the jewel yoke neckline that sparkled like diamonds. The long satin skirt fell onto each step as she glided down.

Being the only one that he'd seen in that hue, he had every hope that Amanda Taylor was the next to be announced. Derrick closed his eyes and smiled a knowing smile as the announcer's words echoed through his head. "The extraordinarily beautiful, Emma Saint-Claire."

Evil laughter rolled silently through him. Derrick was definitely at the advantage. *You can run, little rabbit, but you cannot hide . . .*

Emma paused on the staircase as she watched Colton approach. He looked devastatingly handsome in the tailored tux that matched his raven hair. The perfect bowtie around his neck caught her attention, and she was glad to see him wearing it. It had taken seven attempts to get it to his satisfaction even though it looked exactly the same to her each time. She smiled at the thought.

His black mask fit snuggly against his face. When his emerald gaze swept her body, she couldn't help but shiver from the butterflies in her stomach. She ducked her head and continued down the stairs.

"You look positively lovely, Emma," Colton said as he kissed her hand then pulled her into his arms.

She gave him a playful reprimand. "I don't like that word."

"Lovely?" He smiled a crooked grin and winked.

Emma pulled her hand from his, playfully propping it on her hip. "Extraordinary. And you know I don't like it, Mr. Graves," she grinned.

He thought back to the day at the river when she told him she hated that word. Colton smiled and bent to lightly kiss her lips. "You *are* beautiful Miss Saint-Claire," he reached for her hand, kissing every digit on her fingers, and then her engagement ring. "And you *are* extraordinary. And I'm *well* aware of the meaning of the word and that's precisely why I had him say it," he tenderly stroked her cheek.

Emma couldn't help the smile that played across her lips. "God, I love you!"

"And I love you and your ornate mask."

Colton had picked out Emma's dress for the ball, but she had selected her own mask. The mask itself was cream in color, but very little of that showed through. Shimmering emerald and silver beads were woven throughout casting heavy shadows around the eyes and edges and drawing to a slight peak on her forehead. Wispy emerald green feathers adorned one side, fanning out to create a classic elegant style.

Derrick adjusted his own mask and laughed to himself at the many people who had taken a second glance at it. It was nothing like the ones he had seen there. But then again, *he* was nothing like the people there.

He watched as Amanda and her tall companion made their way to the dance floor. She danced and laughed as if she didn't have a care in the world. And she clung to the man as if he was her world.

Derrick thought about his kids and Jaz and all that Amanda had deprived him of. He palmed the knife in his jacket pocket, but willed himself to calm down.

Even though the game he had planned for tonight was more for the torment of her friends than for her, he wouldn't rush things. By the time any of them realized what was happening, it would be too late.

Reaching out to take two flutes of champagne, Colton thanked the server and handed a glass to Emma. "Let's sit this next one out," he suggested.

Emma nodded her approval and led him to a table near the window where their friends were already seated.

As they passed a guest near the dance floor, Emma locked eyes on his mask. It was alabaster in color and shielded the man's face entirely. A grimacing drama mask was the design. Blood stained tears streamed from each eye and matched the cherry red lips that were wide open as if wincing in pain. Squiggly black lines permeated the forehead and cheeks like fractures. Emma shuddered.

"What's the matter, luv?"

"Did you see his mask?" Emma asked as they continued to walk. Colton hadn't, so she described it. "Why would anyone wear that?"

"Maybe he's confused on the type of function we're holding. Let's not let him ruin our great evening." Colton drew his arm around Emma's waist and continued toward their table of friends.

She hadn't had the chance to talk to Lisa or Cat since they arrived. As she and Colton approached, her gaze fell on her gorgeous friends and the dresses they wore.

Lisa wore a white halter strap gown that flowed over her olive skin like satin. The gown itself was reminiscent of old Hollywood glamour. She paired it with a crimson mask that was over the top - figuratively and literally. It was more of a mini headdress than mask. Emma knew she could never have pulled something like that off, but on Lisa, it looked perfect.

Cat's long black dress was simple in design, but elegant. The open neckline curved into tiny cuffed sleeves that sat just off each shoulder. Their grandmother's midnight cameo brooch gathered the material at the juncture between one sleeve and her bodice. Much like Emma's, Cat's hair was styled in an elegant up do with cascading locks flowing out.

"*Good evening,*" Cat exclaimed in her best Dracula voice as her gloved hand raised a studded black mask on a holding stick to her face.

Everyone chuckled.

"You girls look beautiful," Emma said as she fingered the tear drop pendant that hung from Cat's brooch.

"And you went with an up do." Emma shifted in her chair to give Cat a better look. "These are gorgeous," she said as she traced her fingers over Emma's antique hair pins. "Were they Gran's?"

"Kind of. They were Colton's Gran's," Emma smiled knowing that he would never call his Grandmother, "Gran."

Emma was deep in explaining how she'd come to have them when Colton motioned to the French doors. "There's Mum."

CHAPTER 52

*C*olton removed his mask, rose, and extended his hand to her. Emma removed her own mask and accepted the hand he offered. Waves of nervousness and insecurities gnawed at her. Her heart thundered in her chest as she gave herself mental notes. *Don't say anything stupid, don't snort when you laugh, don't-*

As if he could sense her thoughts, Colton gave her hand reassuring squeezes and winked when her gaze met his own. She smiled a genuine smile that lit up her eyes at his ability to always know how to put her at ease. Colton tipped her chin and brushed a kiss across her lips as they walked.

Mildred stood in the doorway and smiled as they approached.

Emma took in the attributes of her flawless future mother-in-law. She was a timeless beauty in her sapphire sleeveless gown and long white gloves. Her gray blonde swing bob fell just above her shoulders with one side tucked behind her ear. She wore a strand of classic pearls that brought Emma's attention to the collarbones that stood out against her slim frame. Emma immediately felt self-conscious. *I'd need an x-ray for someone to see mine . . .*

She felt her own frame tighten as she stood a little taller, pulling her stomach in as much as possible and smiling a smile that she hoped masked the fact that she felt undeniably, truly inferior.

Colton wrapped his arm around her waist as they continued toward the door. Emma melted into his soothing embrace and was grateful for it.

Seemingly pleased with what she saw, Mildred stepped down into the ballroom and greeted them both warmly.

Colton made introductions.

"Hello, Emma. I'm delighted to make your acquaintance," Mildred said as she kissed each cheek.

Emma smiled at the fact that she had pronounced her name "Emer" just like she'd heard British people do on television. "It's nice to meet you, too," Emma said.

Mildred held her at arm's length, her gaze falling on the emerald dress. "Your gown is quite exquisite, Emma."

A passing server holding a tray full of champagne flutes paused to offer drinks. Colton handed a glass to Emma and then took one for his mother and another for himself.

Turning her attention back to the conversation, Emma motioned toward Mildred's dress. "Thank you. Yours is stunning, too." She felt herself beginning to relax. "I'm glad you're feeling better and were able to join us tonight. I've been looking forward to," *terrified about* "meeting you for some time now. Eleanor, too," Emma added.

Mildred's brows drew together for only a moment, then relaxed as she turned her attention to Colton. "Ah, yes," she said as she slowly nodded her head. "Colton dear, have you shut your phone off again?"

She continued, knowing the answer. Mildred placed her hand on Colton's arm, bracing him for what he knew would be disappointing news. "Eleanor was further engaged, Colton. She was unable to make the trip."

"I checked online and saw that *two* tickets were charged to the corporate account. I'll call in the morning and have the fee adjusted," Colton replied, even though the nagging in his gut told him that no mistake had been made.

"No need, dear," Mildred said as she patted her hand gently on his cheek.

Colton clenched his jaw bracing himself for the words he had every hope that she would not say.

"You really should have checked your messages, dear. I called four times," Mildred smiled warmly, turning her focus to Emma. "And now I see what has caused such a ruckus between my lads."

Emma didn't know how to respond to that; nor did she have time before Mildred spoke again.

"So what I was trying to tell you, Colton, the four messages that I left was to inform you-"

"What the hell is he doing here?" Colton seethed through gritted teeth as he spotted his brother come through the doors.

"-was that Kane was coming, too," Mildred finished.

Colton shot daggers at his brother. Trying to keep his composure, he growled a single word, "Why?"

*Oh shit, oh shit, oh shit e*choed through Emma's head as she glanced from Kane to Colton repeatedly. She gripped her glass, willing herself not to snap it in two as she listened to the exchange between her fiancé and his mother.

Apparently Kane had objected to returning to Brookfield and attending the ball, despite Mildred's relentless requests. Finally, she pressed until he broke and the details of his feelings for Emma, and his rift with Colton had come out.

"That only offers further proof that he should have stayed away. Again, why is he here?" Colton spat.

"Colton, I knew you'd never return home until this issue with your brother was resolved. My goal is to keep my family harmonious. Kane is here because I insisted. Now, let's go speak with him, shall we?"

Well, I seem to have caused 'a ruckus' without saying a single inappropriate word. New record, Emma!

"Mum, I'm happy you're here, but you shouldn't have brought him. I can't so easily forgive the brother who claims to love my fiancé the same way I do. I have nothing to say to him."

Emma inhaled and exhaled. The force of the breath she took in mingled with the butterflies in her stomach that now felt more like dragons. She knew that she should give the two of them the time and space they needed to discuss this and that her presence would only make it worse. "Perhaps you two should discuss this upstairs . . . without me," Emma suggested. She looked at Colton, "There's a sitting area on the balcony of my dressing room if you want to go there."

"Thank you," Colton said as he tugged her chin and brushed a light kiss on her lips. His attention returned to his mother. "Shall we?" He asked as he offered a hand to her. Mildred looked back at Kane, and with hesitation, followed her oldest son.

Without giving Kane another glance, Emma turned on her heels, walking away as fast and as gracefully as she possibly could. She couldn't imagine what he was thinking by coming back here. She couldn't imagine what Mildred was thinking by insisting that he did, and right now, she wanted to impair her *thinking* and forget this calamity altogether, so she tipped her glass up and didn't stop drinking until she'd swallowed the last drop.

She weaved her way through couples on the ballroom floor. Spotting Cat sitting alone at their table, Emma rocked her empty glass in the air, "You coming?" She asked as she continued on her path to the buffet table.

Cat was parched from dancing, so she welcomed the invitation to find a drink. She could also tell by looking at her cousin that something was very wrong. She imagined that Colton's mother had been as snooty as she looked. Cat already had the retaliation planned before she came toe to toe with Emma. She'd find Mildred's champagne glass and squirt a few drops of eye drops in her drink. She didn't know if that would cause someone to become ill, but she had every hope that it would make her uppity ass sick and she'd have to leave. Cat smiled at the thought and was opening her clutch when Emma began to speak.

"Can you believe this?" Without pause for Cat's response, Emma continued. "Can you *believe* that he'd come back here - tonight of all nights?"

Cat's gaze settled on her cousins, "Who, Em?"

Emma knocked back another glass of champagne and spun her cousin around, holding her firmly by the shoulders. Cat snapped her purse and her mouth shut when she spotted Kane stalking closer.

"Holy World War, III! He must have a death wish!"

～

Kane knew that Colton would be less than pleased to see him, but he had hoped that Emma wouldn't have had the same reaction. He couldn't hide the joy that he'd felt when he'd seen her and his mother together - then the stab in his heart when he'd seen Colton kiss her.

Now he followed from a distance as he easily caught site of her emerald dress. He wanted to talk to her. Kane simply planned to tell her that it hadn't been his idea to come tonight and to ask her not to be angry. He laughed quietly at the idea that he'd have the ability to say only that if given the chance.

The sting of rejection was still fresh in his mind from the last time he'd shared his feelings with her. He knew she was affected by him whether she admitted it or not. But he wouldn't press. Not this time.

Emma watched as Kane approached. She cursed the adrenaline that sped through her system – cursed the reaction she always had when he was near. He was dark, and he was dangerous, and something she sure didn't need in her life.

His brown eyes locked with hers. She clenched her teeth and swallowed hard, hoping that her heart wasn't pounding visibly - because on the inside, it was beating indentions into her ribcage. Would her shaky voice give her away when she spoke to him?

Kane grinned a crooked smile that looked so much like Colton's. It brought her back to the thought that she should be angry he was here. She should feel anger and not the excitement that her traitorous body made her feel.

Kane realized that what she needed now was time to adjust to the fact that he was here before attempting a conversation with her. In a move that surprised even him, that's exactly what he did.

Emma and Cat stood to the left of a linen clad table brimming with delectably plump strawberries and bubbly champagne.

Amusement tugged at the corner of his lip when he mistakenly reached for the glass that Emma reached for, too. Her eyes widened at the brief touch and he suppressed the chuckle that threatened to escape his throat. Kane held her gaze for a moment more, grasped another flute of champagne, winked, and walked away.

Emma snapped out of her daze, closing her eyes. She shook her head slowly from side to side. "Damn him," she whispered in a voice barely above a whisper, "and damn me for letting him affect me like this."

Cat had watched the exchange between Kane and Emma in utter disbelief. "Well damn!" She said as she looked at Emma. "You know how in movies when two people come together, and everything in the background blurs away, leaving only the two people visible?"

Emma pursed her lips and glanced at her in irritation.

She didn't miss a beat, "Well, darling, that's called chemistry. And I do believe I've just seen me some."

"Shut up, Cat," Emma said and she meant it. She didn't need anyone calling attention to what she already knew, but what she would never lend voice to.

Cat turned her cousin to face her. "Emma, I know you well enough to know that you are already mentally beating yourself up over that little - whatever that little thing was. But stop it already. You're engaged, not dead."

"He drives me crazy, Cat. And I know he knows it. That's as far as it will go though."

"You know what they say; the grass is always greener on the other side of the pond," she joked, but Emma ignored her.

"Regardless of how . . ." Emma trailed off. "Nothing he has is worth losing Colton over."

"You're overthinking this, Em," Cat said as she drew her arm around Emma's shoulder. "Come on, I just saw Colton and his snooty ass mother sit down at our table."

"She's actually not bad," Emma said as they walked. "I kinda like her, so far."

Cat drew her closer and whispered in her ear. "And it's a good thing, babe, because she's gonna be your mother-in-law one way or another." Cat laughed. Emma did not. "I'm joking," she finally said. *I'm actually not,* she thought.

Colton found himself surrounded by his fiancé, his new friends, his mother, and jovial conversation. Even amidst all the positive aspects, he was still furious that his brother had shown up. He was relieved that Kane was nowhere in sight. He'd deal with him later. He'd told him what would happen if he ever saw him again, and while he may not actually kill Kane, he was quite sure by the time he'd finished with him, that Kane would wish he were dead.

Colton didn't forgive easily and he sure as hell wouldn't forget what Kane had hoped to take from him. Emma's sweet voice lulled him into her story.

" . . . and it was then that Colton decided that glass blowing was better left to the professionals. I had tried it before and was secretly happy that he couldn't do it any better than me," Emma laughed and bumped his shoulder. "I still think he's pretty close to perfect, though," she smiled up at him. "It still amazes me that Dillingham Manor brought us together."

The conversation continued with Mildred recounting some of her grandmother's stories from the journals, then to ones about Colton.

Cat so wanted to interject a story of her own, but had taken an oath on a doughnut box that she would be on her best behavior. She had funny things to say, too, but found that all her stories involved tattooing, criminals, sex - sex with tattooed criminals - or just plain weren't appropriate to share with someone's tight ass Momma. *You take your Momma to bingo not the damn ball!* She huffed to herself.

With Hayden dancing with Mildred, Cat was tired of being left out. She turned to Colton, "Dance with me and I'll tell you all of Emma's deepest darkest secrets!" They all chuckled as he hurriedly ushered her onto the ballroom floor.

When the song was over, Emma was amused by Cat's refusal to let go of her fiancé. She faked whispering in his ear and he mimicked shock at her words.

Emma approached them wagging her finger, still playing along. She was about to cut in, when she spotted Charles Jackson, the reporter from the Lexington Herald who the Lewis' had hired to document the event. Emma was afraid he would leave before she had the opportunity to speak with him, so she altered her plans.

She motioned toward the reporter, "I have to talk Charles for a second, but I'll be back as soon as I can." Emma kissed Colton on the cheek then whispered something in his ear. She pulled away smiling.

Cat could tell by his seductive groan that her cousin had

uttered something entirely unwholesome. *That girl makes me proud*, Cat thought to herself.

Emma watched as a staff member herded Charles down the hall and through the caterer's door. She didn't want to be rude and follow, but couldn't lose her opportunity to speak with him.

She pressed her palms to the heavy wooden door noting the smooth edges of the routered blocks. The eight panel swing door was mahogany in structure and matched the hardwood in the grand room.

When she entered the room, they were talking about specific photos, the man clearly irritated that Charles hadn't snapped the images.

It was at that moment that it occurred to her that with the excitement of the night, she hadn't taken a single picture herself. Emma made a mental note to go back to her dressing room and grab her camera.

She quickly covered a few points with Charles then sent him on his way.

Derrick watched as Amanda walked away from the crowd for the first time tonight. He smiled at the fact that her boyfriend was still on the ballroom floor, as well as her cousin. His heart began pumping harder as his breaths become shallow. Allowing ample time so as not to be suspicious, he finally followed in the direction she had gone.

"Hey Ben, what time did you want to start the game?"

He tightened his fists into painful balls when he heard Geoffrey call out behind him.

Derrick couldn't afford the distraction and didn't

welcome it either. He was curt with his response when he turned to face him. "Eleven o'clock and midnight - just as we discussed! Now, if you'll excuse me," he nearly growled.

His harsh words spewing from behind such an unsettling mask quickly had Geoffrey retreating.

Derrick adjusted his mask, turned again, and fell into a slow pace in pursuit of his prey.

Emma stepped toward the door when she noticed that the strap on her platinum shoe had come loose. She lowered herself onto a short saddle stool. Crossing one leg over the other, she began adjusting the fallen strap.

She looked up when she heard him speak. Adrenaline flooded her system like waves lapping at the shore.

CHAPTER 53

"*H*ello, Emma," Kane's velvety smooth voice sliced through the silence in the room.

Emma's heart thundered in her chest as her head snapped to attention. She was startled by the unexpected voice and drawn to it at the same time.

She poured over the site of him standing before her and cursed herself internally for the reaction he so easily evoked. She was taken aback by his debonair good looks and impeccable dress. Like Colton, his raven locks fell to the shoulders of his tailored black tux. His matching bowtie and crisp white shirt completed the look. Unlike Colton, he wore no mask.

His gaze fell away from her eyes, sweeping her gown and bared legs before returning. "You look positively lovely tonight," Kane smiled warmly.

His smile should have melted her heart and his words warm her soul, but his allure, and the fact that they were alone made her nervous.

Emma uncrossed her legs, allowing her gathered skirt to fall to the floor before attempting to stand. "Please don't go,"

Kane requested as he held his hand out to her. "Just hear me out, Emma." His voice was so gentle that she obliged. He pushed through the frame allowing the door to swing shut behind him.

Watching him stalk across the room toward her, she swallowed hard and said the first thing that came to her mind. "You shouldn't have come, Kane."

"I know," he said as he closed the distance between them, kneeling at her feet. Looking up to catch her gaze, he continued. "I hadn't planned to come back here tonight, Emma. I know how Colton feels, and I understand why." He reached his hand forward toward her fidgeting fingers then stopped himself.

"The morning that you left, Miss Francine gave me a letter. He found it, Kane. He's the one that told me what it meant. He was livid."

Kane laughed. "Ah yes, I received a rather *scathing* message from him." He paused as if he were recalling the words. He shook his head, "Colton's always angry with me for something." He smiled his crooked smile.

"And surely you can understand his feelings!" Emma closed her eyes briefly, regretting her poor choice of words immediately.

A look of hurt crossed his face as he stood. "More than you know, pet." He reached forward brushing his thumb across her cheek before stepping passed her to walk further into the room.

Kane leaned against the granite countertop, crossing one ankle over the other as he watched her. Would she turn to face him or would she leave?

As he waited for her reaction, he appreciated the architecture of the room around him. The white washed cabinets and sienna walls paired with dark countertops to give the room a feeling of warmth. Champagne bottles lined the workspace to his left and empty serving trays littered the island that sat between Emma and himself.

His appraisal turned to the woman before him. He wished he knew her thoughts.

Moments passed; the silence grew thicker and eerily uncomfortable. As she sensed the weight of his stare, she fisted the fabric of her dress around her knees. Smoothing it out, she asked, "Are we finished?"

Low laughter sounded behind her. Emma spun around on the wooden stool, pinning him with a questioning stare.

Kane adjusted his cuff link. "Are we finished?" He repeated before locking eyes with her, "I doubt that very much, but it's your call, really."

Emma exhaled and shook her head. She ignored his insinuation, clarifying what she meant. "Have you said what you came in here to say?"

"I have not. What I need you to know is that it was Mum's idea for me to come back here. What, with the 'discord in the family' and such. She's determined-"

Emma held her hand out letting him know that she'd heard enough. "We know, I overheard some of it and she explained the rest to Colton in length."

Kane tried but failed to suppress the smile that tugged at his lips.

Emma furrowed her brow. "Stop smiling at me like that."

Throwing his arms out to his sides, Kane asked, "like what?"

"Like you know something I don't," Emma replied angrily.

He shrugged one shoulder matter of factly, "What I know,

luv, is that you knew what I was going to say, had the opportunity to walk out of this room, to walk away from me, but you didn't."

"It's called being courteous, asshole!"

The irony in her words elicited a deep chuckle from him. "It's called attraction, sweetheart – *mutual attraction.* You're being ridiculous by denying it. You can act like you're unaffected by me, but I know differently."

Ridiculous, now you're calling me names? Emma pushed to her feet bringing herself flush with his body. She cupped his cheek and gazed into his eyes. "You're right, Kane," she whispered across his lips. "You *do* affect me." She smiled a sinister smile.

Derrick pressed his palms to the door that she had gone through minutes earlier. This was the moment he had waited for all night, the moment when he finally had her alone. As he slowly pushed the door open, he hoped that the hinges wouldn't alert her to his presence; he didn't want to lose the element of surprise.

He swallowed the curse that threatened to spill from his lips at what he saw. *How the hell did he beat me in here!* Derrick thought to himself as he eased the door back shut.

Even though his face was shielded with dark locks of hair and her hand, Derrick knew that the boyfriend had somehow, inexplicably, made it into the room first.

Frustrated, he stepped into the shadows where he awaited his next opportunity.

Kane smiled at the fact that Emma was finally admitting what he already knew. "Yeah?" He urged her to continue.

"Oh, yeah. You remind me why I made the right choice by choosing your brother, *sweetheart,*" Emma laughed, smacked his face lightly, and turned to walk away.

"And I'm going to remind you why you didn't," Kane said one second before he spun her around and pulled her to him.

"Let me go!" Emma implored. She wanted to hate that she was pressed to his chest. She didn't know how she would react to his closeness and honestly didn't trust herself to find out. His mere presence made her thrum with anticipation – a reaction that she berated herself for.

His words feathered across her lips, "You're not going anywhere until you hear what I have to say." Emma pushed against his chest. The gentleness in his voice was a direct contradiction to the firm embrace she found herself in. "Give me this last chance, Emma. Please hear me out."

She was stiff in his arms, but no longer battered his chest. "That's all I ask," he said softly as he held her gaze.

He explained how his focus had changed, how his feelings had changed since that first day he had heard her voice over the speakerphone. "I still don't understand it myself, these feelings that I have no right to possess. And even now as I hold you, I know I should let you go," he said without budging, "but it's so damn hard."

Kane held her and watched as her conflicting emotions morphed from anger, to passion, to understanding, to . . . *fear?*

He was filled with anguish when he felt her body tremble and watched her head drop, refusing to look at him any longer.

Damn! This is not how this was supposed to happen. "Emma," he caressed her cheek, "you have nothing to fear from me."

"I don't," she whispered without meeting his eyes.

"You're trembling, luv. You're afraid of me," At this, Kane dropped his hand from her waist.

She shook her head, "I'm not afraid of you, Kane."

He ducked his head and grasped her chin, tugging it upwards so he could capture her gaze, "Then what *are* you afraid of?"

She sucked in a shaky breath then pushed out, "This." Emma sobbed as Kane enveloped her in his arms holding her protectively – one arm around her waist and one hand pressing her cheek to his chest.

His own heartbeat roared in his ears as he tried to inter-pret the meaning of the single uttered word. It was at this moment that he chose to bare his soul to her.

"Look at me, Emma." She straightened slightly and slowly dragged her gaze up, doing as she was told. "I know that you don't share my exact feelings." She started to speak when he pressed his finger to her mouth, reminding her that it was his turn. "And I know why." Kane caressed her cheek contem-plating his next words. When he felt her relax in his arms, his confession continued. "You're the last thing I think of when I go to bed at night, Emma, and the first thing I think of when I wake." He felt her quiver in his arms. "Sometimes my dreams are vivid, a life with you, and when I awake, I mourn the loss - mourn the love that you felt for me . . . if only in my dreams."

Kane watched as Emma tried blinking away the tears, watched as she bit her trembling lip. "So if just for tonight, please tell me that I'm not imagining this connection between us. Just once, let me hear the words."

Emma shook her head. She could no more say the words he wanted to hear than she could deny that what he said was true. She didn't love Kane, but she felt a magnetic pull to him that could not be explained. She hated herself for feeling this way about another man and hated that she was hurting him at the same time.

"Kane, I can't," *resist you.* She shook her head hoping to shake the truthfulness away. "You have to let me go." *Because I don't trust myself to be this close.*

As if he could read her mind, Kane pulled her closer. "Please say it, Emma," he urged. He felt her bated breath cross his lips and saw the lump she repeatedly tried to swallow. "Tell me you feel it, too, that I'm not alone in this." He waited and still she said nothing, but didn't pull away.

He watched as she furrowed her brows; watched as the pain became unbearably evident in her expression. Kane felt like someone had twisted a knife through his heart. Her unspoken declarations were painfully clear. Emma had said everything she needed to say . . . without saying a word. Her not retreating revealed that she was drawn to him but the silence said that she couldn't love him because she loved another.

Kane realized in that moment that the woman he held in his arms, the woman that he loved, would never be there again once he walked out the door.

He brushed his thumb over her plump bottom lip as he lowered his head. "I'm going to kiss you, Emma."

"No," she protested weakly.

His hand fell on the back of her head and he smiled. "I wasn't asking permission." His gaze lingered on her lips, gauging her reaction. "Kiss you goodbye."

Kane swept his lips against hers delicately. When she didn't object, he turned her, pressing her against the wall as he deepened their kiss. His hands didn't roam her body and seductive words didn't try to persuade her. He had dreamt of the day that she would kiss *him* as she kissed him now, knowing that it was he. As they clung to one another in the lingering kiss, Kane drank in every emotion that she poured into their goodbye and relished the way she pulled him close when her fingers laced into his hair.

Emma was consumed with passion, the weight of his kiss fueling her desire. She savored the feel of his possessive lips against her own and appreciated the commanding body that pressed harder against her as the embrace continued. For once in her life, she was doing the wrong thing. And for a brief moment, it felt so right.

Thoughts of Colton filtered back in along with the reality of what she was doing, what she had done by not denying her forbidden desire. Regret crashed over her as she broke the kiss.

Kane pulled away when he felt her tears cascade over his lips, the sorrow in her eyes revealing to him the words she could never form. He hadn't imagined it. But knowing that Colton was the better man, the better choice for her, his resolve was broken. Because he loved her, he would pursue her no more. "It's ok, pet," he said as he kissed her tears away. "I understand. I love you," he paused, "and you love him."

Emma closed her eyes when he pressed his lips to her forehead.

"I'm sorry to have hurt you, Kane, but I do love Colton. He's good to me." She raised her head to look at him, "and he's good *for* me." She exhaled. "And even though-" she stopped herself from saying the words that would confirm what Kane already knew. She smiled a firm smile. "This is goodbye, Kane."

Kane cupped her cheeks and closed his eyes against the tears that threatened to fall. "I love you," he whispered across her lips before kissing her tenderly for the last time.

As he walked away, he turned. "Goodbye, Emma. My brother is a lucky man to have you."

He forced a smile, winked, and disappeared through the door.

Alone in the silence, she waited for the flood of emotions that she was sure would come. She'd allowed Kane to kiss her, and not only that, she had kissed him back – and enjoyed it. Regret and self-loathing began inching in.

But she had little time for either as a rather sassy Cat could be heard in the hallway. "Cinderella, get your ass out here!"

The door swung open, "Oh, there you are Emmabear!" Cat smiled and sashayed into the room. As she came closer, the smile turned into a frown. Without saying a word, she opened her clutch and started dabbing makeup on Emma's tear streaked face. "It's not exactly your color, lovey, but it'll do. We can't have you looking like the ugly step sisters, now can we?" She held Emma's face in her hands, tilting it from side to side to make sure the base was blended.

"Cat," Emma squeezed her eyes shut, exhaled a forceful breath and bit her lip. When she regained her composure, she continued. "Kane and-"

"You know, Em," Cat said, interrupting, "sometimes you just have to get something out of your system." She pinned her with a hard stare.

"I kissed him," Emma said regretfully.

Cat crinkled her nose as she looked at Emma's mouth, "Yeah, your swollen lips kinda already told me that." She smiled an empathetic smile.

"Then we said goodbye."

"Did you mean it?"

Emma's gaze fell to her engagement ring. "We did. This really was the end for Kane and me."

"Then let this be where your guilt stays, too. I can see it in your eyes that it's over. I saw it in his, too, when we passed in the hallway." She searched Emma's reaction for any signs of regret.

Emma pushed off the wall with a renewed sense of determination. "I've kept my prince charming waiting long enough." She interlaced her arm with Cats as they walked toward the door. "It's time I focus my attention where it belongs – on the only man I love."

Cat could sense that Emma's words were genuine. She didn't know what had been said between her and Kane tonight, but could tell that her cousin had finally put that chapter of her life to rest.

CHAPTER 54

*E*mma walked back into the ballroom where the party was in full swing, Cat by her side. The combined elements of the room thrust her into sensory overload after being in relative solitude. She watched as couples swayed to the music, listened as champagne glasses clanked together in a celebrated cheer, and jumped when lightening lit up the sky at the same time the warm hand slid across her back.

"These secrets displease me very much, luv," Colton growled menacingly as he darted his head between her and Cat.

A shiver ran down her spine as she turned to face him. "What do you mean?" She asked nervously, hoping that he hadn't seen her and Kane.

"Your deep dark secrets, Em," Cat said as she opened her eyes wider in a 'shut up' command. "I spilled them all while I danced with your prince! *Such scandal,*" she laughed and Colton did, too.

He placed a kiss on the tip of Emma's nose. "You act like a

kid who was caught with their hand in the cookie jar," he laughed again.

"Sorry, I think my champagne is just hitting me a little harder than usual," Emma lied.

It was at this time that Colton was approached by Mayor Penny Joseph. She thanked him for planning the ball and asked if he planned to make it an annual event. When he stepped aside to further discuss his motives behind having the ball and plans for Dillingham Manor's renovations, it allowed Cat time to coach her jumpy cousin. "You've got to pull it together, Emma."

Emma nodded, took a few deep breaths and attempted to regroup. She had made a huge misstep with Kane; that much was true. The guilt nagging at her soul from her momentary indiscretion was made all the more powerful as she watched her fiancé. She pinched the bridge of her nose and closed her eyes in an attempt to stave off the tears that threatened to fall.

Hayden stepped out into the night air in an attempt to compose his thoughts. As distant lightening danced across the sky, he leaned against the brick wall and watched the show. A warm, gentle breeze whipped around him signaling that rain was on the horizon.

He closed his eyes in an attempt to block out anything that would distract him. Little good that did. Horses could be heard neighing nearby. *I didn't know the Lewis' had horses.*

Forcing himself to concentrate, Hayden thought about Emma and her stalker. His gut told him that tonight was the night. There was every likelihood that he was here tonight, among them. Hayden thought of all the men he had come in contact with over the last few hours – all of whom were disguised behind masks. *It could be anyone.* The mere thought had his mind racing.

Since the day in the park when Cat had told him about the newspaper article that revealed Emma's identity, he had known that it was a distinct possibility that the stalker would show up tonight, but he had had every hope that he was wrong. *Always trust your instincts, buddy!*

She heard the lure of Colton's laughter and opened her eyes. Emma watched him as he talked to the petite blonde Mayor. He towered over her. Emma drank in his presence - tall, strong, handsome, honorable, charismatic, commanding. *Mine. He's mine,* she smiled at the thought, *and I am his, alone.*

When he saw her watching him, he smiled and winked, then returned his attention to the Mayor.

Emma moved to his side when his conversation ended. Without saying a word, she grasped his hand and led him onto the ballroom floor. Turning her, Colton snaked his arms around her and pulled her tight against him as they began swaying to the music. The closeness afforded her the feel of his strong, safe arms and the wondrous scent that she had noticed about him from the very first day they met. Her mind traveled back to that day, to the wine glass that was actually a bowl, to the squirrel that nearly killed her, to them hiding in the shadows of Dillingham Manor, and to the love that had blossomed since that time.

She looked up and held his gaze, "I love you, Colton."

"And I love you, sweetheart," he said as his lips crushed against her own.

"I was thinking about the first time we came here together, when you gave me dance lessons in the gazebo. I loved that."

He smiled at the memory. "That was also the night that our first kiss was denied us by a pyrotechnic lunatic in a boat," They both laughed. "Do you remember when we were hiding in the upstairs bedroom at Dillingham Manor?" Emma smiled and nodded her head at the memory. "I wanted to kiss you then but was afraid of scaring you. I had just met you, but I wanted to kiss you."

"You can kiss me now to make up for your shortcomings, Mr. Graves," Emma chided.

Colton obliged.

She wrapped her arms tightly around his neck, elbows resting on his shoulders, as he lifted her from the floor. He held her impossibly tight as he possessed her lips. Emma lifted her heels, a motion that pressed their bodies even closer together.

"Get a room you horn dogs," Cat said in passing as she and Hayden made their way back to the table.

Colton lowered Emma back to her feet. "We'll continue this very soon in a great deal of detail," he whispered.

His promising words sent jolts of need straight to her core.

She thumbed toward the door, "Yeah, I'm good to go now - *right now*," Emma nearly pleaded.

Before Colton could provide an answer of any kind, the booming voice drew their attention.

❦

"Excuse me everyone," the tall man dressed in black spoke

into the microphone from the podium. "My name is Geoffrey, and I've been asked to have you solve a Halloween riddle." Excitement filled the air as people eagerly awaited his next words.

~

Emma smiled at Colton. "This is neat," she said. "You just think of everything, don't you?"

He shrugged his shoulders. "The Lewis' must have planned this riddle game. I know nothing of it," Colton said in bewilderment.

~

"Four people have been selected to help solve the mystery: Cat Morgan, Lisa Hernandez, Loretta Townsand, and Francine Jones. Ladies, please come forward to receive your instructions.

Cat looked at Hayden and smiled. He held his hands up in an "I'm innocent" motion.

"Yeah right!" She said as she pushed her chair away from the table and stood.

Hayden quickly assessed the odds of this being the work of the stalker. If it were him, Emma's name would have likely been called. He deducted that Colton must have planned this. He cautiously watched as Cat walked toward the podium.

She approached the announcer. He placed a matte black box tied with a matching ribbon in her hands. A note with her name scrawled across it was tucked inside the ribbon. Cat took the card out and tucked the rectangular box under her arm while she read the words to herself: *solve this riddle if you dare; mystery looms in the midnight air . . .*

Cat untied the ribbon and opened the box, all the while

wondering if Hayden was behind this. He knew that Halloween was her favorite holiday and that spooky riddles were her forte. *This has his name written all over it!* She smiled at the thought. Making her way to a vacant table, she emptied the contents of the box on top as the crowd gathered around her.

One by one the recipients accepted their box and read the cryptic poem attached.

Cat looked at the round table covered in elegant black linen and the tiny puzzle pieces that littered it. She spread them out and then separated them into edge pieces and center pieces. The cardboard itself was white with black squiggles on every piece. Before long, she realized that it was words or a word that she was forming.

With every puzzle worked, they were still no closer to solving the riddles. Finally, Cat took charge and suggested that they try working their puzzle pieces together since everyone had extras. Maybe they were solving one riddle instead of four. Being the assertive person she was, she announced that everyone should come to her table and work their puzzle around hers.

Since every person had worked their puzzle on a different table, bringing them together meant that most of the pieces had to be reworked, as they broke apart on transport. The mystery of the riddle would take even longer now.

"Where are you running off to?" Colton questioned as he tightened his grip on Emma's waist.

She pointed to the table where the puzzles were being worked, "I want to document this, especially if you didn't have a hand in it. Sounds freaky and it will be a great addition for the paper. Besides, Phil will hang me if I don't take some pictures of something tonight!" She giggled.

"Don't go," Colton requested as he placed a tender kiss on her shoulder. "Let's just watch it play out - you know someone has a phone and is recording it."

Emma was determined. "I'll be straight back down, and I'll watch it play out through the camera lens and might end up with a raise once Phil sees this!"

Colton allowed her to slip away from his body, but gripped her fingers as she started to leave. Emma turned to face him. The glimmer in her hazel eyes and flash of a smile caused him to pull her flush with his body as he kissed her passionately. "Hurry back, luv!"

Emma smiled as her fingers slipped from his. She started up the stairway when a tickle of fear raced down her spine. *Could this be him?* She allowed herself to wonder as she stilled her feet in mid stride on opposite steps. *You're being ridiculous, Emma!* She scolded herself and continued up the long staircase while continuing her silent conversation. *You're not living in fear of him, not another day!*

CHAPTER 55

*E*mma entered the dark dressing room. She felt around for the light switch and clicked it on. When the room illuminated and the image came into view, a scream escaped her throat . . . and then a chuckle when she realized it was her own reflection. She shook her head as she clenched her hand tightly to her heart. *"Damn, girl, you have got to calm down!"* She said to herself as she made her way across the room to retrieve her camera.

She stood in front of the dressing table as she hurriedly adjusted the proper camera lens. She could hear the voices coming from downstairs and couldn't wait to get back down there. She knew she had missed something when she heard multiple gasps. Emma couldn't imagine why someone would be upset unless the riddles spelled out someone's misdeeds. *Cat's been behaving lately, so she should be safe.* She giggled at the thought and gave the camera lens the final turn, locking it into place.

"Hello, Amanda," the ominous voice called out behind her.

As if a force field held her motionless, she stilled herself.

Emma dragged her eyes up, seeing his image before her in the mirror. His calm demeanor was as disturbing as the reflection that tore away her defenses, causing the night in Louisville to come crashing back into her mind. Those icy eyes, his hair, his face, the terror, the pain . . . everything came back to her like a train racing through a tunnel.

Where amnesia's darkness had once served as a barrier shielding her mind, the light gave way to razor sharp memories. It was him. He had found her, and Emma found herself paralyzed with fear.

"I told you I'd find you, Amanda," Derrick said as he pushed himself off the door frame and stalked closer. He tossed the mask he had been holding onto the bed.

Breathe . . . just breathe. Her heart hammered inside her chest, her vision began to tunnel, and her stomach churned like a brewing hurricane. A full blown panic attack was setting in. This was it. Emma knew that she had to face him, and she had to be smart about it. *Breathe . . . just breathe.*

Colton's words echoed through her head. *Emma, if he comes for you again, you have to be as calm as possible to remain level headed. You have to think the situation through. Stay focused, breathe. Take comfort in the fact that you've had self-defense training. Do not let him move you to another place. If he does, leave clues if you can.*

Emma met his gaze in the mirror. He was closer now, circling her like prey. She could feel her dress move as he brushed passed the flowing skirt – close enough to strike, but making certain that her fear continued to mount. His shoes scraped the floor with every stride, and at times, she could feel his breath move against her exposed neck. He was toying with her like a viper.

"How did you find me?" Emma asked without turning, already knowing the answer. It was the article. She felt it in her soul. She needed him to talk so that he wouldn't hear the 'click' when her digital camera came to life. She looked down slowly and switched the dial to video, clicking the button. The red light illuminated, signaling that it was on.

All the while, Derrick continued to tell her just how he discovered who she was and where she would be tonight. Either he didn't hear her camera settings or he didn't care because he didn't react. Emma could barely hear anything over the roaring of her heartbeat in her ears.

She brought her gaze back up to the mirror. "I love you, Colton," she mouthed. Grief ate away at her heart as she wondered if maybe she was saying that for the last time. She bit her lip hard, attempting to stop the quivering. Welled up tears finally spilled over and slid down her cheeks. They fell like raindrops and nothing she could do would stop them. Emma brought her trembling hands to her cheeks in an attempt to wipe away the tears. The diamonds in her ring caught the light. *Leave a clue,* she thought to herself. Emma slipped her engagement ring off. Holding it in the palm of her hand, she closed her fingers tightly around it.

The man from Louisville continued his tirade while he circled her.

She turned to face him. Gathering strength she didn't truly possess, she attempted to get information. "Well, now that you know my name, why don't you tell me yours."

"Derrick," he said without hesitation. "Derrick is the name of the person whose life you ruined, you miserable bitch!" With lightning speed, his fist shot out, slamming into her jaw.

Pain jolted through her, driving ripples of agony through her left cheek bone.

"That's for breaking up my family," he said as he loomed over her.

The attack knocked her hard against the table, but not down. Emma was still standing, albeit leaning against the mirror on shaky legs as she fought for balance. In the blink of an eye, he was on her again. He grabbed the loose hair in the front of her head, fisting tightly against the scalp. Pulling her forward roughly, Derrick bashed her head into the mirror with relentless force. Glass shards dug into her scalp, littering the dressing table and all its contents.

Flashes of red light assaulted her vision as blinding pain coursed through her head.

"And that's for Jaz!" He said as he turned to walk away.

Emma brought herself to a standing position on an extremely unsteady frame. She felt around behind her for something, anything on the table she could use. Glass splinters dug painfully into her searching fingers. She didn't have the luxury of fretting over the pain. She had to find something to protect herself with.

The heaviest object she could find was her camera. She had originally hoped to leave it recording as a clue to document his name and face, but after all the jostling, she didn't know if it was working anyway.

Derrick turned to face her once more. The look in his eyes could only be described as pure evil, as was the sinister grin tugging at his lips. Emma found herself looking into a long silver blade. "And this is for my kids!" He brought the knife down as ominous laughter escaped him.

Emma wove her wrist though the camera strap, grasping it tightly a split second before he advanced. She swung it in front of her by the strap with increasing momentum. Derrick cursed loudly when she slammed the camera into his face, his head – where she struck him, she wasn't sure. All she knew was that the blood that she had drawn from him allowed her a moment to run. But turning her back to him proved to be a grave mistake . . .

~

Cat's puzzle consisted of three words: *kindly came for*. It was obviously a phrase or quote. She had done her part; now it was everyone else's turn. She returned to their table. One by one, the additions were fit in.

When she heard the loud gasps, she came back and stared at the riddle before her. It was apparent that something was missing. But the partial phrase that *was* present cast a foreboding that had Cat scrambling backwards.

Hayden took one look at the puzzle then all around as he scoured the room for Emma. This was it. He knew now that this was the work of the stalker. Remaining calm and not causing pandemonium was his intent. Unfortunately for him, he knew Cat was not capable of the same.

The frightening words of the riddle echoed through Cat's head. Hayden had no part in this; that much was clear by his stiff demeanor. She visually swept the room looking for Emma. The green dress would have been hard to miss, but yet, she didn't see her anywhere. "Colton!" She screamed as she made her way through the room.

On his way to Cat, Colton passed the table where the puzzle had been worked. He read the words aloud in passing, "Because I could not stop for death, he kindly stopped for . . ." The color drained from his face. He was an educated man and quite familiar with Emily Dickinson's "Death" poem. He bolted across the room, taking the stairs three at a time. He knew where she had gone. What he didn't know was what he would find when he reached her dressing room. The warm breeze greeted him first as bile raced into his throat. "Emma, Emma -no!" He cried hoarsely over and over, as if he could stop the events that had already been set into motion.

Kane didn't know what was wrong with his brother or why the puzzle had affected him the way it had. All he knew for certain was that it somehow involved Emma, so he quickly followed in Colton's footsteps, as did Cat.

Hayden sent a party guest who was also an officer to follow the trio, then he advised everyone to be seated and informed them all that no one would leave until he'd questioned every last one of them about the riddle.

He searched the room until he found Geoffrey. "You!" He jabbed his finger in the direction of the man. He remembered that Geoffrey had five packages, but that only four of them had been opened. He came to stand toe to toe with the man. "There's another package. Who's it addressed to?" Hayden demanded.

"I was instructed not to reveal the final box until midnight," Geoffrey answered looking up at him.

Hayden grabbed him by the lapels of his jacket, jerking him to his feet as he shook him violently. "Answer me!"

Bryce spotted the fifth box inside the podium. The envelope was void of valuable content – no name or message, just a blank, empty envelope. He opened the box, which was larger than the others and found a completed puzzle that simply read – *me*. He quickly scanned the note inside and asked, "Who's Amanda?"

Scribed in a brownish red hue, which could pass for dried blood, was the two part message:

Because I could not stop for death,
  he kindly stopped for me.

I came for Amanda . . .

CHAPTER 56

*H*e had always heard that when you die, your life flashes in front of your eyes - memorable events, milestones in life, moments in time played out like a movie in fast forward. What Colton didn't know was that, for him, traumatic images caused the same.

He stood paralyzed for what felt like hours as he watched Emma's movie play before him in his mind. He saw her long brown hair shimmering in the sunlight and could almost smell her coconut shampoo. He saw the way her hazel eyes lit up when she looked over her shoulder at him. He watched her sleep, watched her love, and watched the silhouette of her body in the woods as they sought refuge from the storm. He saw the flickering light of the bon fire radiating against her skin at Hurricane Creek. He watched as she bravely battled the demons of her dreams night after night. He recalled the tender moment when they exchanged unity bands, saw the vulnerability in her eyes when she said, "I love you" for the first time, and then the utter disbelief when he proposed sometime later. He saw her body, warm and willing as it moved in a lover's embrace. He imagined her as a beautiful bride, mother to the children they would someday have, the woman he would live out his every tomorrows making happy and keeping safe. Only, he hadn't.

The smell of copper brought him crashing back to a harsh reality as he saw a bloodied and battered room before him. Mocking him. Reminding him that like vapors in the wind disappearing into the night, so had she, his Emma. She was gone.

His heart clenched painfully in his chest and he struggled to breathe. Unable to drag his eyes away from the crimson stains, unimaginable horrors coursed through his mind. This was no movie and it was no dream - perhaps a living, breathing nightmare. And he knew that whatever he was experiencing, it was nothing compared to what was to come for her, for Emma. *Emma*

The room before him lay in complete disarray. Colton blinked in horror as the images inundated his brain. Pooled blood on the floor, on the bed, contents of the dressing table strewn about, the shattered glass of the mirror, her broken camera littering the floor, a syringe, her shoe, large jagged pieces of her blood stained dress – clearly ripped from her body, a bloody hand print on the door that drug across as if she were hanging on . . .

A warm breeze blew through the open French doors. The shifting air swirled dried leaves in a vortex on the veranda causing Colton to snap out of his trance. That's when he saw it. Emma's ring lay just beyond the threshold. Was that intentional? Had she left a clue? He crossed the room and knelt to grasp it, but thought better of it. He knew he had to leave the room undisturbed.

Colton surged onto the patio and bound down the stairs in search of her. The ferocity of the storm picked up. Thunder rolled across the sky matching the fury that he felt. Punishing booms echoed through him. He deserved them.

He vowed to protect her, and he had failed. Painful regret coiled inside him at the thought.

Lightening danced wickedly in the darkness, illuminating the path that refused to reveal her. It was sharp and unforgiving. Plump rain drops pelted his body like the tears that crashed over his cheeks. Colton heard the neighing of the horses as they became more agitated. Like him, they were restless and searching. The storm that raged around him paled in comparison to the one that coursed within him. He had never felt so helpless, so hopeless, in all his life.

The roaring thunder, pounding rain, and the cries of the steed that were waiting to whisk her away in the carriage, those were the only sounds he heard.

Ignoring the rain that battered his skin, Colton searched for any sign of Emma, any other clues that she may have left. The lake road was void of traffic. No one meandered about the property or the drive, no one to bear witness to where she had gone. *Where are you, sweetheart?*

Like a vapor in the wind, she had *Vanished.*

Cat was not one to follow rules – never had been. But when Officer Pearson ordered them into the hallway as he called for backup, she adhered to his command. In the dim light, she leaned against the wall, sinking slowly to her knees. Her black dress fanned out around her like the darkness seeping into her soul. Her mind tried to process all that she had seen. *So much blood.* Regret tugged at her at the thought that this could have been prevented. *I should have done something, anything to keep her safe.* Cat had always been protective of Emma and Emma of her. They were as close as sisters, and the best of friends, which made the reality of losing her all the more painful. She glanced into the room when she heard the obvious sounds of a crime scene being photographed. *This can't be happening.*

Cat's trembling hands scrubbed her face. She began to rock slowly. Thoughts of Emma bombarded her. It was hard to tell where one thought stopped and another began. She traveled back in time in her mind, a time when they were surrounded by people who loved them and kept them safe. She recalled sleigh rides, snowball fights, baking cookies with Granny, and Christmas caroling with everyone they knew. She had taught Emma to ride a bike and a teenaged Emma had taught her to drive a stick shift. She smiled at the memory of singing along to every song on the radio as Emma sang off key-

"Cat," Hayden's soothing voice brought her crashing back to the present. She looked up, grief filled eyes pleading for help.

"She's gone, Hayden. He took her. He *h-hurt* her." A single tear dropped onto her cheek as she sobbed.

Hayden nodded his head recalling the picture attachments that Pearson had texted him. He knelt in front of her, brushing the tear away. "I know, baby." He wanted to tell her that everything would be ok, that they'd get Emma back. *Alive.* Instead, he said nothing of the sort. He couldn't give her false hope, but at the same time, wouldn't be cruel. So he just said nothing.

He looked over his shoulder, gaining the first peek into the room. An officer snapped pictures as he sidestepped Pearson who paced back and forth talking on his phone. He motioned Hayden inside when he saw him.

Turning his attention back to Cat, Hayden brushed a strand

of hair behind her ear. "Listen," he said as he gently tugged her chin, "I need you to go downstairs and give your statement to Officer Reynolds. Can you do that?"

"My statement?" She looked at him incredulously.

"Yes, Gage Reynolds is down-"

"I'll tell *you* my statement, Hayden McAllister, and you be sure to quote me!" Cat's eyes burned with fury as she rose to her feet. Looking down at him, she continued, "When I find that fucker, I'll nail his balls to an electric fence. When he begs for mercy, when the screams have ceased because numbness has finally seeped in, then I'll flip the switch, and watch him fry!"

Hayden exhaled. "Or, on second thought," he pushed up to tower over her, "I'll just tell him that you need some time." *Which will be even worse because that will give you more time to come up with even more intense death threats.*

Kane observed Cat as she passed him walking toward the staircase. She had gotten clearance to leave; he wondered when his turn would come. They were wasting time keeping him for questioning when he could be doing something, anything to help find Emma. The sound of raised voices drew his attention back to Emma's room. Kane watched as Hayden disappeared inside, joining Officer Pearson and the various others who had congregated. Arms folded tightly over his chest, his fingers dug painfully into his bicep. He recalled the scene of her room and moved closer when the officers began speaking in clipped tones.

Kane heard the voices, but couldn't determine who said what.

"Obvious signs of struggle, someone lost a lot of blood, she didn't go down without a fight, he shot her up with something . . ."

The monotone chatter came to an abrupt stop, as did the

clicking of the camera. "Colton," Hayden said, alarmed by his sudden presence.

"Mr. Graves, this is a crime scene. You can't be in here," Pearson urged as tactfully as possible when a deflated Colton appeared in the French doors.

Colton numbly looked at the bloody print on the door, the yellow evidence markers by her ring and syringe, and then to every person in the room as he pushed his way inside, ignoring the protests. He looked all around, the reality of the situation slicing straight to his heart.

He spotted the ominous mask on the bed. *She knew not to trust him. He scared her. If I had only made him leave when she first noticed him.* "Find security footage to see who wore that mask," he pointed to the bed, "that's who has Emma."

Images, voices, and faces all blurred together making the last few hours seem both like an eternity and like no time had passed at all. Colton didn't know when he had gotten into his dressing room, but he had, and now he sat with Kane by his side.

They sat on the bed in similar hunched postures. Their long legs were bent, supporting forearms with rolled up sleeves. Colton's bowtie was gone, while Kane's hung loosely around his neck with the edges pointing down. They had long shed their jackets as well as the top few buttons of their white shirts.

Hayden pulled a chair up in front of them and questioned them in length. "I know your history," he said as he looked from one to the other. "I know you hate each other, but now, more than ever, it's crucial that you two work together in order to help us bring Emma home."

Kane looked over his left shoulder at Colton, "I don't hate you, brother."

Colton lay his weary head in his hands, shaking it slightly from side to side. Bringing his head up, he folded his hands under his chin, looking straight ahead. "Well, that makes one of us then, because at this moment, I hate *me* more than I've ever hated you." He shot a glance in Kane's direction.

Kane nodded his head. He understood what Colton was saying - he hated himself for not keeping her safe.

"But right now," he continued, "I don't have the energy to fight you, Kane. Finding Emma is my only concern."

Emma was the battle line between these brothers, but an unspoken alliance had just been formed. They would work together to find her – regardless of how they felt about each other.

Hayden gathered Emma's friends. He instructed them to keep their routines. "You will work regular hours. Go to the gym at your scheduled time, lunch at the usual time and place. The best way for Emma to get help is if you are where you are supposed to be when she would expect you to be there." He discussed places that she would likely go.

He turned his attention to Cat and Lisa. "You will stay at your houses at night. Bryce, I need you at the cabin, Colton at the Jacobson house, and Kane at Dillingham Manor."

Hayden called for an officer to go to the bed and breakfast, but none were available being that all extra bodies were involved in the search for Emma. He pulled Colton and Kane to the side. "This is against protocol, but you're going to help me expedite the investigation." He made a list of things that he needed. Knowing that Colton should stay at Victorian Gardens in case Emma returned, he instructed Kane to go to the Jacobson House to retrieve the items instead.

Kane walked into the dark room at the bed and breakfast and fumbled for the light switch. As the room came into view, he went to the left side of the bed, the side that Colton said was hers. He automatically drew the pillow up to his face, inhaling deeply. He knew he shouldn't. He had no right. It smelled of her shampoo - fragrant and clean - sending thoughts of her rushing into his mind. There was so much about Emma that he didn't know. Was she a morning person, did she read in bed, how did she sleep? Kane thought about her perfume. He knew she wore it on her wrist. Would the underside of her pillow smell of it? He flipped it over, the light vanilla fragrance that was distinctly her could easily be detected. *She sleeps with her arm under her pillow.* This is something that Colton would know, as he had had the opportunity to watch her sleep countless times and yet Kane could only imagine. *Where are you, Emma?*

He placed the pillow in the bag and sealed it as Hayden had instructed. His next order of business was to retrieve the pink toothbrush out of the right hand drawer of the vanity.

Kane walked into the bathroom after turning on the light. He saw a purple shirt sleeve peeking out of the hamper. He bagged it and a few other items then moved closer to the sink. He opened the drawer in search of her toothbrush. Instead, what he saw made him feel like he'd been punched in the gut. He stared at the stick. "She's pregnant?" Kane said to himself as he stared in disbelief.

He bagged the toothbrush and eased the drawer shut. As he walked out of the bathroom, he looked over his shoulder at the closed drawer. A worrisome look crossed his face as he flipped the switch, casting the room in darkness.

Hayden sat at his desk attempting to organize his thoughts. The harsh florescent lights shone brightly overhead in the office he never occupied at this early morning hour. The five windows to his back remained hidden behind closed blinds and the smell of freshly brewed coffee hung thick in the air.

Photos fanned out in front of him covering paperwork on his desk. Hayden stared at the stranger in the images that Lisa had provided him with. He recalled the day that she called Cat and him to the park to look at them. He had been concerned then, but never dreamed that it would take the horrific turn that it had. He looked at the date stamp on the pictures. *He's been planning this attack for some time – longer than we even know, I imagine.*

Hayden scrutinized the man in the photos more closely. Subtle hints of wiry hair could be seen sticking out from underneath the hat he wore – or maybe it was just a fuzzy image, it was hard to tell. His clothes were baggy offering no description of his body type, and the mirrored sunglasses he wore distracted from any distinct facial feature. Or did they? Hayden pulled the image closer. Maybe a scar on his cheek. It was hard to tell. Even with photo proof, somehow the stalker managed to hide in plain sight.

Hayden shoved back against his desk and propped his feet up, one ankle crossing over the other. He threw his stress ball into the air over and over again, allowing the reprieve while he cleared his mind.

After a few moments, he scooted back to work mode and thumbed through the photos. They weren't much to go on with his hat and sunglasses, but maybe one of their tech guys could decipher a usable image.

He brought his coffee cup to his lips as Colton's words echoed through his head. *"I wanted tonight to be perfect for her. I planned to surprise her with a horse drawn carriage ride. That's how I intended to end this evening - making her every wish come true. Instead, fate dealt us a cruel hand."*

Hayden nodded his head. *Fate was cruel indeed, my friend.*

Hayden popped the security footage from the ball into the player. The Lewis' had turned it over to the police willingly making him thankful for one less obstacle. It revealed little about the man he was looking for. The only time the stalker was within range, he either had his back to the camera, or his face was shielded by his mask or hand. He fast forwarded to the end of the video, vowing to watch it more carefully the second time around. Just as he was ready to dismiss the footage altogether, he saw them. Hayden lurched forward and watched in horror as a lifeless Emma was mercilessly tossed into the trunk of a black car as if she were nothing more than discarded trash.

Colton drove up the winding river road just as the sun began to rise. The tears in his eyes reflected painfully against the harsh rays. How could the sun give birth to another day? Did it not know what had happened, that his Emma had been snuffed out like a worthless flame?

Bloody images taunted him.

He stepped out of his truck and was greeted by a deep

chill in the air. The storm that had mocked him just hours earlier now had lain the path for frigid temperatures. Ignoring the bite of the crisp air, he stood at the property's edge and gazed down on the river. His world had been turned upside down.

Miss Francine met him at the door. She offered breakfast, coffee, or whatever he needed. Colton smiled, attempting pleasantries. That was all he could manage. He turned the corner to walk up the stairs and was bombarded by a husband and wife who quizzed him about the evening and offered to help in the search for Emma. News travels fast in a small town.

He knew they meant well, but right now he had to put distance between himself and everyone, so he excused himself and entered the solitude of his room.

The sunlight shone brightly through the sheer curtains, illuminating the bed. It was as empty as he felt. He walked around to sit on her side. Colton ran his hand against the cold sheet, sorrow welling deep inside him. He stretched out and allowed himself the private moment to grieve, to think about her.

Driving away from Victorian Garden's, knowing that they were no closer to finding her, was *the* most horrific night of his life. He had watched as officers and staff members alike walked away. Would they go home and sleep well feeling that their jobs were done? Was this just a run of the mill thing to them? Could they not know that his whole world was shattering all around him?

Colton walked into the bathroom and turned the water on. When steam began to rise, he stripped down and stepped into the shower. Leaning against the opposite wall, he allowed the hot water to massage his back, to soothe him.

Colton leaned his head back into the stream of water and blindly selected shampoo from the shelf. The smell of coconut filled the shower and filled him with agony at the same time. *I won't let you down, Emma - I'll find you.*

With a plush towel wrapped around his waist, Colton stood at the sink and stared at his own weary reflection. He ran water over his toothbrush and reached for the toothpaste. Not finding it in his drawer, he looked in Emma's. His dropped toothbrush danced against the vanity and then floor as Colton stared in complete shock at what he saw. He picked up the pregnancy test. Words escaped him as he stumbled backwards and slid against the wall to his bottom. *She's pregnant?*

Thoughts of Emma crashed all around him. "I'll find you *both*," he finally managed to say as he cradled his head in his hands.

CHAPTER 57

$\mathcal{W}$ild realities had always played out in Emma's dreams. Sometimes they were triggered by an event that had occurred during her day causing her to recall a person or place that she hadn't thought about in a very long while. Other times they simply were images that flashed into her consciousness without rhyme or reason.

Today she had awoken having had the most vivid dream of her life. Only, the throbbing in her head and the taste of copper in her mouth made her realize that she had awoken to the reality of a living nightmare.

The unforgiving stone floor below her cheek was icy cold and stabbed into her flesh like thumb tacks. A deep chill encompassed the body that she willed to move, but couldn't.

Emma lay on her left side and struggled to open her eyes. *What's wrong with me?* She wondered, but only wondered because even speaking the question required too much energy. Every instinct within her told her to get up, get out, or at least ready herself for the battle. *Where am I?*

Her memories were cloudy and her thought process slow. Instead of focusing on filling in the blanks, which caused her head to throb painfully, she took a moment to just listen to her surroundings.

She heard someone talking. A man's voice. *Who is that?* She wondered.

He spoke again. "I'll be gone longer than I planned," she heard him say. The icy cold truth shook her into awareness as adrenaline coursed through her system charging her brain into action. It was him. *What was his name? "Derrick is the name of the person whose life you ruined, you miserable bitch!"*

A tear streamed down her face and a sob escaped her throat. She hadn't meant for it to. She watched in horror as he stiffened, lowered the phone he'd been talking on, and slowly turned to face her. A flickering lantern illuminated his figure and cast an ominous shadow on the floor and wall as he walked towards her ever so slowly.

She tried to push up on her hands, but her body refused to follow commands. She tried to pull her legs up in an attempt to stand, but nothing would move. *He drugged me.*

Her brows drew together as fear sunk deep into her soul. She was helpless, lying there waiting for his attack. He stalked closer. Slowly. Enjoying the look of fear in her eyes.

"Get up!" He ordered. Emma had given herself the same command but her body still lay motionless. He kicked her in the ribs. "I said, 'Get up!'"

She didn't know what he had given her that would be so unforgiving to a body to paralyze it from movement, but at the same time, be so sadistic that it allowed her to feel the pain. "I can't," she whispered, "I can't move." Emma found herself taking violent blow after blow, unable to move and unable to stop the pain, and unable to stop the darkness that eventually claimed her.

~

It had been three days since anyone had seen or heard from Emma. Three days since she'd known a day without violent blows to every part of her body.

Sweat soaked strands of hair clung to her face as she gazed across the dim room at the flickering lantern. Eyelids heavy, the silhouette of her kidnapper blurred in and out of focus as he walked away. Her heart hammered in her chest and the room began to swirl. Emma had talked herself off a ledge before and she'd do it again, she would, but right now her fight was gone. Battered and exhausted she fell against the rough stone wall, sliding down. She ignored the pain they caused for they couldn't rival the ache coursing through her head as she fought to find balance. And they certainly couldn't compare to the painful void in her heart created from being separated from Colton. *Colton.* Tears stung her eyes at the thought of him.

Emma drew her arms tightly around her knees when she reached the cold, cruel floor, wincing at the sound of Derrick's *humming*? He'd hit her, hard. Her head and body throbbed from days of abuse. Days, she knew, because he had taken great pleasure in reminding her.

Even in the dim light, her dark hued bruises were evident. Fist sized discolorations so purplish blue that they looked black streaked across her arms and legs. She could only imagine what her face looked like. Emma licked her throbbing lips and hissed a protest. She brought a finger to her busted mouth and felt the deep stinging split on her bottom lip. Pulling her hand away, she caught site of her injured knuckles.

One thing that she'd learned about her captor over the past few days is that he was only interested in fighting her if she offered a struggle. No way in hell was she going to let him beat her unconscious again without leaving marks of her own, so this time, she fought. She knew it wasn't wise. *"You little bitch!"* He had yelled when Emma hit him. She knew she'd only have one chance and she'd made it count.

Larger than her in every way, the pendulum swung in his favor. Still yet, she was no one's punching bag.

If Derrick had thought that she would simply lie down and die, he was sadly mistaken. For just a moment, she found joy in the fact that she had fought back, and given the chance, she would again. But right now, she was spent.

As she willed her heart to steady in her chest, Emma listened to the howling wind as it whistled through a crack in the door. A tiny beam of light filtered through the same crack reflecting off the gems in her dress top.

She was still no closer to determining where she was. All she was certain of is that she now sat in a small stone building with a gravel floor. The razor sharp edges of the jagged rocks dug into the skin on her bare legs. She tried adjusting her weight, shifting from leg to leg, but relief was not to be found.

She looked around the sparsely furnished space for any hints. Derrick stood at a table with his back to her, wiry hair stood out against the hint of light. *A table and a lantern; both could be used as weapons.* She didn't know if the open room was part of basement or a structure that she'd passed by before. She also didn't know if she was even in Brookfield.

Derrick kept the damp room minimally lit – if at all. Emma was sure his reasoning was solely to maximize her fear.

Darkness encompassed the room as Emma's heart constricted in her chest. The last time this happened, he beat her until she lost consciousness. She could hear the scrape of Derrick's shoes across the gravel as he stalked closer. *Oh, God, not again.*

She tried to push herself up but her legs were like jelly. Resting her head on her bent knees, she uttered reassuring words to herself. *"You can do this. It'll be ok. You'll survive this."*

Emma could hear him breathing. Her breath hitched in her throat when she felt a piece of gravel skid across her bare foot. She couldn't see him and she couldn't move. She was paralyzed with fear. Derrick wanted her to know he was close. Close enough to strike. Moments passed. She waited. Tried to stand again, but was brutally dragged back down to the floor.

A hard hand fisted in her hair as he settled roughly beside her.

One hand knotted painfully in her hair, his other caressed her shoulder with tender, reassuring pats. "Shhh, Amanda," he whispered in her ear. "Shhh." The cruel tug on her hair paired with the tender embrace served to confuse the senses and utterly terrify her at the same time. A sob escaped her throat. "Amanda?" He asked with feigned concern. When Emma didn't answer, he tugged her head back painfully.

"Leave me alone!" She cried out as her head banged against the stone wall.

Un-fisting his hand, he stroked her hair gently then began to speak in whispered tones. He was so close that she felt his warm breath brush against her skin causing her stomach to churn. "Amanda, I heard what you were saying," a cruel laugh swept across her cheek. "And it's not ok," he said as he grabbed her and held her in an unwanted embrace. *"You're* not going to be ok." He stroked her cheek then pulled her head to his shoulder. "And you most certainly won't survive this." Emma quaked in his arms as fear welled up inside her. He hugged her close pinning her arms to her side as she fought to push him away. "Shhh, hush now, little one, it won't be over soon." Derrick paused then evil laughter echoed through the room.

Emma felt bile rise into her throat. She didn't know what was worse, being beaten by him or mock comforted as his deceptive tone spewed vile words and threats. She knew how to make him release her, though, so she did the very thing that would guarantee it.

Emma tried to pull away. He tightened his grip. "Let me go you sick fuck!" She turned her head and spat directly in the direction of his voice.

"You stupid cunt!" Derrick said as he shoved her away, jumping to his feet. The brunt of his fury was evident mere seconds later as searing pain shot through her side and head. He kicked her merciless, darkness claiming her consciousness once more.

~

Much to Hayden's dislike, Colton did not keep his usual schedule, as instructed. There was no way he would sit around and let an understaffed local police department handle her case when he had the funds to maximize the efforts. While he searched for Emma during the day with his private security team, another team member stayed behind in his room until he excused them when he returned for the evening. His nights were filled with readying the house on Oakland Hills for her arrival.

Colton had been pleased when the current tenants vacated the property early after hearing Emma's story on the news.

Tonight; however, he drove the long, broken driveway to

Dillingham Manor. He didn't know why he went there. He just wanted to be surrounded by her things, Colton supposed. Her letters, photos - anything that she had left behind – anything new to look at that might spark an idea.

As the house came into view, his headlights shone on Kane's rental car. The brothers had been getting along surprisingly well since their mother returned to England, but Colton wondered how long that would last. *It never lasts for long.*

Shifting the truck into park, he stepped out into the cool air and was greeted by the unmistakable cry of an electric guitar. The house was dark with the exception of the windows in Emma's room where the music came from.

He approached the house, finding the entryway unlocked – just as it was supposed to be in case she returned there. Colton walked down the hall to Emma's door, stepping inside. The pulse of the drum masked his presence, allowing him to enter unnoticed. Kane stood in the far corner jabbing the punching bag like it was his worst enemy. He hadn't heard Colton come in and only turned to acknowledge him when the music shut off.

With taped hands, Kane wiped sweat from his brow and caught his breath. His black shorts absorbed the moisture as he wiped his hands on them before reaching for a dumbbell and crossing the room. He lowered himself to the bed.

"I see you've made yourself at home," Colton said dryly nodding to the punching bag.

Kane lifted the weight in a bicep curl. "I hope you don't mind." Lowering it to the floor, he repeated the rep.

Colton looked around at the drab room. "I don't care what you do." He turned his focus to Emma's desk. Colton rifled through papers in the drawers, not knowing what he was looking for. He searched blindly for anything that might give him a clue as to where she was. Returning the papers, her calendar caught his attention. *"Lunch with Cat,"* was written on every Monday in October. The word *"Colton"* was written in purple ink between two solid hearts. It was scribed on one very special day - the day they were engaged. He couldn't help but smile as he traced his fingers over his name.

Colton thought about Emma and the pregnancy test he had found. He ducked his head blowing out his frustration.

"We'll find them, Colton," Kane said, offering genuine compassion. "We won't stop until we bring them home."

Them? He turned and pinned Kane with a hard stare. *How the hell would he know before I did?* "You said *them*, how the hell did *you* know?"

Kane dropped the weight to the floor when he saw the anger in Colton's eyes. Holding his hands up, he attempted to defuse the situation, "I found the test when Hayden sent me to retrieve her things from your room. I swear, I didn't know."

"And neither did I." Colton couldn't comprehend why Emma would keep such a secret from him. They had talked about it. She knew that he wanted children right away, knew he would be ecstatic with the news. "Why wouldn't she tell me?" He asked, meaning the question for himself.

"Maybe it's not yours," Kane blurted out without meaning to. He snapped his mouth shut as he saw the fury raging in Colton's eyes. "I didn't- I mean-"

Colton was rising to his feet as the question came out of his mouth. "What did you say?" He asked, then repeated as his fist connected with Kane's jaw. "You think she's a common whore?" Another blow. "Answer me!"

"Colton, no!" Kane managed to say through the assault, but it fell on deaf ears.

And just like that, the truce between brothers had come to an abrupt end as a ruthless battle ensued. Colton could not believe his ears when Kane made such an asinine assumption. Not only was Emma missing, stolen from him to face unimaginable horrors, but his brother assumed the baby wasn't Colton's. It was the proverbial straw that broke the camel's back.

Colton picked up the dumbbell and propelled it at Kane's head. He didn't care if he killed him. He'd threatened to do that very thing, and he always tried to keep his word. Let the chips fall where they may.

Kane ducked a split second before the weight hit him. It disappeared straight through the wall behind Emma's bed.

It should've hit a brick wall, but instead, they could hear it rolling - as if it had been propelled into another room.

"What the hell?" Colton asked as he peered past Kane. Kane turned and stared at the gaping hole in the wall. A putrid smell wafted past their noses – the smell of a room long shut off from the world.

The brothers scurried across the bed, shining a flashlight into the cavity. Darkness encompassed the room with the exception of a four poster bed that was slightly illuminated by the light filtering through the hole.

"Am I seeing what I think I'm seeing?" Kane spared Colton a glance. "Could that be Leah's room?"

Colton nodded his head slowly as he caught his breath. "I believe it could be the very room that holds the secret to Dillingham Manor." Colton ran his hand along the wall. "The structure of this room always puzzled me." He shook his head as he thought. "When Grandmother's journal said that the room was sealed shut, I assumed they had sealed the door, I had no idea they would add a wall to seal off the room. They never wanted it found."

"I didn't think it really existed," Kane said.

"Nor did I," Colton waved his hand as if dismissing the room altogether. "But right now, I cannot deal with another thing," he said as he eased himself off the bed and back into the chair. "I just can't."

Kane motioned to the wall behind him, "I'll seal this back up. No one will know but us." He pointed to Colton and then to himself, "You focus on finding Emma, and I'll assist in any way you need."

Colton stood and crossed to the door without regard to Kane's offer. The last thing he wanted or needed was Kane helping him in any way. He reached for the door knob.

"Colton," Kane said, getting his attention. "I really am sorry. I'm sorry that Emma is gone, I'm sorry about what I said, and I'm sorry that we are on the outs once again."

Colton turned to look at him. "Sorry is a good description for you, brother!" He held his gaze for a moment more. "Piss off Kane," he said as he disappeared through the door.

CHAPTER 58

*S*taring down at the yellow note pad, Hayden let the pen roll from his fingers onto the desk. He exhaled and nodded his head as a smile tugged at his lips. *Smart girl,* he thought to himself.

When the forty-eight hour window had closed, he had feared the worst. For days he had stared at the blank pages of the notepad - frustrated, no solid evidence to record. Today, however, he gazed again at the nearly two dozen notations that had come from a very unlikely source - Emma herself.

He popped the SD card that had been in her camera out of his computer. *Damn smart.*

The card had been badly damaged and originally thought useless for evidence, but after some time in the hands of their tech team, it appeared that most of the data had been retrieved.

Hayden had swiped the card from the evidence locker as soon as it was tagged. No one knew he made a copy before returning it.

Emma was well known in Brookfield for her photography, so they were certain that she'd have some useful images on her camera. At the very least they'd hoped for a distant picture that could be enlarged enough to see the stalkers face. Instead, Emma had delivered them more – much more. They had tapped a goldmine.

Hayden clasped his hands behind his head and thought about what he'd do with the information he'd just learned. The conflict inside him played tug-of-war with his sense of duty. He couldn't keep this from Cat, couldn't keep it from Colton . . . and wouldn't keep his job if anyone found out he'd leaked information.

He glanced at his watch and thrummed his fingers on his desk. His mind made up, he pulled the phone from his pocket and dialed Colton's number. After a brief conversation, they made plans to meet - off the record.

The turn signal blinked noisily as Colton turned onto the narrow road. The gravel beneath the tires of his truck crunched as the wheels rolled slowly over them. He knew that Emma had traveled this road countless times, and he'd give anything in the world to have her by his side now. He spared a glance at the passenger's seat and wondered how it was possible to feel crowded by emptiness.

His headlights illuminated the barren trees that lined the path of Oakland Hills. Much like himself, the treasures they once held were lost.

Colton backed the truck up to the little white house that would become their home. He'd kept himself busy over the last few days doing necessary repairs. They served two purposes – sprucing up the house and keeping his mind from being idle. An Idle mind created chaos. He had to remain level headed. So he worked. Day and night, he worked.

After tugging the machine to the edge of the tailgate, Colton hefted it to the ground and onto a hand truck, wheeling it into the house. The smell of fresh paint greeted him. As he gazed onto the caramel hued walls, he hoped that Emma would approve of the color. He liked its richness and thought it made the home feel warm, or would help it to once the renovations were complete.

Colton's appraisal traveled over the open floor plan. So far, he'd managed to add crown molding and paint to the walls. He also added a custom mantle to the fireplace. He looked behind him at the empty dining room and crossed to the kitchen to set the two stools on top of the bar alongside paint supplies. A clean paint tray filled with rollers, brushes, and tape sat neatly in the crook of the bar, a plastic sheet nestled around it protecting the surface underneath.

The sound of Colton's boots echoed throughout the room as he returned to the great room. He stared down at the faded wood floors and then to the drum sander. Forgoing instructions, he went straight to work scraping away worry and despair from the tired boards – if only he could do the same for himself.

As he worked around the hearth of the fireplace, Colton's mind drifted with the repetitions. He allowed the break from reality and watched as a wonderful fantasy played out in his head; he welcomed it, even.

He imagined a roaring fire illuminating the room. Leaning against the sofa, Emma stretched out by his side in the floor. She was dressed in a long satin gown with matching ivory robe. The fabric felt cool against his bare chest as he leaned against her body. He felt her hands in his hair as he kissed and caressed the swell of her growing belly. He looked up to capture her gaze, the glow of her golden skin warming his heart. Colton thought the baby would be beautiful, like Emma.

His mind fast forwarded in time.

He watched as a little figure toddled down the hallway peering into each room. Her chestnut curls fell loosely against her white dress and bounced lightly with every uneven step she took. "Sophie," he called out behind her, but she continued on her quest. "Sophie Elizabeth," he said a little louder. When she turned, emerald eyes stared back at him. He smiled when she batted her thick black lashes.

She shrugged her little shoulders. "Mama?" She asked, her tiny hoarse voice lending an eclectic British accent.

Colton closed his eyes against the pain that he could not endure. His heart ached for Emma and the Sophie Elizabeth of his imagination. He had never felt so empty, so alone.

The hand that closed over his shoulder giving him a gentle shake pulled him from all his thoughts – real and imagined. Colton slammed Hayden into the wall as the sander spun of its own accord.

Hayden knew that it was risky walking up on him, but with the roar of the machine, his voice had been drowned out. Now he found himself being released from a deadly choke hold as Colton eased his hand away from his throat and yanked the plug on the sander.

Hayden gave him time to adjust, to get his anger under control. "I would ask you where you were just now . . ." he trailed off.

"Where I was?" Colton asked shaking his head, "where I was was somewhere between heaven and hell."

Colton walked to the refrigerator and pulled out two beers. Twisting the tops off, he handed one to Hayden and grasped his own between two fingers as they walked to the bar, lowering the stools. "You wanted to talk to me about something?" Colton asked.

Moments passed before Hayden spoke. "I came here to tell you about a lead we got today."

Colton's head snapped to attention as he waited for his next words.

"But after some consideration, I think I want you to see for yourself."

Hayden retrieved his laptop and opened the lid. After inserting the card, he turned to Colton. "Your security team received this anonymously," he glanced away, "and we never had this discussion."

Colton nodded his head. "What are we looking at?"

Hayden smiled. "One brave girl who I'm damn impressed with." He turned the screen to face Colton. "Some of this will be hard to watch. Press play when you're ready. I need to call Cat." Hayden stepped outside, giving Colton the opportunity to view the video in private.

Colton clicked the arrow and waited for the video to load. Hayden hadn't given him much to go on, so he had no way to prepare for what he was about to witness. He shot forward, pulling the screen closer when Emma came into view. She wore the emerald gown from the masquerade ball and a sheer look of terror. He knew without being told that the tall, lean man in the reflection was her stalker.

He watched as she coached herself. *"Breathe,"* she urged. *"I love you, Colton,"* she had mouthed. The tears that streamed down her face matched his own at her profession. He was so proud of her composure and calculated discussion that coaxed details out of the man that she feared. She'd provided them with a solid image of his face and his name.

She'd also provided them with the reason that the man knew where to find her, the newspaper article. Guilt bore down on Colton like a wine press. *This is my fault.* Before sorrow could claim him, another emotion prevailed – rage.

Colton watched as the man delivered ruthless blows to the woman he loved, watched as a cascade of shattered glass fell in front of the jolted camera lens like a crystal shower. "I will kill you!" Colton seethed as his fists drew into tight balls. Then he watched as the camera blurred and heard the impact as a man's voice screamed out a curse. The splatter of blood through the cracked lens spiraled the video into total darkness.

Colton pulled the phone from his pocket. Selecting the number, he called the team lead of his security detail, verifying that a package had been received. He ended the call and played the video again.

He must have watched it a dozen times when he heard the door close behind him.

"I know it was difficult to watch, but I wanted you to see-" Hayden couldn't think of the right words to fit. "She's smart, Colton. She's thinking." *She may just survive this.* "And you can see by the end of the clip, she's brave; she didn't go down without a fight."

"That's my girl," both men turned when Cat's voice filled the room. She dropped her purse and keys to the hearth then crossed the room. Taking the seat beside Colton, Hayden stood at her back with his hands on her shoulders as she watched.

She and Colton sat in silence as they played the video repeatedly only stopping when the images faded to black from a drained battery.

Receiving the phone call he knew was coming, Hayden drove into work for an "unexpected" briefing. He had bent the facts many times over the years, as was sometimes necessary, but tonight he knew that he'd be blatantly lying to the police chief. He would feign surprise, along with the rest of the officers, during roll call and sing the praises of the tech team when it was revealed that useful data was extracted from Emma's camera card. No one at the station knew that he'd made a copy of it. And no one would.

Hayden knew that Colton's team had more resources and a concentrated focus - that alone improved the odds of bringing Emma home. And that's why he did what he did.

Colton grabbed himself another beer and sat one down in front of Cat. For the last bit, they had sat with their forearms resting on the bar, sharing stories about Emma.

Cat turned on the stool, leaning her back against the bar, mirroring Colton's new position. She looked at the improvements he'd made. Pointing her bottle to the empty space above the fireplace, she made an offer. "I'm gonna paint a picture that would look perfect there."

Colton shook his head. "I appreciate the offer," he said

gently, "but I already have something in mind." He gave her a sideways glance. Returning his focus on the space, he nodded. "Our wedding photo will go there. I'm going to find her and marry her as soon as she's ready."

"Then I shall make the first toast at your wedding!" Cat said as she clanked her bottle against his. "To Emma."

Colton sat forward and slowly peeled the label from his bottle. "You know what I don't understand?" He asked as he continued the rip the paper slowly. "Why was she drinking?"

"When?" Cat asked.

"At the ball. I can't comprehend why she was drinking."

"Oh, I don't know, Colton," Cat said as her sassiness rose a notch. "Maybe it was because she was scared to death to meet your mother," *or that your brother confuses the hell out of her!* "Or that she simply likes the taste of champagne. What does it matter?"

"What does it *matter*?" He repeated as he looked at her in confusion. "It matters because she's pregnant."

"She's-" Cat felt like she was choking on air. "Wait, what?"

Colton looked down at the dark knot in the floor. "I found the test in the vanity drawer," he looked at Cat. "It had a line. She didn't even tell me."

A flood of relief rushed over her as she curled her hand over Colton's wrist. "She didn't tell you, Colton, because she's not pregnant."

"But I-"

Cat held her hand up to stop him from talking. "I know what you found, and can certainly understand why you thought that, but I can put your mind at ease. That was not her test; it was Lisa's. And only one line meant Lisa was not pregnant. There's no way Emma would risk the life of a child by drinking while pregnant."

As she explained the story behind Lisa's request, Colton found her words fading into the background. Even though he was relieved that an innocent child wasn't in harm's way, he couldn't help the tiny sense of loss that he felt.

Finding himself alone in the house once more, Colton resumed his task until the last board was stripped. In a way, Cat's revelation did to him what the machine had done to the floor, peeled away a layer of stress. For that, he was thankful.

Satisfied with the results of the floor, he glanced at his watch and decided to call it a night. With his hand on the light switch, he gave the room an once over. An image of the curly topped toddler drifted into his mind. Little Sophie Graves would come into his life one day, but for now his focus could be on bringing Emma home.

The room fell into darkness as he closed the door behind him.

CHAPTER 59

*C*at pulled up to the tattoo shop and shoved the gearshift into park. The last place she wanted to be after the sleepless night she'd had was work. The video had played over and over again in her mind causing sleep to elude her; she imagined that Colton had suffered a similar fate.

She lowered her visor and opened the mirror. A quick peek revealed that a few touchups were needed. After smearing on some eyeliner and lip gloss, she tugged long tendrils loose from her messy ponytail. Satisfied with her appearance, she stepped from the truck and up the steps to her shop.

At the toll of the bell tower, Cat turned and looked across the street. The closing door at the Journal caught her eye. Her gaze instantly drifted to Emma's dark office window. A stab of sorrow punched her gut.

What she wouldn't do to see Emma giving her customary hello with the shuttering blinds. Cat smiled at the memory as she turned and pushed through the doors of the shop.

With a harsh eye, she assessed her new assistant. And had she remembered that she'd actually hired one, she would've still been in her bed. Nevertheless, she stared at Erin who was dressed all in black, just like Cat. They quickly ran through the rules and the day's schedule as Cat readied her work station.

Jazz music poured from the speakers, soothing her soul, relaxing her.

The ding at the door alerted her that the first client of the day had shown up. Cat walked to the front and assessed him. She was underwhelmed with his poser appearance – bandana, scuff-free motorcycle boots, and a leather jacket that hadn't seen a cross county ride, let alone a cross country one. She'd seen his type before – a Billy badass wannabe. As she led him back to her station, he spouted about having aspirations for a full back piece and claimed to ride a soft tail custom. In reality, a set of lips grinding into existence against his shoulder would have him running for the door and the foot powered scooter than he likely had chained up at the parking meter.

Cat knew this, but as a business owner, she had to listen to his crap and feign interest.

She directed the sandy haired man to stretch out on his belly so she could examine the placement for his wolf tattoo. Poking on pudgy people didn't interest her, but nevertheless, this was the profession she had chosen. The cry of the gun drowned out his incessant hisses and mundane words. Cat silently worked, the repetitive motions soothing her as she laid the charcoal ink in and wiped the excess away.

"...and that's when I said she deserved it. That nosey bitch is always up in somebody's business," he said.

Time to feign interest. "Who's that?" Cat asked not giving two hoots about what he was saying.

"That chick, Emma, who works at the Journal."

Cat's gun came to a stop as she leaned against the man's back. She placed her elbow directly onto his abused skin, ignoring his cries. "Let's try that again," Cat said with her face up to his ear. "What's this about Emma?"

Maybe he wasn't as dumb as she originally thought because he started back peddling like crazy. She could see from the wild pulse in his neck that he was afraid. Cat laid the gun needle to his carotid artery. "I have a question for you," she asked as the man turned his neck to look at her. "Do you know what happens when a person's artery is pumped full of tattoo ink?"

"No!" The man cried out in a shaky voice.

"Neither do I," she said as she fired the gun to life. Cat laughed as she watched him crawl off the table, stumbling away from her as he struggled to get to his feet.

"You're crazy," he called out, running for the door.

"You have no idea," Cat answered, blowing the tip of her tattoo gun.

Derrick shoved Emma roughly through the doors, sliding the bolt into place. She fell to her knees as her face skidded across the straw. She ducked her head and attempted to stand but the heavy foot that fell on her back crushed her down, forcing debris into her mouth.

Emma turned her head, coughing violently as she tried to clear her airway. The simple act alone caused every muscle in her tired and battered body to protest. She ached. Her head, her stomach, her arms from the hands that were tied behind her back, her legs . . . all over, she ached.

Derrick hooked the toe of his boot in her bound hands, bending her back cruelly. Emma cried out when she felt the burn of her muscles as they struggled to adjust to his latest abuse. "Shut up, bitch," he ordered unsympathetically as he pulled his foot away, sending her careening back to the barn floor. "I'm tired of hearing you scream."

Emma felt a warm trickle flow from her nose and tasted copper when the blood dripped onto her lips. She turned her head and wiped her face on the blue dress she'd been forced to change into days ago. The sole of Derrick's boot moved past her head, shocking her back to her current hell. She braced herself for his kick, but it didn't come.

He moved across the room. With his back to her, he worked. She could see a laptop sitting atop stacked hay bales and could hear the feverish strokes of the keys as he moved across them.

Emma quietly worked herself onto her knees, then attempted to stand.

Derrick barked out a cruel laugh. "Just because my back is to you, Amanda, doesn't mean I don't see you."

When he moved to the side, she saw her image come into view in the right corner of the laptop. He was filming her.

"We're going to send a greeting to your boyfriend," Derrick said cheerfully. He looked from her to the computer screen and then back again. "Let's go ahead and move you over a skosh to the left so that you're centered." He turned his back again. "He's going to-"

Emma sprang to her feet and bolted for the door.

Derrick was a cruel captor and allowed her to reach it. Realizing that she couldn't grasp the latch, she kicked her foot to release it. But it was in vain. Dragging her mercilessly back by her hair, he slung her across the room to the barn floor. Derrick smiled at the camera then slammed his fist into her cheek.

≈

Three sport utility vehicles with blackened windows fell in line with one another as they kicked up dust on the rural Kentucky road. Colton and his security team raced toward the weak signal they had locked on to. He was in the back seat of the middle caravan following a streaming feed from a laptop. His team lead sat at his side and quietly assessed the footage. Images pulsed in and out of focus but were clear enough that Colton could see the rough treatment that Emma endured. Even though it was hard to watch, at least he knew she was still alive, and for that, he owed the police sergeant a debt of gratitude.

Once again, Hayden had come through for him and given his team the jump they needed. Even though the signal that had been transmitted to the police department was supposed to be untraceable, Colton's team had been able to break it. Now they searched.

Barns and houses dotted the landscape around them. The heavy machinery which proved beneficial to the livelihood of the farmers proved detrimental to his efforts. Metal was jamming the signal, as Derrick likely knew it would, prolonging the search.

With haystacks to their back, Derrick settled in beside Emma and brushed the dirt from her pale blue dress. He tsked when she tried to pull away.

"I'm sure your boyfriend will be happy to see you," he said as he popped the top button on her dress.

Emma's eyes filled with tears, awareness crashing over her as his intent became clear. "No!" She screamed out, her voice thick and rough. She scrambled to the side until the overturned fence spool hit her hip. Derrick threw his legs over hers. Trapped.

She worked the rope that held her hands against her back.

Allowing her fear to mount properly, Derrick took a moment to provide the explanation that she hadn't asked for. "I asked myself a question. I said, 'Self, what could I do to Amanda that would be even worse than killing her boy toy and making her watch?' And then it came to me," Derrick looked at his reflection in the computer screen and smiled a proud smile. His voice grew darker as he turned to face her. Grasping her chin hard, he continued, "I'm going to ruin you right before his eyes. Can you imagine how he'll feel, Amanda?" Derrick cocked his head to the side waiting for her reply. When she didn't offer one, he did, "I think you can and that's why I changed my plan. He'll watch as his whore of a girlfriend lies there helpless as I take my pleasure in any form I like. And he'll listen to your screams. He'll be a fingertip away, but there's nothing he'll be able to do to stop it," Derrick smiled. "Then, when I'm finished with you, I'm going to slice your worthless throat and let him watch as the last drop of blood slowly drains from your body. You *knowing* that he's hurting is the best way I can hurt you. It's a delightful plan, really, don't you think?" Derrick leaned in closer, ripping another buttonhole free. She spit in his face.

"You're a psychopath!" Emma screamed.

Derrick leaned back with scornful disapproval. "Correction, Amanda. I'm a *sociopath*. As a doctor of psychiatry, I relate well to society. And, while I understand that I'm hurting you," a sinister smile tugged at his lips, "I just don't give a fuck!"

Emma felt her legs being jerked forward as he pushed her thighs roughly apart. She tried to close her legs, but he was too strong.

Derrick pulled back slightly to undo his pants. When

Emma felt the disgusting evidence of his arousal against her leg, a new found fight rose up in her. She knew this was her last chance to get away, so she used the only weapon she had as she worked one hand free.

Emma lunged forward with more speed than her aching muscles should have been able to accommodate. She bashed her head against his with a fury that would rival any blow he'd given her, then she jammed the butt of her hand hard against his nose.

"Fuck!" Derrick screamed out as he fell backwards grasping his face.

Emma sprang to her feet.

"Run, Emma," Colton screamed at the monitor as though she could hear him. He had watched in horror as Derrick rose above her with the intentions of raping her. Even though Colton was proud of her spirit, and her ability to fight through the fear, he wanted her to run. "Please," he pleaded. "Please, sweetheart, just get out."

The caravan sped furiously to a halt, tossing Colton against the passenger's seat in front of him. Agents poured out around them leaving doors open and weapons drawn. The buzz of machinery drowned out the chatter around him.

Colton looked at the vast acreage housing one homestead and numerous barns. She was in one of them, but would he get there in time? His legs carried him forward despite the protests of his team.

Emma's foot shot out like lightening against Derrick's face. She watched the splatter of blood as it lashed against the haystack to his side. Again, he groaned and gripped his face weakly, obviously addled. She now had the upper hand and would not lose it. With all the force she could muster, Emma stomped the gaping zipper at his crotch. "That's for taking me away from Colton."

Derrick bellowed in pain and turned his head. A cruel foot landed against his eye. "And that's for taking me away from Cat." When he attempted to rise, Emma's deadweight fell directly into his chest. She could feel the crunch of his bones below her knees and heard the sounds as they tore through his chest. "And that's for causing me to live in fear of you." Teardrops spilled onto her cheeks as she rose to her feet.

Derrick writhed in pain as screams of agony echoed through the barn. His eyes popped open in horror when he felt Emma's foot against his neck. He pressed his hand to her ankle but didn't possess the strength to stop her. He cried out when she stepped down, bearing her weight fully on one foot, crushing his windpipe.

Emma sank to her knees and gazed into the lifeless eyes of her abductor. As she worked to free her other hand, her mind drifted back over the last year. She thought about the stalker who she'd lived in fear of and the grandparents' whose deaths had thrust her in his path. She thought about Cat, her constant cheerleader, and then to the love of her life. When her mind floated to Colton, tears spilled onto her cheeks.

Sounding a sigh of relief, she rose to her feet and let the ropes fall to the floor.

With stiff, achy arms, Emma unbolted the door and walked into the bright light. She squinted her eyes against the assault. The sun was warm against her skin, a direct contradiction to the nipping breeze. Exhaustion was quickly claiming her. She felt disconnected from her surroundings; even the buzzing machinery seemed faint now. Looking across the field, Emma saw flashing lights coming around the dusty bend in the distance. For the first time in a long time, she no longer felt fear. Still yet, she was thankful for her rescuers. Fatigue guiding her steps, Emma's legs began to grow heavy. She stumbled, falling to the ground. She tried to pull herself up, but the effort was too great. "It's over," she cried, tears streaming down her face. Emma lay against the cool earth blinking heavily at the three black sport utility vehicles. They sat in a pyramid form, all twelve doors splayed open. She knew within reason that they were there to help her, too, if only she could make them see her. The fight in her gone, her eyes slipped shut.

Colton had just sprinted from the second barn when he saw the door of the third inch open. "Thank you, God," he cried out when he saw Emma emerge, her gait unsteady and slow. Relief washed over him, but so did fear. Where was Derrick? "You have to run, sweetheart. Please."

Emma took only a few steps before falling to the ground. Moments passed. She didn't get back up. Colton felt bile rise in his throat.

He kept an eye trained on the doorway of the barn as he rushed to her side. Agents dressed in black hurried passed him, pouring inside the building with their weapons drawn. Colton could see the rise and fall of her chest. She was alive. He closed his eyes briefly in silent praise. Dropping to his knees, his gaze poured over her body as tears stung his eyes. He stared in disbelief. "What did he do to you, luv?" Colton's stomach lurched. Bruises in varying shades of black, brown, purple, green, and yellow covered her entire body. Every exposed surface was bruised, cut, and scraped. Her eyes were black and swollen. Dried blood streaked across her cheek, leading from the split in her busted lip.

Afraid to touch her, but not willing to leave her on the cold ground, Colton scooped Emma up, cradling her in his arms. He shrugged his jacket off and wrapped it around her. Gently rocking her back and forth, he whispered tender reassurances to her.

"I'll kill him for what he did to you, Emma," Colton declared.

"That won't be necessary," the voice beside him called out.

Colton looked up, seeing Hayden kneeling by his side. Hayden motioned toward the barn as a man entered the building. The reflective words on the back of his jacket clearly identified him as the corner.

Colton glanced back at Hayden.

"There's not a jury in this land that would convict her, either," Hayden declared.

Emma felt herself floating through the air. The strong arms that surrounded her were safe and familiar. "Colton," she whispered, barely audible.

"I've got you, luv," he whispered again and again as he held her to his chest. "It's going to be ok."

Emma believed him and knew it would. She burrowed her face into his shirt, inhaling his cologne. She smelled the light scent of leather and realized that his jacket was wrapped around her.

Emma felt the soft cot underneath her and heard an array

of voices as questions of every kind were hurled in her direction. She opened her eyes when the blanket tucked firmly around her. Colton was by her side, caressing her cheek.

"Hey, there," Emma squeaked out.

Colton bent forward and kissed her lips ever so gently. "Hi, yourself," he said as tears filled his eyes to the brim, cascading over.

CHAPTER 60

*T*he days following the nightmarish events of her abduction had now turned into months in the small town of Brookfield, Kentucky. Emma felt life slowly returning to normal, the relentless pursuit of the media finally dying down. No longer could she say her only claim to fame was the fact that she didn't have a middle name.

Sinking down into the plush red chair, the softness enveloped her like a cloud of cotton. Since her return, Emma had learned to slow down and take time to appreciate the small things in life. Her gaze poured over the home that Colton had made for them while she was gone. Plush white sofas filled the room, a direct contrast to the walnut floor and chocolate traveler's chest they used for a coffee table. Black and bronze framed art stood out against the caramel walls that had gained tasteful crown molding since she last lived here. Above the fireplace, a gorgeous walnut mantle sat against stone construction. She looked at the inscription in the wood. Emma and Colton's names were perfectly centered and sat situated between two dates – the day they met and the day they would wed, which was two days from now. She laughed at the relatively small time span. *Sometimes you just know.*

She looked at the small bowl atop of the mantle. A smile tugged at her lips. The bowl was their "wine goblet" and was filled with pine cones and decorative twine balls in shades of red, tan, and black.

Emma gazed out the long window to her side and watched as snowflakes gently piled on top of her car. There were few things on earth that she loved more than her grandpa's old car, but snow was one of them. As she watched, she tucked her legs to her side and sipped the steamy hot chocolate from her mug. When she leaned to place the cup on the side table, relief washed over her at the realization that there was no more pain.

One thing she'd learned through it all is that she was tougher than she ever thought possible. Her battered body had healed; her emotional scars would, too. Emma held her arms out in front of her and smiled at the evidence that the bruises that had once mocked her, reminding her of the worst days of her life, had faded into a memory. The night terrors weren't gone completely, but they were ceasing – likely the result of therapy. *Therapy*, she thought to herself and laughed. *I always thought therapy was for weak minded individuals. Then I decided that it was for survivors - people who refused to be the victim one day longer.* "Guess I should write that down."

She reached for the table again and pulled a leather bound journal from the drawer. Emma leaned back in the chair and ran her fingers along the ornate swirls of the vintage brown leather.

The day her therapist had suggested she record her thoughts, Colton presented her with the case. He'd seen it in a window display of a secondhand shop and thought that Emma would appreciate its unique style. He was correct in that assumption as vintage things always appealed to her more than something new and shiny.

Emma turned her focus back to the heavy journal in her hands. She uncoiled the thin leather strip that bound the edges together and gazed inside at her entries. What started out as daily blurbs had expanded into stories that told the tale of a life worth living.

When she was originally told to record her thoughts, Emma wondered why anyone would sit down and pour their every inner thought onto paper, but she'd found that once she got started, things began to click. In the beginning, she tried writing her feelings down. She didn't want to relive them, so she chose to use her journal as a diary until her next appointment. What was the therapist going to do, spank her if she did it wrong? She laughed at the thought.

Emma secured her hair with the pencil that had rolled out and was pleased that it had stayed. Flipping back to the beginning, she read what she had written.

Day 1: This is stupid.

Day 2: Not feelin' it.

Day 3: My feelings? I don't like to talk about my feelings. And I don't like being put in a box. We're gonna do this my way, and I'm going to start by stopping with the numbering of days. If I get to it, I do. If I feel like writing, I will. This is me taking charge, and it's a good feeling.

Emma skipped ahead until she saw pages filled with entries.

Today Colton and I went to Dillingham Manor. He didn't tell me why we were going, only that I needed to bring my new camera.

I love to take pictures, so I didn't question it. When we pulled into the drive, I saw the house with new eyes. For once, I didn't see the dilapidated boarding house that sat just off Penn Way. I saw a flawed shell of a home that, with a little work, would reveal the beauty it once held. I guess that's like me, blemished but not broken.

When we walked inside and entered my old bedroom, I saw Kane. I froze immediately. With him and Colton, you just never really know what you're gonna get. One minute they're fighting, the next they're getting along, but maybe that's what having a sibling is like. I couldn't say.

Anyway, all my furniture was gone and the room sat empty with the exception of a huge box of tools and some lighting. "What are we doing?" I asked Colton because frankly, a vacant room isn't much to photograph, or not that vacant room, anyway. He handed me a pair of safety glasses and then plugged a saw into an orange extension cord. Extending his arm, he offered the power tool to me. I laughed. I couldn't help it. I'm not much of a crafty girl! He explained that after I saw what was on the other side of the wall, that the request to bring my camera would make sense.

I placed my camera in the safety of the closet and dunned my stylish plastic glasses. "I'm ready for my chemistry experiment, teacher." Colton and Kane both laughed. Colton said I looked adorable in the huge glasses that covered both my eyebrows and cheekbones. Kane said nothing - I'm guessing that was wise. I pulled my ponytail into a mini bun and was thankful that I'd chosen to wear jeans and a sweatshirt for this outing.

Taking the pencil from Kane, Colton drew a large square on the wall and instructed me to trace it with the saw. What were they thinking? No amount of trauma would make me forget that I don't like do-it-yourself projects because I don't do them well! Anyway, I placed the saw to the wall and pulled the trigger as he instructed. The jagged blades cut through the lead path and I blew the dust away when I'd finished. Colton pointed to his feet and I sat the saw down. I jumped when the pad of his fist struck the wall, knocking the sheetrock to the other side. Kane shined his flashlight and I looked inside with wide eyes not believing what I saw before me. Colton and Kane were plastered on each side of me - the three of us staring in silent awe.

They only turned when they heard the shuddering lens of my camera. I wanted to document this step by step, so I had slipped from their sides silently. For so long, I had yearned to see deeper inside the walls of Dillingham Manor, although, I meant that figuratively. I always felt that a secret lay within the corridors, but I honestly had no idea it was on the other side of the wall from where I slept night after night.

I took a picture of the wall beside where my bed used to be and showed them the rugged blemishes of the drywall. Time and time again, I had lain in bed and ran my fingers over those grooves, always wondering but never knowing what caused them. Nodding to Colton, I returned my camera to closet and he and Kane took turns cutting into the wall.

Deciding it was safe, we all three climbed through the hole after I grabbed my camera again. When Colton hooked a light up, we realized we'd stepped back in time. I took pictures of Leah's room before anything was disturbed. It was surreal being in there. The air was still and musty, almost nauseatingly so. Thick dust covered everything in sight. The windows were bricked over from the outside. That, paired with the wall that had been constructed, showed a parents' attempt at confining the hurt. My heart ached for them at the mere thought.

I was going to say that I couldn't imagine having a hurt so deep, but not long ago, I killed a man who caused a fear so deep that I would have done anything to keep from reliving it. We all have our own brick walls, I guess.

With the exception of fallen ceiling tiles and crumbling plaster, Leah's room was free from clutter. I shot Colton and Kane an odd glance when I saw a dumbbell lying in the floor near the bed. I knew this was a modern addition. "Don't ask," they both requested. Knowing their history, I didn't.

A four poster bed sat in the center of the room with night stands holding oil lamps on either side. An antique dressing table with four rounded drawers sat adjacent to the bed. A swipe of my hand revealed a pattern of painted rose and ivy. I know it had been beautiful at one time. The attached dusty mirror that sat above it was round in shape, but the ornate wood that housed the glass was scalloped giving it a classic Victorian feel. A small, broken stool was overturned underneath the drop vanity ledge that held an empty rectangular jewelry box, hairbrush, and a dust caked cameo broach.

As fascinated as I was over the structural stuff, I wanted to delve deeper. I wanted to peek inside the wooden chest at the foot of her bed, flip through books on her bookcase . . . I wanted to see how someone of this era lived, what they loved, what interested them. So I did.

I perused Leah's small bookcase. Blowing the dust from the titles sent me into a sneezing fit, but once I recovered, I saw books of many types. A black bible with pages so brittle, I was afraid to turn them sat between genres of classic fiction, mysteries, and a handwritten book of fairytales in a pink casing. I suspected the latter was the favored genre since someone had taken the time to write certain stories by hand. I wondered if Leah had had aspirations of becoming a writer someday.

While Colton and Kane discussed the safety of the room, I covered as much ground as possible taking in my surroundings and snapping photos. I fell to my knees in front of the chest. The crying hinges reminded me that I was opening a time capsule. A violin with its deteriorating bow lay atop woven Afghans and blankets. I photographed every layer as I peeked deeper inside. A book of poetry was buried in the folds of the first blanket. I thought it odd that it wasn't on the shelf with the rest of the novels. When I opened the cover, the inscription within *made me laugh. Penned in beautiful scroll handwriting were the words, 'I hate poetry. No one really understands it, signed Leah.' I laughed because I had thought the same thing countless times! I imagine that the book was hidden as a means of not having to read it. Between the fabric of the next blanket laid a vintage lace and eyelet dress that I wondered if Leah had intended to be her wedding dress. The fabric was yellowing, but I'm sure it had been a pristine white when it was carefully placed inside. At the bottom of the chest lay a blue glass jar. Its contents were held in place by a wire and gasket closure and was wrapped in four handkerchiefs with intricate lace edges.*

When I released the wire from the lid, the clanking contents inside grew my curiosity. Having heard the pinging noise, Colton and Kane came to investigate. We all knew that we had found the treasure that Martin and Nancy had intended to steal. Silver and gold certificates were stashed inside along with half penny coins which I had never even heard of. There was regular money, too, but nothing of the goldmine that that was rumored. Maybe it was a lot of money at one time, either way it was cool to find such rare currency.

As we crawled back into current day, leaving Leah's bedroom behind, Colton and Kane made plans to have the contents moved so we could inspect them more carefully.

When I woke up this morning, I didn't know what the day would hold, what I would do, or how I would feel. As always, Colton surprised me with a revelation that, in turn, revealed a little about myself. Like Leah's room, some things aren't meant to be hidden away. I'm going to try to be more open about the things I experienced, but everyone needs to bear with me if I put up a wall from time to time.

Emma closed the journal, hugging it to her chest. The hot chocolate had warmed her bones and she felt a glorious nap on the horizon. She gazed at the lit Christmas tree through heavy eyes; the multicolored lights were gorgeous. She appreciated them for only a moment as the drippy kitchen sink lulled her into a peaceful slumber.

She woke to the sounds of giggles - her own. The wet tongue that lapped across her naked toes tickled. She bent down and scooped up the little fur ball, placing his fat little hiney in her lap. Colton had insisted that she needed a guard dog and assured her that this jet black pup from the humane society would grow into a fierce protector one day.

With a yap, he rolled onto his back and wiggled in her lap. Emma obliged and scratched the smooth warm skin of his underbelly. After a few moments, he hopped down and turned around, letting out a tiny bark. "He has me well trained," Emma said as she rose to her feet. As they walked toward the door for his potty break, she looked down at him, "I still say he should have named you Betty." Jett's low whine protested as if he knew she was calling him a girl name. Emma giggled and opened the door to the snowy landscape, watching his furry black figure disappear into the storm.

CHAPTER 61

With Jett safely back inside and snuggled in his bed by the roaring fire, Emma settled back into her comfy chair. The snow outside continued to pile up, and she did a mental scan of the pantry wondering if they had ingredients for snow cream. A nod of her head told her tummy it would be getting some unwholesome goodness before the night was over. The thought made her smile.

Emma glanced at the clock on the wall. It was a while still before Colton would be home. He and Hayden had met at the Tavern to discuss a possible business endeavor for a new security company. The two had formed a tight friendship in the weeks following her ordeal and Emma was happy that they had. Like Colton, Hayden was a good man.

A fluttering sound drew her attention to the vertical column leading into the dining room. Its four sides were brimming with brightly colored Christmas cards they'd received from their family and friends. It was customary in Emma's family to display the cards until after the New Year, so keeping with tradition, the open cards were taped to the column for all to see. She and Colton had decided not take down their Christmas decorations until after they'd returned from their honeymoon. And in true Colton fashion, he hadn't told her exactly where they were going.

Turning her attention back to the journal that she'd neglected to write in earlier, she chose to read a few more passages. Emma told herself that she'd read one entry, maybe two, then jot down her thought for the day.

Today Colton and I went to Cat's house to celebrate Christmas Eve. Mom and Dad wanted us to come to Texas to spend it with them, but I didn't want to. Is that bad? It probably is. I swear I don't have Mommy/Daddy issues. It's just that I wanted to be home for Christmas, our home.

Anyway, it was a good day being surrounded by our friends. Lisa and Bryce were there, and of course, Hayden, too. Cat and I cooked up a mean feast - turkey, dressing, and all the fixin's. We even schlucked out that nasty cranberry sauce that no one eats. We didn't bother slicing it. It just lay there on the dish with its can-formed jellied rings staring back at us. Gross, but it's tradition. You just do it. The boys were impressed with our culinary skills and we all ate until we about popped – as you should on a holiday!

When we were preparing the banana pudding, we needed to do a double check on the ingredients. Opening Gran's wooden recipe box sent a flood of memories our way. Some sad, most good, and some hilarious like our first attempt at roasting a turkey.

We recalled that day fondly. Under the patient guidance of Granny's watchful eye, we pulled it off, but not without a hiccup or two. Cat and I were seventeen, and cooking was not our forte. I'll never forget it. Giving us enough rope to hang ourselves with, Granny watched as we put the turkey in the roasting pan and socked it in the oven. As we stood at the stove trying to figure out if we were supposed to cover it or not, she walked up between us and cleared her throat. "Girls," she said as she draped her arms around our waists looking up at each of us, "you're gonna have to fish that turkey right back out." She laughed because we had stuck it in the oven with the bag of parts still inside. I had argued if they didn't want us to bake it all, they shouldn't play hide and seek with its grab bag of mystery parts! In the end it turned out fabulous just like today's meal which in a way is like me. Well, I don't know about the 'fabulous' part, but the persistent part. It often takes several attempts to get it right, whatever "it" might be, and sometimes you face unexpected hurdles. Whether it be a mystery bag of parts or a hodgepodge of emotions, you have to deal with what's thrown your way. Persistence.

With everyone rested from the meal, we decided to carry on an American tradition – holiday football, guys against girls. The odds were certainly in their favor, but we had no intentions of playing fair.

In a crazy way, this was therapeutic. For obvious reasons, being approached from behind still caused momentary panic in me. My therapist suggested overcoming my fear by facing it in a safe, secure environment.

Back to the game: Each team member was given a flag and a member of the opposing team given the corresponding color. Mine was yellow, appropriately so, approach with caution.

The sun was gorgeous, but the wind chilled me to the bone until we started playing. I watched as the players fanned out in the yard. All us couples had matching flags, so nothing in me made me think that a game of actual football was happening as per the rules.

Hayden tossed the ball to Colton. That was my cue to chase him and take his flag. His long legs ate up the yard in pursuit of their goal line. Hayden and Bryce cheered him on and warned that I was approaching – those turds! Just before he reached the pergola, which was their goal post, I swiped the flag from his pocket. "That wasn't very nice, luv," he said as he turned and scooped me up into his arms. I laid my head on his chest, inhaling his cologne. I told him that this wasn't the typical way to play football, packing off the enemy. Colton ignored my advice and rewarded me with a kiss. I said to heck with the rules and wrapped my arms around his neck, kissing him back. By the time we made it across the yard to the others, my legs had wrapped around his waist. Who knew that football could be so delightful!

The game nearing an end, we had just one touchdown left to make before we were declared victors. Cat threw the ball to me. Just like all the times before, I had a momentary panic knowing that I would be chased. I knew it would be Colton who came after me, and I willed myself not to panic. The vibrations that sped behind me threatened to send my heart racing. Being that we were playing with modified rules, it was apparent that he planned to take me down this time just as Hayden and Bryce had done to my friends. "Just breathe," I told myself. "It's Colton and you're safe." I could hear his boots as they pounded the ground in pursuit of me. I felt a shift within me, felt the worry fall away. The trepidation I had felt now turned into anticipation. I was eager to feel his arms around me, his breath against my cheek, hear his voice in my ear. The tree line of pines was just ahead. I was two steps away from scoring the victory for Team Girl when I felt the flag being tugged from my jeans' pocket as his arms shot out around my waist. Shrieks of delight escaped my throat as Colton gently hauled me off my feet and lowered us both to the ground . . . onto the cold, snowy ground. I found myself caged in, staring into his heated emerald eyes.

"Are you ok?" He whispered.

"Yes," I said almost breathlessly as my hips rose to meet his of their own accord.

A low groan spilled from his lips. Apparently the chase excited him, as it had me. Suddenly the last thing that I felt was fear. And the last place I wanted us to be was in the company of others. It had been weeks since we'd made love. I knew as he lowered his lips to mine that that dry spell was over. My body called to him and his to me.

When his scorching kiss ended, I looked at him braced above me on his forearms. "I was so close," I said. "I almost made a touchdown!"

Colton's fingers flipped the end of one of the braids that I'd donned just for the game. "I could be persuaded to let you reach that goal line, luv," he said as an eyebrow shot up in a challenge and his lips tugged into a seductive grin.

God, how I love this man!

I wrapped my arms around his neck and pulled his weight on top of me. He felt good and even though I was dominated, I knew I was safe. My thoughts were derailed by the familiar stir of desire pulsing through me. "Let's go home," I whispered as I weaved my fingers into his hair, pulling him in for a lingering kiss.

Pulling away slightly, his bated breath crossed my lips as he gazed into my eyes. He didn't say a word. His hips that bore harder against my own was his only answer. "Now," I pleaded.

"Now," he repeated as he cupped my cheeks and ravaged my lips once more.

"Game's over!" Bryce declared when he saw us meshed together in a lover's embrace. And it was. It was over. We said our goodbyes and headed back here to our little house where we didn't even make it past the living room. It was a nice homecoming. Very nice.

I wondered why Colton and I hadn't been intimate since my return. He's been so patient. We both have healthy sexual appetites, so it wasn't making sense to me, wasn't clicking until today when I had an epiphany. I realized that the thought of taking pleasure from making love felt wrong after what Derrick had attempted to do to me. He no longer has that control. I'm breaking the chains that bind me one link, and one day, at a time . . .

Reaching up, Emma pulled the pencil free that secured her hair. With locks flowing around her shoulders, she flipped to the next empty page. She recalled the thought that she'd had earlier and quickly jotted it down.

Therapy. I always thought therapy was for weak minded individuals. Then I decided that it was for survivors, people like me, who refuse to be the victim one day longer. I think it's ironic that, in the end, the chosen profession of the man who terrorized me is the very thing that will help me break these crippling chains. I won't allow him to dominate my fear and continue to control me from the grave. This is me, Emma Saint-Claire, the survivor.

And on an unrelated note, Colton will be home in a few minutes and I must say, reading about our football game has me flushed and ready to welcome him home in a proper manner. He can't get here fast enough!

Emma closed the journal and swirled the leather strip around it, securing its contents. She placed the book and pencil back in the side table drawer and crossed to the front door to look out. She couldn't suppress the happiness she felt when she heard the crunching of packed snow and saw the tip of Colton's truck coming up the drive.

Colton stepped from the truck and walked across the yard. He wore black from head to toe making his six and a half foot frame look even taller. He smiled when he saw her watching him so intently. Emma would never tire of his devilish crooked grin. "See something you like, luv?" He asked teasingly in his delectable accent.

"See something I love, luv," she corrected as she gave him a tender kiss on the lips when he reached the porch.

Colton hefted the box under his arm and turned to lock the truck with his key fob.

"What's that?" Emma asked pointing to the box as he moved passed her and into the comfort of the warm house.

"Some of the books from Leah's room. I thought you'd like to see them." He dug in the top of the box and pulled out a dusty cover, the pink handwritten one. "I thought this would be especially interesting to you."

Jett bolted across the room jumping at Colton's legs and yapping until he bent to give him attention. A few moments were all he needed before padding down the hall and disappearing into the bedroom. "Our guard dog is rather lazy, don't you think?"

Emma laughed but was more focused on the book.

Emma and Colton sat on the sofa that faced the fireplace. He relaxed with his feet propped on the traveler's chest with Emma stretched out the opposite direction, head in his lap. She opened the cover of the pink book and read aloud as he ran his fingers through her hair, massaging her scalp. All the tales you would expect a little girl to love were recorded. Emma turned the page to the final entry. The gasp that escaped her throat drew Colton's attention away from her silky mane and onto the book that she held. Not only had Leah included classic fairytales of princesses, gingerbread houses, and giants in the sky, but she'd jotted down one that originated in the small town of Brookfield, Kentucky - Little Victoria and the Williams' Bridge. What made it all the more interesting, Leah herself was listed as the author.

Emma sat forward, turning to look at Colton. "Can you believe that all this time, all these people thought that Little Victoria was real, had claimed to have seen her, even?" She could tell by the smile on his face that he could believe it and had known even before handing her the book.

"And that's why I thought you'd find this one particularly interesting," Colton said as he tapped the book then the tip of her nose.

Emma curled against his side. Colton caressed her hip with the arm he had draped over her and she traced circles on his thigh with her fingers as they recapped the day.

They talked about his successful business meeting with Hayden. The idea for the security company had been born when Hayden was suspended from the police force one week ago. When asked under oath if he'd leaked information to Colton's security team, Hayden's response was a resounding "Yes!" He added that expediting the search to save the life of a fellow citizen was more important to him than following protocol and a bogus chain of command.

Publicly, having a rogue cop opened the department up for up for legal repercussions they couldn't afford. Privately having Hayden as an ally, who didn't have to follow by the same rules, was a tremendous advantage and one that the police chief looked forward to exploring.

With Colton's financial resources and the former police sergeant's expertise, it looked like the security team of Graves-McAllister would become a reality.

"What about Regal Engineering?" Emma asked as she gazed at him, gauging his reaction.

Colton thought for a moment. "Kane is perfectly capable of assuming his role there. He's a fierce businessman and fine engineer. I'll retain my status within the company leaving me with the power to override any jackass decision he might surprise someone with," Colton laughed, "but mainly I'll stay in the shadows because I feel he can do it." A look of concern crossed his face. "Eleanor may tell him to piss off the first time he tries to boss her, though. That'd be fun to watch." They both laughed.

Emma thought about her own job at the Journal. Much to Colton's dislike, she'd tried to return weeks ago. The concern of well-meaning citizens had halted any productivity she'd tried to accomplish. Knowing that things would be like that until the hype of her ordeal died down, Phil asked her to take a leave of absence. It was best for her and for the Journal, he'd offered. Maybe he was right.

She had found that she was enjoying writing in her journal and thought maybe she'd like to explore the idea of writing for a living.

"I've been thinking about going back to work," Emma glanced at Colton for his input. He nodded his head for her to continue her thoughts. She shrugged her shoulders, "Maybe I could start out as a freelance writer for the Journal or another publication. I enjoy writing, and working behind the scenes might be the best thing for me right now."

Emma noticed that Colton was tracing her scarred wrist with his fingers. He brought his lips to the marred flesh, brushing them gently over her sensitive skin. For so long, she'd seen her scars as a reminder of the terror she experienced and as a constant reminder of the fear that suppressed her. Even though they were ugly, she hoped in time that she'd be able to view the hash marks as the day she changed her own destiny by altering his course . . . someday.

"I just want you safe, luv," Colton said, pulling her back in the conversation. "I want you happy, and I want you safe." He looked into her eyes, "So I'll stand behind you whatever you choose."

Emma thought for a moment. "Maybe I could do a

segment on historic homes and thrust Dillingham Manor into a positive light as we do renovations. We could publish some of your grandmother's journal entries about life in the early nineteen hundreds. It would be an interesting read."

"It would indeed," Colton remarked, proud that Emma had come so far.

EPILOGUE

*R*hythmic strokes of piano keys filled the silence as a familiar melody seeped into the room. Stained glass windows, exquisite floral arrangements, and rich architecture surrounded them. But all he saw was her.

Extending his hand forward, he brushed his thumb lightly down her cheek. Daniel Saint-Claire had always prided himself with being a strong man, but in this moment as he gazed upon his baby girl, *strong* was not in him. His arms were folding around her before his actions were even realized.

Emma willingly fell into the tender embrace that he offered. With her head on his shoulder, she felt the gentle quake of his chest. Like her, his composure was failing. "What are you thinking about, daddy?" She asked, her voice thick with emotion.

"What am I thinking about?" He let out a weak laugh then tugged her closer. "I'm simply wondering where the time went. How did we get here, to your wedding day so quickly?" Daniel thought for a moment before he continued. "It seems like only yesterday when you were born. I remember when you learned to walk and can still see your tiny uneven steps as you toddled between Claire and me. And now, here we are on your wedding day where we'll witness unchartered steps once again." He released his hold to gaze into her eyes. "Are you sure this is what you want, angel? It's not too late to back out."

Emma's hazel eyes fell upon the ruggedly handsome man with salt and pepper hair. He was ready to whisk her away at the word go, this much she was sure of. She glanced at the arched doorway to her left. Three steps forward and the doors would swing open, the white carpet pointing her like a compass into the arms of the man she loved. Three steps back and the street side exit would lead her out into the world she'd always known.

A smile played across her lips as she turned her focus back on her father. Holding her shoulders a little taller, Emma leaned up on her tiptoes and placed a delicate kiss on his cheek. "I'm sure, daddy, I've never been more certain of anything in my life. Colton's a good man."

He nodded. "I think that's true. There's no doubt he loves you."

She smiled. "And I love him."

Taking a deep breath, Daniel reached into his jacket pocket feeling the smooth edges of the small rectangular box. He felt the vibration as the button was pressed, the same vibration that the attendant on the other side of the door would feel which alerted him to the fact that the bride was ready.

Emma gave her father a final hug before threading her hand through the crook of his arm. "I love you, daddy," she whispered.

He squeezed her hand. "I loved you first, baby girl."

Colton stood at the altar resisting the urge to loosen his bowtie. Even though his brother and Cat tried to make idle chit chat, it did nothing to lessen his angst. He felt as if he'd stared at the attendants for hours. They were unmoving in their statue like stance; their still hands grasping the handles that he willed to turn. A thousand thoughts raced through his mind. *Why was it taking so long? Had she changed her mind? Had it, indeed, been too soon as her therapist had warned?* As scenarios continued to inundate his brain, his appraisal fell on the guests.

He saw his future mother-in-law and her sister, his own mother and assistant, several of Emma's friends along with his friends, Hayden and Bryce. Smiling faces of countless others blended together as they faded into the crowd.

He glanced at his watch.

"Colton, unless you want CPR to be the only kiss you get today, you'd do well to relax," Kane smiled at his own whispered comment which his brother ignored.

"You have the rings, right?"

Kane patted his breast pocket, "Right here."

"No one knows Emma like I do," Cat whispered, attempting to calm the nerves of the uncharacteristically jumpy groom. "Everything is fine. I know for a fact that there's nothing in this world that she wants more than this. Nothing."

Colton closed his eyes. He recalled the night they'd exchanged unity bands in the snowy Canadian cabin. He smiled inwardly at the thought that she had no idea that was also their honeymoon destination.

The crescendo of the wedding march pulled him from his reflections as the church doors sprang free. One by one, guests rose and turned to witness what he had already seen. She was stunning.

The moment their gazes collided, everyone else in the room ceased to exist. His eyes traveled her voluptuous curves that were enveloped in white satin. The sleeveless gown she wore was simple, but elegant. Anticipation coursed through him as he watched her approach.

Daniel placed her hand in Colton's who immediately brought it to his mouth. He feathered tender kisses across her fingers. When she turned her hand to cradle his face, his chest swelled with pride.

Warm hands fell on her cheeks seconds after the final vows were spoken.

"Ladies and Gentlemen, It's my great honor to present to you Mr. and Mrs. Colton Graves." The crowd buzzed with excitement, clapping hands and congratulations erupting into the room. "You may kiss the bride."

Colton gazed into her misty eyes then his appraisal fell on her lips. He lowered his mouth to hers and kissed her tenderly. With fingers flexing against her skin, he deepened the kiss. Emma's body fell flush with his, her hands weaving into his hair as she pulled him closer. The searing kiss that passed between them was a testament to the passion they felt for one another. Reluctantly, they pulled away and turned to face their guests.

The church doors opened. Emma and Colton Graves found themselves ducking between twin crowds of revelers who pelted them with bird seed as they made their way down the stairs to the waiting limo.

As they reached the car, Emma held her bouquet of stargazer lilies high above her head. She rocked it back and forth signaling her intent. Keeping with the time honored tradition she turned her back and tossed the arrangement.

She glanced over her shoulder to see who had caught it and laughed at the dazed look on her cousin's face. The crowd erupted with laughter when Cat finally said the words she was thinking, "Well hell!"

Emma and Colton scurried into the limo. As it drove away, his hands immediately fell on her thighs, pulling her to his side. He placed a passionate kiss on her lips then lowered her down against the cool leather seat.

"We won't have time," Emma whimpered.

Colton's eyebrow hitched upwards at the same time her skirt did. "I told the driver to take the long way."

Emma wrapped her arms around his neck, tugging him closer. His lips caressed hers as precise fingers traced the juncture of her thighs. Gazing down on her, his hungry eyes mirrored her own. "Spread your legs, luv."

Liquid heat flooded her core with anticipation at the smooth sound of his command.

∾

One year later . . .

Emma crossed the room to the arched window, pulling the curtain aside. From her vantage point of the upstairs bedroom, she saw the headlights of Colton's truck come into focus. A smile tugged at her lips. She could hear the sound of snow crunching under his tires as he meandered closer.

Pulling her robe tightly around her, she descended the semi-winding staircase, appreciating its classic beauty.

In her lifetime, Emma had known unmeasurable heartache and despair. This house was once a source of that. As she moved on, she noted how those feelings were all but a fleeting memory now.

She took a moment to appreciate the renovations they'd done. With Colton's finances, the design possibilities were nearly endless. However, echoes of the past called to them both, assuring that the only design Dillingham Manor would receive was the one it graced Brookfield with at the turn of the century, over a hundred years ago.

Mahogany floors, moldings, and doorways were reclaimed to the best of their ability. What they couldn't reclaim, they replicated. Modern conveniences blended with vintage architecture, lending a comfortable feel to the historic home.

Moving closer to the door, Emma glanced across the vast entryway toward the room she used to occupy. She smiled; glad she and Colton had made the decision. In keeping with the Dillinghams' original wishes, Leah's room - along with her possessions - was hidden away from the world, a bookcase spanning the brick wall backing up to it. Classic titles lined the shelves, as did photos of the room it concealed. To anyone who stumbled across them, the photos appeared to be an amazing portrayal of another place in time. As is common in life, the only corridors we're granted passage to are those areas the author wishes to reveal. And even then, sometimes secrets still lie in plain sight . . .

Emma crossed to the heavy wood door with prominent oval window, easing it open. A cool blast of air assaulted her as she gazed upon her husband. With careful footing, he padded along - grocery bag in one hand, a package, and various other mail in the other.

"How's my girls?" Colton asked before kissing Emma on

the lips, then on the belly. The door closed behind him as she took the loot from his hands, moving toward the kitchen.

"We're good," she answered, "now that you're home, that is."

Emma sat the mail on the counter and dug the container out of the grocery bag. She reached for a spoon. Colton's arms slipped around her waist as he rubbed her ever growing belly. His warm breath fell on her ear. 'Sophie wants ice cream,' he chuckled as he repeated the request she'd texted him earlier. "Classic use of the 'daddy card,' luv!"

Emma's head fell back against his shoulder, joining in his laughter.

Colton played tug-of-war with Jett as Emma stood at the counter thumbing through the mail. She opened a box from Kane. He'd sent an array of baby things in preparation for his niece's arrival - dresses, sleepers, blankets, toys, keepsakes . . . the bounty was unending. Emma didn't know if his new girl-friend had selected the items or if he had. Either way, they were fun to dig through.

Turning her attention to the stack of mail, she picked up a card. Peeling it open, a smile tugged at her lips when she read the engagement announcement. Hayden was a good man, and she knew he'd make her cousin very happy.

As evening turned into night, Emma and Colton settled into bed. Instead of reaching for her Sudoku puzzle – her nightly routine – tonight, she chose her journal. Unwinding the leather strings from the fastener, she flipped to an empty page – a recent entry catching her attention.

Today was my baby shower. It was so much fun! Gender reveals are all the rage these days. And while I love a mystery, I still wanted to do this my way. Jett, our beloved pound pup, was the announcer. While everyone expected the cake to contain the answer when we cut into it, neither a pink nor blue center was to be found. The guests were thoroughly confused. It wasn't until Jett made his appearance wearing a pink shirt that said "It's a girl!" that everyone understood. We got lots of stuff, had all kinds of food, and were surrounded by friends and family that we love dearly. It was a great day.

Yesterday, I did a private gender reveal with Cat. She came over here after work to look at our new nursery furniture. It really is beautiful. We went with a vintage theme. The cream dressing table is an antique replica of the one that's sealed off downstairs in Leah's room. And the crib and rocking chair, in the same distressed hue, is equally as gorgeous.

Cat thought she was just looking at the furniture until she came closer to the crib. A satin pillow near the head of the bed caught her eye. Scrolled across it in beautiful pink cursive writing was the baby's name – Sophie Elizabeth. Cat squealed with delight when she saw it. She snatched the pillow up, examining the workmanship. She knew it was just like the ones we had as babies, the ones that Gran made us.

"It's beautiful, Em," Cat said as she hugged the pillow close to her heart," then she laughed. "Between you and me, this baby doesn't stand a chance! I can't wait to buy her her first 'Pink Lady' jacket."

Leave it to Cat. I can only imagine the things she'll buy for my baby in the name of fashion.

Emma giggled as she read the entry, then she flipped over to the next blank page. Pressing her pen against it, she began to write . . .

"I once made the statement that Dillingham Manor was where I laid my head at night, but it would never be a place that I called home. It was a statement that, thankfully, has proven untrue. Tonight, as I drift off to sleep, I do so with Colton by my side, and

our little Sophie Elizabeth set to make her arrival in two weeks. Or a fortnight, as my fancy ass husband would say. As I write this, as she stirs around inside me, it occurs to me that everything I need is right here under this one roof, this home I've come to love, Dillingham Manor . . ."

~*~ The End ~*~

ACKNOWLEDGMENTS

First and foremost, I'd like to thank Bru and Tyler, my husband and son. Thank you for your encouragement during this book writing process. Lord knows it took me long enough! Thank you for understanding that when I'm in "writing mode," I can't live in two worlds; I'm either present in this one, or I disappear into my world of fiction. Thanks for still being there when I reemerged. I love you guys so much. You are my rocks.

I'd like to thank my lifelong best friend and cousin, Audrey "Cat" Clowers. It's because of you that I wrote a book in the first place. You encouraged me to try my hand at fiction. I swore I couldn't do it, but you thought differently. You were my sounding board and also the one who told me that I "need to learn to say things on the outside." You made me a better writer, and I love you for it. You are my Boo.

To my niece, Natosha Reeves, thank you for your influence. You inspired me without your ever realizing it. I'll tell you about it someday. You are my levelheaded advisor.

To my friend, Jill VanDyke, thank you for the encouragement and always being willing to read the next chapter. You are an enabler in the best possible way.

To my dear friends, Jamie Lovell and Penny Wilbur, thank you for reading my early versions – even when I changed them multiple times. And then changed them again. And Jamie, thank you for providing me with dialog for one of my favorite scenes. And Penny, you were right; I really did use everyone's name but my own. Now I've taken it a step further and included last names. You girls are my original beta readers.

To my editor, Tracy Stephen, thank you for taking a jumbled-up mess and making it presentable. Also, thank you for not beating me over the head with those ellipses I love so . . . You are a grammar wizard.

To my friend, Cheryl Pardington, you have been a wealth of knowledge to me. Thank you for the guidance in a world I knew nothing about. You are a lifesaver and a key reason this book is ever seeing the light of day. I can never thank you enough.

To my soul sisters - Cathy "Lynn" Eaves, Kathy Yates, Cassie Green Bradley, and Tonya Stevens, y'all are angels! Some of you read my book, some didn't. And that's ok. But, you all gave me encouragement, feedback, or ideas along the way - even if you didn't realize it. To my soul brothers - Brian Eaves, Matt Yates, Brent Bradley, and Nick Stevens, I can't forget you guys. I received positive and hilarious feedback from you guys that encouraged me to keep writing. Thank you, my soul brothers.

To my cousin, Amy Maggard Sizemore, thank you for reading and for the wonderful feedback and suggestions you gave me.

To my friends, Amy Collins, Amanda Smith, Tracy Cruse, and Leslie Pasley, I want to say thank you. I've received amazing feedback from you girls along the way.

To my friend, Erin Garrison Johnston, thank you for reading and allowing me to bounce ideas off you on those midnight walks. A good many ideas were borne on those moonlit walks.

To my friend, Liz Lester, thank you for brainstorming with me.

To my friend, Carmen Reyes, thank you for the random reminders that I really should publish my book and for reading it. Twice. You are wonderful.

To my cousin, Kim Sipple, thank you for reading. You gave such detailed and heartfelt feedback, it made me cry. You are good for a writer's soul.

To my friends who are too numerous to list, and those who need to remain anonymous, the ones I called "My Little Reading Group," thank you for reading my book.

To that guy in high school who sent me the black carnation for Valentine's Day, I suppose I should thank you, as well. When all the other girls got beautiful flowers surrounded by delicate baby's breath, you unintentionally gave me a storyline for this novel. It was embarrassing and disturbing at the time. It's not now. That's a good lesson for everyone. It's not about what happens to you; it's about what you turn it into.

To Keisha Webb Gentry, you are one of the only people I know who reads a book cover to cover. I know you will delight in finding your name here! Thank you for reading my book. Also, thank you for years of laughter over those Gummi Bears. You know what this means. By the way, they no longer sell them. I looked.

To my friend, Johnathan Tussey, thanks for letting me bounce some ideas off you. The advice was much appreciated. Should you ever read this book, I'm positive my next round of advice will be of the biblical sort. And you *know* I'm laughing as I write this.

In case I never write another book ever again, I better thank my parents, Clay and Peggy Lovett Covey, and my siblings, Tony Pennington and Kim Pennington Huffman. Some have read my book, some haven't. But, you all have provided a lifetime of memories, some of which have inched their way into this novel.

I'd like to thank my friend, Shane Simmons. "You need to stop hiding your talent!" Those were the words you said to me. Thanks for the wake-up call, friend.

As is always the case, I know I have unintentionally left some amazing people off this list. Just know that I appreciate you all. Every single person who has touched my life and lent an ear, a suggestion, or a life lesson, thanks for helping shape me.

ABOUT THE AUTHOR

Amelia Blake was born and raised in Hyden, a quaint town in southeastern Kentucky. At an early age, she penned clandestine paranormal mysteries - nothing more than a page in length and always quickly discarded. As a forlorn teen, she began to write poetry. Her collection was stored in a ratty old notebook and tucked away out of sight.

Throughout her life, she wrote tales that would evoke laughter in anyone who read them. Of course, this was all before the age of internet. Shortly after high school, Amelia's home was destroyed by fire. She and her family lost everything they had, stories and poems included.

Thinking that writing was nothing more than a hobby, she laid her pen aside and focused on her education and starting a family. Years later, her old soul caught up with her as she felt that familiar pull once more. She has since written countless stories of non-fiction, reflective articles, and this novel, *Vanished.*

Her purpose in sharing this with you is to urge you not to give up on *your* dreams. She'd tell you that it's never too late to dream a new dream, just as it's never too late to explore one previously set aside.

In the powerful words of Aerosmith, "Dream on. Dream on. Dream until your dreams come true."

Listen to your soul when it whispers. It recognizes the things you can't - danger, love, opportunity . . . It's your compass. Follow it.

~ Amelia Blake

Visit me on facebook
facebook.com/amelia.blake.5059

Made in the USA
Lexington, KY
26 July 2018